Sabine Baring-Gould

**A Book of Fairy Tales**

Sabine Baring-Gould

**A Book of Fairy Tales**

ISBN/EAN: 9783337025328

Printed in Europe, USA, Canada, Australia, Japan

Cover: Foto ©Andreas Hilbeck / pixelio.de

More available books at **www.hansebooks.com**

# A BOOK OF FAIRY TALES

### RETOLD BY S. BARING GOULD
### WITH PICTURES BY A. J. GASKIN

LONDON: METHUEN AND COMPANY
36 ESSEX ST. STRAND: MDCCCXCV

# PREFACE

THE Fairy Tales in this little book are, with two exceptions only, those which delighted our fathers and grandfathers in their childhood.

In the form in which we have them they are not older than the end of the seventeenth century. The majority of them were written by Charles Perrault, whose collection of Fairy Tales appeared in 1697, dedicated to one of the royal family of France. It contained 'Blue Beard,' 'The Sleeping Beauty,' 'Puss in Boots,' 'Riquet and his Tuft,' 'Hop-o'-my-Thumb,' 'Little Red Riding-Hood,' 'Cinderella,' 'The Wishes,' etc. To each of these tales was added a moral in bad verse. The morals have been forgotten, the tales are immortal. But although written by Perrault, he did not invent the stories, they were folk-tales which he wrote in simple words as they had been told him in his childhood, or as he had seen them in earlier collections.

'The tales of Perrault,' says Dunlop, 'are the best of the sort that have been given to the world. They are chiefly distinguished for their simplicity, for the naïve and familiar style in which they are written, and an appearance of implicit belief on the part of the relater, which, perhaps, gives us

v

668655

additional pleasure, from our knowledge of the powerful attainments of the author, and his advanced age at the period of their composition.'

The success attained by Perrault's little collection animated others to write Fairy Tales. Such were the Countess D'Aulnoy, Madame Murat, and Mademoiselle de la Force. But only the first of those approached Perrault in charm of style, and gained a lasting hold on posterity. She told the imperishable tales of 'The Fair Maid with Golden Locks,' 'Gracieuse and Percinet,' and 'The White Cat.' Among a host of imitators none wrote stories that have lived, except Madame de Beaumont, who published her collection in 1740, and in it is 'Beauty and the Beast,' a tale that has gone through successive stages of simplification, till it has assumed a form tolerable to childish minds.

Almost as soon as Perrault's tales became popular in France, they were translated into English, and speedily became indispensable in the nursery. It is to be regretted that the popularity which attended them caused the disappearance of a great many of our own home-grown folk-tales. Attempts were made in England to win the ears of little folk by fairy tales. A couple of volumes were published in 1750, but they lacked precisely that quality which was so conspicuous in Perrault, and so certain to ensure success with children—simplicity, both in structure of the plot, and in diction. Though the stories in this collection have some merit, they have none of them gained a hearing.

It was otherwise with Grimm; he did in Germany on a more extended scale what Perrault did in France, and Grimm's Folk-Tales won their way to children's hearts at once, and have established therein an empire, which cannot be shaken. Grimm's success was due to the same cause as that of Perrault.

The stories in this little book are all, with two

exceptions, known in every nursery. What I have
done is to rewrite some of them—I may say most
of them—simply, and to eliminate the grandiloquent
language which has clung to some of them, and
has not been shaken off.

Madame D'Aulnoy sinned greatly in style, but
nothing like the degree to which others sinned.
The original 'Beauty and the Beast' is intolerable
in the dress in which it was sent into the world.

What Perrault did was to take traditional tales
and clothe them in the language that was adapted
to children of the end of the seventeenth century.
The tales were not original; what he did was to
print them undisfigured by fine language.  His
great merit consists in having thought them worthy
to be published.  Perhaps the stories want telling
a little differently to children at the close of the
nineteenth century.

I have thought so—and have so dealt with some,
but not all, of these tales.

If I have made a mistake, I am quite sure of one
thing, that the printer has made none in using
such a beautiful type as can try no eyes; and the
artist has made none in supplying such delightful
illustrations.

If I have made a mistake, then I appeal to the
tender hearts of the little people in the nursery—
and I know they will pardon me, not only because I
promise to make them up a set of really delightful
old, old English Fairy Tales, but mainly because
the childish heart is ever generous and forgiving.

S. BARING-GOULD.

# CONTENTS

# JACK AND THE BEAN STALK

IN the days of King Alfred, there lived in a lonesome part of England a poor widow with her son Jack. She had a cottage, a meadow, and a cow-shed, and one cow to eat in the meadow, sleep in the shed, and supply the cottage with milk and butter.

The widow had one son, his name was Jack, and he was a thriftless, idle lad, without thought for his mother or the morrow. She had to do all the work and he had all the pleasure.

If the widow had not petted and spoiled her boy, he would have been a comfort to her instead of a trouble. If she had made him work instead of letting him run idle, he would have been happier.

As her poverty increased, and Jack increased at the same time, and required larger shoes, longer stockings, and more broadcloth for his back, the mother disposed of all her little goods one after another, to supply his necessities. He brought nothing into the housekeeping but took a great deal out, and he had not the wits to see this.

At length there remained only the cow to be disposed of, and the widow, with tears in her eyes,

A

said to her son: 'Jack, my dear boy, I have not money enough to buy you a new suit of clothes, and you are out of elbows with your jacket, have knocked out the toes of your boots, and worked your knees through your breeches. Nothing remains for us but to part with the cow. Part with her we must; I cannot bear to see you in rags and disreputable.'

Jack said his mother was quite right to consider his personal appearance.

Then the widow bade him take the cow to market and sell her. Jack consented to do this.

As he was on his way he met with a butcher, who asked him whither he was going with the cow.

Jack said he was going to market to sell her.

'What do you want for her?' asked the butcher.

'As much as I can get,' answered Jack.

'That's spoken sensibly,' said the butcher. 'And now I know with whom I have to deal. It's always a pleasure to treat with a man of business habits and with plenty of intelligence. With him one knows where one is, but with a fool and a scatterbrain—I ask—Where are you?'

'Exactly,' said Jack, 'Where are you?'

Jack was vastly gratified at being called a man, and a man of business to boot, and with plenty of intelligence on top of that.

'Come,' said the butcher; 'between you and me, as business men, what will you take for the cow?' Now, he had in his hands some curious beans of various colours, red and violet, spotted purple and black. Jack had never seen the like before, and he looked curiously at them.

'Ah!' said the butcher, 'I see you are a chap as knows what is what. In one moment, without speaking a word, them eyes of yours went into my hand, looking at my scarlet-runners. There is no cheating you, you know the value of a thing by the

2

outside girth, you do. Well—if I was dealing with any one else, I'd say, three scarlet-runner beans for the cow, but as you're an old hand, and a wary bird, I'll give you six.'

Jack eagerly closed the bargain. Such a chance might never occur again, so he gave the man the cow, and walked home with the six beans in his hand. When his mother saw the beans, and heard what Jack had to say, her patience forsook her; she threw away the beans in a rage, and they were scattered all over the garden. The poor woman was very sad over her loss; she cried all the evening, and she and Jack had to go supperless to bed.

When Jack awoke next morning he was surprised that the sun did not stream in at his window in the manner it was wont to do, but twinkled as through dense foliage. When he rose from his bed, and went to the window, he saw to his great astonishment that a large plant had sprung up in the night and had grown in front of the cottage, and that its green leaves and scarlet flowers obscured the light from entering his chamber as fully as of old. He ran down-stairs into the garden, and saw that the beans had taken root, and had sprung up; the stalks were entwined and twisted like a stout trunk, or formed a ladder, and this mounted quite out of sight, for the clouds as they drifted by passed across the bean without reaching the top.

Jack very speedily resolved to climb the bean stalk and see whither it mounted.

In the meantime his mother had come forth, no less astonished than himself. But when he told her it was his intention to scramble up the bean stalk, then she entreated, threatened, and forbade him—he must not go. He would run extraordinary risks; he would break her heart.

Jack had been too long his own master, and too

3

regardless of his mother's feelings to pay attention
to what she said.  He put his hands to the tangle
of stalks and found it extremely easy to climb.
So he set to work and began his ascent, pausing
at intervals to look round and observe the scenery
as it grew small below him.
After scrambling for several hours, he passed
through a thick layer of flaky cloud, and found

that the uppermost shoots and tendrils of the bean
were there.  They had fallen over and were strag-
gling across the upper surface of the cloud.
Looking about him, Jack discovered that he was
in a very strange country.  It appeared to be a
desert, without tree or shrub, here and there were
scattered masses of stone, and here and there also
were masses of crumbling soil.

4

Jack was so fatigued that he sat himself down on a stone and thought of his mother, and the distress she was in, and a pang of remorse entered his heart. Then he heard the croak of a crow, and looking up, he saw a black bird perched on a rock. It said to him: 'Korax! Korax! I am a fairy, and I will tell you why you are here. Your father was a great man, and rich, and one day a cruel giant came and killed him and carried off all his goods, and unless your mother had hidden herself with you in the sheep-pen, he would have destroyed you both as well. She fled with what little she could collect together, carrying you on her back, and she has lived ever since in great poverty, and her poverty and sorrows have not been lightened by any signs of consideration and deference shown by you. I am speaking to you now, not that I care for you or desire to do you good for your own worthless sake, but because I am grateful to your mother, and I know that I cannot give her greater pleasure than by serving and saving you, and I hope that in future you will behave better to her. You must know that though I am a fairy, my power is not continuous, every hundred years there comes a time when it fails, and I am obliged to live on earth subject to extreme poverty and privation, and to be reduced to the utmost destitution, and that I can only be released from this condition by one who will give me to eat her last crumb, and to drink her last drop, and will comb my head with her golden comb.

'Now, yesterday, whilst you were away driving the cow to market, I came begging to your mother's door. She was so good, so charitable, that she gave me the last particle of bread that remained in the house, and the last drop of milk that remained in the pan, and then, seeing that I was without any of those articles of toilette which

5

make life happy, she seated me on a stool, and
with her golden comb, the only article of luxury
that remained to her, she combed out my long
black tresses. Now, no sooner had she done this,
and spread my black hair all over me, than I was
transformed into a crow, and as a crow I flew
away, and a crow I remain until I can peck the
three golden hairs out of the mole that grows on
the tip of the giant's nose, that is, of the giant who
slew your father.

'In order to reward your mother, and also to advance my own interest, I flew over you as you were
making a great ass of yourself with the butcher,
who was laughing in his sleeve to think what a
greenhorn you were, and how easily gulled by
a little vulgar flattery, and I dropped among the
scarlet-runner beans three of a very different kind
from those the butcher was giving you; and it is
these three magical beans out of fairyland that
have grown to such a size, and up which you have
climbed.

'You are now in the country where lives the
giant.

'You will have difficulties and dangers to encounter, but you must persevere in avenging the
death of your father, and in doing all you can to
enable me to get the three gold hairs out of the
mole at the end of the ogre's nose. One thing I
charge you strictly: do not let your mother know
of your adventures till all are accomplished; the
knowledge would be more than she could endure.'

Jack promised that he would obey the directions
of the fairy. Then she said: 'Go along due east
over this barren plain, you will soon arrive at the
ogre's castle.'

Then the crow spread its wings and flew away.

Jack walked on and on, till at last he saw a
large mansion. A woman was standing in the
doorway. He accosted her and begged a morsel

of bread and a night's lodging, as he was desper-
ately hungry and excessively weary. She expressed great surprise at seeing him, and said
that it was an uncommon thing for a human being
to pass that way; for it was well known that her
husband was an ogre, who devoured human flesh
in preference to all other meats, that he did not
think anything of walking fifty miles to procure
it, and that usually he was abroad all day quest-
ing for it.

This account terrified Jack; nevertheless, he was
too weary and famished to think of proceeding
farther; besides, he remembered the injunction of
the fairy to avenge his father's death. He entreated the woman to take him in for that night
only, and to lodge him in the oven.

The good woman at length suffered herself to be
persuaded, for she was of a compassionate disposition. She gave him plenty to eat and drink
in the kitchen, where a pleasant fire was burning.
Presently the house shook, for the giant was approaching; and the woman hastily thrust Jack into
the oven.

Next instant the giant entered, and holding his
nose high in the air, shouted in a voice of thunder:
'Ha! Ha! I smell fresh meat.'

'My dear,' answered his wife, 'it is only the calf
we killed this morning.'

The ogre was appeased, and called for his meal.
The good woman hastened to satisfy him, and
spread the table and put on it a pie that would
have taken ten men to consume it in ten days.
The ogre finished it at a sitting, and when he
had done he desired his wife to bring him his
crimson and gold hen.

Jack could look through a crevice in the door of
the oven, and he saw that the giant's wife, after
having removed the supper, brought in an osier
cage, and out of this cage took a hen that had the

most magnificent plumage ever seen, shot with green and gold and crimson. When the giant said, 'Lay!' then at once the hen laid an egg of solid gold that shone like the sun.

The ogre amused himself a long while with the hen; meanwhile his wife was washing up the supper things in the back kitchen.

At length the giant wearied of the somewhat monotonous sport and fell fast asleep by his fireside, and Jack now stole out from the oven, tucked the hen under his arm, slipped through the house door and ran as fast as his legs could carry him due west, till he reached the head of the bean stalk, and he descended it rapidly and successfully, always carrying the hen under his arm.

His mother was overjoyed to see him; he found her crying bitterly, and lamenting his fate, for she had made sure he had come to a shocking end through his rashness.

Jack showed her the hen. 'See, mother,' said he, 'here is an end to our toil and trouble. Now I hope to make some amends for all the grief I have caused you.'

The hen laid them as many eggs as they desired; they sold them, and in a little time were rich enough to buy cows, and a new suit for Jack, and a best gown for his mother.

But Jack was not easy. He recollected the command of the fairy, that he was to avenge his father, and work for her release from the form of a crow. Accordingly he made up his mind to climb the bean stalk and visit cloudland once more.

One day he told his mother his purpose, and she tried to dissuade him from it, but as she saw that he was firmly resolved to do what he said, and with her fears to some extent allayed by the successful issue of his first expedition, she desisted from her attempt. Moreover, she did not know what

8

dangers he would run, for, obedient to the instructions of the fairy, he had told her nothing of the ogre that lusted after human flesh, and of his concealment in the oven.

Knowing that the giant's wife would not again willingly admit and harbour him, he thought it necessary on this occasion to totally disguise himself. Accordingly with walnut he dyed his hands and face black, and put on the new suit which had been purchased out of the money brought by the sale of the golden eggs.

Very early one morning he started, and climbed the bean stalk. He was greatly fatigued when he reached the top, and very hungry. Having rested for some time on the stones, he pursued his journey to the ogre's castle. He reached it late in the evening; and he found the woman standing at the door as before.

Jack accosted her, and begged that she would give him a night's lodging and something to eat. She replied that the giant, her husband, ate human flesh in preference to all other meat; that on one occasion she had taken in and hidden a beggar boy, who had run away carrying off something that her husband prized greatly. Jack tried hard to persuade the woman to receive him, but he found it a hard task.

At length she yielded, and took him into the kitchen, where she gave him something to eat and drink, and then concealed him in the clothes-hutch. Presently the ogre entered, with his nose in the air, shouting: 'Ha! Ha! I smell fresh meat.'

His wife replied that a kid had been killed that day, and this kid he doubtless scented.

Then she hastened to produce his supper, for which he was very impatient, and constantly upbraided her with the loss of his hen.

The giant at last, having satisfied his voracious appetite, said to his wife: 'Bring me the money-bags that I took out of the castle down on the earth.'

Then Jack knew that it was his father's money the ogre was going to look at. He peeped from his hiding-place, and saw the woman enter carrying two money-bags into the room. She placed them before her husband, who at once opened them and poured forth from one bezants, that is to say gold coins, and from the other deniers, that is

to say silver coins. The ogre amused himself with counting out his money; and Jack, peeping from his hiding-place, most heartily wished it were his.

At length the giant tired of the great mental exertion of counting. He put back the money into the bags, tied them up, and fell asleep.

Jack, believing all was secure, stole from his hiding-place, and laid hold of one of the bags.

Then a little dog that was lying under the table began to bark, and Jack, fearing lest the giant should wake, slipped back into his hiding-place. He however remained unconscious, snoring heavily; then the wife, who was washing-up in the back kitchen, came in and called the dog to attend her.

The coast was now clear. Jack crept out of the hutch, and, seizing the bags, made off with them, as they were his father's treasure which had been carried away by the giant.

On his way to the top of the bean stalk, the only difficulty Jack had to encounter arose from the weight of the bags, which burdened him immensely. On reaching the bean plant, he climbed down nimbly, carrying the treasure of gold and silver with him, and on reaching the bottom gave them to his mother. They were now well off, and might have exchanged the cottage for a handsome house, but Jack would in no way consent to this, for he knew that he had not as yet avenged his father, and released the fairy.

He thought and thought upon the world above the bean stalk, and his mother saw that he was meditating on another expedition.

She was sorrowful, as there was really now in her mind no need for anything further; but she knew how resolved her son was when he had made up his mind to anything, and that it was not in her power to dissuade him from it.

One midsummer day, very early in the morning, Jack reascended the bean stalk. He found the plain above the clouds as before. He arrived at the giant's mansion in the evening, and found his wife standing at the door. Jack had disguised himself so completely that she did not recognise him. He had painted his face and hands with red ochre. When he pleaded hunger and weariness in order to gain admission, he found it very difficult indeed to persuade her. At last he prevailed, and was concealed in the copper. When the giant returned in the evening, he lifted his nose and bellowed: 'Ha, Ha! I smell fresh meat.'

'Some crows have brought a piece of carrion and have left it on the roof,' said the wife.

'I said fresh meat,' retorted the giant; and notwithstanding all his wife could say, searched all through the kitchen. Jack was nearly dying with fear, and wished himself at home; and when the ogre approached the copper and put his hand on the lid, Jack thought his last hour had struck. The giant however forbore from lifting the lid, and threw himself into his chair, storming at his wife, whom he accused of having lost him his hen and bags of money.

She hastened to dish up supper. He ate greedily, and when satiated, bade the woman bring him his harp. Jack peered from under the copper lid, and saw the most beautiful harp that could be imagined. It had a head like an angel, and wings. When the harp was placed on the table, the giant shouted 'Play!' whereupon the harp played the most beautiful music of its own accord. The giant listened, and fell asleep. Meanwhile his wife had finished washing-up and had retired to bed.

Jack crept from the copper, and laid hold of the harp. But the harp had instinct, and it cried out: 'Master! Master! Master!'

The giant woke, rubbed his eyes, stretched himself, and looked about him. He had eaten and drunk so much that he was stupefied, and he did not understand what had happened, in the first moment of being aroused.

Meanwhile Jack ran away with the harp.

In a while the giant discovered that he had been robbed, and he rushed after Jack, and threw great stones at him, which Jack fortunately evaded. As soon as he reached the bean

12

stalk he began to descend, and he ran down as nimbly as might be.

The giant pursued him, and began to follow down the bean stalk.

Jack, on reaching the bottom, called for a hatchet. His mother, who saw the danger, immediately brought one; and Jack with the axe hewed through the stalks near the root; consequently the whole mass with the giant on it fell to the ground, and the fall broke the neck of the ogre.

Immediately hovering overhead appeared the black crow. It swooped down and picked three golden hairs from a mole that was on the end of the giant's nose. No sooner was that done, than the crow was transformed into a lovely fairy.

Jack's mother was not a little delighted when she saw the bean stalk destroyed, for now Jack need no longer climb it. He was now allowed by the fairy to tell the whole story; and he not only did this, but begged his mother's pardon for dis-obedience in past years, and promised to amend.

He kept his promise, and what with the hen that laid golden eggs, and the bags of bezants and deniers, and the marvellous harp that played of its own accord, Jack and his mother no longer suffered poverty or felt tedium.

 MILLER left all he had to his three sons. To the eldest he gave the mill; to the second he gave the ass; to the third the cat.

Very sad was the youngest over what fell to him. The two eldest were not kind, they managed very well together. The first ground the corn into flour, and the second took it about in sacks on the ass and sold it. But the third could do nothing with the cat but keep the mill clear of rats and mice. One day he said: 'I am very much alone and very poor in the world, and I live on the charity of my brothers. They will soon turn me out, and then I shall die of hunger and cold, whenever my cat has devoured the last mouse.' The cat heard him, came and rubbed himself against his legs, and said: 'Do not be troubled, dear master. Have a pair of boots made for me, and give me a sack, and you will soon see that you are better off with me than are your brothers with the mill and the ass.'

The young man had got a piece of gold in his pocket; it was all the money he had. He spent that in getting a pair of very handsome boots for his cat, and he also got a sack, as puss required.

14

When the cat had got what he had asked for, then he drew on his boots—they were topped with crimson leather—and he threw the sack over his shoulder, and went away to a warren, where there were many rabbits. Then he put some sow-thistles and some bran at the bottom of the sack, and throwing himself down as though he were dead, he waited till some foolish young rabbit should come and be snared.

Nor had he long to wait, for very soon a silly bunny came up, and attracted by what was in the sack, went in. Then the cat drew the cords that shut the neck of the sack and killed the rabbit.

Very proud of what he had done, he went to the king's palace, and asked to speak with his Majesty. He was readily admitted, when, marching in his boots to the foot of the throne, he made a profound bow, and throwing down the rabbit on the steps of the daïs, said: 'Sire, the Marquess of Carabas has enjoined me to present you with a rabbit from his warren. With onion sauce, boiled, your Majesty will find it excellent.'

'Tell your master,' answered the king, 'that he could hardly have afforded me a greater pleasure. My cook never dreams of sending me up rabbit, on which I dote. Thank him cordially from me.'

Next day the cat concealed himself in the standing corn, with his sack open. Soon two partridges entered; he drew the strings and caught them. Then again, he went to the palace, and presented them to the king in the name of his master, the Marquess of Carabas.

The king was delighted, and ordered that the messenger should be given something to drink. The cat asked for a saucerful of milk—he touched nothing stronger, said he; on principle he was a teetotaller.

The cat continued his course; he caught in like manner, pheasant, woodcock, snipe, teal, wild-

15

duck, fieldfare, and kept the palace larder pretty
well supplied with game during the season.

One day when the cat knew that the king was
going out a drive beside the river, along with his
daughter, who was the loveliest princess in the
world and heir to his throne, the cat said to his
master: 'If you will follow my advice, your fortune is made. You have but to bathe in the river,
at the spot I shall point out to you, and leave the
rest to me.' The young fellow did as was advised,

without understanding what was the purpose of
the cat. Whilst he was in the water, the carriage
of the king drew near; it was gilded and had glass
windows, and was drawn by cream-coloured horses
with gold and red trappings.

The cat now began to run up and down the
bank, screaming: 'Help! help! my master, the
Marquess of Carabas, will be drowned.'

The king hearing the cries, put his head out of the window and bade the coachman draw up. Then he recognised the cat which had brought him so many good things. He called the cat to the carriage-side and asked what distressed him.

'Sire!' answered the cat, 'whilst the most noble the Marquess of Carabas has been bathing some thieves have run away with his clothes. I am afraid if he remains much longer in the water he may have cramp and go under.'

In fact the cat had carried away his master's poor, mean garments, and had hidden them under a stone.

The king, who was not merely compassionate, but also generous and not above feeling gratitude for services rendered, at once ordered his attendants to go back to the palace for the most splendid suit they could find. 'I believe,' said the king, 'there is a very fine suit made for me some twenty years ago, when I was courting. I was then less corpulent than at present. You will find it in the lower right-hand drawer of the mahogany chest. I have little doubt it will fit the marquess to a nicety—that is, if he is a graceful man—I was immensely graceful twenty years ago.'

Owing to the minute and exact instructions given by his Majesty, the suit, which was exceedingly splendid, was soon found and brought to the lad in the water, who quickly clothed himself in it and then came to the coach door to pay his respects to the king and the princess.

The youth looked so engaging in the dress in which his Royal Highness had been invested when he went courting her mother, that the princess immediately lost her heart to him, and felt that the world to her would be a blank without him.

The king was also touched, for the sight of the youth in this suit—which he became, rather than the suit became him—awoke old feelings of senti-

mentality in the bosom of the king; he wiped his
eyes, and entreated the most noble marquess to
enter the carriage with him and his daughter;
and nudging the princess, he whispered: 'I was
like that when I went a-sweethearting.'

The cat, delighted that his schemes had so well
succeeded, ran on ahead of the carriage; and
having passed through a field in which harvesters
were cutting and making stacks of golden corn,
he said to them: 'Good people! unless you tell the
king who is coming this way that these cornfields
belong to the Marquess of Carabas, you will all be
made mincemeat of.'

The harvesters were somewhat alarmed at the
appearance of the cat in boots; they were exceedingly afraid of being made into mincemeat.

Presently the gilded coach of the king passed.
He stopped it and inquired of the peasants to
whom these splendid fields of grain belonged.

They answered, as they had been instructed, 'To
the most noble the Marquess of Carabas.'

'Upon my word!' said the king, addressing the
miller's son, 'you have a noble heritage.'

The young man bowed and blushed; and the
king and princess were pleased at his modesty.
The king nudged his daughter, and whispered:
'I was tremendously shy—when I went a-courting.'

The cat ran ahead, and came into a meadow in
which were mowers making hay. He said to
them: 'Good people! unless you tell the king who
is coming this way that these meadows belong to
the Marquess of Carabas, you will all be pickled
like young walnuts.'

When the king soon after came into the meadow
and smelt the sweet hay, he bade the coach stop,
and he inquired of the mowers to whom the
meadows belonged. They answered, as instructed,
that they belonged to the most noble the Marquess of Carabas.

'Goodness!' exclaimed the king, addressing the miller's son, 'you have indeed a noble heritage.'

The young man stammered something unintelligible. The king nudged his daughter, and said in a whisper: 'I also stuttered and stammered when I was paying my addresses to your mother.'

The cat ran on, and passed through a forest in which woodcutters were engaged thinning the timber.

He halted, and addressed them, and said: 'Good people! unless you say that all these woods belong to the Marquess of Carabas, you will all be stewed in your syrup like prunes.'

When soon after this the king's coach entered the woods, the king called to the driver to stop, and he signed to a woodcutter to come up. He asked him whose forests these were, and he replied that they belonged to the most noble the Marquess of Carabas.

'Well, I never!' exclaimed the king to the miller's son, 'you have verily a splendid inheritance.'

The poor lad was so bewildered that all he could do was to respond with a sickly smile.

The king nudged his daughter, and whispered: 'I also sniggered when I asked your mother to name the day. She said my snigger was more eloquent than words.'

The cat ran on, and saw at the end of the wood a magnificent palace. He went in, and found that it belonged to an ogre, who was also a magician and enormously rich, for all the lands through which the cat had run belonged to the domain of this palace. The cat asked leave to see the ogre. He said he could not think of passing that way without paying him his respects.

The ogre received him with civility; even ogres enjoy flattery.

'I have been informed,' said the cat, 'that you are so clever and so profound in your acquire-

19

ments, that you can transform yourself into any
shape you like. But this may be merely idle
gossip, not based on any foundation of truth. For
myself I never believe half the tittle-tattle I hear.'
'But it is really true,' said the ogre.
The cat smiled incredulously.
'I will at once show you my power,' said the ogre;
and in a moment transformed himself into a lion.
The cat was so frightened that he made a bolt
out of the window and ran up the water-pipes and
did not rest till he was on the roof. This was
difficult for him, because he wore boots, and boots
are calculated for a high-road, and not for scrambling.
After some time, he plucked up courage to descend.
'What do you think of my power now?' asked
the ogre, who had resumed his former shape.
'I think that your power is great,' answered the
cat, 'yet hardly all that I should have thought
had I given belief to what is said.'
'How so?' asked the ogre.
'I heard, for instance, on my way here, that you
were a great bear.'
'I can make myself that in a moment,' answered
the ogre.
'I am sure you are that already,' answered the
cat courteously. 'Others said you were an awful
bore—or boar—I did not ask them to spell the
word.'
'I can transform myself into that instantly.'
'I am certain you need no transformation to be
that most completely,' said the cat, with a bow.
'I also heard that you were in reality quite insig-
nificant as a personage, and a nobody. Now, any
fool can puff himself up into something greater
than himself, but it takes a wise man to make
himself appear less than he really is—Can you do
that?'

20

'In a moment,' answered the ogre, and he changed himself into a mouse.

Instantly the cat was on him and had eaten him.

Then he walked to the gate of the palace, and arrived there just as the royal carriage drove up.

'I wonder whose magnificent palace this is?' said the king.

Then the cat ran down the steps, opened the door of the carriage, and said: 'Your Majesty—welcome to the palace of the most noble Marquess of Carabas.'

'Why, this is truly a surprise,' said the king. 'What a splendid inheritance is yours, Marquis! Give my daughter your arm. We will pick a crumb with you, Carabas. I'm vastly hungry with my drive.'

The miller's son clumsily offered his arm as bidden to the princess. Her father nudged her, and whispered: 'I also was a great gawky when I proposed to your mother.'

Then all entered the great hall, and the king could not contain his surprise and admiration at all he saw. The cat ran down into the kitchen and ordered up a cold collation, and into the cellars, where he chose out the best wines; and the king said he had never enjoyed his victuals so heartily as that day. Then turning to the miller's son, he said: 'If you like, Carabas, you shall be my son-in-law. Say: I adore you—will you be mine? to the princess. I did that when I solicited the hand of her mother.'

The miller's son did not wait to be told this a second time. The princess at once accepted him, and they were married and lived happily.

The cat became a great lord, and had no occasion to run after and eat mice.

CINDERELLA

THE PRINCE TAKES CINDERELLA FROM HER HOME

22

# CINDERELLA

HERE was once a gentleman, a widower, who took for his second wife a lady who was a widow with two daughters. He, for his part, had a daughter by his first wife.

The second wife was extremely proud and haughty in her demeanour, and her two daughters had inherited their mother's qualities.

The gentleman's daughter by his first wife was most amiable and gentle, in which points she resembled her own mother.

No sooner had the marriage taken place than the ill-humour of the stepmother became manifest. She became jealous of the good qualities in the child, which made her own daughters appear by contrast the more disagreeable. She put upon her all the meanest tasks, and held her to them with inexorable severity. The young girl had to clean pots and pans, to scrub the floors and sweep the steps. She was obliged to do all the servile work of the house, and be as a slave to her half-sisters. For a bed she was given an old straw paillasse in an attic, where it was cold, and where ran the rats, whereas her sisters occupied the best

23

rooms in the house and feather-beds. They had also in their rooms cheval glasses in which they could admire themselves from top to toe.

The poor girl endured all without complaining. She did not dare to speak to her father about it, because he was completely under the thumb of his new wife. Moreover, he was much engaged in business which carried him away from home for weeks together, and she considered that if she were to speak to him about her treatment, her step-mother and sisters would serve her still worse as soon as his back was turned. When she had done her daily tasks, she was wont to creep into a corner of the fireplace, and sat among the cinders, for which reason her eldest sister called her Cinder-slut, but the second who was not quite so ill-tempered as the other, called her Cinderella. Although, poor girl, she was given the shabbiest clothes, and the dirtiest occupation, she was a hundred times more beautiful than her sisters in their finest dresses.

It happened that the king gave a ball, to which were invited all persons of quality. Amongst others the two young ladies of the house received invitation. No one thought of Cinderella, for no one knew of her existence; or if at any time they had known, they had forgotten her since she had been banished to the kitchen.

The two daughters of the lady were greatly excited about the ball; they discussed how they should be dressed and how they would have their hair done up, and what jewels they would wear.

'For my part,' said the eldest, 'I will wear red velvet and lace, and a turban of red and yellow, with an ostrich feather.'

'And I,' said the younger, 'I shall wear sere green velvet and satin embroidered with gold, and I will frizzle up my hair and tie it with amber silk ribbons.'

24

When the time approached they made Cinderella
lace them, and patch them, and paint them, and
frizzle them, and shoe them.

'How would you like to be at the ball?' asked
one of the sisters of Cinderella.

'As for me!' answered she, 'I do not think a
king's palace is the place for me, nor would my
sooty and soiled gown appear to advantage in a
ball-room.'

'That is true indeed,' laughed one of the
sisters. 'That would be a rare joke to see you at
the ball.' 'And what a fool you would look if
the prince asked you to dance a minuet,' said the
other.

For two days before the ball, the two damsels
ate nothing; they were desirous to have the small-
est waists of any ladies who appeared, and in
lacing them, Cinderella broke a score of laces

25

before she had got them done up tightly enough
to satisfy their vanity. When it came to patching,
the sisters were extremely particular. 'I,' said one,
'will have a square patch on the top of my nose.
I think it will heighten my complexion.'
'And I,' said the other, 'will have a round one in
the middle of my forehead. It will make me so
interesting.'
When the young ladies departed with their
mother, then Cinderella was left quite alone in the
house.
She sat herself on a heap of ashes in the corner
of the fireplace and began to cry.
Then all at once the hearth opened, and up
through it came a little woman with a red cloak
and a black pointed hat. This was her godmother,
who was a fairy.
The fairy godmother asked Cinderella why she
was crying.
Cinderella could only stammer—'I wish—Oh, I
wish . . . I wish . . . I wish . . .'
'I see clearly,' said the godmother, 'that you also
would like to go to the ball; is it so?'
'Indeed—indeed—I should,' sobbed the poor girl.
'Very well, then, so you shall. Go into the garden
and bring me a pumpkin.'
Cinderella at once went to pick the finest she
could find; it was yellow streaked with green.
She took it to her godmother, but had no idea
what would be done with it.
The fairy scooped out the inside, leaving only the
skin. Then she tapped it with her staff, and in
a moment it was changed into the most beautiful
coach, gold and green.
'Now,' said she, 'bring me the mouse-trap.'
Cinderella obeyed. In the mouse-trap were six
little mice. The fairy opened the door and as the
mice ran out, she give each a tap with her rod,
and it was transformed into a beautiful horse with

26

flowing mane and tail. She then attached the
six horses to the coach, the horses were all of a
beautiful brownish grey.

'What are we to do for a coachman?' asked
Cinderella.

'Fetch me the rat-trap,' said the godmother. The
girl did as desired. In it were three rats. The
fairy took the fattest, and with a touch of her wand
changed him into a pompous and dignified coachman.

Then she said, 'Go into the garden, and you will
there find six lizards behind the watering pot,
bring them to me.'

No sooner had Cinderella done what was commanded, than the fairy changed them dexterously
into six sleek lackeys, which mounted behind the
coach and hung on to it with all the grace and
facility as if they had been bred to it.

The fairy then said to Cinderella: 'There now, you
are set up with a conveyance in which to go to
the ball.'

'That is very true,' answered the girl, 'but, alas!
my clothes are so mean and soiled, that I shall be
ashamed to get out of my beautiful coach.'

'That is easily remedied,' said the fairy, and she
touched the garments worn by her godchild.

They were at once changed into the most splendid
silk, studded with diamonds.

'And now to make you complete,' said the fairy,
'I give you two glass slippers, the only ones there
are in the world.'

When Cinderella was thus dressed, she mounted
her carriage, and thanked her godmother gratefully. The good fairy said to her: 'I am well
pleased that you should enjoy yourself. But remember to leave before midnight. If you remain
a moment after the last stroke of the clock, then
your carriage will turn into a pumpkin, your horses
into mice, your driver into a rat, your flunkeys into

lizards, and all your beautiful garments will revert
to the condition of dirty, patched rags.'

Cinderella promised her godmother to remember
what she had said, and to return most certainly
before midnight.

Then she started, with a heart bounding with joy.

When she arrived at the palace, it was announced
to the prince, the king's son, that a lady in the
most splendid equipage ever seen was at the gates,
and that she would not give her name.

The prince at once ran out to salute her and
invite her to the ball. He gave her his hand to
help her to descend, and led her into the great hall
where the company was assembled.

Then a great silence fell on all. The dancers
ceased dancing, the musicians ceased playing, and
the gossips ceased gossiping, all were eager to see
the strange princess.

On all sides were heard whispers of, 'What a
radiant beauty!—what superb jewels!—what an
exquisite dress—who could have been her milliner?
—What a style in the doing of her hair—who could
have been her hairdresser?—What wonderful
slippers, who could have been her shoemaker?'

The king, although old, could hardly take his
eyes off her, and he whispered to the queen, that
except herself, he had never seen a greater beauty.
The queen, who was old and fat, accepted the
compliment gracefully, and smiled. All the ladies
observed Cinderella attentively, and endeavoured
to engrave in their memories every detail of her
dress, so as to get their next ball-dresses made
like it. The son of the king seated Cinderella in
the most honourable place, danced with her, and
himself brought her refreshments. As for himself,
he could eat nothing, so taken up was he with
attention to her, and in admiration of her beauty.

Cinderella seated herself by her sisters, and was
very civil to them. She gave them some of the

oranges the prince had peeled for her, and talked
to them most sweetly. They were lost in astonishment, and never for an instant recognised her.

Presently Cinderella heard the clock strike a quarter to twelve. Then she rose, made a graceful courtesy to the king and queen and to the company, and hastened away. On her return home she found her godmother in the chimney corner. She thanked the fairy for the favour granted her, and begged that she might be allowed to go to the ball at the palace on the following night, as the prince had expressly invited her.

Whilst she was thus talking, she heard the coach drive up that conveyed home her sisters and their mother. She hastened to the door, opened for them, yawned and rubbed her eyes, and said: 'How late you are! It must be past one o'clock.'

'Ah, ha!' exclaimed her eldest sister, 'you have missed something. There has been not only a most splendid entertainment, but there arrived at it a most illustrious princess, so beautiful, that she nearly came up to me.'

'And to me,' said the second.

'And she was most superbly dressed—her taste was almost equal to mine.'

'And to mine,' said the second.

'She was very civil to us, and gave us some of her oranges. Indeed—for ease and graceful courtesy, I should say she came almost up to me.'

'And to me,' said the second.

Cinderella listened to all that was said with great interest; she asked the name of the princess. But that—said her sisters—'is not known; the king's son did his utmost to find it out and failed. He says he would give a great deal to know it.'

'O dear, dear!' said Cinderella, 'I should like to see her; do, dear sisters, let me go with you to-

morrow night, spare me some of your clothes. I
should like to see this princess.'

'Hoity-toity! this is a fine idea!' exclaimed the
sisters. 'We should die of shame to be seen at a
great ball with such as you—and have it known
too that we were related.'

Cinderella expected this refusal. She was not
sorry; she would have been sorely embarrassed if
the sisters had consented to lend her their clothes,
and take her with them.

Next evening the sisters departed for the ball,
and all happened as on the previous night. This
time Cinderella was even more splendidly dressed
than on the first night.

The king's son was all the evening at her side,
and said to her the prettiest things imaginable.
Cinderella was so happy that the time passed
unobserved; and she forgot what her godmother
had said to her; so that she heard the first stroke
of twelve when she supposed it was only eleven
o'clock. Then she sprang from her seat and fled
as swiftly as a fawn.

The prince followed her, but could not overtake
her; however, in her flight she let fall one of her
glass slippers, and as the prince stooped to pick
it up she vanished. Cinderella arrived at home,
panting, in her soiled and patched dress, on foot,
without coach and attendance, nothing of all her
magnificence remained except the odd glass
slipper.

The prince inquired of the guards at the palace
gate if they had seen a beautiful princess pass,
and which way her coach had gone; but they
declared that no one except a scullery-maid had
passed that way; and upon looking for her coach,
it was nowhere to be seen.

When the two sisters returned from the ball,
Cinderella asked them if they had enjoyed themselves, and if the beautiful lady had been there;

they replied that she had, but that she had fled at the stroke of twelve and had left behind a glass slipper—the most lovely that could be conceived; that the king's son had picked it up, and that he had been quite disconsolate after she had disappeared, and had refused to dance or to eat or drink anything, but had sat in a corner sighing and looking at the glass slipper.

On the following morning the town was aroused by the blowing of trumpets, and, upon the people coming out to know the occasion, they found the royal heralds with a chamberlain and guards, and an attendant carrying a crimson velvet cushion, upon which was placed the glass slipper. The chamberlain announced that all single ladies were to try on the glass slipper, and that the prince had declared he would marry the one whom it would fit.

The slipper was tried first on the princesses, then on all the noble ladies, then on all the court ladies, but in vain; their feet were too large. Then it was tried on in the town by the daughters of the citizens, and the chamberlain brought it to the house of the sisters. The eldest saw at a glance that her foot would not go in, so she made an excuse, ran into the kitchen and cut off her toes. But even so her foot would not fit into the shoe, and she was obliged to abandon the attempt. Then it was offered to the second sister. She saw at a glance that it was too small for her foot, so she ran into the kitchen and cut off her heel. But even so she could not get her foot into the glass slipper.

The chamberlain was about to leave when he caught sight of Cinderella in the chimney corner, and he requested her to try on the glass slipper.

The sisters set up a loud laugh, and said the idea was ridiculous! However, the chamberlain insisted on it, and no sooner was the glass slipper put to her foot, than it slipped on as if made for it.

The amazement of the sisters was great, but it was greater still when Cinderella produced the other slipper—the fellow—from her pocket, and put it on her foot.

Then the hearth opened, and through it rose the fairy godmother. She touched Cinderella, and her clothes became more beautiful and costly than those she had worn at the balls.

Then her sisters recognised her as the princess they had seen and admired. They threw themselves at her feet and implored pardon for all the injuries they had done her. Cinderella raised them and kissed them, and said that they could make up for the past by loving her for the future.

The fairy godmother then said that Cinderella must go to the court in a splendid equipage, whereupon, as by magic, the gilded coach drawn by six greys, with the pompous coachman on the box, and the six lackeys behind, drew up at the door.

In this she drove to the palace, where she was well received by the prince, who thought her more beautiful by daylight than by that of candles.

A few days after, there was a grand marriage.

After that Cinderella got her sisters to lodge in apartments in the palace, and after a little urgency, two noblemen were persuaded to marry the sisters, who sincerely promised and vowed on their side to be better-tempered in their married state than they had been as spinsters. And the noblemen promised and vowed, on their part, if they did not, they would give them shabby clothes, and smut their faces till they became amiable again.

# VALENTINE AND ORSON

## CHAPTER I

PEPIN, King of the Franks, had a sister named Bellisance, who was exceedingly beautiful, and who was asked in marriage by many kings and princes.

The lady's choice fell upon Alexander, Emperor of Constantinople, who came to the court of King Pepin to marry the princess. Great rejoicings took place on the occasion in all parts of the kingdom; and soon after the marriage the emperor took his leave, and carried his lovely bride in great splendour and triumph to Constantinople.

The Emperor Alexander's prime minister was a selfish and subtle man; unhappily his influence with the emperor was very great. This man, observing the gentleness and sweetness of the Lady Bellisance, began to fear that she would undermine his influence, and he wickedly resolved to seek the destruction of the innocent empress. The emperor was of a credulous and suspicious temper, and the prime minister found means at length to infuse into his mind suspicions of the empress. One day when the emperor was alone, he entered

c                    33

the apartment, and throwing himself at his
master's feet, said: 'May Heaven guard your
majesty from the base attempts of the wicked and
treacherous! I seek not the death of any man,
nor may I reveal the name of the person who has
intrusted to me a dreadful secret; but, in the most
solemn manner, I conjure your majesty to beware
of the designs of your empress; for that beautiful
and clever lady is faithless and disloyal, and is
even now planning your dethronement. Alas!
my heart is ready to burst with indignation, to
think that a lady of such charms, and the sister
of a great king, should become so dishonourable
and wicked.'

The emperor giving perfect faith to his favourite's
tale could no longer restrain his fury; and abruptly
leaving him, he rushed into the apartment of
the empress, and in the fiercest manner dragged
the fair Bellisance about the chamber by her
long and beautiful hair. 'Alack! my dear lord,' she
cried, 'what causes you to commit this outrage?'

'Base wretch!' he exclaimed, 'I am but too well
informed of your wicked proceedings;' then dash-
ing her with violence upon the ground, he left her
speechless. The attendants of the empress finding
her lying senseless on the floor, uttered loud
screams, which presently brought all the courtiers
into the chamber.

Every one was sorry for their amiable queen;
and the nobles demanded an audience of the
emperor, to represent to him the wrongs he had
done to an honourable lady, with whom no one
before had ever found any fault. But the emperor
was still blinded with passion, and to their repre-
sentations he answered: 'Let no man dare to
defend a woman who has basely betrayed me.
She shall die; and they who interfere in her behalf
shall partake in the dreadful punishment that
awaits treason.'

The empress on recovery from her swoon, fell upon her knees, and thus addressed the emperor: 'Alas! my lord, take pity on one who never harboured an evil thought against your person or dignity; and if not upon me, at least I implore you have compassion on your two children! Let me be imprisoned or put to death, if it so pleaseth you; but, I beseech you, save my poor children!'

The rash emperor, misled by the false tales of the prime minister, would not hearken to her; and the courtiers, perceiving that nothing could mitigate his rage, removed Bellisance from his presence.

Her faithful servant, Blandiman, now threw himself at her feet, exclaiming, 'Ah! madam, let me prevail on you to quit this unhappy place, and suffer me to conduct you and your children to your brother, the good King Pepin. Innocent and noble lady, follow my counsel; for if you stay here the emperor will bring you to a shameful death.'

'No, my faithful servant,' replied she; 'I cannot follow your advice. If I should steal away privately from the court, it might be said I had fled because I was guilty. No; I had rather die the most cruel death than bear the blame of that of which I am innocent.'

The emperor so far relented, that he would not pronounce sentence of execution upon his queen; yet, as his mind was continually excited by false accusations against her, he resolved to banish her from his dominions, and immediately commanded her to quit Constantinople. At the same time he published an edict, forbidding all persons, on pain of death, to assist or succour the unfortunate lady, allowing her no other attendant than her servant Blandiman, whom she had brought with her from France. Sentence having been thus pronounced, the queen, Blandiman, and the two children,

hastened away. As she passed through the city,
she was met by multitudes of people lamenting the
loss of so good an empress. When she had left
Constantinople, 'Alas!' cried she, 'in what unhappy hour was I born, to fall from so high an
estate to so low a condition as I am now in!'

As she was thus complaining and weeping with
anguish, her servant said to her, 'Madam, be not
discomforted, but trust in God, who will keep and
defend you.'

He had hardly spoken, before he espied a fountain,
which he and his lady at once approached. After
refreshing themselves at the fountain, they proceeded towards France. Many weary days and
nights had been spent in travel, when, arriving in
the forest of Orleans, the disconsolate princess
was so overcome with grief and fatigue, that she
sank, and was incapable of proceeding farther.
Her faithful attendant gathered the fallen leaves
and the moss to make a couch for her on which
to rest, and then hastened away, to seek some
habitation where he might procure food for his
unfortunate mistress.

During Blandiman's absence the empress fell
asleep, with her two infant boys laid on the couch
beside her, when suddenly a huge bear rushed
out of the forest, and, snatching up one of the
children in its mouth, disappeared with its prey.
The wretched mother, distracted at the fate of her
child, pursued the bear with shrieks and lamentations, till, overcome with anguish and terror, she
fell into a swoon near the mouth of the cave into
which the bear had carried her child.

It happened that King Pepin, accompanied by
several great lords and barons of his court, was
that same day hunting in the forest of Orleans,
and chanced to pass near the tree where the other
little boy lay sleeping on his bed of moss. The
king was astonished with the beauty of the child,

who opened his eyes as the king stood gazing on him, and, smiling, stretched out his little arms, as if to ask protection. 'See, my lords,' said King Pepin, 'this lovely infant seems to ask my favour. Here is no one to claim it, and I will adopt it for my own.'

The king little imagined it was his nephew, the

son of his sister Bellisance, that he now delivered into the hands of one of his pages, who took the babe to Orleans to be nursed, and gave it, by the king's orders, the name of Valentine, because it was found on S. Valentine's day.

Blandiman, who had now returned, after looking in vain for assistance, missed his mistress; and after searching the forest for her, he at length

espied her on the ground, tearing her hair, and
uttering piercing cries of grief. 'Ah, Blandiman!'
she exclaimed, 'can there exist in the world a
being more encompassed with grief and sorrow?
I left Constantinople the mother of two beautiful
children, my only comfort under my bitter sorrow.
A ravenous bear has now snatched one from my
arms, and a no less cruel beast of prey has doubtless devoured the other. At the foot of yonder
tree I left it when I pursued the bear; but no
trace of either of my children remains. Go, Blandiman, leave me here to perish, and tell the Emperor
of Constantinople to what a horrible fate, by listening to evil counsel, he has destined his innocent
wife and children.'

At this moment they were interrupted by the
sudden appearance of a huge giant, who immediately attempted to seize the empress. Blandiman sprang to his feet, stepped before him, and
began to draw and defend himself. His efforts,
however, were unavailing: the giant prevailed,
and slew him; and throwing the unfortunate lady
over his shoulder, proceeded towards his castle.

## CHAPTER II

MEANTIME the bear that had carried away the
infant, bore it to its cave, and laid it down unhurt
before her young ones. The young bears, however, did not devour it, but stroked it with their
rough paws; and the old bear, perceiving their
kindness for the little babe, gave it milk, and
nourished it in this manner for the space of a
whole year.

The boy became hardy and robust; and as he
grew in strength he began to range the forest, and
attack the wild beasts with such fury that they

used to shun the cave where he continued to live
with the old bear, who loved him with extreme
fondness. He passed eighteen years in this kind
of life, and grew to such wonderful strength,
that he was the terror of the neighbouring
country. The name of Orson was given to him,
because he was nurtured by a bear; and the re-
nown of this wild man spread over all France.
He could not speak, and uttered no other sounds
than a wild kind of growl to express either his
anger or his joy. King Pepin often entertained
a great desire to see this wild man of the woods;
and one day rode with his retinue into the forest
of Orleans in hopes of meeting him. The king
left his train at some distance, rode on, and
passed near the cave which Orson inhabited.
On hearing the sound of horses' feet, the wild
man rushed upon the king, and would have
strangled him in an instant but for a valiant
knight, who galloped up and wounded Orson with
his sword. Orson then quitted the king, and,
running furiously upon the knight, caught him
and his horse and overthrew both. The king,
being quite unarmed, could not assist the knight,
but rode away to call the attendants to his rescue.
However, before they arrived on the spot, the
unfortunate knight was torn to pieces, and Orson
had fled to the thickest part of the forest, where,
notwithstanding all their endeavours, they could
not discover him. The noise of this adventure
increased every one's terror of the wild man, and
the neighbouring villages were nearly abandoned
by their inhabitants.

Valentine, in the meanwhile, had been educated
in all kinds of accomplishments with the king's
two sons and his fair daughter, Eglantine.
Nothing could exceed the fondness of the young
people for each other; indeed, there was never a
lovelier princess than Eglantine, or a more brave

and accomplished youth than Valentine. The king observing his inclination for arms, indulged him with armour and horses, and after creating him knight gave him a command in his army that was about to march against the Saracens. Valentine soon distinguished himself above the other leaders in battle. He fought near the king's side; and when his majesty was taken by a troop of the pagans, Valentine rushed through their ranks, slew hundreds of them, and replacing the king on his horse, led him off in triumph. Afterwards, when the Saracen city was besieged, he was the first to scale the walls and place the Christian standard on the battlements. By his means a complete victory was obtained, and peace restored to France.

Having conquered the Saracens, Valentine returned to the court of King Pepin, and was received with loud acclamations by the people, and joyfully welcomed by the Princess Eglantine. The distinctions and favour showered on him raised the envy and hatred of the king's sons, who plotted together to destroy Valentine.

It happened very shortly after the return of Valentine from his victory over the Saracens, that a petition was presented to the king by a deputation of peasants, praying relief against Orson, the wild man of the woods; the fear of whom was now become so great that the peasants dared not go out to till their fields, nor the shepherds to watch their flocks. The king immediately issued a proclamation, saying, if any man would undertake to bring Orson dead or alive to the city, he should receive a thousand marks of gold.

'Sire,' said his sons, 'we think no person is so proper to undertake this enterprise as the foundling Valentine, on whom your majesty lavishes such great favours, and who, it seems, aspires to the hand of your daughter. Perhaps if he conquers the savage with his sword, you will not think it then too much to reward him with the hand of our sister Eglantine.'

Valentine saw through the malicious design of the king's sons; and the king himself wished to protect him, and advised him not to encounter such an enemy.

'Pardon me, my liege,' replied Valentine; 'it concerns my honour that I go. I will encounter this danger, and every other, rather than not prove myself worthy of your majesty's favour and protection. To-morrow I will depart for the forest at break of day.'

When the Princess Eglantine heard of Valentine's determination, she sought to turn him from his purpose; but finding him inflexibly resolved to attack the wild man, she adorned him with a scarf, embroidered by her own hands, and then retired to her chamber to pray for his safety.

At the first dawn of morning Valentine arose, put on his armour, and with his shield polished like a mirror, he departed for the forest. On his arrival there, he alighted, tied his horse to a tree, and penetrated into the thickest part of the wood in search of Orson.

He wandered about a long time in vain; till coming near the mouth of a large cave, he thought that might be the hiding-place of the wild man. Valentine then climbed a high tree near the cave; and scarcely was he seated among the branches, before he heard Orson's roar in the forest. Orson had been hunting, and came with a swift pace, bearing upon his shoulders a buck he had killed.

Valentine could not help admiring the beauty of his person, the grace and freedom of his motions, and his appearance of strength and agility. He felt a species of affection for the wild man, and wished it were possible to tame him without having recourse to weapons. Valentine now tore off a branch of the tree, and threw it at Orson's feet; who, looking up and espying Valentine in the tree, uttered a growl of fury, and darted up the tree like lightning. Valentine as quickly slipped down on the other side. Orson seeing him on the ground leaped from the tree, and, opening his arms, prepared in his usual manner to rush upon and overthrow his antagonist; but Valentine holding up his polished steel shield Orson suddenly beheld, instead of the person he meant to seize, his own wild and terror-striking figure. Upon Valentine's lowering the shield, he again saw his enemy, and with a cry of transport prepared to grasp him in his arms. The strength of Orson was so very great, that Valentine was unable to defend himself without having recourse to his sword. When Orson received a wound from the sword, he uttered loud shrieks of anger and surprise, and instantly tearing up by the roots a large tree, furiously attacked Valentine. A dreadful fight now ensued, and the victory was a long time doubtful; Orson received many dreadful wounds from the sword of Valentine, and Valentine with great difficulty escaped from being crushed to death beneath the weighty club of Orson. At last Valentine's skill prevailed, and the wild man was conquered, and lay prostrate on the ground at his feet.

Valentine now made signs to Orson that he wished him to accompany him, on which he quietly suffered his hands to be bound; and Valentine having mounted his horse, the two brothers proceeded towards Orleans.

## CHAPTER III

WHEREVER they passed, the people on seeing the wild man, ran into their houses and hid themselves. When Valentine arrived at an inn where he intended to rest during the night, the terrified inhabitants fastened their doors, and would not suffer them to enter. Valentine made signs to Orson, who placed his shoulder against the door, and forced it open in an instant; upon which the people of the inn all ran out at the back-door, and would not venture to return. A great feast was in preparation, and there were plenty of fowls and good provisions roasting at the fire. Orson tore the meat off the spit with his hands, and devoured it greedily; and espying a caldron of water, he put his head into it and drank like a horse.

In the morning, Valentine resumed his journey, leading Orson as before. On arriving at the city, the inhabitants shut their doors, and ran into the highest rooms to gaze upon the wild man. When they reached the outer court of King Pepin's palace, the porter in a great fright barred the gate with heavy chains and bars of iron, and would not be prevailed upon to open it. After soliciting admittance for some time, and being still denied, Valentine made a sign to Orson, who, tearing up one of the large stone posts that stood by, shattered the gate to pieces. The queen, the Princess Eglantine, and all their attendants, fled to hide themselves when they heard that Orson was arrived; and Valentine had the greatest difficulty to persuade them to believe that Orson was no longer furious and savage as he had been in the woods. At length the king permitted him to be brought in; and the whole court soon gathered in a crowd in the apartment, and were much amused by his wild actions and gestures, although they were very cautious not to come near him. On Valentine's making signs, he kissed the king's robe, and the hand of the Princess Eglantine; for Orson had now become so attached to Valentine that he would obey him in all things, and would

43

suffer no other person to attempt to control him. If Valentine went for a moment out of his sight, he would utter cries of distress, and overturn every one that stood in his way, while he ran about the palace in search of him; and he slept at night in Valentine's chamber on the floor, for he could not be prevailed to lie on a bed.

Very soon after the capture of Orson, a herald appeared at the court of King Pepin, from the Duke of Aquitaine, summoning all true knights to avenge the cause of the Lady Clerimont, daughter to the noble duke, who was held in cruel captivity by Atramont, the black knight: the herald proclaimed that whoever should conquer him would receive the hand of the lady in marriage, together with a princely dowry. This knight was so famous for his cruelty and his victories, that the young lords of the court all drew back, and were unwilling to enter the lists; for it was known that he was defended by enchantment, and it was his practice to hang upon a high tree all the knights whom he had defeated. Valentine, however, offered himself without hesitation; and though he did not intend to ask the lady in marriage, he nevertheless determined to attempt her rescue from the hands of the giant.

Valentine, followed by Orson as his squire, soon reached the castle of the black knight, and immediately demanded the freedom of the captive lady. This was refused, and the two knights at once began the combat. The fight was long and equal. At length Atramont demanded a parley: 'Knight,' said he to Valentine, 'thou art brave and noble; behold, yonder hang twenty knights whom I have overcome and put to death: such will be thy fate; I give thee warning.'

'Base traitor,' replied Valentine, 'I fear thee not; come on—I defy thee.'

'First,' rejoined the black knight, 'fetch me

44

yonder shield; for in pity to thy youth, I tell thee, unless thou canst remove that shield, thou canst not rescue the lady, nor conquer me.'

Valentine approached the shield; but, in spite of all his efforts, he could not loosen it from the tree, though it appeared to hang on only a slender branch. Valentine, breathless with his exertions to pull down the shield, stood leaning against the tree, when Atramont, with a loud laugh, exclaimed, 'Fly and save thyself, fair knight; for since thou canst not move the shield, thou art not destined to be my victor. Further, know there is no one living who can subdue me, unless he be the son of a mighty king, and yet has been suckled by a wild beast.'

Valentine started on hearing these last words, and immediately ran to Orson, and led him to the enchanted shield. On Orson's raising his arm towards it, it dropped instantly from its place. A loud blast of wind rushed through the trees, the ground rocked beneath their feet, and the black knight trembled and turned pale; then gnashing his teeth he seized his sword, and attacked Orson with desperate fury. At the first blow, Atramont's sword broke in pieces upon the enchanted shield. Next he caught up a battle-axe, which also snapped instantly in two. He then took a lance, which was shivered to atoms in the same manner. Furious with these defeats, he threw aside his weapons, and trusting to his great strength, attempted to grasp Orson in his arms: but Orson, seizing him as if he had been a mere child, dashed him on the ground, and would have instantly destroyed him, had not Valentine interposed to save his life. Orson continued to hold him down till some chains were brought, when, in despite of the furious struggles of the black knight, Orson bound him in strong fetters, to lead him away a prisoner.

45

Atramont, finding himself conquered, addressed
himself to Valentine, and said: 'This savage man
is my conqueror, and there is some mystery in his
fate. Hasten to the castle of the giant Ferragus,
where, if you can conquer him, you will find a
brazen head, kept by a dwarf, that will explain to
you who this savage is. You will also be able to
set at liberty all the captives whom he keeps confined in his dungeons.'
He then directed them on their way to the
giant's castle; and after they had rested and
refreshed themselves, they took their departure.


## CHAPTER IV

THEY had to pass over many a hill and valley,
and through wild and trackless forests; at last
they came in view of the giant's castle, to which
the entrance was by a bridge of brass. The building itself was of marble, and the battlements were
surmounted by golden pinnacles, which glittered
richly in the evening sun as the two brothers approached the castle. Beneath the bridge of brass
a hundred bells were fastened by a strange device,
so that neither man nor beast might pass over
without a loud alarm being given. The moment
the two travellers began to cross the bridge the
bells sounded, and immediately the great gates of
the castle were thrown open, and a huge giant
stalked forth, bearing in his hand a knotted club
of steel. He immediately summoned them in a
voice of thunder to lay down their arms.
'Yield, you caitiffs!' said he, 'or I will make you
food for the wolves and birds of prey. No one
comes here and escapes with his life so long as
I can wield my good club.'
'Vain boaster,' replied Valentine, 'I scorn you

and your threats! I come determined to force the brazen gates of your castle and to set free your prisoners.'

With these words he put spurs to his steed, and aimed his trusty spear at the giant's head. The first thrust made the giant bleed, and he, in his turn, aimed a desperate blow at the knight. This happily missed, and left Valentine an opportunity of attacking the giant with his sword, which he did with the greatest courage, aiming blow after blow, first on one side, then on another, with the utmost agility and skill. But at last the giant, mad with pain and rage, saw that his adversary was beginning to flag, and found opportunity to deal him a tremendous blow with his mace, which laid both horse and rider senseless on the ground. He now grinned a hideous grin, and, stooping down, he was about to aim a second blow, exclaiming, 'Now, caitiff, breathe thy last.' But before he could raise his arm to strike, two tremendous blows descended upon his own head, and the monster fell groaning to the earth. These blows came from the knotty club of Orson, who, seeing his friend's danger, ran up just in time to save him. The giant was dead; and, with Orson's care and attention, Valentine soon began to recover.

They now began to search the giant's castle, both to set free his captives and to find the dwarf who would give the promised explanation. As they went through the gloomy apartments and dungeons, they found the bones of many murdered knights who had been overcome by the giant, and at last, in a little dim cell lighted by one small window, they found a lady lying on the ground and bathed in tears. At their entrance she lifted up her eyes and begged for mercy. Valentine gently raised her, and assured her that they were come to succour her, that the giant was killed, and that the castle-gates were thrown open. They

47

then led her out of the dungeon into one of the
apartments of the castle, and supplied her with
food and wine, and attended to all her wants.

They then inquired her name and her story,
when she related to them her whole history, as it
has been already told, from the time of her marriage to the hour when the fierce giant slew her
trusty attendant, and carried her off by force to
the castle. But, when they heard her name, and
that she was sister to King Pepin, they were
beyond measure amazed and overjoyed; for they
had often heard the sad story of the Empress of
Constantinople, and how the emperor, after she
had gone, had discovered the treachery of his
prime minister, and had made long and anxious
search for his wife and children, but in vain.

## CHAPTER V

VALENTINE and Orson determined to set out
for the coast of France as soon as the Lady Bellisance was able to travel, knowing how overjoyed
the old king would be to see his long-lost sister.
But, before taking their departure, they went to
search for the dwarf, who at last was found in one
of the turrets of the castle, and who immediately
expressed his willingness to serve his deliverer,
now that his cruel master was dead.

They desired him to lead them to the chamber
where the brazen head was kept, which he immediately did. Valentine fixed his eyes upon the
head, anxious to hear what it would say concerning his birth. At length it spake thus: 'Thou,
O renowned knight, art called Valentine the Brave,
and art the man destined to be the husband of the
Princess Eglantine of France. Thou art son to the
Emperor of Greece, and thy mother is Bellisance,
sister to King Pepin of France. She was unjustly

48

banished from her throne, and after many wander- VALEN-
ings, she was seized by a giant and confined in a TINE AND
dungeon of this castle, where she has been for ORSON
twenty years. The wild man, who hath so long
accompanied thee, is thy brother. You were both
lost in the forest of Orleans. Thou wert found
and brought up under the care of King Pepin thy
uncle, but thy brother was stolen and nurtured
by a bear. Proceed to France with the innocent
empress, thy hapless mother. Away, and prosper!
These are the last words I shall utter. Fate has
decreed, that when Valentine and Orson enter this
chamber, my power ends.'

Having thus spoken, the brazen head fell from its
pedestal, and in the fall was broken into a thousand pieces.

The two youths stood for a moment fixed with
astonishment; they then joyfully embraced each
other, and rejoined the empress to tell her the
extraordinary news they had just heard. Imagine
her surprise when she saw before her her two long-
lost sons. To describe her emotions on this joyful
occasion would be impossible.

After the first transports were over, they prepared
for their departure. The stables of the giant's
castle furnished them with horses; and everything
else necessary for their journey was found in its
well-stored recesses. So, taking with them the
dwarf as their servant, the whole party proceeded
towards France.

The meeting of King Pepin and his dear sister
was, we need not say, a happy and joyful one. A
courier was immediately despatched to Constantinople to inform the Emperor Alexander of the
arrival of his empress at the capital of France.
The messenger found him still mourning the loss
of his innocent queen, and refusing all comfort
from those around him, from the thought that by
his own folly and rashness he had been the cause

of her banishment and death. The news was like life to the dead; and the emperor, as soon as he had sufficiently collected himself to give the proper orders, set off with his whole court to meet his long-lost queen, and to bring her back in triumph to her throne. His delight was still further increased when he saw the two youths his sons, and embraced them for the first time since they were children.

Great rejoicings, feasts, dances, and tournaments were held in honour of these events in all parts of the French king's dominions; and, in due time, the emperor and his queen, accompanied by Orson, took their departure for their own country. Valentine remained at the court of his uncle, and was shortly after married to the fair Princess Eglantine.

At the death of the monarch they succeeded to the empire, and were blessed with a long and prosperous reign.

by kind and good people, who would give them food and shelter.

But the poor little children were so frightened and confused that they did not understand in which direction to go. They waited a long while for the man, and, as he did not come back, they wandered in the wood ; and in place of getting out of it, by a sad mishap they turned, and went back into its very depths.

These pretty babes, all hand in hand,
  Went wandering up and down ;
But never more could see the man
  Approaching from the town.
Their pretty lips with blackberries
  Were all besmeared and dyed ;
But when came on the darksome night,
  They sat them down and cried.

Thus wander'd these poor innocents
  Till death did end their grief ;
In one another's arms they died
  As wanting due relief.
No burial this pretty pair
  Of any man receives,
But Robin-redbreast, piously,
  Did cover them with leaves.

It must now be told how that the wicked uncle got no rest in mind or body. Nothing prospered with him. His fields were blighted, and his cattle died in stall. His barns caught fire, and his substance wasted.

He had sent his sons in a merchant-ship to Portugal, and a violent storm arose, wrecked the vessel, and his sons were drowned.

So badly did the uncle fare, that, in seven years, all his lands and goods were in pawn or lost ; and himself smitten with an ague that never left him, but made him shiver and shake.

E          65

As for the man who had left the Babes in the wood, he was convicted of a robbery and thrown into prison, when he confessed the whole story—how he was hired by the uncle, how he had fought with and killed his fellow, and how he had deserted the children in the wood.

Thus it was the whole story came to the light of day.

## PRETTY MARUSCHKA

AR away in the hazy purple of antiquity, when all stepmothers were wicked, and all younger sons were successful, there lived on the confines of a forest a woman who had two daughters: the one her own, the other only a step- child. Naturally, the love of the mother was concentrated on her own Helena, and, as naturally, she disliked Maruschka, who was the fairest, the gentlest, and the most pious of the two girls.

Little did pretty Maruschka know of her own surpassing beauty—a fact proving to us how remote from the present age was that in which these damsels lived. Her hair was like the waving gold of the cornfield when the wind soughs over it, and her eyes were as the blue forget-me-not which smiles and glimmers in a quiet nook by the brookside. She was slim and graceful; her step was light, for her heart was free. Wherever she went she brought cheerfulness and smiles; like the little golden sunbeams which pierce among the tree-shadows of a forest, and light up unex- pected beauties where all before was gloom; now painting a saffron butterfly, now kindling an

67

emerald moss-tuft, now making a scarlet lily flame
against the dusk of the forest glades behind.

Helena was dressed by her mother in gay colours
for Sunday and Feast-day, but poor little Mar-
suchka had only a dingy grey gown, cast off by
her sister. Helena wore black shoes with silver
buckles, but pretty Maruschka clattered up the
churchyard path in wooden clogs. Helena wore
a false gold chain of great links round her neck,
but her half-sister had only a turquoise-coloured
ribbon and a little silver cross with a crystal in
it—that was her only ornament—and that had been
given her by a lady whom she had guided into the
road, when she had lost her way in the forest.

As the mother and the two girls went to church
on Sundays, the lads were all in the yard hanging
about the tombstones; and the old woman heard
them whisper, 'There is pretty Maruschka;' but
never once did they say, 'See pretty Helena.' So
she was angry, and hated the golden-haired, blue-
eyed maiden. At home she made her do all the
hard work—scrub the floors, cook the victuals,
mend the clothes—whilst Helena stood all day
before her glass, combing her hair and adorning
herself with trinkets, and wishing it were Sunday
that she might flare before the eyes of the young
men in the churchyard.

Helena and her mother did all that lay in their
power to make the little girl's life miserable. They
scolded her, they beat her, they devised schemes
of annoyance for her, but never could they ruffle
the sweet temper of Maruschka.

One day, in the depth of winter, Helena cried out,
'Ah, me! would that I had a bunch of violets in
my bosom to-morrow, when I go to church. Run,
Maruschka, run into the forest and pluck them for
me, that I may have them to smell at whilst the
priest gives us his sermon.'

'Oh, my sister!' answered Maruschka, 'who ever

68

heard of violets being gathered in midwinter, under the deep snow?'
'Idle hussey!' screamed Helena; 'go at once and fetch them. Have them I will, and you shall not come back without them.'
Then the mother chimed in with, 'Mind and bring a large bunch, or you shall not be taken in here for the night. Go!' and she caught her, thrust her from the house, and slammed the door behind her.
Bitterly weeping, the poor maiden wandered into the forest. The snow lay deep everywhere, undinted by human foot; white wreaths hung on the bushes, and the sombre pine-boughs were frosted over with snow. Here were the traces of a hare, there the prints of a badger. An owl called from the depths of the forest. The girl lost her way. Dusk came on, and a few stars looked through the interlacing boughs overhead, watching Maruschka. An icy wind moaned through the trees, shaking the pines as though they quaked with mortal fear, and then they bent their branches and shot their loads of snow in dust to the ground. Strange harp-like sounds reverberated through the gloom, and gratings of bough on bough, which seemed as though the wood demons were gnawing at fallen timbers. Now a great black crow, which had been brooding among dark firs and pines, startled by the footfall and sobs of the maiden, expanded his wings, and, with a harsh scream, rushed away, noisily, sending the life-blood with a leap to the girl's heart. Suddenly, before her—far up on a hill-top—a light appeared, ruddy and flickering. Maruschka, inspired with hope, made for it, scrambling up a rocky slope through deep snow-drifts. She reached the summit, and beheld a great fire. Around this fire were twelve rough stones, and on each stone sat a man. Three were grey-bearded, three were middle-aged, three were

youths; and the last three were the youngest and fairest. They spake not, but looked intently on the roaring flames. He who sat in the seat of honour had a long staff in his hand. His hair was white, and fluttering in the cold wind.

Maruschka was startled, and watched them with astonishment for a little while; then mustering courage, she stepped within the circle and said:—

'Dear, good friends, please suffer me to warm myself a little while at the fire, for, indeed, I am perishing with cold.' He with the flowing white hair raised his head, and said—
'Yes, child, approach. But what brings you here?'
'I am seeking violets,' she answered.
'Violets! It is not the time for violets, when the snow lies deep?'

'Ah, sir! I know that well; but sister Helena and mother have bidden me bring them violets, and if I do not I must perish in the cold. You, kind shepherds, tell me where I may find violets!'
Then the white aged one arose from his seat, stepped to one of the blooming youths, put his staff into his hand, and said—
'Brother March, take thou the pre-eminence.'
Then the Month March sat himself on the chief stone, and waved his staff over the fire. Instantly the flames rushed up and blazed with greater brilliancy, the snow began to thaw, the hazel-bushes were covered with catkins, and glossy buds appeared on the beech. Green herbs thrust up through the moist soil, a primrose gleamed from a dusky bank, and a sweet fragrance of violets was wafted by on a gentle breeze. Under a bush, the ground was purple with their scented blossoms.
'Quick, Maruschka, pluck!' ordered March. The girl hastily gathered a handful. Then she cour-tesied to the twelve Months, thanked them cordially, and hurried home.
Helena was amazed when her half-sister came with the bunch to the door. She opened it to her, and the house was filled with the delicious odour.
'Where did you find them?' she asked.
'High up on the mountain, under a hawthorn bush.'
Helena took the flowers, and set them in her bosom. She let her mother smell at them, but she never gave one to Maruschka.
When they came home from church next day, Helena cast off her gay shawls, and sat down to supper. But she had no appetite for what was on the table. She was angry with her sister; for all the lads had fixed their eyes on Maruschka, and had not even been attracted to her by the fragrant bunch of violets. 'How beautiful is Maruschka

to-day!' had said some of the older people; and none had spoken a good word of her.

So she sat and sighed, and hated the pretty girl more and more.

'Oh that I had strawberries!' she said. 'I can eat nothing this evening but strawberries. Run, Maruschka, into the forest and gather me a dishful.'

'Dear sister, this is not the time of the year for strawberries. Who ever heard of strawberries ripening under the snow?'

But the stepmother angrily exclaimed: 'Run, Maruschka, fetch them at once, as your sister has ordered, or I will strike you dead;' and she thrust her from the door.

The poor girl cried bitterly; she looked back at the firelight which glimmered through the casement, and thought how warm it was within, whilst without it was so piercingly cold. But she dared not return unless she had with her the desired fruit. So she plunged into the forest. The snow lay deep, and nowhere was a human footprint. Snow began to fall in fine powder, whitening her shoulders, clinging to the folds of her grey dress, and forming a cap of ice on her golden hair. In that dull rayless night there was no light to show the blue ribbon, which strayed among the tree boles, or to twinkle on the crystal of the silver cross.

Presently Maruschka saw, high up on the summit of a rugged hill, a blazing fire. She scrambled to it, and there she found the Twelve sitting solemn and silent around the flames, and the Ice Month, with his staff, sat still on the seat of honour.

'Dear, good friends, please suffer me to warm myself a little while at the fire,' she asked in a beseeching voice; 'for, indeed, I am perishing with cold.'

Then the one with the drifting white locks raised his head and said—

72

'Yes, child, approach. But what brings you here?'
I am seeking strawberries,' she answered.
'Strawberries! It is not the time for strawberries when the snow lies deep?'
'Ah, sir! I know that well; but sister Helena and mother have bidden me bring them straw-berries, or they will strike me dead. You, kind shepherds, tell me where I may find strawberries.'
Then the white Ice Month arose from his seat, stepped across the area to one of the young men, put the staff into his hand, and said—
'Brother June, take thou the pre-eminence.'
Then the Month June sat himself on the chief stone, and waved his staff over the fire. Instantly it glowed like molten gold, beams of glory streamed from it through the forest, and it shone like a sun resting on the earth. Overhead, the clouds flamed and curled in wreaths of light-tinted rose, carnation, and purple, athwart a sky blue as the forget-me-not. Every trace of snow vanished, and the earth was buried in green. The trees were covered with rustling leaves. Blue-bells gleamed under their shadows, and then died away. Red-robin blushed in tufts, and then shed its ragged petals. Wild roses burst into glorious flower, and the soft air was charged with the scent of the sweet-briar. From among the forest-glades called, in cool notes, a wood-dove. The thrush began to warble, and the blackbird to pipe. A bright-eyed squirrel danced among the fresh green leaves on the tree-tops. Beside a brown stone was a patch of sloping green. It was dotted with little white stars with golden hearts. Now the leaves drop off, and the hearts swell, and flush, and glow, and become crimson.
'Quick, Maruschka, pluck!' said June.
Then the girl joyfully hurried to the slope, and gathered an apronful of the luscious strawberries.

73

She courtesied to the twelve Months, thanked them
cordially, and hurried home.

Helena was astonished as she saw her come to
the house, and she ran to open the door. The
whole cottage was fragrant with the odour of the
strawberries.

'Where did you gather them?' asked Helena.

'High up on the mountains, under a brown rock.'

Helena took the strawberries, and ate them with
her mother. She never offered even one to pretty
Maruschka.

Next day, Helena had again no appetite for her
supper.

'Oh, if I had only ripe apples!' she said; and
then, turning to her sister, she ordered, 'Run,
Maruschka, run into the wood and gather me
some ripe apples.'

'Dear sister, this is not the time of the year for
apples. Who ever heard of apples ripening in an
icy wind?'

But her stepmother cried out, 'Run, Maruschka,
fetch the apples as your sister has required, or I
will strike you dead.'

And she thrust her from the door into the cold
winter night-air.

The maiden hastened, sobbing, into the wood; the
snow lay deep, and nowhere was there a human
footprint. The new moon glimmered in a clear
sky, and sent its feeble beams into the forest deeps,
forming little trembling, silvery pools of light, which
appeared and vanished, and formed again. And a
low wind whispered a great secret in the trees, but
so faint was the tone that none could make out
what it said. There was a little opening in the
wood; in the midst stood a grey wolf looking up
at the moon and howling; but when Maruschka
came near, it fled, and was lost among the shadows.
The poor maiden shivered with cold, and her teeth
chattered. Her lips were purple and her cheeks

74

white; and the tears, as they formed, froze on her long eyelashes. She would have sunk on a snow-drift and died, had she not seen, up high on a rugged hill-top, a blazing fire. Towards it she made her way, and found it to be the same she had seen before. Round about, solemn and silent, sat the Twelve, and the Ice Month was on the seat of honour, clasping the staff of power.

'Dear, good friends, please suffer me to warm my-self a little while at the fire,' she asked, in suppli-cating tones; 'for, indeed, I am perishing with cold.' Then the one with the long white hair and frosty beard raised his head, and said: 'Yes, child, ap-proach; but what brings you here?'

'I am seeking ripe apples,' she answered.

'Ripe apples! It is not the time for ripe apples, when the snow lies deep?'

'Ah, sir! I know that well; but sister Helena and mother have bidden me bring them ripe apples, or they will strike me dead. You, kind shepherds, tell me where I may find ripe apples.'

Then the Ice Month arose from his seat, stepped to one of the elder men, put the staff into his hand, and said—

'Brother September, take thou the pre-eminence.' Then the Month September sat himself on the chief stone, and waved his staff over the fire. Whereat it glowed like a furnace, red and fierce; sparks flew about, and volumes of glaring hot smoke, like the vapour of molten metal, rolled up to heaven. In a moment the snow was gone. The trees were covered with sere leaves; the oak foliage was brown and crumpled, that of the ash yellow as sulphur; other trees seemed leafed with copper. Stray leaves floated past and were whirled by little wind-eddies into rustling heaps. A few yellow flowers shook in the hot air. Pinks hung over the rocks, covering their faces with wandering shadows. Ladyfern waved and wafted its pleasant

odour. A constant hum of bees and beetles and flies
sounded through the wood. Maruschka looked
about her for apples, and beheld a tree on whose
branches hung the ruddy fruit.

'Quick, Maruschka, shake!' commanded September. Then she shook, and there fell an apple;
she shook again, and there fell another. 'Quick,
Maruschka, hasten home!' said the Month.

Then she courtesied to the Twelve, thanked them
cordially, and returned to the house of her stepmother.

Helena marvelled not a little when she saw the
red apples.

'How many have you plucked?' she asked.

'Only two.'

'Where did you find them?'

'High up, on the mountain-top, on a tree weighed
down with them.'

'Why did you not gather more? Did you not eat
them on your way home?' asked Helena, fiercely.

'Oh, dear sister, I have not tasted one! I shook
once, and down fell an apple; I shook twice, and
there fell another. I might not bring away more.'

Helena struck her, and drove her to the kitchen.
Then she tasted one of the apples. Never before
had she eaten one so sweet and juicy. The stepmother ate the second.

'Mother!' exclaimed Helena, 'give me my fur
dress. I will go to the hill and bring some apples.
That hussey has eaten all she took except two.'
Then she wrapped herself up, and hurried into the
wood. The snow lay deep, and nowhere was a
human footprint. Helena lost herself; but presently
she was aware of a hill, and a fire burning at the
summit. She hastened to the light. There she
saw a great blaze, and round it sat the twelve
Months, silent and solemn. He with the long
snowy locks sat on the seat of honour, holding
the rod of power. Helena stared at them, then,

76

pushing through the circle, went to the fire, and began to warm herself.

'What seek you here?' asked the Ice Month, with a frown wrinkling his white brow.

'That is no business of yours,' answered Helena, sharply, over her shoulder.

The Ice Month shook his head, and, raising his arm, waved the staff over the fire.

Instantly the flames sank, and the fire was reduced to a glowing spark. The clouds rolled over the sky, and, bursting, discharged snow in such quantities that nothing was visible in earth and heaven but drifting white particles. An icy wind rumbled in the forest and roared round the hill. Helena fled. Everywhere white fleeting spots—whirling, falling, rising, scudding! She ran this way, then that; she stumbled over a fallen log, she gathered herself up and ran again; then she plunged into a deep drift; and the white cold down from the breast of heaven whirled and fell, and rose, and fleeted, and danced this side of her, and dropped here on her, and rested there on her, and lodged on this limb, and built up a white heap on that limb, then bridged over one fold and filled up another. She shook herself, and the particles fell off. But then they began their work again: they spangled her with white, they wove a white net, they filled up the interstices of her lace, they built a mound over her arm, they buried her foot, they raised a cairn above her bosom. Then they spun a dance around the white face which looked up at them, and began to whiten it still more; lastly, they smoothed the sheet over her, and the work was done.

The mother looked out of the window and wondered that Helena did not return. Hour after hour passed, and her daughter came not.

'Maybe the apples are so sweet that she cannot eat enough,' thought the mother. 'I will go seek them too.'

77

So she wrapped herself up in a thick shawl and went forth.

The snow lay deep, and nowhere was a human footprint. She called Helena, but received no answer. Then she lost her way. The snow fell, and the wind howled.

Maruschka sat over the fire and cooked supper. Mother and sister came back no more.

# BEAUTY AND THE BEAST

THERE was a merchantman once, who was very rich.

He had three daughters, and he spared no expense to provide them with an excellent education.

His daughters were beautiful; but the youngest so excelled her sisters that, from earliest childhood, she was called the Beauty, and afterwards this name slipped into, simply, Beauty.

But the real cause why she was so much more admired than her sisters was that she was amiable and they were not; and the sweetness of her disposition shone out in her face and made it doubly sweet. No frown ever spoiled her fair brow; no pout was ever on her pleasant lips. She possessed the charm of good temper which makes even a plain face agreeable.

The merchant's elder daughters were idle, ill-humoured, and proud; and people did not consider them as beautiful, because they saw only the bad temper that was in the expression of their faces.

The pride of the young ladies was so great that they despised all such as were of their own rank in life, and wished to be the friends of noble ladies and princesses. They hunted after grand

79

acquaintances, and met with many mortifications accordingly. They gave themselves great airs, and, to show the world how high in life they were, they held up their noses. Their whole time was spent in balls, operas, and visiting and driving about.

Meanwhile, Beauty kept to her books; and, when not at work, she loved in kindly way to go among the sick and poor, and comfort them. Thus it came about that she was as much beloved by the poor as she was admired by the rich.

As it was well known that their father was a well-to-do man, many merchants asked the girls in marriage; but all these offers were refused, because the two eldest had set their minds on marrying only nobles, and the youngest had no wish to be married at all.

Beauty's great desire was to be with her father when he was old and feeble, and to be then his comfort.

One unhappy day the merchant returned home, very downcast, to inform his children that his ships had been wrecked, his head clerk had defrauded him, and that the firms which owed him money were bankrupt. He was, therefore, a ruined man. Beauty wept because her father was unfortunate and unhappy, and asked him what was to be done.

'Alack, dear child!' he replied, 'I must sell this house, and go to live in a cottage in the country; and we shall have to work with our hands to put bread into our mouths.'

'Well, father,' said Beauty, 'I can spin and knit and sew very neatly. I daresay I shall be able to help you.'

The elder daughters said nothing, but resolved to marry such of their rejected lovers as were richest. They speedily found, however, that their rejected lovers rejected all their advances, now that they were poor.

be for him if the children were to die before they
grew to years of discretion, for then he would have
the little boy's three hundred pounds a year, and
the little girl's five hundred pounds. He kept
them in his own house for a twelvemonth and a
day, and then he formed a wicked device to get
rid of them both.

There were two wicked men who lived not far off,
who were ready to do any bad act if paid for it,
and he sent for these men, and bargained with

them to take the babes out into the greenwood,
and to kill them there. His wife, their aunt, was
a good and kind woman, and would never have
consented to such wickedness, whatever gain it
might bring, so he told her an artful tale, that it
was his purpose to send the children to a friend of
his in London, who would see to their schooling.

He then gave over the two children to the men
with whom he had agreed, and told them that they
were going to London where were toy-shops, and

as many toys to be had for the asking as their
hearts could desire.

Away then went those pretty babes,
   Rejoicing at that tide,
Rejoicing with a merry mind,
   They would a cock-horse ride.

The two men conveyed them into the wood; and,
as they went, the children talked to them of what
they would do when they got all the pretty toys in
London town. And one of the men, who was
softer-hearted than the other, became sorry for
what he had taken in hand to do. But the second
man was hard, and he would not listen to his
fellow, and said he would kill them outright.
So they fell from words to blows; and they drew
their swords and fought; and he who was most
merciful in heart slew the other.
Now, when he saw that his fellow was dead, he
thought he might be taken and hanged for murder,
and that he must fly; but he could no ways see
what he could do with the poor babes, who stood
sobbing—frightened at seeing the men fighting.

He took the children by the hand,
   Tears standing in their eye,
And bade them straightway follow him,
   And look they did not cry.
And two long miles he led them on,
   While they for food complain;
'Stay here,' said he, 'I'll bring you bread
   When I come back again.'

Then he went away, and never came back. He
ran from the wood, and tried to escape into a
distant part of the country. Now, he had brought
the poor babes on very near to the edge of the
wood, and not a mile from where there were some
cottages, and he thought that they would make
their way out from under the trees and be found

On the other hand, such as had admired Beauty pressed their services on her, and would gladly have shared their fortunes with her. She, however, could not think of deserting her father when he was reduced to low estate. She felt she must abide by him, and work for him.

Very soon, the grand house in town was sold, as well as all the rich furniture, and the merchant and his daughters retired into the country.

Beauty now rose at four o'clock every morning. She cleaned the house, laid and lighted the fires, prepared the breakfast, and put flowers on the table. Then she cooked the dinner, and made the house tidy. She was happy, and sang like a lark over her work, and slept peacefully, and had pleasant dreams.

Meanwhile, her sisters grew peevish, dissatisfied, and miserable. They would not work; and, as they had no occupation and no amusement, the days dragged along and seemed as though they would never end. They did nothing but regret the past, and grumble over the present. As they had no one to admire them, they neglected their personal appearance and became veritable dowdies.

Perhaps they perceived that the contrast between their sister and themselves was not to their advantage, for they became spiteful in their manner to Beauty, and held up their hands and declared that she had always been fit only to be a servant.

'It is clear as daylight,' said they to Beauty; 'that Nature made you to occupy a menial position, and now you are in your proper place. As for us, we are ladies. We can't soil our fingers, we can't dust the furniture, we can't scrub the floor. We are above such things.' ·

The merchant heard, after a while, that there was some chance of retrieving part of his fortune if he made a journey to a country where one of his richest vessels had been wrecked. He must claim what had been recovered from the sea. Accordingly, he bade his daughters farewell, and he did so in a hopeful spirit, for he believed he would get back enough to make their life more comfortable. Before leaving, he asked his daughters what they would desire him to bring for them on his return, as a little token that he remembered them.

The eldest asked for a diamond necklace. The second wished for a whole suite of pearls. The youngest said, 'Dear father, bring me a white rose.'

So the father kissed all his daughters, and departed. He was successful; and had recovered so much of his property that he hoped to reopen his business, and in time recover all that was lost. When he prepared to return home, he remembered the requests of his daughters, and bought diamonds for the eldest and pearls for the second; but he sought everywhere in vain for a white rose. This distressed him greatly, as his youngest daughter was his favourite child.

Now, as he was on his way home, he lost his way in a wood. Night was closing in, and as the merchant was aware that there were wolves, bears, and wild boars in that country, he was very anxious to find a shelter for the night.

Presently he perceived in the distance a twinkling light, and he urged his horse in that direction. But, to his surprise, instead of coming to a woodman's hut, he found himself in front of a magnificent castle, to which led a stately avenue, composed of orange and lemon-trees hung with fruit.

He did not hesitate to pass down this avenue, and, at the end, he came to the steps leading to the front gate, and through the open door shone the light that had attracted him.

He entered, having first knocked at the door, and looked round him expecting to see servants. But no one responded to his knock, and the hall was

82

wholly deserted. He passed through several galleries and empty rooms—all illuminated and all empty—and finally stayed his course in a smaller apartment where a fire was burning, and a couch was prepared as if for some one to lie on it. Being very tired and cold, he cast himself down on the couch and fell asleep.

After a pleasant and refreshing slumber he awoke, and found he was still alone; but a little table stood by him, and on it was spread a delicious repast. As he was extremely hungry, he sat at the table, and partook of all the good things on it. Then he threw himself on the couch again, and again fell asleep.

When he awoke, the morning sun shone into the room, the little table was still at his side, but on it was now spread an excellent breakfast.

The merchant began now to be very uneasy at the intense stilness of the house, and perplexed at seeing no one. He left the little room and entered the garden, which was beautifully laid out, and was full of flowers. 'Well,' said the merchant to himself, 'this wonderful place seems to have no master. I will go home and bring my daughters to it, and we shall be able to claim it as our home; for I discovered it, and it belongs, as far as I can see, to no one.'

He then went to fetch his horse, and, as he turned down the path to the stable, he saw a hedge of white roses on each side of it. Thereat the merchant remembered the request of his youngest daughter, and he plucked one to take to her.

Immediately he was alarmed by hearing a horrible noise. Turning in the direction of the sound, he saw a frightful Beast, which seemed to be very angry, and which exclaimed—

'Who gave you permission to gather my roses? Was it not enough that I suffered you to lie on my couch, and warm yourself at my fire, and eat my

supper and breakfast? Your insolence shall not
go unpunished.'

The merchant, terrified at these words and threats,
dropped the rose, and casting himself on his knees,
cried: 'Forgive me, sir; I am sincerely grateful
for your hospitality, which was so profuse that I
hardly thought you would grudge me one rose.'

The Beast's anger was not mitigated by this speech.
'I pay no regard to your excuses,' said he. 'You
shall most certainly die.'

'Alas!' exclaimed the merchant. 'Oh, Beauty!
Beauty! why did you ask this fatal thing of me?
The white rose you desired will be the death of
your father.'

The Beast asked the merchant the meaning of this
exclamation, and the merchant then related the
story of his misfortunes, and of the requests made
by his daughters. 'It cost me nearly all I recovered of my fortune,' said he, 'to buy the diamonds
and pearls for my eldest girls; I did not think I
was doing any harm in plucking the poor little
white rose for my youngest.'

The Beast considered for a while, and then said—
'I will pardon you on one condition, that is, that
you will give me one of your daughters.'

'Oh!' exclaimed the merchant. 'If I were so cruel
as to buy my own life at the expense of one of my
children, what excuse could I make to bring her
here?'

'No excuse is needed,' answered the Beast. 'If
she comes at all, she will come willingly. Let me
see if any one of them be brave enough, and loves
you dearly enough, to come here and save your
life. You seem to be an honest man. I give you a
month in which to return home and propose to
one of your daughters to come here to me. If none
of them be willing, then I expect you, on your
honour, to return here to your death. Say good-
bye to them for ever.'

The merchant reluctantly accepted this proposal. He did not think any of his daughters would come; but it reprieved him for one month, and gave him an opportunity of saying farewell to them, and of settling his affairs.

He promised to return at the appointed time, and then asked permission to set off at once.

But the Beast would not allow this till the next day. 'Then,' said he, 'you will find a horse ready for you. Go in, and eat your dinner, and await my further orders.'

The poor merchant, more dead than alive, went back into the palace, and into the same room in which he had rested before. There he found a most delicious meal prepared for him. He was, however, in no mood to eat; and if he swallowed a few mouthfuls, it was only lest he should anger the Beast by refusing all food from his table. When he had finished, he heard a trampling in the passages, and, shortly, the monstrous Beast appeared, who repeated the terms of the agreement they had made; and he added—

'Do not get up to-morrow until after sunrise, and till you have heard a bell ring. Then you will find your breakfast prepared for you here, and the horse you are to ride will be ready in the courtyard. He will bring you back again when you come with your daughter a month hence. Farewell! take a white rose for Beauty; and remember your engagement.'

The merchant was only too glad when the Beast went away, and though he could not sleep for sadness of heart, yet he lay down on the couch. Next morning, after a hasty breakfast, he went to gather the rose for Beauty, mounted the horse, and rode swiftly away.

The gloomy thoughts that weighed on his mind were not dispersed when he drew up at his cottage door. His daughters, who had been uneasy at his

85

long absence, were prodigal of their embraces, and, seeing him ride home on such a splendid horse, they felt quite sure that he had been successful in his journey. He gave his elder daughters the gems and pearls they had desired, and, as he handed the rose to Beauty, he sadly said, 'You little know, my darling, what this has cost me.'

This saying greatly excited the curiosity of his children, and they gave him no rest till he had told them the whole story from beginning to end.

The elder daughters urged him to break his promise and remain at the cottage; but their father said that a promise was a promise, whether made to a king or a pauper, a man or a beast, and that he must fulfil it. Then the two eldest were very angry with Beauty, and told her that it was all her fault. If she had asked for something sensible this would not have happened.

'If it be my fault,' answered Beauty meekly, 'it is only fitting that I should suffer for it. I will, therefore, go back with my father to the palace of the Beast.'

At first her father would not hear of this, but Beauty was firm.

As the time drew near she divided all her little possessions between her sisters, and said good-bye to all she loved.

Now, it must be told, that when Beauty had received the white rose she put it in water, and when she had heard how it was won, and what it entailed, she had wept nightly over it, and her tears falling on it seemed to have preserved it in its beauty, for at the end of the month it was as fresh as when first picked; and the scent was so sweet that it perfumed the whole house. She put the white rose in her bosom, when the day came for departure, and she mounted on a pillion behind her father to depart.

The horse seemed to fly rather than gallop; and

86

Beauty would have enjoyed the journey if it were not for the dreadful prospect of the Beast at the end of it. Her father constantly urged her to dismount and turn back, but she would not hearken to this.

At last they reached the avenue of orange trees, and then a wonderful sight was seen. Every orange was like a globe of light; the oranges were

deep yellow, and the lemons pale yellow, and all shone like lamps. Moreover, beautiful lights played about the palace, and sweet music murmured among the trees.

'The Beast must be very hungry,' said Beauty, 'if he makes such rejoicing over getting such a little mouthful as myself.'

The horse now stopped at the foot of the flight of

steps leading to the gate, and when she had dismounted, her father led her through the halls and
galleries to the little room in which he had rested
and been regaled when there on his former visit.
Again the fire was burning, and on the table a
lavish supper was spread.

The merchant knew that this was meant for them;
and Beauty, who was rather less frightened now
that she had passed through so many rooms without seeing the Beast, was willing to begin, for her
long ride had made her hungry.

They had hardly finished eating, before they heard
tramp, tramp! stump, stump! It was the sound
of the beast approaching; and Beauty clung to her
father in terror, which was heightened when she
saw how greatly alarmed he was.

But when the Beast entered, like a brave and a
courteous girl she stood up, mastered her fear, and,
making a low courtesy, said: 'I thank you, Mr.
Beast, for my pretty white rose.'

Then the Beast was pleased. He saw the little
flower in her bosom, looking white and fresh as
when first picked; and he said, somewhat gently—
'Did you come quite willingly, Beauty?'

'Yes, Mr. Beast,' said Beauty, and dropped another
courtesy.

'And will you be willing to remain with me, when
your father is gone? I will not eat you—my food
is only crystallised rose and violet leaves. I eat
nothing more solid or less æsthetic.'

'Yes, Mr. Beast,' answered Beauty; and the
thought that she was not to be eaten revived
her courage, and she dropped another little
courtesy.

'I am well pleased with you,' said the Beast. 'You
shall stay. As for you,' he now turned to the
merchant, 'at sunrise, to-morrow, you must depart.
When the bell rings, rise quickly and eat your
breakfast, and you will find the same horse wait-

ing to take you home; but remember, you must never venture to seek my palace again.'

Then, turning to Beauty, he said: 'Take your father into the next room, and help him to choose presents for your sisters. There are two portmanteaus there. Fill them with whatever you like to send home. All are yours, and at your disposal.'

Then the Beast made a clumsy bow, put his paw to his heart, and said: 'Good-bye, Beauty; good-bye, merchantman.'

Beauty was very sorrowful to have to part with her father, and much dismayed at the thought of being left alone in the great palace with no one but the Beast. However, she promptly obeyed his orders. The room they entered was full of the costliest objects, the most splendid dresses, and the richest jewelry. After making a selection, she put them in the portmanteau which she intended to contain the presents for her sisters. Then she found a trunk full of gold coins, and with them she stuffed the second portmanteau, which was for her father.

But Beauty and her father much doubted whether the horse could carry the load. However, on reaching the courtyard, there they saw two horses beside that on which the merchant had ridden. They moved the portmanteaus down, and strapped them on the pack-horses' backs. Then the merchant bade his daughter a tender farewell with many tears, and rode away.

Then Beauty wept bitterly, and wandered sadly back to the room in which she had eaten. She soon found herself so sleepy that she threw herself on the couch and closed her eyes, and was at once in the world of dreams.

Now, in her dreams, she saw something very strange. She thought that there stood before her a Prince, handsomer than any man she had ever

seen, wearing a crown of white roses on his head.
He said to her: 'Beauty! your fate is not as
forlorn as you suppose. Be true-hearted as you
are beautiful, and all will be well in the end.'

Beauty awoke, after a long sleep, much refreshed.
She then began to explore the palace. The first
room she entered was lined with looking-glasses,
and Beauty saw herself reflected on every side.
Then she saw a bracelet hanging down from a
chandelier. She took it, looked at it, and saw
that from it hung a locket, and in this locket was
the portrait of the very Prince she had seen in her
dream.

The next room she entered was tapestried round
with foliage, and it was full of musical instruments.
Beauty knew how to play some of them; and she
amused herself for some time trying them, and
playing the different ballad tunes that came into
her head. First she sang—

There was a fair maiden, all forlorn,
  With hey! with ho! for the rain;
And she sat herself down all under a thorn,
  The poppies are red in the grain.

Next she sang—

There rode a knight when the moon shone bright,
  He rode to the lady's hall;
He sang her a lay, bade her come away,
  And follow him at his call.
He courted her many a long winter night,
  And many a short winter day,
And he laid in wait, both early and late,
  For to take her sweet life away.

Then she sang—

There came an earl a-riding by,
  A gipsy maid espied he;
O nut-brown maid, to her he said,
  I prithee, come away with me.

I 'll take you up, I 'll carry you home,
   I 'll put a safeguard over you ;
Your slippers shall be of Spanish leather,
   And silken stockings all of blue.

And last of all she sang—

Green gravel ! Green gravel !
   The grass is so green,
The fairest young damsel
   That ever was seen.
O Beauty ! O Beauty !
   Your true love is dead,
He sends you a letter
   To turn round your head.

Then Beauty was tired of singing and playing, and
she went into the next room, which was a library,
and it was full of books. She pulled down several
and looked at them, and thought that surely it
would take her all her life to read the books she
saw there.

Then she walked in the garden, and wondrous
were the flowers and the fruit there. Never had
she seen so many and such beautiful flowers ; never
had she tasted such delicious fruit.

At last day declined, and she came indoors. A brilliant light illumined all the rooms; she found supper
prepared for her, and she seated herself to eat.

Then she heard, tramp, tramp ! stump, stump !
and in came the Beast.

He asked her if she thought she could be happy in
his palace ; and Beauty answered, that everything
was so beautiful that she would be very hard to
please if she could not be happy. Then he asked
if he might sit down and eat his meal with her.

'Oh ! what shall I say ?' cried Beauty, for she knew
that she could not eat in comfort, with him munch-
ing crystallised rose-leaves and violets out of a
bon-bon box on the other side of the table.

91

'Say exactly what you think,' he replied.

'Oh! no, Beast!' said Beauty, hastily.

'Since you will not—good-night, Beauty,' he said;
and she responded: 'good-night, Beast.'

When she was asleep she again dreamed of the
mysterious Prince.

Next day she found a room in which were silks
and canvas and needles, and all sorts of articles
for embroidery.

Then she entered an aviary full of beautiful birds,
which were so tame that they flew to Beauty as
soon as they saw her, and perched on her shoulder
and hands.

The day passed a little more heavily than the last,
and Beauty began to long for some one to talk to,
and even was pleased when at supper she heard
the tramp, tramp! stump, stump! of the Beast
coming along the passages.

She now put a chair on the side of the table opposite her, and when the Beast said, 'May I sit
down and eat with you, Beauty?' she answered,
'Oh! please do, Beast!'

That night she dreamed of the Prince again, and
he smiled at her and looked pleased.

Next day she walked in the woods, and she saw
deer there, fleet and graceful; and she came on
fish-ponds in which were gold and silver fish. She
went to the music-room and tried to play and sing,
but became tired of her loneliness, and wished
greatly for supper, when the Beast would appear
and she could talk with him, and hear him talk.

When day declined, and the palace was lighted up
for supper, then she waited impatiently for the
tramp, tramp! stump, stump! and when the Beast
came in she ran to meet him, dropped a courtesy,
and said, 'Please, Beast, can you play and sing?'

'Yes, Beauty.'

'Would you play and sing with me, sometimes?'
she asked.

'Certainly, Beauty! if you wish it.'

Next day when she entered the music-room, the Beast was there, and she found that not only could he play very charmingly on many instruments, but also could sing a rich bass. They made together quite a charming little concert, singing duets and playing different instruments, and this wore the morning away.

In the afternoon, Beauty was quite dull by herself. She wandered in the library, looking at one book after another, and she could not choose which to read.

So at supper she ran along the gallery to meet the Beast directly she heard his tramp, tramp! stump, stump! and, dropping a little courtesy, she said: 'Please, Beast! will you tell me what books to read?'

'Certainly, Beauty!' he answered; and next day she found him in the library, and he read with her, and explained to her difficult passages, and so a very pleasant morning was passed.

In the afternoon, Beauty walked in the garden, admiring the flowers, and wishing that she knew their names. At supper, when she heard the tramp, tramp! stump, stump! of the Beast, she ran to meet him, and, taking one of his paws in her hand, said: 'Please, Beast! will you walk in the garden with me?'

'Certainly, Beauty!' he answered; and next day when she went into the garden there he was, and he was able to tell her all about the flowers, their names and their properties, and whence they came.

That evening, at supper, she said to the Beast: 'Please, Beast! may I make you a pair of slippers?' 'Certainly, Beauty!' he answered. 'But my feet are very big and clumsy.'

'Oh!' said she, 'not half so big and clumsy as those of an elephant.'

So she amused herself in embroidering for the
Beast a pair of slippers. The ground was tur-
quoise blue, and on it were white roses, with
stamens of gold, and the pods for seed were
scarlet. Never before or after were such beautiful
slippers made.

That night she dreamed that she saw the Prince.
He looked at her, smiling, and showed that he wore
her slippers—which she had made for the Beast—
and they had shrunk to the size of his finely-formed
feet.

One day she was in the forest, and she thought:
'Oh! how nice it would be to ride out hunting, but
how dull to ride all alone!'

So that evening at supper, she ran to the Beast,
when she heard his tramp, tramp! stump, stump!
and, catching hold of both his paws, she said:
'Please, Beast! will you go hunting with me?'

'Certainly, Beauty!' he answered.

Next day there was a fine hunt, and Beauty
enjoyed herself vastly.

One day, when Beauty was walking in the garden
with the Beast, she passed with him by the hedge
of white roses, and she put out her hand and
picked one. Then he said to her: 'Beauty, will
you marry me? If so—give me the white rose.'

'Oh! what shall I say?' cried Beauty; for she was
sorry to offend the Beast, who had been so kind to
her, and such an agreeable companion, and so
eager to forestall all her wishes; but, at the same
time—he was a Beast.

He said, seeing her hesitation: 'Say just what you
think.'

Then Beauty answered hastily, 'Oh! no, Beast!'

That night she dreamed of her Prince, and that he
looked sad and wobegone.

So everything went on for a time, until at last,
happy as she was, Beauty began to long for the
sight of her father and sisters; and one evening,

94

seeing her look very sad, and her eyes red, the
Beast asked her what was the matter.

Beauty had quite ceased to be afraid of him. She knew that he was gentle and kind in spite of his ferocious appearance; and clever and learned in spite of his being such an animal; and quite dainty and courteous in his manners, though a Beast.

She answered, that she was longing to see her home once more.

Upon hearing this, the Beast seemed greatly affected. He sighed, and said: 'Ah! Beauty, will you desert your poor Beast like this? Is it because you hate me that you want to leave me?'

'No, dear Beast,' answered Beauty, softly. 'Indeed I do not hate you, and it would make me very unhappy if I thought I should never see and talk with you again. But I do long greatly to see my father. Let me go, if only for two months, and I promise to return to you, and stay with you the rest of my life.'

The Beast said: 'I can refuse you nothing, and that you well know. Take the four boxes; you will find in the room next your own, and fill them with whatever you like to take away with you. But remember your promise, and return when two months have expired, or you will find your faithful Beast dead. You will not need any carriage to bring you back. Only say good-bye to your father and sisters the night before you come away, and then, in your room, turn this ring I give you on your finger, and say: "I wish to be with my Beast again."'

As soon as Beauty was by herself, she hastened to fill the boxes with all the rare and precious things she saw about her. Then she went to bed, but could hardly sleep for joy. And when at last she did begin to dream of her beloved Prince, she saw him lying stretched on the grass, sad and weeping.

95

When she opened her eyes, she could hardly
believe her senses. She was in a very different
place from the palace of the Beast. The room
was neat and comfortable, but not splendid.
Where could she be? She dressed herself hastily,
and then saw that the boxes she had packed were
in the room.

Whilst she was wondering where she was, she
heard her father's voice. She at once left the
room, and, seeing him, threw herself into his arms.
She was, in fact, in the new house to which her
father had removed from the cottage, when his
fortunes were improved. Her sisters were greatly
astonished to see her. All embraced her with
demonstrations of the greatest joy, but her sisters
were not in heart glad to see her. Their jealousy
was not extinguished.

She was made to tell her story, and it filled all
with astonishment. But when she said that her
stay with them was limited to two months, then
her father was sorrowful, but her sisters secretly
rejoiced.

Her father had much to tell her, and her sisters
had made many acquaintances, and the time was
spent in going about making visits and in receiving company. Nevertheless, somehow, Beauty
did not feel as happy as she had been with her
Beast. The time had come at last when she ought
to return; but her father was so sorrowful when she
spoke of departure, and there was always something arranged for the next day for which she was
expected to remain, so that she did not fulfil her
promise exactly. Besides, she so loved her father
that she could not make up her mind to bid him
good-bye.

One night she had a dreadful dream. She thought
she was back again in the Beast's palace, and that
she was walking through the rooms seeking him.
Not finding him anywhere, she went into the

garden and called him, but received no answe.
At last, having reached a portion of the shrub-
beries that was allowed to run wild, she heard
groans issuing from a cave.
She penetrated into it, and found the Beast
prostrate on the ground, and apparently dying.
He reproached her with having forgotten him and
broken her promise, and reminded her of what he
had said, that her absence protracted beyond the
two months allotted to her would be death to him.
Beauty was so terrified by this dream that she
sprang from her bed, hastily clothed herself, ran
to her father's room, roused him, said farewell;
then she did the same to her sisters, and, still
agitated with the thoughts of the dying Beast,
turned her ring and wished herself back again in
his palace.
Hardly had she done this before she was again in
the little chamber in which she had spent so many
agreeable hours. She looked about; no Beast was
there. Then, although it was night, she ran out
into the garden, calling him and seeking him. She
was still searching for him when the grey of dawn
appeared. Then she was able to find her way,
and she sought the wilderness she had been in, in
her dream, and at last lit on the cavern of which
she had dreamed.
In fact, from this now issued the most lamentable
sighs and groans.
She ran in and saw the poor Beast stretched on
the earth, and evidently exceedingly weak and
suffering.
'O Beast! Beast!' she cried; 'I am so sorry!
So heartily sorry that I have delayed my return.
Oh, tell me you will recover!'
'Nothing now will restore me but one thing,' he
answered in a faint voice.
'Tell me what that is, and it is yours.'
'The rose,' he answered—'the white rose. You

will find it growing over the mouth of this cave. But, remember—if you give me that, you give me yourself with it. You accept me as your husband.'

In a moment, without speaking, Beauty sprang out of the cave and hastily plucked a beautiful white rose that hung down over the mouth.

Returning to the poor Beast, she gave it him, and said: 'Dear Beast!—indeed I am yours. I love you with all my heart.'

'Will you kiss me on my snout?' asked the Beast. 'Indeed—indeed I will,' answered Beauty.

At that moment the sun rose and poured its golden beams into the cave, and made the walls glitter and twinkle like a cave of rainbow, and indeed they were all of ruby, carbuncle, amethyst, topaz, emerald, and every imaginable stone.

The reflection was so dazzling that Beauty having kissed the Beast covered her eyes. When she drew her hands away he had disappeared. In his place stood her long-dreamed-of, beautiful Prince. Then he took her by the hand, and said: 'Dear Beauty, to you, to your faithfulness and goodness, I owe my delivery. I have been bewitched by a cruel fairy, who said I should remain in the form of a hideous monster until some maiden would consent to be my wife, and in token of her consent give me a white rose, and kiss me on the mouth. This is my palace, I have an immense kingdom and innumerable treasures. You shall be my queen, and we will make your father happy, and, if possible, your sisters shall be made contented. I shall never forget what you have done for me, and all my life shall be devoted to rendering you happy.'

# THE YELLOW DWARF

NCE upon a time there lived a queen who had an only daughter, whom she loved so excessively that she never corrected her faults or thwarted her wishes. The consequence of this folly was, the young lady grew up very self-willed and unamiable. Her great beauty made her likewise very proud. She was called All-fair, and the fame of her beauty spread through all the surrounding courts, and many princes became so enamoured as to offer her marriage. But the princess rejected them all, much to the annoyance of the queen, her mother, who was very anxious to see her daughter well married. When she found all her entreaties were of no avail, she resolved to go and consult the Fairy of the Desert respecting the best course to be adopted towards her stubborn daughter. It was, however, difficult to gain access to this fairy; for she was guarded by two fierce lions. The queen, however, knew of a certain cake that would appease their fury, and enable her to pass by them. Providing herself with this, she set out privately towards the fairy's dwelling. After walking several miles, she became so excessively weary that she lay down under a tree, and fell into a sound sleep.

Suddenly she was awoke by the roaring of the
lions, who were approaching her. She jumped up
and seized her basket of cakes to appease their
fury; but, alas, it was empty! The poor queen
was in an agony of terror, not knowing what to do.
It was impossible to escape from the furious lions,
and there appeared no other prospect for her than
a cruel death. At this moment she heard a noise
in the tree, which attracted her attention; and on
looking up, she saw an ugly yellow dwarf, about
three feet high, picking oranges.

'Ah, queen,' said he, 'you are in great danger!
These lions have destroyed many; and how will
you escape, seeing you have no cakes?'

'Alas,' said the queen, weeping, 'I know not; for
I have lost my cakes.'

'There is but one way,' replied the dwarf. 'I know
what has brought you here; and if you will
promise me your daughter in marriage, I will save
you from the lions; if not, they shall devour you.'

The queen, horrified at the thought of sacrificing
her beautiful daughter to such a hideous creature,
made him no answer; but a terrible growl from
the lions, who were just ready to spring upon her,
so terrified her, that she gave her promise, and
then fainted away. When the queen came to herself she was in bed in her own palace. All that
had passed seemed as a dream; nevertheless she
was so persuaded of its reality, that her spirits
gave way, and she sank into such a state of
melancholy that she cared for nothing.

Princess All-fair loved her mother very tenderly,
and she grieved to see her in such a state of
dejection. After trying in vain to ascertain the
cause of the queen's sorrow, that she might
comfort her, the princess determined on paying a
visit to the Fairy of the Desert, to ask her advice
on the subject. All-fair, having provided some
cakes for the lions, started secretly on her danger-

ous journey.  It so happened that she took the same road as her mother had taken, and accordingly arrived at the unlucky orange-tree.  Attracted by the luscious appearance of the oranges, she put down her basket and plucked some to eat.  Whilst the princess was enjoying the fruit, she heard the roaring of the lions, which were advancing towards her.  Alarmed at this terrible sight, she hastily

picked up the basket to take out some cakes; but she found to her great sorrow that the basket was empty.  All-fair, overwhelmed with terror, wrung her hands and sobbed aloud.  The hideous Yellow Dwarf now made his appearance, and asked the princess what had brought her to that place.  She told him she was going to consult the Fairy of the Desert as to the cause of her mother's sorrow.

'Oh,' replied he, 'you need not go any farther to ascertain that. I can tell you the cause. She has promised you to me in marriage, and now is so ungrateful as to repent of her promise.'

'What!' exclaimed the princess; 'the queen, my mother, promised me to such a hideous creature as you! Impossible!'

'Oh, very well,' replied the Yellow Dwarf; 'as you please, young lady. The lions will soon punish you for your insolence.'

The lions were about to seize on poor All-fair, when she cried to the Dwarf, 'Oh, save me! and I will promise to marry you, rather than be eaten by these monsters.'

On saying these words she fainted from terror. When she recovered from her swoon, she found herself in her own apartment, and round one of her fingers was a ring of red hair, so tightly fastened that she could not remove it. The princess now became as melancholy as her mother. The queen and all her court were greatly distressed at the alteration in the princess, and they concluded that the most likely way of diverting her thoughts would be by urging her to marry. The princess listened to their proposals, and at length consented to marry the King of the Golden Mines, who had long tried to gain her affections. This king was exceedingly rich and powerful.

When all was agreed upon, preparations were made to celebrate the nuptials in the most magnificent style. The King of the Golden Mines expended large sums of money in purchasing all that was splendid and gorgeous, and the palace glittered with gold and precious stones.

At length the day arrived for the celebration of the marriage: but as the party were proceeding to perform the ceremony, they saw an ugly old fairy approaching them, riding on a box drawn by two peacocks. Coming up to the queen, she shook her crutch in a malicious manner, saying, 'Oh, oh, this is the way you perform the promise you made to my friend the Yellow Dwarf. I am the Fairy of the Desert, and I will not allow such unfaithfulness to my friend to go unpunished; therefore decide whether you will marry him or die.'

This unexpected appearance of the fairy filled the queen and princess with the greatest alarm. But the King of the Golden Mines drew his sword, and going up to the fairy, he said, 'Fly, wretch! or I will strike off thy head.'

The king had no sooner uttered these words than the box flew open, and out started the Yellow Dwarf, seated on a huge wild cat; who, placing himself before the fairy, said, 'Hold, rash youth! your rage must be vented against me; I am your rival and enemy. I claim the princess, who is pledged to me by the ring of hair on her finger.'

'Hideous monster!' exclaimed the prince, 'you are too contemptible to be noticed by me.'

The dwarf, enraged at this scornful speech, drew his sword and challenged the king to fight. Immediately the air was darkened; and amidst lightnings and thunder the two peacocks were transformed into giants of enormous size, who stood on each side of the Yellow Dwarf, vomiting fire. All the spectators were terrified at this fearful sight, excepting the King of the Gold Mines, who with undaunted courage attacked his terrible enemy; but his brave heart sank within him when he saw the Fairy of the Desert, mounted on a fiery dragon, advance towards his beloved All-fair and strike her to the ground. The king hastened to the assistance of his lady; but the dwarf flying before him on his cat, seized All-fair and carried her off.

The fairy, having fallen in love with the king, carried him aloft in the air, and conveyed him to a frightful cavern, and chained him up; hoping thus to make him forget All-fair, and secure him for herself. But finding this plan unsuccessful, she changed herself into a lovely girl, and going to the king she removed his fetters, and placed him by her side in a chariot drawn by swans, which flew rapidly through the air. In their flight they passed over a palace of polished steel, the brilliance of which attracted the king's notice, and on looking down he saw All-fair weeping bitterly in the garden.

The princess, attracted by a noise in the sky, looked up, and saw to her great sorrow the King of the Gold Mines seated in the chariot with the fairy. Stung to the heart at this sight she inwardly reproached the king with want of fidelity to herself, and piteously bewailed her unhappy condition. The poor king still loved her tenderly, and would have rejoiced, if he could, to have thrown the fairy from the chariot, and hastened to her rescue. But the chariot passed swiftly on, until they approached a magnificent palace on the sea-coast, at which the swans descended. The fairy then alighted and led the king into the palace, in which was everything that could delight the eye.

The king knew that his companion was a fairy, and he suspected she was the Fairy of the Desert, although she appeared as a lovely young woman. He resolved therefore, to ingratiate himself with her if possible, and to conceal his dislike of her, in the hope that he might have some opportunity of escaping. The fairy, supposing her charms had now made some impression upon the prince, allowed him to walk beyond the gardens of the palace.

One day as he was walking by the sea-shore, he was surprised by the appearance of a mermaid, which spake to him in a melodious voice, and said: 'I am aware, O king, of the attachment existing

104

between you and princess All-fair; I know also the misery you endure, and am come to release you from it. I am an enemy to the Fairy of the Desert and the Yellow Dwarf; if you, therefore, will trust to me, I will deliver you and the princess out of their power.'

The king gratefully accepted the proffered aid; and seating himself on the mermaid's back, promised to do all that she should direct. They then sailed off; and as they went, the mermaid told him all that had befallen the princess, and that she was now confined in the steel castle of the dwarf.

At length they drew near to the place, when the mermaid told him that he would have many powerful enemies to overcome before he could reach his beloved princess. 'But,' said she, 'if you take this sword,' which she then gave him, 'and follow my directions, you will be able to destroy them all. Beware lest the sword fall from your hand; for if you once lose possession of it, you will not be able to recover it, and certain destruction will fall upon you.'

The king promised to use the utmost caution; and after warmly thanking the mermaid for her kind services, he started for the castle. The first danger he encountered was two enormous lions, which guarded the outer gate. He advanced boldly towards them, and with one blow laid them dead at his feet. On reaching the inner court the king was assailed by six fierce dragons of prodigious size, but he quickly destroyed them with his magic sword. The king then entered the castle, and was met by a band of lovely females, who forbade his entering, telling him that they were appointed to guard the castle, and that their lives would be forfeited if they allowed any person to enter. The king was so moved by their entreaties that he could not resist them, until he heard a voice say: 'Strike, or the princess is for ever lost.' He now saw this was a cunning trick of the dwarf to ensnare him, and without hesitation he attacked and scattered them. The king then advanced to the place where he had seen the princess, and throwing himself at her feet he declared his unalterable love for her.

The princess drew herself from him and said: 'Did I not see you riding with the Fairy of the Desert? Is that your fidelity and love?'

The king related to her all the circumstances; and while talking he thoughtlessly dropped the magic sword, which the Yellow Dwarf seeing from behind a bush, sprung forward and seized.

'Now,' said he, 'you are in my power; and unless you consent to give up the princess to me, I will at once destroy you.'

The king replied: 'No, never will I do that! I scorn the terms you propose.'

The malicious dwarf immediately struck off his head. This dreadful spectacle broke the heart of the poor princess, and she fell upon the body of her beloved and died.

The kind mermaid grieved over the fate of these faithful lovers; and resolving to unite in death those who were so cruelly separated in life, she transformed them into two trees, which grew side by side, and intertwined their branches.

# HOP-O'-MY-THUMB

AS it fell upon a day there lived a wood-cutter and his wife on the outskirts of a great forest. They had seven children, and all were boys. The eldest was ten, and the youngest seven years old.

The parents were very poor, and the children were nearly the same age, for they were twins, with the exception of the youngest, and unable to earn their bread.

The father was sore puzzled how to provide for them. What made matters worse was that the youngest was very sickly and weak. When he was born, he was but the size of a man's thumb, and this made his father call him Hop-o'-my-Thumb. This poor child bore the blame of whatever went amiss in the house; he was always thought to be in the wrong; he was, however, far more clever than was supposed. Indeed, he had more sense in his little noddle than in all those of his brothers put together. He spoke very little, but then he kept his ears wide open.

Just as Hop-o'-my-Thumb had reached his seventh year, the land was afflicted with a great famine, and food became so dear that the woodcutter and his wife found great difficulty in getting even dry

bread for their family. At last they spent their
last penny, and knew that when they had finished
the loaf that was then in the house they must
starve.

Very sad and wretched were the pair that evening
as they sat over the wood fire, thinking of what
awaited them. The children had been long in bed,
and were, as the parents thought, asleep, and
knew nothing of the miseries of the coming day.

'My dear wife,' said the woodcutter, breaking a
long silence, and his voice sounded hoarse and
hollow, 'my dear wife, I have something to say
to you. I cannot bear to see our poor dear children
die of the slow pangs of hunger. I think we had
better take them into the forest to-morrow, and
leave them there. It is possible that the fairies
may take pity on their innocence and helplessness,
and carry them off to live with them. At any rate,
we shall be spared seeing them die, and hearing
their cries for food.'

'Oh, husband,' said the poor startled woman,
'how can you think of so dreadful a deed? Have
you forgotten that the wolves which haunt the
woods would be much more likely to eat the poor
babes up than the fairies to feed them? Oh, no,
no! I will never consent.'

But the husband was a man who, when once he
had resolved on a thing, was not easily turned
from his purpose; so he talked, and argued, and
scolded his poor wife, till he made her give an
unwilling consent to his proposal.

'Heaven, you see, has left us to starve,' he said;
'therefore we need not care what we do, or what
becomes of us.'

These were foolish and wicked words. Heaven
never forgets us, and the woodcutter ought to
have been patient and have waited till help came,
or else he should have died bravely without daring
to do wrong. But he had lived very long in the

forest, and had not been taught what is right and what is wrong.

Weeping very bitterly, the wife at last went to bed, and soon after her husband followed. As he closed the door of the room behind him, you might have seen a little dark object creep out from under the bench on which the woodcutter and his wife had been sitting. This was none other than Hop-o'-my-Thumb. He fixed his sharp little eyes on the red embers, and seemed lost in thought. Then he nodded his head, and he crept out of the room into a large closet where he and his brothers slept.

Hop-o'-my-Thumb had not intended to listen to what his parents were saying. He had been very cold in bed from hunger, and having found that the warmth of the fire made him feel better, he had stolen softly under the bench, meaning to give himself a good warming before he went to sleep. But when he heard his father's resolve to leave them in the wood, he was afraid to let him know that he was there, and scarcely dared breathe till his father and mother were gone to bed.

As you may suppose, Hop-o'-my-Thumb slept little that night. He was glad when he saw the dawn peep in at the window; then he rose, without waking his brothers, and went down to the brook near the hut, and filled his pockets with smooth round pebbles, as white as snow.

By-and-by the woodcutter called out, in a cheerful voice:

'Get up, my little sons, and come with me into the wood. I will give you a treat. You shall help me to bind the fagots.'

Now the little boys very much liked to help their father, feeling proud to be useful.

'And I will go with you,' said the mother, though she gave a deep sigh as she spoke.

They each had a slice of bread for breakfast, and then they all set out for the forest.

That morning was lovely. The leaves were
glistening with dew, and the birds were singing
on the branches. Everything looked fresh, and
Hop-o'-my-Thumb could hardly believe that any
one could be so cruel as his father and mother
intended to be. But he took care as he went
along to drop the pebbles, and no one noticed
what he did. The trees gradually closed in, so
that they had to walk separately, and about ten
feet apart, and thus they followed each other in a
long line ; the youngest coming last. When the
thicket opened a little, the woodcutter began his
work, and the children helped him, picking up the
smaller branches and binding them into fagots.
Hop-o'-my-Thumb did the same.

Whilst they were thus employed, the parents stole
away unperceived ; and as soon as they were out
of sight, hurried to their house, leaving their poor
little boys alone in the forest.

By-and-by the sun went down, and Peter, the
eldest boy, cried—

'Father and mother ! where are you ? It is growing dark. Is it not time to go home ?'

But no voice answered him; only the echo cried,
'Home ! home !' mocking them.

The little boys ran hither and thither, calling on
their parents, and at last, finding that they were
left alone, they all huddled into a group, with their
arms round each other, and began to cry. Then
Hop-o'-my-Thumb spoke—

'Do not cry, brothers, for I can show you the way
home.'

The little boys were glad when they heard him say
this; and they crowded round him, asking eagerly
why their father and mother had left them.

Then Hop-o'-my-Thumb told his brothers all that
he had overheard.

'But do not fear,' he added; 'I have strewn
white pebbles all the way we came, and these will

guide us out of the forest. Only we must set out
at once, before the darkness falls.'

So holding on to each other, the little string of
children followed Hop-o'-my-thumb, who looked
for the pebbles which he had thrown behind him
as he came along in the morning. The moon was
shining, and by its light the pebbles glistened as
snow, so that by their aid all safely reached the
door of the woodman's hut. There, however, they
paused, afraid to go in, since they knew that their
parents wished them dead.

Meanwhile, the woodcutter and his sorrowful
wife had reached their dwelling before sunset, and
had scarcely entered the room, where no sound of
little feet would, they believed, ever be heard
again, than they were struck with remorse and
horror.

Before either of them could speak, they heard a
cheerful voice at the door—

'Here, Hugh, woodman,' it cried, 'I have brought
you help in time of need. The squire is sorry for
the distress you are in, and has sent you some
rabbits. A good many, too, because he knows
you have a large family. "Give those who have
children the largest share," he said to me this
morning. So, there, you have seven times as much
as your neighbours.'

The woodcutter turned pale, and trembled as he
heard those words. Here was help come (chiefly
for the sake of the children) and he had cast them
forth to perish! He could scarcely find voice to
thank the forester for the gift. The good-natured
fellow thought that his husky accents came from
want, and nodding good-naturedly, he said—

'Ay, ay, I'll thank my master for you. Now,
Goody, make haste and cook your goodman some
food, for he looks half-starved.'

Then he hurried away to carry help to another
suffering family.

112

You may imagine that the pair had little appetite for the supper thus sent to them.

'Oh,' cried the wife, 'if only—if only our babes were here to partake of this good food. But no! the wolves are devouring them. My pretty ones will be eaten up in the lonely forest!' and she gave herself up to passionate grief, threw herself on the floor, and would not be comforted. Meantime her husband, though feeling very miserable, made up the fire, and began to roast a pair of rabbits. When ready, he bade his wife come and eat some of the food.

'No, no,' she cried, 'I will not eat it. I want my children; where are my darling babes?'

'Here we are, mother,' cried seven little voices all at once outside the door, and with a cry of delight the woman opened it, and saw her sons hand in hand standing close to it.

She clasped them in her arms, and wept and laughed, and kissed them, as if she were mad with joy; and then she drew them in, and washed their faces and hands, and made them sit down, and fed them from her own plate before she would taste a morsel herself. As to her husband, he also was very glad.

Whilst the supply of rabbits lasted they lived very comfortably and merrily; and the little boys, when seated by the fire, would often repeat how wise Hop-o'-my-Thumb had been to strew pebbles along the way, and thus the father learned how his plan had been defeated.

But the famine grew worse and worse, and the lord of the manor could no longer supply his tenants with food, for all the rabbits in his warren and in the woods had been killed and eaten. The woodcutter again grew morose, and once more determined to take his boys into the wood and there lose them. But as he was sure his wife would never consent to this, he persuaded her one

day to go into the nearest town and beg for help;
and while she was away, he again told his sons to
accompany him. But this time he watched Hop-
o'-my-Thumb, and took care that the child did not
get any pebbles. However, as he gave each boy
a slice of bread, poor Hop-o'-my-Thumb thought
that would do as well, and as he walked he took
care to throw crumbs of bread all along the path-
way.

By-and-by the father proposed a game of 'hide-
and-seek' amongst the trees, and as the children
played at it, he managed to slip away and leave
them alone in the forest.

When they were tired of play, and found that their
father had once more deserted them, they began
to cry bitterly, but Hop-o'-my-Thumb said:

'Do not weep, my dear brothers, I will take you
home.'

And he began to look for the path, by the crumbs
of bread. Alas! the birds had eaten them all up!

Hop-o'-my-Thumb did not, however, despair.

'My dear brothers,' he said, 'we were protected
before; we shall not be deserted now. Do not let
us waste the short time of twilight in tears, but
hurry on, and see if we can find a shelter for the
night.'

They all said they would do whatever he told
them, for they saw that he was wiser than they
were. So Hop-o'-my-Thumb led the way and they
endeavoured to find a beaten track. But now
night closed in, and a high wind raged in the
forest; the trees creaked and groaned, till the
terrified children expected to be beaten or crushed
by their mighty boughs.

Every now and then they heard in the distance the
howl of the wolves; a heavy rain poured down and
soaked their thin garments; their feet slipped in
the mire, and they fell repeatedly.

At last Hop-o'-my-Thumb climbed to the top of a

114

high tree. From this height he could look all around, and he perceived a light in the distance.
He took notice in which direction it lay, descended to the ground, and led his brothers in the way that led to it. However, it was long before they could see the light as they trudged along, and they were beginning to despair, when they came suddenly on it, and found that it proceeded from a large house on the outskirts of the wood.

They knocked at the door at once, and it was opened by a good-natured-looking woman, who asked what they wanted. Hop-o'-my-Thumb told her that they were poor children who had lost their way in the forest, and begged that she would take pity on them and give them a night's lodging. The good woman, seeing these seven poor little babes, with their long hair wet and draggled, hanging round their sweet faces, and their soft imploring eyes, wept for pity, and answered—

'Ah, my poor darlings! You do not know whither you are come! This is the house of an ogre, who eats little children.'

'Alas, madam!' said Hop-o'-my-Thumb, 'what shall we do? If you do not give us a night's shelter the wolves will devour us, and sooner than that we should prefer to be eaten by the ogre. But, perhaps, he will have pity upon us, and spare our lives at your entreaty.'

The ogre's wife, who hoped that she might be able to hide them from her husband till the next day, yielded to the children's entreaties, and let them in. She told them to sit down and warm themselves by the fire, which was large enough to roast a whole sheep for the ogre's supper.

Now she was the giant's second wife; he had killed her father and mother, and had carried her off, against her will.

Just as they were beginning to get warm they heard a loud knocking at the door.

'Here comes my husband,' said the woman, in a
whisper; 'make haste, and let me hide you.'
And she concealed them as well as she could under
the bed. But it is difficult to conceal seven boys.
Then she went and admitted her husband.
The ogre asked if his supper were ready and his
wine drawn, and immediately seated himself at
the table. The sheep was served at once; it was
still half raw, but he liked it all the better.
When he had eaten it he looked about him, and
spied a little shoe lying near the fire.
'What is this?' he asked, in a terrible voice. 'You
have had children by the fireside—where are they?'
'Husband, how can you be so silly?' said the
poor trembling wife; 'surely that is only our
eldest daughter's doll's shoe.'
The giant might have been deceived, but just at
that moment poor Peter, who had caught a cold,
happened to sneeze.
With a savage roar the ogre jumped up, and
dragged the seven pretty children from under the
bed, where they were hidden.
'Ah!' said he to his wife, 'this is the way you
deceive me, is it? It would serve you right if I
were to eat you; but you are serviceable to me,
you do my cooking. However, these children come
just as I wanted them. Three ogres are coming to
dine with me the day after to-morrow, and they
will greatly enjoy such a feast. The children may
not be fat, but they are tender.'
The poor boys cast themselves at the ogre's feet,
and, with many tears, besought him to spare them;
but they had fallen into the power of the most cruel
of the ogres, who had no pity. He answered their
prayers by telling his wife that he would have them
roasted and served up with apple sauce.
He then got his axe, and was about to cut off their
heads, when his wife said—
'It would be better to keep them for a day or two,
116

and feed them up, for as you see they are half-
starved, and terribly thin.'

The giant took up Hop-o'-my-Thumb and pinched his arms.

'You are right,' he said; 'they must be fattened. This child is nothing but skin and bone.'

So their long want of food saved their lives for the nonce. Then the woman, with real pleasure, but as if to oblige her husband, brought them a good supper, and coaxed them to eat, and they were so hungry that they were glad to do so, although they were trembling with fear. Meantime the ogre sat down to the table, and, being very merry at the thought of the delicate dinner he would give his friends, he drank a great deal of wine; more by a dozen glasses than usual, and thus he grew so tipsy that he was obliged to go to bed early. Then the good woman put the seven little boys to bed in the same room with the giant's own daughters by his first wife, who was dead, and they were just about their ages. These seven little ogresses had very white skins, small eyes, and little noses and mouths, like other children; but they had long and sharp teeth—far apart. Though they were too young to do much mischief, they were as cruel as their father, and would bite pieces out of little children whenever they could get at them. The ogresses had been in bed some time, and were fast asleep. They lay side by side in a big bed; each of them wore a golden crown on her head. The ogre's wife put a nightcap on each of the boys.

Now Hop-o'-my-Thumb was afraid that the giant might change his mind, and kill them in the night; so, as soon as the good woman was gone, he took off the gold crowns from the heads of the little ogresses, and put them on his brothers and himself; and he set the nightcaps on the little girls' heads. This was a very wise proceeding. The

ogre was so tipsy that he could not sleep, and as
he lay thinking of the nice meal his guests would
make, he forgot all about the fattening up, and
determined to kill the boys and have them cooked
for his breakfast.

So he got out of bed, took his axe, and went to
their room in the dark. Then he felt the beds,
and finding the crowns on the boys' heads, he took
them for his daughters, left them and went to the
other bed, and cut off the heads of the young
ogresses. Satisfied with what he had done, he
went back to bed, not knowing, of course, what a
mistake he had made.

As soon as Hop-o'-my-Thumb heard the ogre
snoring, he awakened his brothers, and told them
to make haste and dress and follow him. They
obeyed, and Hop-o'-my-Thumb stole with them
downstairs, and opened the back-door, without
making the least noise. Then they climbed over
the garden-wall and got into the road.

They ran as fast as they could all night, not knowing which way they went.

When the ogre awakened in the morning he said
to his wife: 'Go upstairs and dress those seven
boys for breakfast.'

The wife was delighted to hear him speak, as
she thought, so kindly; for she had no idea that
he meant 'cook' by 'dress,' but believed that he
wished her to put on the little boys' clothes for
them. So she ran upstairs. But when she entered
the bedroom she was horror-struck to find that
her seven step-daughters had all lost their heads.
She gave a scream and fainted away.

The ogre, who thought his wife had been gone a
long time, at last went in search of her, and when
he saw what had happened he was full of rage.

He shouted till he had brought his wife to her
senses.

Then the weeping woman said: 'Husband, if you

had not been so cruel, this would never have happened!'

'It is all the fault of those imps of boys,' roared the giant; 'they stole my daughters' crowns and put their nightcaps on my daughters' heads. I will follow them and punish them. Go fetch me my seven-league boots.

The woman obeyed, and the ogre, having put on his seven-league boots, sallied forth and strode over the country in search of the children.

But Hop-o'-my-Thumb was on the watch, perched at the top of a poplar-tree, and when he saw the giant stalking over mountains, and crossing rivers at a single step, he descended, and said to his brothers: 'Let us hide in this hole under a rock.'

He had observed the cavity before, and when his brothers were all inside it, he covered it with stones and boughs, and then hid himself under a dock-leaf, for he was sure the giant would not find so small a being as himself.

The ogre, who had been striding about in all directions, was now tired with his journey, and felt inclined to rest. It so chanced that he lay down close by the very spot where the seven children were concealed. As he was much exhausted by going about the country searching for the boys, and in every direction but the right one, he soon fell asleep, and began to snore so loud that the little fugitives were terribly frightened.

But Hop-o'-my-Thumb drew his brothers gently out of the hollow, and bade them make haste home while the giant slept, and not trouble themselves about him.

When they were gone, Hop-o'-my-Thumb crept quietly to the ogre, and gently drew off his boots and put them on his own legs. The seven-league boots were fairy boots, and would adapt themselves to any size of foot, consequently they suited

Hop-o'-my-Thumb exactly, and he set out in them
at once.   But as he was quite sure that the giant
would pursue him in order to recover them, he did
not take the road homewards, but went off in an
opposite direction.

As he had expected, the giant woke up a few
minutes afterwards, and, finding his wonderful
boots gone, was in a towering passion.  He looked
about for them, and finding the trace of the huge
heel, he at once pursued Hop-o'-my-Thumb.   But
what chance had his bare feet against the seven-
league boots?   Hop-o'-my-Thumb, looking back,
beheld the giant blinded by his fury striding over a
precipice.   He saw how that the ogre missed his
footing, and fell crashing down to the bottom.
The rocks echoed with the noise of his fall, as his
huge form dashed from crag to crag, and Hop-o'-
my-Thumb held his breath with awe.

'Poor children have reason to be glad you are
gone,' thought the boy, 'and I dare say your kind
wife will not be sorry.'

Hop-o'-my-Thumb was now both tired and hungry,
so he made haste to lead his brothers home.

The very day after the father had left his children
in the wood, the forester again called at the
cottage.   This time he brought some flour and
half a pig, the lord of the manor having sold some
land to buy food for his people.

He was surprised to find only the wife at home,
and she crying bitterly.

'Why, good wife, where are all your children?' he
asked; 'and where is my little friend Hop-o'-my-
Thumb, of whom my lord is quite fond?'

The bereaved mother answered only by a burst of
tears.   Then the man, suspecting that something
was wrong, insisted on knowing the truth, and the
broken-hearted woman confessed all.   He set off at
The forester was much shocked.   He set off at
once for the village, called together the neighbours,

and went and took both the woodcutter and his wife prisoners.

So when the six brothers returned home with Hop-o'-my-Thumb, they found nobody in the woodman's hut. However, in the excitement of the moment, the villagers had left the bacon and flour in the cupboard, and so Hop-o'-my-Thumb said—

'Let us get some food while we can.'

And he made a fire, cut rashers off the bacon, made a few cakes of flour and water, which he baked in the oven, and gave his brothers a good dinner.

They were much surprised when night came and still their parents were absent; but they shut up the house, said their prayers, and went to bed, hoping that father and mother would soon return and tell them what they had better do. However, as they did not come, the boys resolved to stay a little longer at home, and, as they had plenty of food, they managed to live very comfortably.

Meantime, in his dreary prison, the woodcutter had time to reflect on his crime. His wife never ceased reproaching him for it.

'What do you think,' she would say, 'will be the judgment of our good squire on you?'

The husband had not a word to answer. Indeed, he was so unhappy that he rather wished to be well punished.

At last the boys became seriously alarmed at the absence of their parents.

'Ah! Hop-o'-my-Thumb, and we used to despise you!' said the eldest brother. 'We see now how mistaken we were. Can you help us now to the sight of father and mother?'

'Well, I shall go into the village to-morrow and find out where they are,' said Hop-o'-my-Thumb.

Then they sat chatting and laughing round a wood-fire, which danced and crackled as if it, too, were glad, and cast a ruddy glow upon the seven little happy faces laughing round it.

The next morning early Hop-o'-my-Thumb put on
his seven-league boots and was in the village in a
moment, for it was only ten miles off. He found it
in a great state of commotion. The people were
gathered together on the village green, talking all
at once. So Hop-o'-my-Thumb went up to them,
and asked a woman what was the matter.

'Oh, my little dear,' said she—she was a stranger,
and did not know Hop-o'-my-Thumb. 'Oh, my
dear, the squire has just held a court and condemned a cruel woodcutter and his wife to death.
The wicked people had cast forth seven innocent
babes to be eaten by the wolves.'

'Ah!' thought Hop-o'-my-Thumb, 'those are my
father and mother. I am only just in time.'

So he stepped home again, and said to his
brothers—

'Make haste and walk as fast as you can to the
village, and show the squire that we are yet alive.'
So the six brothers set out and walked as fast as
their little feet could carry them.

Then Hop-o'-my-Thumb, taking them by the hand,
led the little string of boys to the house of the
forester, who was greatly astonished to see them
alive and well.

Hop-o'-my-Thumb related his adventures, and the
forester insisted on taking them to the squire, who
listened to their story with great interest. Of
course, as the children were not dead, the woodcutter and his wife were not put to death; but the
squire, though he restored the mother to her
children, kept the father in prison for two months
as punishment.

Then the squire sent some of his soldiers, conducted by Hop-o'-my-Thumb, to the ogre's house,
to see what had become of his wife.

They found that she had gone away to her kinsfolk
in the country whence the ogre had carried her off,
and the squire, on whose land the dwelling stood,

at once bestowed it and all the ogre's wealth on Hop-o'-my-Thumb.

So Hop-o'-my-Thumb took up his abode in that once dreaded house, and lived there with his father, his mother, and his brothers.

His seven-league boots made them all rich, for whenever any one wished to send letters, or make inquiries at a distance, they sent to Hop-o'-my-Thumb and asked him to go for them, and as he was paid a large sum for every journey, or we may say step, he took, he became a very wealthy man.

# WHITTINGTON AND HIS CAT

 MERCHANT once upon a time,
  Who had great store of gold,
 Among his household placed a boy
  Sore pinched by want and cold;
No father and no mother watched
  With love o'er this poor boy,
 Whose dearest treasure was a cat,
  His pet, and only joy,
That came to him beseechingly,
 When death was at the door,
And kindly to relieve her wants
 He shared his little store.

This boy was called Richard Whittington. He
had lost his father and mother, and, having no
friends, had come up to London to seek his fortune.
London streets, he had been told, were paved with
gold. Alas! he found them only deep in mud, and
hard—hard with stones.

After many privations and disappointments, and
when nearly starved, he was taken into the house
of a merchant named Fitzwarren.

In this house he would have lived very happily, if
it had not been for the cook, who was very ill-
natured, and who would beat him with the broom,

124

and made him turn the spit on which was the
roast meat, like a dog.  He was given a room in
the garret, in which to sleep, which was overrun
with rats and mice.  But Dick had brought up
from his country town with him his dear cat, and
this cat soon drove away the tormentors.

A grateful cat ! no mice might live
    Where she put up to dwell,
And Whittington could sweetly sleep
    While puss watched o'er his cell.

Now it happened that soon after this, the merchant,
Mr. Fitzwarren, had a ship ready to sail with
various commodities, which were to be sold or
exchanged for others, whereby he would gain great
profit.
Now it was customary at that time for a master
to ask his servants if they would like to venture
their little savings in the same vessel, and so give
them a chance of turning their money over and
increasing their little stores.
Now all the servants in Mr. Fitzwarren's house
gave up something to embark in the venture, and
the master asked Dick Whittington what he would
put into the ship.  But poor Dick had nothing
save his pussy-cat, and rather than not have some
share in the venture, but with tears in his eyes, he
gave up his cat, at the advice of Alice, the merchant's daughter.  So says the ballad—

Now by the strand a gallant ship
    Lay ready to set sail,
When spoke the merchant, 'Ho! prepare
    To catch the fav'ring gale;
And each who will his fortune try,
    Haste, get your goods on board,
The gains ye all shall share with me,
    Whate'er they may afford;

From distant lands where precious musks
    And jewels rare are found,
What joy to waft across the seas
    Their spoils to English ground!'
So hasted then each one on board,
    With what he best could find,
Before the ship for Afric's strand
    Flew swiftly with the wind.
The little boy he was so poor,
    No goods had he to try,
And as he stood and saw the ship,
    A tear bedimmed his eye,
To think how fortune smiled on all
    Except on his sad lot—
As if he were by gracious Heaven
    Neglected and forgot!
The merchant and his daughter too,
    Fair Alice, marked his grief,
And with a gentle woman's heart,
    Intent on kind relief,
She bade him bring his cat to try
    Her fortune o'er the sea;
'Who knows,' she said, 'what she may
      catch
    In gratitude to thee!'
With weeping and with sore lament
    He brought poor puss on board.
And now the ship stood out for sea,
    With England's produce stored;
And as she sped far out of sight,
    His heart was like to break;
His friend was gone that shared his crust,
    Far sweeter for her sake.
Humble his lot the merchant knew,
    But knew not that the cook
With blows and cuffs the boy assailed,
    And surly word and look,
Until his life a burden seemed,
    Too grievous to be borne,

Though Alice oft would pity him,
    So lowly and forlorn.

The cross-grained cook was very angry at the kindness shown to poor Dick by Alice, and she treated him more roughly than before, and sneered at him for having sent his cat to sea. 'Do you suppose,' she said, 'that your cat will sell for sufficient to buy a stick wherewith I may thrash you?'

At length poor Whittington could endure this harsh treatment no longer, and he resolved that he would run away and seek his luck elsewhere. So he packed up his few goods in a bundle, and started one morning, All Saints' Day, which is the 1st of November, and he walked as far as Holloway; which was then all fields, and there were no houses. There he sat himself down on a stone, which to this day remains, and is called 'Dick Whittington's Stone,'[1] and he was very sad to think how solitary he was in the world, and how badly he had fared. Moreover he could not tell which way he should go. While he was thus considering, the bells of Bow Church, which at that time were only six, began to ring for service, and their sound, borne on the breeze, seemed to say to him—

'Turn a-gain, Whitt-ing-ton,
Thrice Lord Mayor of Lon-don.'

The same words would come with the chime of the bells again, and over again into his head. He tried to laugh and began to cry. And still the bells rang on—

'Turn again, Whittington,
Thrice Lord Mayor of London.'

He shook his head and stood up, and took a few

---

[1] It now forms part of a lamp-post.

127

steps along the road to Finchley. But he had not gone far before he heard the bells again calling out—

'Turn again, Whittington,
Thrice Lord Mayor of London.'

And somehow, he did not fancy the Finchley road, so he turned back and he now took the road to Enfield. But he had not taken many steps along that way before again he heard Bow bells, and they still sang in his ear—

'Turn again, Whittington,
Thrice Lord Mayor of London.'

Then he laughed through his tears, and said to himself, 'Lord Mayor of London! That is a strange notion; but after all, Mr. Fitzwarren was good to me, and so was Mistress Alice, and perhaps I can bear the ill-nature of the cook, if I have the thought before me that I shall be Lord Mayor of London and ride in a coach.'

So Dick walked back by the way he had come, and got into his master's house before the cook came downstairs.

Now, the very first news which came to his ears that morning when he got back to the house were glad tidings.

Good news he quickly hears,
How that a richly laden ship,
    Amid ten thousand cheers,
Had entered port from distant climes
    Full freighted with their gold,
By traffic gained for English wares
    In honest barter sold.
With shout and song the crew rejoiced—
    Not less the folk on shore—
Told of adventures strange and rare
    Among the blackamoor;

128

And how their king was glad to see
    Our English sailors bold,
Who sat and ate and drank with him
    From cups of purest gold.
Once on a day, amid their cheer,
    When healths went gaily round,
How were the crew amazed to see,
    In swarms upon the ground,
Unnumbered rats and mice rush forth
    And seize the goodly cheer,
While stood the wond'ring guests aloof,
    O'erwhelmed with dread and fear.
'Oh!' said the king, 'what sums I'd give
    To rid me of such vile
Detested brutes, whose ravages
    Our bed and board defile!'

Now when the captain and sailors heard this, they recollected the cat of Dick Whittington; so they told the king that they had an animal on board which would rid him very speedily of all the vermin.
'Bring the beast to me,' said the king, 'and if it be as you say, I will lade your vessel with gold dust in exchange for it.'
So the captain sent a sailor to the ship, whilst a second dinner was being got ready. The sailor soon caught the puss, tucked her under his arm, and arrived at the palace in time to see the swarm of rats rush in to eat up the second meal that had been served.
Now when the cat saw and smelt the rats, whish she went out of the sailor's arms, and away she rushed upon the rats, and nipped and killed them one after another, and those who saw her, and had time, fled to their holes like wind.
The king laughed and kicked his feet about, and clapped his hands, and was so delighted that he said he must and would have the beast, even if it cost him half his kingdom.

I       129

The captain now called the cat to him and showed
her to the king, who at first was afraid to touch
her, but after a while, to show his manliness and
his royal fearlessness, put out a finger and touched
the cat, who at once began to purr. The king had
never heard this sound before, and it frightened
him, and he went under the table. But presently
he put out his head from under the table-cloth
to ask if all was safe. When he was assured that
the cat would do him no harm, then like a man
and a hero he came back to his place, and becoming bolder, with impunity patted the cat. After
a while even the queen summoned courage to
caress the cat, and say: 'Puss! Puss!' whereupon
the cat stepped into her lap, coiled herself up, and
went to sleep. The king was now quite determined to have the cat. He bargained with the
captain to buy all the rest of the ship's cargo, but
in payment for the cat he gave ten bags all full of
the finest gold dust.
The captain then took leave of the king, and
having a fair wind set sail for England, and after
a prosperous voyage arrived safely in London
port. This was the news that reached Dick
Whittington that morning of All Saints' Day
when he returned to his master's house, and now
as he heard it he no longer thought that the Bow
bells told what was impossible, as he was master
of ten great sacks of gold dust.
Now the cook was jealous and went to Mr. Fitzwarren and told him that all the treasure was too
much for a poor scullion. But the master was a
good man, and he said: 'God forbid that I should
rob the boy of a single penny; he shall have all the
gold dust to the last pinch.'
Then he sent for Dick, but the boy said: 'I have
only hobnailed boots and cannot go into the
parlour.' However, Mr. Fitzwarren insisted, and
he came in very modestly, and his master told him

all the truth about his good fortune, and called
him Mr. Whittington.

Poor Dick was overwhelmed with his good luck, and wanted the master to take half of it; but Mr. Fitzwarren said: 'No. It is all your own; but what I will do is to advise you how to dispose of it.'

Now Dick was so kind-hearted, that he made a present of some of the gold to all his fellow-servants, and to the captain and sailors of the ship. He did not even neglect the cross-grained cook.

After this Mr. Fitzwarren sent for a tailor, and had Dick dressed as a gentleman, and told him he was welcome to live in his house till he could provide himself with one of his own.

When Whittington's face was washed, and his hair curled, and he was dressed smart, then he looked a very handsome fellow, and that Miss Alice thought. She who had formerly looked on him with compassion, now considered him fit to be her companion, and soon afterwards her suitor; the more so because Mr. Whittington was constantly making her the prettiest presents imaginable.

At the end of three years Mr. Fitzwarren, perceiving the affection of Mr. Whittington and his daughter for each other, consented to unite them in marriage; and accordingly a day for the wedding was soon fixed, and they were attended to church by the lord mayor, the aldermen, the sheriffs, and a great number of the wealthiest merchants in London. There was a grand entertainment afterwards, at which the poor were feasted as well as the rich.

History tells us that Whittington and his lady lived in great splendour, and were very happy; that they had several children; that he was sheriff of London, and three times afterwards lord mayor;

that in the last year of his mayoralty he entertained King Henry the Fifth, on his return from
the battle of Agincourt; upon which occasion
the king knighted him by the style and title of
Sir Richard Whittington.

It is told that he then entertained the king at a
great banquet, when King Henry said: 'Never
had a prince such a subject.' To which Whittington replied: 'Never had a subject such a prince.'

Sir Richard Whittington constantly fed great
numbers of the poor: he built a church, and added
a college to it, with lodgings, and a yearly allow-
ance to thirteen poor scholars. He also erected
a great part of St. Bartholomew's Hospital in
Smithfield.

History has not told us what became of the property left by him for the support of the church and
the thirteen poor scholars; but it is believed it
was seized by King Henry VIII. at the time of
the Reformation, as that king seized upon many
of the lands which were left for religious purposes;
but those which Whittington left for building and
endowing almshouses met with a better fate; and
Whittington's almshouses remain to this day.

Here ends the story of Whittington and his cat;
from which we may see how that honesty and
industry met with success; and that charity and
piety are the best ornaments of the rich.

# DON'T-KNOW

HERE was once upon a time a king whose wife, the queen, became mother in the palace of a little son called Dan. And at the same time, even to a minute, a mare in the stable had a little foal. Therefore the king gave the foal to his son Dan.

When the young prince was old enough, he was sent to school, where he learned to read and write and cypher. Now not a single day passed but before going to school he went into the paddock where was his foal, and talked to it and patted it.

Now it happened that war broke out, and the king was obliged to go to battle, and he intrusted his queen and boy to the care of a prime minister. Now the queen was a wicked woman, and she entered into a plot with the prime minister to seize on the reins of government, and to establish herself sole sovereign in the land. But because the prince was clever and observant, the prime minister had to be very cautious lest his plans should be found out. And as the prime minister schemed to get the king killed and then to marry the queen, he determined also to get rid of the Crown Prince.

133

And in order to do this, he put a dagger in his bed
with the point upwards, so that when Prince Dan
went to bed, the dagger might pierce him through.
Now the little prince went as usual into the paddock to stroke his little horse, and he saw that
it looked sad and woebegone.
So he said to it : 'Little horse! what ails you to-
day?' but as the groom was by, the foal only hung
his head and said nothing.
Now when school was over, Prince Dan came back
to see his little horse, and again he asked : 'Little
horse! what ails you to-day?'
Then the foal said: 'Nothing ails me; but the
prime minister wants to kill you.' Then he told
the prince of the plan for his murder; and he told
him what he was to do that night.
So when darkness came on, Dan would not go to
bed at all, but slept on the sofa.
The prime minister saw he had failed in this
scheme, but thought he would poison Dan with
toffee : for of toffee the prince was passionately
fond.
Next day as he went to school he visited the foal.
And the little horse said to him: 'My king's son,
be on your guard, and take no toffee,' and he told
him the plan of the prime minister.
When the prince came home he was offered some
delicious-looking toffee, but he refused to touch
any.
Then the prime minister saw that this scheme of
his was unavailing. So he went to the queen and
he said to her: 'Tidings have just arrived that the
king is unexpectedly returning; and we are not
yet prepared for his destruction; and I believe that
Dan's foal tells him everything. Now pretend to
be very ill, and say that the doctors order you the
heart of the foal as the sole thing that will set you
on your feet again.'
Now very soon the king arrived, and was sorry to

find the queen ill, and she told him all that the
prime minister had put in her mouth.

Then the king said: 'Certainly, I will have the foal
killed, and you shall eat its heart; only wait till
Dan returns from school, that he may say good-
bye to his little horse.'

Now the king walked to meet Dan as he came back
from school, and told him that he must kill the foal.
So Dan said: 'Certainly, dear father, you must do
what you see fit; only first of all let me pull on my
riding breeches, and take my little whip and gallop
round the paddock once on my little horse's back.'

Then Dan ran to his foal, that looked sad and
woebegone, and told it what his father had said,
and what he had desired.

The foal said to him: 'Call for a glass of wine, and
drink to your father's health and the failure of your
mother's and the prime minister's plans; then
jump on my back, I will carry you far away.'

He did so. When he had pulled on his riding
breeches and taken his whip, he asked for a glass
of wine, and kneeling before his father, said: 'I
drink to your health, father, and to the failure of
my mother's and the prime minister's plans, who
have sought to dethrone you and to kill me.'

Then he jumped on his foal's back and away, away
he rode.

Now when the king had heard those words, he
wondered and examined into the matter, and then
all came out; so he had the prime minister hung,
and he put the queen in prison.

In the meantime the little horse had galloped
away, away over land and sea, and never halted
till it came to England and to the city of London.
There, at the outskirts, it halted, and said: 'Now
go into the town, but never speak any other word
but Don't know to whatever is asked you, till
I give you leave.'

The prince promised this, and leaving his foal in a
136

meadow outside London, he went alone into the
great town. Those who met him asked him who
he was, but he answered only 'Don't know.' They
inquired of what country he was. He replied only
'Don't know.' They further asked his occupation.
He said only 'Don't know.'

Now after a day or two it was told the king
that there was a handsome lad going about
London, who could say no other words but 'Don't
know.'

So he sent for him and asked him his name, and
received the answer 'Don't know.' 'Very well,'
said the king, 'be it so. You shall be called Don't-
know.' Then he sent him into the kitchen to be
scullion there, but gave strict orders to the cook
not to maltreat him in any way.

Now it was usual for the servants to go to church
on Sundays, and one only to remain at home and
prepare dinner.

When it came to Prince Dan's turn to be alone in
the kitchen, then he took ashes and strewed it
over all the meat.

When the cook came home he was angry to see
the good meat all spoiled. He said: 'Why, what
have you done this for?'

Dan replied: 'Don't know.'

'Do you know that you deserve a good hiding.'

'Don't know.'

But as the king had ordered that the lad was not
to be maltreated, the cook did not dare to beat him;
but he went to the king and begged that he might
be taken out of the kitchen and put elsewhere.

So the king placed him with the gardener.

Now it was the custom in the garden for the gardeners to go to church on Sunday, and one to
remain behind to guard the garden.

When it came to Dan's turn to be at home, then
his little horse came trotting up to him, and he
brought him a bridle, and said: 'Shake the bridle

137

and at once you will have a splendid horse to ride and grand clothes to put on.'

So Dan shook the bridle, and immediately a chestnut horse stood before him with a red suit of clothes over the saddle, and all the accoutrements were of copper.

Then Dan jumped on his back and rode round and round the garden, till all the beds were trampled and spoiled. Then he leaped off the horse, which vanished along with the splendid red garments Dan had worn.

Now it fell out that the king's third daughter, the youngest of his children, had not gone to church that day, as she had a bad cold. She had been looking out of the window, and saw all that had happened.

When the gardeners came back from church, they were very angry, and they said to Dan: 'Who has been here spoiling the flower-beds?'

'Don't know.'

'Why did you not keep proper guard?'

'Don't know.'

'Were you asleep or awake?'

'Don't know.'

'I hope,' said the head-gardener, 'that you know one thing, which is that you deserve a hiding?'

'Don't know.'

It took a dozen men a whole week to put the garden in order again, and a month before any flowers grew in it.

Then again it came to Dan's turn to remain at home while the rest went to church.

The princess had told no one of what she had seen. Again she had a cold, and so she remained at home. And this is what she saw:—

No sooner were all at church, and Dan thought himself alone, than he went into the garden and shook the bridle, whereupon a white horse appeared with a white suit of clothes adorned with silver over the saddle. Dan drew on the suit, jumped into the saddle and rode up and down the garden trampling all the beds. When he was tired he jumped off, and at once the horse and the white clothes disappeared. The princess had seen all this.

When the gardeners came home and saw the mischief done, they were very angry, and they asked—
'Why did you not keep proper guard?'
'Don't know.'
'Who have been in the garden, making this mess?'
'Don't know.'

You may well believe, that if the king had not given strict injunctions to the contrary, they would have beaten Prince Dan black and blue.

Again the princess said nothing, and resolved on the same Sunday in the next month to pretend to be unwell, so as to stay at home and see what would happen.

Now when the Sunday came, when it was Dan's turn to keep guard, the princess remained in the palace. This time she opened her window and leaned forth to see the better.

Dan shook the bridle and immediately a yellow horse appeared, and over the saddle was a dress of cream colour all woven with gold thread.

He jumped into the saddle and rode up and down and around the garden, and when he came near the open window, where was the princess, then he leaped on the saddle, and kissed her on the mouth.

Now when he had ridden sufficiently, he dismounted, and instantly horse and garments vanished.

When the gardeners returned they were furious.
'Who has been here? There are horse hoof-prints!'
'Don't know.'

'How is it you don't know? Did you keep your eyes shut?'

'Don't know.'

Well—the king thought it was high time to have his three daughters married. So he had them advertised in all the daily papers :—

> WANTED, three desirable husbands, for three eligible Princesses. Must be of Royal blood, good looking, cleanly in their habits, and not given to chewing or smoking or snuffing tobacco. Apply: Buckingham Palace. N.B.—No post-cards.

The king was very amiable, and he said to his daughters: 'My dears, I positively don't want to force any undesirable husbands on you. I give you free liberty to pick and choose and take whomsoever you like.'

'Any one, revered father?' asked the youngest. 'Is not royal descent a sine qua non?'

'So long as he is cleanly in his habits and person, and doesn't chew, snuff, or smoke, I will not insist on that requirement,' said the king.

Troops of princes came to London, all aspirants after the hands of the princesses, and every one was scrupulously clean, and none were devoted to tobacco.

The king had them all trotted out in the yard before his daughters, and the eldest chose her husband, then did the second the same, both desirable princes. But the youngest did not find any to her mind, so she said to the king: 'Father, may I have one of the court?'

'By all means—if cleanly in his habits, and not addicted to the filthy habit of snuffing, chewing, or smoking tobacco.'

'Will you have them all up?' asked the princess.

So all the court was brought forward and marched

140

in the front yard of the palace before the princess, but not one pleased her.

Then she said: 'Is every member of the court here?'

'All but that miserable Don't-know,' said the head-gardener.

'Send for Don't-know,' asked the princess, and the prince Dan arrived.

Then she went straight up to him and kissed him on the mouth, and said: 'That's the boy for me.'

Now when the sisters and the princes who were to be their husbands saw and heard this, they were greatly shocked and offended. However, the king was so good-natured, and his youngest daughter so persistent, that there was no help for it, and the three princesses were married the same day. But as the two eldest sisters and their princes were extremely disgusted at the youngest sister's choice, and as they represented that it was not proper for them to live in the palace, the king had the potato-house cleared out, in which the potatoes were usually kept through the winter, and fitted up as the house of Don't-know and his wife.

Now one day, soon after the wedding, there was to be a hunt. So the two princes, as they rode out to the chase, passed the potato-house, and saw Don't-know outside. They laughed and said: 'Brother-in-law, are you coming out for some sport to-day?'

'Don't-know.'

'We suppose you never rode a horse in your life?'

'Don't know.'

'Nor killed any game?'

'Don't know.'

So away they went, laughing to each other about this silly brother-in-law of theirs.

Now when they were gone, Dan shook his bridle, and at once the red horse appeared and the red

and copper garment. He put it on and mounted,
and away he went after his brothers-in-law.

As he approached them, they did not know him,
and they said one to another: 'Who is this great
prince who rides this way?'

They waited till he came up and then asked if he
would join them. Now the horse had given him
leave to speak whilst in his gay garments, so he
answered and said: 'I have already chased.'

'What have you caught?'

He held out a golden pheasant.

Then the princes longed to be able to take this
home with them and show it as their capture. So
they begged him to give them the pheasant. He
said he would do so if they would give him the
rings off their fingers. To this they consented.
They gave him their rings, and he gave them the
golden pheasant and rode away, and got fast
home, jumped off the red horse, and stood by the
door of the potato-house when they came home.

As they drew nigh, the princes showed the golden
pheasant and shouted: 'Brother-in-law, do you
not admire our skill in the chase?'

'Don't know,' was all he answered.

Next day there was to be another chase in the
forest. The princes rode by the potato-house,
and said: 'Brother-in-law, will you come out with
us to-day?'

'Don't know.'

But when they were gone he shook the bridle,
and immediately the white horse appeared, with
the white suit of raiment adorned with silver. He
mounted and rode after his brothers-in-law.

They had been unsuccessful that day and were
discouraged. They said: 'Here comes that prince
again in most splendid raiment and on a magnificent horse. Who can he be?'

When Dan came up, they saluted him respectfully
and asked if he would have sport with them that

day. He replied that he had already been engaged
in the chase and had got a beautiful white swan.
They were very desirous to have this, but he said
he would take no money for it, only if they would
allow him to heat their rings red hot and stamp
the signets on their heads, under the hair, then
would he give up the snowy swan.

They thought no one would see if branded under
the hair, so they consented. He branded them
both with their own seals, gave them up the swan
and galloped home. The horse and his white
vesture disappeared, and as they came home they
saw him lounging at the door of the potato-house.
They held up the beautiful swan, and said: 'See,
brother-in-law, what luck we have. Don't you
wish you were as clever as we?'

'Don't know.'

'Ah! but you know you are a fool and we are
wise.'

'Don't know.'

They rode into the palace laughing, and got great
credit for having killed the swan.

Next day there was another hunting party. Again
the princes laughingly taunted Dan—

'Will you come a-hunting, brother-in-law?'

'Don't know.'

'You haven't got a horse to ride, we suppose?'

'Don't know.'

'Nor bow and arrows?'

'Don't know.'

'But you know you are a fool?'

'Don't know.'

When they were out of sight, he shook the bridle,
and now a gold yellow horse stood before him, and
a splendid crocus yellow garment woven with
gold thread. He put on the dress, mounted and
galloped after the princes. When he drew near
they said to one another: 'Can this be the same
prince we have seen twice before?'

They waited till he came up, and then saluted him
with the profoundest respect, and inquired if that
he would hunt with them that day. He replied
that he had already done his hunting, and he
showed a gold fawn that he had killed.

When the princes saw this, they were mad set to
have the fawn, and they begged him to let them
have it; but he said he would give it up only on
condition that they each allowed him to brand
them on the back with something.

Well—they were so set on having the gold fawn
that they agreed, and he burned on their backs
the symbol of a pair of gallows. Then he rode
home, and had changed everything before they
arrived; and when they came, they bragged about
their hunting and showed the gold fawn they had
killed.

'You couldn't do this, could you, brother-in-law?'
they asked. He only replied from the door of the
potato-shed: 'Don't know.'

Now it happened that the great King Cuckoo of
Ireland, who had been subject to the King of
England, was so set on being independent, and
even of subjugating England, that he gathered a
great army, and came over and marched against
London. The king sent out an army to oppose
his advance under one of his sons-in-law, but it
was defeated; then he sent another under the
second, and that was defeated also. So now the
king gathered together all the remnant of his
forces, and determined to take the field in person,
he would command the centre, and each of his
sons-in-law the wings. The two princes went to
the potato-shed, and said: 'Come on, brother-in-
law, the land is in danger, you must fight as well
as we.'

'Don't know,' answered Dan.

'Don't you know how to handle bow or spear?'

'Don't know.'

144

'If we are defeated again, all will be up with every one of us,' said the princes.

'Don't know,' answered Dan.

Now as soon as they had marched out of London, Dan shook the bridle, whereupon his own little horse came trotting up to him, and he had on his back three portmanteaus. He said to his master: 'See, take these portmanteaus. In one is an army of soldiers, in another are munitions of war, in the third is plenty of money. The day is going against the king. Quick, put on the suit of armour you will see provided, jump on my back, and ride to the rescue of your father-in-law. But first unpack the portmanteaus.'

So Dan immediately opened the leather boxes. And when he had opened the first out marched an army of men. And when he had opened the second out rolled cannons and cannon-balls, and hay for the horses, and food for the men. And when he had opened the third he found in it gold, wherewith to pay the soldiers, and gold is said to be 'the sinews of war.' So he mounted his little horse and rode at the head of his army to the battlefield, and he arrived just as the centre was giving way, and when the two wings were turning to flight. He rushed forward with his men and fell on King Cuckoo with his Irish, and utterly routed them, and took their banner, on which was inscribed 'Home Rule for ever,' and sent the Irish flying, tumbling head over heels, away, away, as fast as their legs could run, in the direction of their native isle.

Now as soon as he had gained the victory he hastily withdrew with all his men till he had got behind a belt of trees, and then he packed all his troops once more into their portmanteau, and put in all the munitions of war into the second, and returned as quickly as he could to London, jumped off his little horse, and stood lounging at the door

of his potato-shed, when the king and the
princes and the army returned, playing and
singing and whistling and dancing 'Rule Britannia, Britannia rule the waves, Brit-tons never,
never, never, will be slaves,'—least of all to
Paddy.

And as the princes passed by the door where stood
Dan, 'Ah, ha! brother-in-law,' they said, 'where
were you to-day when we gained the victory over
King Cuckoo?'

'Don't know.'

'What would you have done had you been in
battle? Run away, of course.'

'Don't know.'

'And where would you be now, but for our
victorious arms?'

'Don't know.'

A grand banquet was given that evening. And
much wine was drunk, and toasts were proposed,
and the two princes bragged of what they had
done, and no one said a word about the mysterious
assistance that had been given just as fortune had
declared against the English arms.

But presently the king got up on his feet, and at
once every one began to hammer on the table, and
say 'Hear! hear!'

Then the king said: 'Ladies and gentlemen,
princes and princesses of the blood royal, dukes
and marquesses and earls, and viscounts and
barons, and baronets and knights and squires,
and all in your several degrees,—I hope you will
listen to the few words I venture to utter.'

'Hear! hear!'

And one of the princes thundered out 'Encore!'

'I have listened,' said the king, 'with surprise and,
I am fain to admit, sorrow, and heard every one
present boasting about his great deeds, and no
one saying a word about that gallant and most
mysterious hero who seemed to drop from the

146

clouds, and without whom we should have been
compelled to—to—to cut and run.'
'No, no!'  'No, no!'
'Yes—I repeat it,' said the king.  'The wings
under the masterly direction of my sons-in-law,
had received the order "Right about face,—cut!"
the centre under my august self was giving way.'
'No, no!'  'No, no!'
'It is of no use our shutting our eyes to facts,' pursued his majesty.  'We should have been jolly
well licked'—he paused—the expression was
hardly diplomatic, he corrected it to 'we should
have met with a serious reverse, but for the assistance of our mysterious ally.  I drink, gentlemen
and ladies, princes of the blood royal, dukes, etc.
. . . to the very good health of our deliverer this
day.  By the way,' added the king, sitting down,
'where is son-in-law number Three?'
Every one of the guests looked in every one else's
face, and said—
'Don't know!'
And the servants behind the guests looked about
the grand banqueting-hall, and they also said—
'Your most gracious Majesty—don't know.'
And the footmen on the stairs looked up and down
the staircase, and the porter at the gate looked at
them, and they at him, and said: 'Don't know.'
Just then was heard martial music.
A magnificent band was heard playing—and the
tune that was being played was, 'See-e-e the con-
quering her-er-er-o comes!'
And presently large bodies of soldiers appeared,
infantry and cavalry, in magnificent uniform, and
surrounded the palace, and then riding on a gold-
coloured horse in golden armour, with a white
horse at his side, on which rode a lady in cloth of
silver, came a prince.  He was attended by a number of equeries and staff officers, and he descended
from his horse at the palace gates, gave his hand

to the princess, let her alight, and then strode up to the gates.

The porter said: 'Your name, sir?'

'Don't know.'

Then the porter, who had quite lost his head at all the magnificence, said to the first footman—

'His Serene Highness Don't-know.'

And the first footman shouted to the second—

''Is 'Iness Don't-know.'

And the second shouted to the third, with great emphasis—

'His Haugust 'igh and Mightiness Don't-know.'

And so the announcement ran up the stairs, but with a few strides the new-comer reached the top of the grand state stairs, and the princess with him, and they walked into the banqueting-hall— and lo! every one stood up and cheered, for they recognised the conqueror in that day's battle.

Then Prince Dan, for it was he, bowed his knee to the king, and said: 'Sire and father-in-law, I am the youth who has for all this while answered to every question asked me, Don't know. Now I am released by my little horse from the necessity of making this answer. Why imposed on me, goodness only knows, but I made the promise, and a promise, sire and father-in-law, is, I need hardly say, a promise and must be kept. I am of royal blood, being the son of the very puissant King of Cloudland. I came here, and here your youngest daughter chose me to be her husband. Your two other princes, sons-in-law, are humbugs. Here are their rings that I took from them. If you will lift up their hair you will see them branded with their own signets. If you will strip their coats off their backs, you will find them marked with a pair of gallows between their shoulder-blades. If you have the least doubt, sire and father-in-law, that it is I who assisted in this glorious day, here is your own pocket-handkerchief which you gave me. In

148

the midst of the fray I was slightly wounded in the arm; when you saw the blood flow, you pulled out your red silk pocket-handkerchief and insisted on binding it about my arm. I restore it to you. I am healed. The kingdom of Great Britain is henceforth safe from the humiliation of annexation through subjugation to the neighbouring isle.'

There was immense applause, and even the humbled princes, the brothers-in-law, had sufficient grace to say: 'Encore, encore!'

Then the king said: 'It is obvious to me and to all, that I must make this victorious hero heir to my throne, though he has married only my youngest daughter. Hitherto we have only known him by the name of Don't-know. We would all like to know what is the real name by which he may be known in history.'

Now the writer of this story is fain to say that at this point his authorities fail him. In Cloudland the prince was indeed called Dan, but not so in English history. If therefore it be asked by what name this prince may be looked for in the catalogue of English sovereigns, he is obliged to admit 'Don't know.'

MIRANDA NCE upon a time there lived a king who had three beautiful daughters, the youngest of whom, named Miranda, was the most amiable, and was her father's favourite.

The king was very superstitious, and had great faith in dreams.

One day he asked his daughters to tell him the subject of their dreams the foregoing night.

The eldest said that she had dreamed that he gave her a gown, the gold and jewels of which shone bright as the sun and stars.

The second said that she had dreamed that he gave her a golden distaff and spinning-wheel, for her to spin linen.

The third said that she had dreamed that her father came to her and held a golden basin with water in it, and had said to her: 'Come and wash your hands.'

The king was very angry with Miranda for her dream, and he thought that it could have but one signification, that she would dethrone him, make herself queen, and turn him into her servant.

As he was a very suspicious and jealous man as well as superstitious, he worked himself to such a pitch of unrest over this thought, that all his love was changed to dislike, and fear took the place of regard. He determined to have his once darling daughter put to death, so as to bring this dream of hers to naught.

For this purpose he commanded the captain of his guard to carry Miranda into the forest and kill her; and that he might be sure of its being done, he ordered the officer to bring her heart and tongue to the palace, threatening him with instant death should he disobey his orders.

The captain, with much sorrow, went at an early hour to the princess's apartment, and told her that the king had sent for her.

She arose immediately and followed him, accompanied by a little Moor, called Patypata, who held up her train; also by a young ape, called Grabugeon, and by a little dog, called Tintin, which ran by her side.

Not finding the king in the garden, where the captain said he was taking fresh air, she was advised to seek him in the forest, whither it was said he had gone to see the does and deer. She resolved on following him thither.

But as they went on the sun rose, and the princess saw it sparkle in the tears that ran down the cheeks of her conductor.

She gently asked him the cause of his sorrow.

'Alas, madam!' he said, 'how can I be otherwise than sad at heart? The king has ordered me to kill you, and to carry your heart and tongue to him; and if I do not this, he will put me to a cruel death.'

The innocent princess became pale when she heard this, and said to the captain: 'Are you hard-hearted enough to kill one who has never injured you, but has ever spoken in your favour to the king.'

'Do not fear, princess,' he answered, 'I will sooner suffer death myself than hurt a hair of your head.

MIRANDA But is it possible for us to find out some method of persuading the king that you are dead?'

'What way can we discover,' asked Miranda, 'since he will not be satisfied unless he sees my tongue and my heart?'

At these words the little Moor, who was warmly attached to her mistress, came and threw herself at Miranda's feet, and said: 'Dear madam, let me be the sacrifice, I shall be but too happy to die for your preservation.'

'No,' said the princess, kissing her, 'your life ought now to be as dear to me as my own.'

The young ape, Grabugeon, next advanced, and said: 'Truly, princess, your slave, Patypata, is likely to be more serviceable to you than I can be; therefore I offer you my heart and tongue willingly.'

'O my dear Grabugeon!' replied Miranda, 'I cannot bear the thought of taking your life away.'

Her faithful dog Tintin then cried out that he could not bear the thought of any one but himself dying for his beloved mistress. In short, after a long dispute between Patypata, Grabugeon, and Tintin, which of them should suffer death instead of the princess, Grabugeon nimbly climbed to the top of a tree, and throwing himself down, broke his neck. The captain, with much persuasion, got leave of the princess to cut out his tongue, but it proved too small to serve to deceive the king with it.

'Alas! my poor ape,' exclaimed the princess, 'thou hast lost thy life without doing me any service.'

'That honour,' interposed the Moor, 'is reserved for me,' and she instantly ran upon the knife wherewith the captain had cut out Grabugeon's tongue.

But here, also, the intended service failed, as the poor Moor's tongue was too black to pass for Miranda's.

The princess bursting into tears and lamentations

MIRANDA for the loss of the Moor and of the ape, her dog
Tintin exclaimed: 'If you had accepted my offer,
there would have been none to regret but myself,
and real service would have been done you.'

Miranda was so overwhelmed with grief, that she
fainted away; and when she came to herself, the
captain was gone, and the little dog was lying dead
beside the ape and the Moor.

Having buried her three favourites in a hole under
a tree, she began to think what she must do for
herself.

As the forest was not far from her father's court,
and she might easily have been discovered and so
bring destruction not only on herself but also on
the captain, she travelled as fast as she could walk,
though in an opposite direction, till at last she was
almost ready to expire with weariness.

Then hearing the bleating of sheep, she supposed
that she was approaching some shepherds with
their flocks, and she exerted all her remaining
strength to reach the place, in hopes of finding
some relief.

But how great was her surprise, when she came to a
spacious plain, to see a large ram, as white as snow,
with gilded horns, and a garland of flowers about
his neck, lying on a bed of orange blossom, and
shaded from the sun by a tent of cloth of gold. A
hundred sheep richly adorned were in attendance
on him.

Miranda became motionless with astonishment,
and looked about for the shepherd of so extraordinary a flock, when the noble Ram approached
her, and said—

'Draw near, lovely princess, and be not afraid of
such gentle creatures as are we.'

'What!' exclaimed the princess, starting back, 'is
it possible that you can speak?'

'Why not, madam,' answered the Ram, 'when your
dog and your ape spoke? They did it because

endowed with the gift by a fairy. May not the
same be the case with me? Be not surprised, but
tell me what has brought you here.'

'A thousand misfortunes,' answered Miranda. 'I
am forced to fly from the rage of a cruel father.'

'Come then with me, madam,' said the Ram, 'and
I will conduct you to a place where you will be
secure from discovery, and be treated with the
utmost respect.'

The Ram then ordered his chariot, which was large
enough to hold two persons with ease, and was
lined with blue velvet, and drawn by six cashmere
goats. The princess placed herself in it, and the
Ram got in after her, and drove to the mouth of a
cave, which though stopped by a large stone, was
opened when the Ram touched it with his foot.

Miranda, having descended numerous marble steps,
was exceedingly surprised to find herself in a
strange country, in a plain enamelled with flowers,
where played fountains of fragrant essences.

Here and there clumps of trees formed a habitation
for birds; and when Miranda passed, they flew
out in the form of tartlets, cheese-cakes, sponge-
cakes, and biscuits, all supplied with wings.

The princely Ram told Miranda that he had reigned
here for several years, and had sufficient cause for
grief. He required but little persuasion to tell his
sad story.

'Born and educated as a prince,' said he, 'I came
into possession of one of the most delightful kingdoms in the world, and I was much beloved by my
subjects and respected by foreigners. Being fond
of hunting, as I was one day pursuing a stag, he
took me to a pond, into which I imprudently
plunged my horse after him. Instead of finding
the water cold, I found it to be extremely hot; and
the pond dried up all of a sudden, and there shot
out of a hole in the earth a terrible fire. Then the
bottom of the pond sank, and I went down a long

MIRANDA way till I reached the bottom of a sort of well, with flames all round me.

'Then I saw an old hag before me, who said, "Fiercer flames than these are needed to warm thy heart."

'"Alas!" said I, "who complains of my coldness?"

'"I do—I, an unfortunate wretch who adores you without hope."

'Then the fire disappeared, and I knew now that this old woman was a terribly powerful fairy.

'"What, Ragotta," said I, "was this done by your orders?"

'"By whose else, think you?" she answered. "Have you not known for a long time that I have loved you? Consider how low I stoop—I, a fairy, to desire the affection of a man such as you."

'"You ask what I cannot give you," I answered, "neither do you go the right way to work to win my love."

'"What do you object to in me?" asked the fairy.

'"In the first place you are old."

'"Old!" she exclaimed, "I can transform myself and make myself young and beautiful."

'"And you have a moustache," said I.

'"That I can pluck out," she answered.

'"And one eye is looking in one direction, the second eye in another."

'"I can put one of them out," she said.

'"In a word," said I, "I can never love you."

'In a rage she struck me with her wand, and said:

'"You shall feel my resentment. Be a Ram, and continue so, till some king will suffer you to sit on his throne and drink out of his cup."

'I found myself at once changed into my present shape, and my courtiers were turned into sheep.'

Miranda was struck by so remarkable a story; she paid the Ram some civilities, but she could not encourage him with hope of regaining his form, for it seemed to her impossible to believe that any king

156

would suffer a ram to ascend his throne and drink MIRANDA
out of his cup.

Miranda remained for some time in the beautiful
land to which the royal Ram had conducted her.
At last news reached her that her eldest sister was
going to marry a great prince, and that extensive
preparations were being made for the nuptials.
These tidings were brought her by a swallow.

Miranda asked the Ram's leave to go to her sister's
wedding, and this was granted; but the Ram
insisted on her going in most magnificent apparel.
She arrived at the King's court just as the marriage
of her sister was about to take place.

When Miranda arrived, her appearance caused a
general flutter of astonishment and admiration, as
she was dressed in shining silver tissue set with
pearls, and no one had ever seen so magnificent
a dress; and indeed she was so lovely that many
—the gentlemen especially—looked only at her face,
whilst the ladies examined, admired, and were
jealous of her gown. The king especially observed
her with great attention.

When Miranda saw this, she became alarmed lest
he should give orders to have her stopped; so she
stole away before the ceremony was concluded
and hastened back to the realm of the royal Ram.

The Ram had been waiting with the utmost
impatience for the return of Miranda; and as soon
as he saw her, he ran towards her, and gave many
tokens of passionate fondness for her.

So Miranda remained again some time in the
pleasant realm of the royal Ram.

Then it fell out that a swallow came and twittered
in her ear, and told her that the king was about
to give his second daughter in marriage to a great
prince.

Miranda begged leave to attend this wedding also.
The Ram could not refuse, and he insisted that
she should wear a still more splendid dress, all

MIRANDA of cloth of gold with diamonds woven into it, and a crown of gold and diamonds on her head, and also he made fast a diamond to every single hair of her head, and also to each of her eyelash hairs, and to those that formed her brows. Thus she twinkled and blazed with splendour.

As soon as Miranda had arrived at her father's court, the king at once ordered all the gates to be closed. When the ceremony was over, he went up to her, and begged leave to escort her to the banqueting-hall.

Miranda would have fled, but found all the doors fast. Then the king led her into the hall, and hasted and brought a golden basin with water for her to wash her hands in.

Miranda immediately fell at his feet, saying: 'Sire! behold, my dream is fulfilled. I am your third daughter, and you have offered me water in a golden basin.'

When the king heard this—he recollected the features of his daughter Miranda, and was filled with shame and sorrow. He cried out: 'O my dear daughter! forgive the cruelty of a father who deserves death for the way in which he treated you. Now what can I do to make amends for my past injustice?'

'Sire,' answered Miranda, 'grant me a single favour!'

'I will grant you anything you ask,' answered the king.

'Sire!' said she, 'suffer a Ram to sit on thy throne, and to drink out of thy cup.'

When the king heard this he was much astonished and became red in the face, and did not know what answer to make. Nevertheless, because he had made the promise before all the court and all the friends and visitors from foreign kingdoms who had come to the wedding, he gave his consent.

158

It must be told that the Ram waited and became
impatient because Miranda did not return. So at
last having lost all patience, he resolved to venture
to the court, where he asked admittance, but was
refused by the guards at the gates. However,
Miranda, having received the king's promise, went
down, and when the gates were opened, then she
saw the Ram outside.

Full of joy inexpressible she conducted him into
the throne-room, and herself carried him up the
steps and seated him in the throne. Then she ran
and fetched wine in the king's own cup and offered
it to him.

No sooner had the Ram drunk out of the royal
cup, seated in the royal throne, than the spell that
had been cast over him came to an end, and he was
changed back into his original form, a beautiful
prince, and immediately, with immense rejoicings,
was married to Miranda.

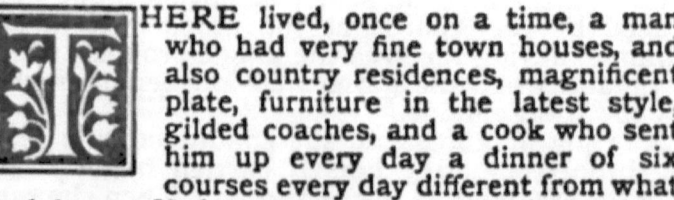HERE lived, once on a time, a man who had very fine town houses, and also country residences, magnificent plate, furniture in the latest style, gilded coaches, and a cook who sent him up every day a dinner of six courses every day different from what had been. Unfortunately for him he had a blue beard. This made him so hideous and frightful, that there was not a woman or girl who did not run away when he appeared.

One of his neighbours, a lady of quality, but very poor, had two daughters of the most amiable dispositions, and both very lovely.

The man with the blue beard asked for one in marriage, and left the choice to their mother.

Neither would hear of taking him because of his blue beard. Moreover, it was commonly reported that he had had several wives, and no one could say exactly what had become of them.

Blue-beard invited the lady with her daughters to visit him in one of his country places. He at the same time asked many of the neighbours there, and he gave entertainments in succession for a week. There was one uninterrupted series of dances and picnics, of hunting parties, of dinners; there was really no time for sleep; there was such splendour displayed in the house, such fertility of resource in the master for their amusement, that the company present thought they never had enjoyed themselves more, and that after all, if the owner of the place, and the giver of the festivities had a blue beard, he had wealth enough to gild it; and that a good deal might be forgiven a man who had such plate, such a cook, such furniture, and who dearly loved giving parties.

The youngest of the lady's daughters considered that it would be a very pleasant thing to be mistress of so grand an establishment, and to be looked up to by all the neighbourhood as the person of most consequence therein.

She felt her aversion for Blue-beard decrease, and finally consented to accept him. The entertainments were now prolonged for another week, at the end of which time a magnificent wedding took place, to the great satisfaction of the young lady's mother, who thought she had disposed of her daughter to the greatest possible advantage.

At the end of a month, Blue-beard told his wife that business required him to absent himself for six weeks or a month, and he begged her to amuse herself as best she could during his absence. She was to invite her friends to visit her, and to entertain them.

'Here,' said he, 'are the keys of two large linen-chests; here are those of my plate-chest; here are those of my money-boxes, and also of all my jewels; and here is a key that opens all the doors and cupboards throughout the house. You see this little key? that pertains to the cabinet at the end of the long picture gallery. You may open any closet and cupboard and chamber throughout my house, with the single exception of that little cabinet. I strictly forbid you to enter or look in

L 161

there under pain of my extreme displeasure, and
of forfeiting all my love for you, and all your
happiness for the future.

She promised exactly to observe all that he commanded, and, after he had warmly embraced her,
he mounted his equipage and drove away.

The neighbours and friends did not wait to be
invited to come to the country house, and to relieve
the dulness of the young bride; and they were
extremely desirous of being shown everything in
the house, and of turning out all the cupboards,
a thing they had never before ventured to do, they
had not even asked to be allowed to do, so great
was their dread of Blue-beard.

Now, however, that he was away, they scattered
through the house, they ran upstairs and down,
they pried into every chamber, they explored every
cupboard, and searched every drawer. They
examined all the furniture, they went through
all the house-linen, they examined and admired
the tapestries, the carpets, the curtains, the cover-
lets; then they looked through all the plate to
make sure that it was of real silver and gold,
and not plated wares. They turned over all
the books in the library, they tried on all the
family jewels, they even examined all the bottles
of preserved fruit, and pots of crystallised ginger,
in the storeroom. The mistress of the house
took little pleasure in seeing and showing all
these treasures to her friends, for she was most
inquisitive to know what there was in the cabinet
at the end of the picture gallery. Indeed, so impatient was she to satisfy her curiosity, that she
deserted her guests, and when they were all
engaged elsewhere, she slipped into the gallery
by herself and put the key into the door which
she had been forbidden to open.

She paused there for one moment, with a little
hesitation, because she remembered her husband's

threats; but her curiosity overcame all scruple of disobeying him, and fears for herself, and she tremblingly opened the door of the cabinet.

At first she saw nothing, for the windows were all shut. But after a while her eyes became accustomed to the gloom, and she saw that the floor was all stained with blood, and that along the walls hung the dead bodies of a great many young women. These were the wives Blue-beard had married in succession, and had put to death, one after the other.

She thought she would have died of horror, and the key which she had withdrawn from the door dropped from her hand.

After a while she recovered her senses, picked up the key, fastened the door, and hastened to her bedroom, to throw herself on a couch and compose her mind. But she could find no rest, so violent was her agitation, and she begged her sister, who was called Anne, to dismiss her guests, on the plea that she was ill and could not entertain them further.

When alone, the young wife noticed that there was a stain of blood on the key. She at once tried to wash it off, but neither soap nor water would remove it. Then she rubbed the key with sand-paper, but this was equally in vain. If she rubbed out the stain of blood on one side, it broke out on the other side of the key.

Blue-beard returned from his travels that same evening. He said that he had received letters whilst on his journey which informed him that the business on which he had started had come to a satisfactory termination, and that his presence was no longer needed.

His wife did all that she could to show him that she was delighted at his return. But she called to her a little foot-page, and said: ' Run, run, as fast as your feet will bear you to my home. My two

brothers are there, just returned from the wars.
Bid them ride and spur and never slack rein till
they have reached this place and saved me.'

Next morning Blue-beard asked for his keys, and
his wife restored them to him with a hand that
trembled so that he suspected what had happened.
He looked at the keys and said: 'I miss that of
my cabinet. Where is that?'

'I must have left it upstairs,' she said.

'Do not fail to bring it me,' he said, in a stern
voice.

There was no help for it. She was obliged to
produce the key.

Blue-beard looked at it with a frown. 'Why is
there blood on this key?' he asked.

She was too frightened to answer.

'You have been in the cabinet, which I forbade
you to open and enter. Very well, madam, you
shall go in again and this time remain there, hung
to the wall beside the other ladies you saw there.'

She threw herself at her husband's feet, weeping
and entreating pardon, with all the marks of
sincere repentance for her disobedience. So
beautiful and distressed was she that she might
have melted a heart of stone, but that of Blue-
beard was harder than stone.

'You must die, madam,' said he, 'and that instantly.'

'If I must die,' she replied, looking at him with
eyes bathed in tears, 'give me at least time to say
my prayers.'

'Very well,' he answered, 'I grant you a quarter
of an hour, not a moment longer.'

When she was alone, she summoned her sister,
and said to her: 'Sister Anne, I pray you, mount
the tower, and see if my brothers are coming.
I sent them word to come without delay. When
you see them, sign to them to speed their fastest.'

Her sister immediately ascended to the battle-

ments of the tower, and looked away in the direction of her home. The poor trembling and
weeping bride called to her after a few minutes:
'Sister Anne! sister Anne! is there any one
coming?'

'I see nothing,' answered her sister, 'but the sun's
beams glancing, and the motes dancing, and the
grass is green and growing, oh!'

Blue-beard in the meanwhile had got a great
cutlass from the armoury, and he called to his
wife: 'Come down, come down, or I'll draw you
by the golden locks of your crown.'

'Grant me one moment longer!' answered his
wife. She cried again to her sister: 'Sister Anne!
sister Anne! is there any one coming?'

'I see nothing,' answered her sister, 'but the sun's
beams glancing, and the motes dancing, and the
grass is green and growing, oh!'

'Come down, come down this very moment,'
shouted Blue-beard. 'Time is up, come down,
come down, or I'll draw you by the golden locks of
your crown.'

'I am coming directly. Suffer me to pull on my
shoe,' said the unhappy wife. Then again she
called to her sister: 'Sister Anne! sister Anne!
do you see any one coming?'

'I see,' said the sister, 'I see a cloud of dust
springing, and I hear harness ringing, and the
grass is green and growing, oh!'

Then Blue-beard roared forth: 'If you do not
come down at once I shall come up and fetch you.'
But his wife said: 'Suffer me to pull on the other
shoe, and then I will come down.' And now again
she called: 'Sister Anne! sister Anne! is there
any one coming.'

Sister Anne replied: 'I see armour glancing, and
two horses prancing, and your brothers ride fast
to the castle, oh!'

Blue-beard would not tarry any longer, and his

166

wife could find no further excuse for delaying to come down. So she slowly and tremblingly descended the stairs. With hair dishevelled and with her face bathed in tears she threw herself on her knees, and begged him to spare her life.

'It is of no avail,' answered Blue-beard; 'die you must and shall.'

Seizing her by the hair—her golden hair—with one hand, and brandishing the cutlass with the other, he prepared to strike the fatal blow.

'Stay! stay!' she said; 'I have on my neck the beautiful chain you gave me.'

'Take it off, lest it turn the edge of my sword,' said he.

She obeyed with fingers that shook as if she had the palsy. Again he raised the cutlass above her head. 'Stay! stay!' she said; 'I am wearing my white bridal silken dress, and it will be all dappled and stained with my heart's blood.'

'Take it off,' he said. She obeyed slowly, so great was her fear. Then she knelt down again, and again he raised the cutlass to strike off her head, when she cried out: 'Stay! stay! the parrot is in the window, and he will talk and tell how you have killed me.'

'That is true,' said Blue-beard; and he removed the cage and put it in another room.

Then he came back, and raised the cutlass, and said: 'I will not be put off again.'

But at that moment a loud knocking was heard at the gates, which made Blue-beard pause.

The gates were burst open, and two young men in shining steel armour, with their swords drawn, rushed in. They flew upon Blue-beard and pursued him as he attempted to escape; they overtook him before he had mounted the platform on top of the castle, and ran him through the heart with their swords.

The poor wife, almost dead with terror, was un-

able for some time to find words wherewith to
thank her brothers for this timely rescue.

As Blue-beard left no heirs, his wife inherited
all his immense fortune. She bestowed part of it
as a marriage dower on her sister Anne, who was
shortly after married to a young nobleman who
had long loved her.

Some money she spent in buying castles and lands
for her brothers. With what remained she was
still vastly rich, and she was soon married to a
generous-minded young man, a companion-in-arms
and friend of her brothers, and his love and courteous treatment soon made her forget the cruel
usage she had received from Blue-beard.

'I give you the keys,' said he, on their marriage
day, 'that open everything I possess, and all the
secret chambers of my heart. You may look in all,
and where you will, and you will find nothing
that I desire to hide from you—for you will find
nothing anywhere but love for you.'

'And I,' answered his wife, 'will never allow myself
henceforth to peep and peer into what does not
concern me.'

# THE FAIR MAID WITH GOLDEN LOCKS

A
S it fell upon a time, there lived in Golden Land a beautiful princess, whose hair was like the finest gold, and waved and rippled down her back and reached the ground, and she was called the fair maid with golden locks. She always wore a crown of China roses on her head, and dresses of the softest and palest pink, or blue, or white embroidered over with diamonds; so that wherever she went and whenever she moved she twinkled like a laburnum bush covered with dew on a May morning.

Now it fell out at this very time that there was a certain king, and as he had heard so much of the fair maid with golden locks, he sent an embassy to Golden Land to ask her hand.

The ambassador arrived in Golden Land with his message, but the princess refused the king's offer. She said she was over young to marry yet.

Then the ambassador set off sadly on his way home. When he arrived in the city where the king was waiting impatiently for him, every one was much disappointed because he returned alone, for every one had expected he would have brought with him the fair maid with golden locks to be their queen.

Now there was at the court a young man, who was very clever and very handsome. His name was Charming. Most people liked him, and he was a favourite with the king, but for that very reason several of the courtiers were envious and sought his destruction.

One day Charming said without consideration, that if he had been sent to Golden Land, he would not have returned with a refusal.

This was quite enough for his enemies. They at once went to the king and said : 'Charming has been talking in a very insolent manner. He says he is such a good-looking fellow that Princess Golden-locks would never have refused him.'

When the king heard this, he was inflamed with rage, and gave immediate orders that Charming should be thrown into prison and fed with only one slice of bread without butter on it, and plain water every day, till he grew old and grey and ugly. So the guards seized on Charming and carried him away to the dungeon. There he lay for many days on straw, and ate only the piece of dry bread and drank only the pipkin of water allowed him.

One day he said sadly to himself: 'How is it that I have offended the king? I am his most faithful servant, and have done nothing against him.'

The king chanced to be walking by the tower when he said this, and he overheard the words of Charming.

The enemies of the young man tried to make him walk on, and disregard what he had heard, but the king insisted on Charming being brought before him. The young man was released, and bending on one knee, he kissed the king's hand, and asked how he had offended.

'You made a mock of me and my ambassador,' said the king, 'and you declared that if you had been sent you would not have returned without the fair maid with golden locks.'

170

'No more would I,' answered Charming; 'I would have made such a description of your majesty, that the princess would have been all impatience to jump into your majesty's arms.'

The king now saw that Charming had been evil and falsely spoken of; he took the young man back into his favour, and said to him—

'So be it. You shall go on an embassy to Golden Land; and if you return without the princess, I will cut off your head.'

Charming said he was content to run the risk.

The king desired to give him a fine equipage and many servants and heralds to blow trumpets before him; but Charming said that all he wanted was a good horse, and to take with him his little dog Dulcet.

So next day he started at early dawn, and rode all alone, save that his little dog Dulcet ran beside him.

Charming carried with him a notebook, and whenever a happy thought struck him which could go into his description of the king he was going to give to the fair maid with golden locks, he got off his horse, sat down, and wrote it, for fear of forgetting it.

He wrote—

'My master the king is a very great lord,
His stomach is round and his shoulders are broad.'

'That goes splendidly,' said Charming, and he rode on a little way. Then a new idea struck him. He got off his horse and wrote—

'His temper is high, but his mind it is low,
He croaks when he talks like a carrion crow.'

Then he got on his horse again. After a while he thought of some more words in commendation of the king, so he got off and wrote—

'His great moustaches they twist and twirl,
To win the heart of each right-minded girl.'

Once as he was sitting by the water, trying to find
a rhyme to 'bandy legs,' and sorely troubled because he could not make a suitable line ending in
eggs, a little golden carp that was rising after a
fly sprang out of the water and fell in the grass
beside him, and remained panting, unable to return
to its proper element.
'Poor little fish!' said Charming.
He put his hand down, took the carp, and threw it
back into the water.
The carp was delighted to be again in the refreshing coolness of the water. She swam up to the
bank, and said—
'Thank you, Charming, for what you have done.
You have saved my life, and when you need my
help I will give it you.'
Another day, as Charming was riding along, he saw
a raven in great distress. It was pursued by an
eagle, that would have devoured it, had not the
young man quickly discharged an arrow from his
bow, and killed the eagle.
The raven perched on a tree, nodded its head, and
said—
'Thank you, Charming, for what you have done.
You have saved my life, and when you need my
help I will give it you.'
Night came on, and Charming rode through a
wood. The moon shone as clear as the day and
painted the ground silver, where it pierced between
the branches and leaves.
Presently Charming saw what seemed to him a
great lump of snow, but it was making a great
noise. He went up to it and found that it was a
white owl caught in a gin. Charming at once
released the poor bird, and the owl hopped on to a
branch, and said, 'To whoo!'

'Do you ask to whom you owe your release? To me,
Charming,' answered the young man: 'you should
speak good grammar, and say To-whom and not
To-who.'

'Thank you, Charming,' said the owl, 'for what
you have done. You have saved my life, and when
you need my help I will give it you.'

These were the only three adventures of any importance that befell Charming on his way to
Golden Land.

When he arrived at the palace of the princess, he
saw how magnificent it was. Pearls seemed to be
as plenty as pebbles, and diamonds as common as
dust. He thought to himself: 'If the princess con-
sents to leave all this, and come with me to marry
my master—I shall be much surprised. And yet—

'"His great moustaches they twist and twirl,
To win the heart of each right-minded girl."'

When he appeared before the princess, his little
dog Dulcet would come in with him. He was so
well-dressed and so handsome, that the guards
saluted him respectfully, and a messenger was sent
to the princess to announce the arrival of another
ambassador.

The princess was vexed; however she consented
that he should be allowed an audience.

Then Charming approached her throne, bearing
himself modestly, and showing the profoundest
respect. When he looked up he was so struck
with her beauty that he put his hand over his eyes
as though dazzled. She was in one of her most
beautiful dresses, and was covered with rosebuds.

Then she graciously bade Charming approach; so
he kneeled on one knee, and gave her an eloquent
description of his lord and master—

'My master the king is a very great lord,
His stomach is round and his shoulders are broad.

His temper is high, but his manners are low,
He croaks when he talks like a carrion crow.
His great moustaches they twist and twirl,
To win the heart of each right-minded girl.
He has a nose in the midst of his face,
And a couple of ears in their proper place.
His eyes are round and his mouth is wide,
What more would have an exacting bride?'

'That will do,' said the princess. 'You are so
amiable and so eloquent, that I would gladly oblige
you and marry such a beautiful and interesting
king, but I must tell you that I have promised not
to marry till I receive a ring which I lost a month
ago. I was walking by the river-side, when I
chanced to draw off my glove. In so doing I slipped
a very valuable ring off my finger, and it fell into the
water. I cannot think of listening to any proposal
of marriage till that ring has been restored to me.'
Charming was much surprised at this declaration.
He bowed, and begged the fair maid with golden
locks at least to accept the little dog Dulcet he
had brought with him. She replied that she did
not want any presents, and dismissed him.
All night long Charming tossed on his bed, and
lamented—
'How am I to find the ring that fell into the river
a month ago?' said he. 'It is not possible. I
shall lose my head.'
Dulcet heard him, and said—
'My dear master, do not despair. Let us at all
events try what we can do. We will go down to-
morrow morning to the river-side and peer into the
water.'
Charming thought this absurd; he gave the dog a
little impatient slap.
At the first glimmer of dawn, Dulcet began to frisk
about, and insisted on making his master come out
with him, and walk by the river-side; and there

174

they wandered up and down, but could see no ring
in the water.

Charming had almost made up his mind to return to his lodgings, when he heard his name called. He looked about, but saw no one. Then he walked on, but again heard a voice that called: 'Charming! Charming!'

'Who calls me?' he asked.

Dulcet, who was very small, and ran close to the water's edge, cried out, 'Master, I see a golden carp coming.'

And sure enough there was a carp, and it said to the young man: 'You saved my life in the meadow where grew the poplar trees, and I promised to repay you. Take this, it is the ring of the fair maid with golden locks.'

Charming took the ring out of the carp's mouth, with many thanks, and he and little Dulcet, which gambolled and barked about him, returned to the palace.

Some one told the princess that he was asking to see her.

'Ah! poor fellow,' said she; 'he desires to say good-bye.'

Then Charming entered, and making a profound bow, approached: he gracefully bent his knee, and handing her the ring, said—

'Madam! I have done your bidding. Here is what you had lost. Now will you marry my master, who is the greatest king and most attractive man in the world—

'" His great moustaches they twist and twirl,
To win the heart of each right-minded girl.
He has a nose in the midst of his face,
And a couple of ears——" '

'Enough,' said the princess,' I have heard that already, and would really be moved to accept the king by the eloquence of your speech and the

175

melodiousness of your lines, but that I am determined not to marry any one so long as I am pestered with the addresses of an ogre named Gallifron, who eats human beings as a monkey eats chestnuts. Before I can listen to your proposal, you must kill Gallifron and bring me his head.'

Charming bowed profoundly, and said—

'Madam, I can at least die in your cause.'

This was said so gracefully that the princess was moved with pity, and said all she could to dissuade Charming from attempting to fight the giant. But it was of no use, he went forth, obtained suitable armour, and mounting his horse rode in the direction of Gallifron.

Every one he met told him what a terrible ogre Gallifron was, and nobody dared go with him as a guide. However, Dulcet frisked at his side, and said—

'Dear master, whilst you are aiming at the monster's breast I will bite his shins, and when he stoops you can deal blows at his head.'

Charming praised the little dog's plan, but had no great opinion of its success.

At last he drew near to the ogre's castle, and saw that all the ground about it was strewn with bones. Presently he heard Gallifron coming. His head was taller than the highest tree. As he came on, he roared like a bull—

'I gobble them up, both old and young,
  Gorroo—gorroo—gorroo.
If old and tough, they are better hung,
  Gorroo! gorroo! gorroo!
If young, at once I snap off the head,
  Gorroo! gorroo! gorroo!
I'm never happy but when full-fed,
  And now—I will dine on you!'

Charming with great spirit answered him—

176

'Don't count your chickens before they are hatched,
Nor sell your pullets before they are catched.
There is many a slip
'Twixt the cup and the lip.
And to catch a sparrow you'll even fail
Till a pinch of salt is dropped on its tail.'

The grammar was not perfect; Charming ought not to have said 'catched,' which was vulgar, but 'caught' would not rhyme with 'hatched.' Besides he was too frightened to be in a truly poetic mood. Gallifron was very furious, and he roared, and rushed at Charming, swinging his iron club, and would certainly have killed him had not at one and the same moment Dulcet flown at his shins and bitten them, and a raven darted down out of the rock and pecked at the giant's eyes, and beat his face with its great black wings. Consequently his blows fell harmlessly upon the air, and Charming, rushing in, gave him strokes on his knees, which brought him to the ground, and then standing over him, he hacked off his head.
Then the raven croaked out—
'You see I have not forgotten the kindness you once showed me. To-day I have fulfilled the promise I made to repay you.'
Charming thanked the raven with all his heart, and then, mounting his horse, he rode away, with the giant's head at his saddle-bow.
On reaching the capital, the people came out in crowds and welcomed him, and shouted with joy, and the church bells rang out merry peals.
The princess asked the meaning of this, and was told that Charming had killed Gallifron, and was returned unhurt bearing his head.
Charming now requested an audience, and the Fair Maid with Golden Locks could not refuse it. He entered, with many bows, and kneeling at the

foot of the throne put down the ogre's head at her feet.

'Madam,' said he, 'I have accomplished the task you set me, and now let me hear that you will

listen to the suit of the most accomplished and powerful of kings—

'My master, the king, is a very great lord,
His stomach is round, and his shoulders are broad ;
His temper is high, but his manners are low ;
He croaks when he speaks——'

'That will do,' interrupted the princess. 'I have no doubt that the king is all that you have depicted him in your resounding verse. But I have, you must learn, the greatest horror of growing old and ugly, therefore I have determined most decisively never to marry till I can take with me a phial of the Water of Perpetual Beauty. This water has the most marvellous properties. Beautiful things never decay and wither, and ugly things become beautiful when washed with it. If any one is young he never wears old if washed with it, and one who is old can be renovated with it to look perfectly young.'

'Princess,' said Charming, 'you, at least, need never employ this water; but I am an ambassador who must do all I can to obtain your hand for my master. Will it please you to tell me where this water is to be found?'

'It is at no great distance from this,' said the princess. 'It flows out of the rock at the bottom of a deep and gloomy cavern, and is guarded by two dragons with fiery eyes who will allow no one to pass them.'

'Madam,' said Charming, 'I fly to my death. My death will be sweet because dying for you.'

When Charming had departed the Fair Maid with Golden Locks said to her ladies: 'Surely he will never undertake this adventure. I would not have him die for worlds. I only said it because I really have no heart to marry his master.'

She was extremely concerned when she heard that he was already departed in quest of the Water of Perpetual Beauty.

Charming went on his way taking Dulcet alone with him. When he came within sight of a great black mountain then he knew he was not far distant from the fountain. He dismounted and turned off his horse to graze, and let Dulcet amuse himself with catching flies.

He went forward and soon saw the mouth of the cavern, from which issued puffs of smoke with flames; this was caused by the breathing of the

dragons who guarded the fountain of the Water of
Perpetual Beauty. He approached as near as he
dared, and saw the hideous monsters spotted black
on yellow writhing about the coils of their slimy
and monstrous bodies.

Charming had brought with him a flask: he now
drew his sword and resolved to penetrate into the
cavern and get the water, or die in the attempt.

At that moment he heard a voice calling, 'Charming! Charming!'

'Who calls me?' asked he, looking round.

'Who! who! who!' was the answer.

'Exactly what I want to know!' said Charming.
Then he saw a white owl sitting among the rocks.
The white owl said to him: 'You saved my life
when I was in the gin. Now I will do all I can to
repay you. Trust me with the phial. I can thread
the interstices of the rocks and penetrate to the
bottom of the gloomy cavern, and shall fill the
flask from the fountain of Perpetual Beauty for you.'

Charming was only too glad to give up the phial,
and the owl flitted with it into the cavern without
either of the dragons caring to stop her, even if
they noticed her; for bats and owls were the
common inhabitants of such places.

Presently she returned, with the phial filled with
the limpid and sparkling liquid. Charming thanked
her with all his heart, and joyfully hastened back
to the capital town.

He went straight to the palace and presented it to
the princess.

She could not now make any further excuses, and
she prepared to go with Charming to marry his
master, the king. But, in her heart, she would
much rather have had Charming as her husband.

At last they reached the king's great city, and he
came out to meet the princess, and escorted her
to his palace with a great retinue, and a magnificent marriage was celebrated.

Then the Fair Maid with Golden Locks told the king of all that Charming had done, how he had recovered her ring that had been lost, how that he had slain the ogre, and how that he had obtained for her the Water of Perpetual Beauty.

Now Charming's enemies were jealous of him because he had succeeded so well, and especially the ambassador who had failed was so filled with envy and spite that he resolved on Charming's destruction.

So he went to the king and said: 'I suppose that the Fair One with Golden Locks is often talking to you of Charming.'

'Certainly she is,' answered the king.

'It is very clear,' said he, 'that she thinks more of him than of you.'

'Yes,' said another; 'and Charming has been saying that your majesty was too great a coward to face the ogre, or to get into the cavern where were the dragons, and too stupid to find the ring, and so you sent him.'

'Did he say that?' exclaimed the king. 'Throw him into the lowest dungeon.'

So they took Charming, who had served his master so faithfully, and shut him up in prison; and he had none with him save his little dog Dulcet, and with the dog he shared his bit of bread and sup of water, which was all the nourishment that was allowed him.

When the Fair Queen with Golden Locks heard what had been done, she cast herself at the king's feet and implored him to set Charming free, but the more she entreated the more stubborn he became.

Now it happened that the king took it into his head that if his queen washed herself with the Water of Perpetual Beauty he might just as well do the same himself, and then he would always remain young and lovely. So he went into her

room, where he knew was the phial standing on
a shelf.

It had fallen out, however, that one of the queen's
maids had been chasing a spider in that boudoir,
and in trying to kill it had upset and broken it,
and spilled all the precious water.

Not knowing what else to do, as she was not an
honest girl who had the courage to speak the
truth and tell what she had done, she swept the
bits of broken glass together, and then remember-
ing that there was a phial very similar in the
king's room, also filled with clear water, she went
there, and without saying a word to any one, took
this and put it on the shelf in the queen's room,
precisely where had stood the flask that contained
the Water of Perpetual Beauty.

Now the water in this bottle was used by the king
for getting rid of those people in his realm whom
he desired to destroy without a fuss and a trial.
It was a most deadly poison, and if a face were
bathed in this water, he who was thus washed,
shrivelled up, and died on the spot.

The king went into the queen's boudoir, and seeing the phial on the shelf, immediately took it,
poured out some of the water into the hollow of
his hand and bathed his face with it. He at once
fell down, withered up, and was dead.

There was, as may well be guessed, great con-
fusion in the palace when the tidings spread that
the king was dead. Dulcet ran to the queen,
plucked at her skirts, and bade her not forget
Charming. So she sent for the gaoler and bade
him immediately knock the chains off the hands
and feet of the prisoner. There was a grand
funeral for the king, and then, as there was no
heir to the kingdom, and the nobles and council
thought it would be well to keep the two kingdoms
united, they resolved that the Fair Queen with
Golden Locks should reign over both, and that she

should chose a husband, who should be king over
both the realms.
When she heard this, then she said that she would
not choose any one else but Charming.
Everybody was delighted that he should be
sovereign, and the wedding, which took place after
a decent interval for mourning over the death of
the king, was as splendid as can well be imagined.

# JACK THE GIANT KILLER.

I N the days of King Arthur there lived
in Cornwall a lad named Jack, who
loved to hear the wonderful deeds
done by King Arthur and the knights
of his Round Table, which were
greatly noised abroad.

Jack did not see why he himself
should not achieve as great adventures as Sir
Lancelot du Lac, Sir Gawain, or Sir Kay.

At this time there lived many giants in Cornwall.
Not far from Jack's father's house, on the top of
S. Michael's Mount, lived one who was the terror
of the neighbourhood. His name was Cormoran,
and he had a voracious appetite. When he
required food, he came down from his castle, and
seizing on the flocks and herds of the poor people,
would cast an ox over his shoulder and stuff his
wallet with sheep, and stride back to his dwelling
thus supplied.

This had been his manner of life for many years,
and the country round Mount's Bay was nearly
ruined through him.

After Cormoran had stuffed himself well with meat,
he usually remained at home for a good many
days, till his supply was exhausted.

Jack took advantage of this circumstance, and

one night he dug a deep pit before the gateway
into the castle, and covered it with sticks and
heather, and over that he laid sods of turf.
When this was done, he blew a loud blast with his
horn, and this roused Cormoran from sleep. He
issued from his castle in a great rage, and when
he saw Jack he roared with a voice of thunder,
'Who are you, that you dare to disturb me?'
Then he charged from his gate with great strides,
so as to catch Jack and kill him; but at the very
second step he took, he went headlong into the
pitfall Jack had prepared for him.
Jack at once ran to the side of the pit, and as the
giant tried to scramble out, he aimed at him with
his pick-axe, cleft his skull, and the ogre fell back
dead.
Jack now ran home in great glee to tell his friends
what he had done. The whole country was moved
at the news, and resolved to show to Jack some
token of gratitude for having delivered it from
such an encumbrance. They therefore presented
him with a sword and belt on which was written
in pearls—

'This is the valiant Cornishman
  Who slew the giant Cormoran;'

and they named him Jack the Giant-killer.
But this only whetted Jack's desire to achieve
fame, and kill giants.
The news of what he had done had reached the ears
of another equally greedy giant, named Blunderbore, and he resolved on chastising Jack for having
killed Cormoran.
Jack heard of this, and he therefore resolved on
being beforehand with Blunderbore, by attacking
him before he got under way to punish him.
The giant lived in a castle in the depths of a great
forest. Jack started in quest of him, and shortly
before reaching the castle sat down to drink of a

clear stream that sprang out of the rock ; and as
the day was warm, and Jack had walked a long
way he fell asleep.

Whilst he was in this state, Blunderbore came to
the spring to fill his pitcher, and seeing a youth
lying there, he stopped and read what was written
on his belt.

'Ha-ha!' roared the giant, as he caught him up.
'Now I have got you, and you shall not escape
me.'

Jack awoke with a start to find himself in the grip
of the giant.

He pretended to be still asleep, and the giant
carried him into his castle and threw him into a
dungeon. Whilst Jack lay there he heard many
sighs and groans issuing from other prisons ; and
a voice which said—

'Haste, gallant stranger, haste away,
  Before you fall the giant's prey ;
  He's gone abroad, but with another,
  He'll soon return, his savage brother,
  A monster dread and cruel, who
  Will torture ere he butchers you.
  Then, gallant stranger, haste away
  Ere you become the giants' prey.'

'That is all very good advice,' said Jack, 'but
somewhat impracticable. When I am locked up
in a prison, how can I get away?

He crawled up into his window and looked out.
Then he saw the giant Blunderbore, who had
gone away, was returning with another giant
more hideous than himself.

Jack, perceiving in one corner of his dungeon a
very stout cord, used for binding prisoners, he
made a slip-knot at each end, and as the giants
walked under the castle walls he threw the loops
over their heads, pulled them tight, and tied the
cord to his window bars. You may believe that

186

the giants struggled, kicked; but the more they struggled the tighter grew the slip-knots, and at last they were quite choked and dead.

He now pulled at that bar of his window to which the giants had been attached, and which they in their struggles had almost torn out of its socket. He easily slipped between it and the next bar, and finished the giants with his sword.

Then seizing the keys which hung from the belt of Blunderbore, he entered the castle and examined all the prisons. In one he found three ladies hung by the hair of their heads to nails, and almost starved to death. Jack at once released them, and asked how they came to be there. They informed him that the giant had killed their husbands, and then had hung them up as Jack had seen, that they might starve. Jack then very gallantly offered them the keys of the castle and bade them live there.

He then bade them farewell, and departed for Wales. Jack now travelled as fast as he could. At length he reached a handsome mansion and knocked at the door. Then out came a Welsh giant. He was rather dismayed at this, but did not allow the giant to see it. He said he was a traveller who had lost his way, and that he sought a night's lodging. Thereat the giant welcomed him and escorted him in, and gave him a room with a good bed in it.

Jack undressed and went to bed, but could not sleep, although he was very weary. Presently he heard the giant walking backwards and forwards in the next room, muttering to himself—

'Though here you lodge with me this night,
  You shall not see the morning light,
  For with my club I will kill you quite.'

'Oh! is that your intention!' thought Jack. 'I must see if my wits will help me.'

Then he got out of bed and put a great log of
wood in his place, and concealed himself in a
corner.

About midnight the giant entered the room, and
with his cudgel struck several heavy blows on the
bed, in the very place where Jack had laid the log.
After that, thinking he had killed the sleeper, he
stumped back to his own room.

Early in the morning Jack put a bold face on the
matter, and walked downstairs and found the
giant at breakfast, and very much surprised the
ogre was at seeing him.

'Halloo!' said he, 'you here! How did you sleep
last night?'

'Pretty well,' answered Jack. 'I should have slept
better, had not a rat given me three or four slaps
with its tail.'

This speech mightily surprised the giant, but he
said nothing. He then brought out two huge
bowls of hasty pudding, one of which he set before
Jack, and the other he took himself. Jack, instead
of eating his, contrived to pour it down his neck
into a leather bag which hung before him.

When they had finished, Jack said—

'Now I can do what you cannot. I can run a
knife in here,' pointing to his bag, 'without killing
myself.'

He then seized the knife, plunged it into the
leathern bag, and out fell the pudding.

The giant was surprised at this, and not liking to be
outdone in such a matter, he also seized the knife,
plunged it into his body, and died on the spot.

Now Jack ransacked his house, and found in it
four great treasures: a cloak which would make
those who wore it invisible, a cap of knowledge
which when put on told one all one desired to
know, a sword of sharpness that would cut through
anything it touched, and shoes of fleetness which
when worn made the wearer run like the wind.

Jack now took these four treasures and went on his way.

He travelled over high hills and moors, and came into a forest whence he heard cries issue. He went in their direction, and saw a giant dragging along a knight and his lady by the hair of their heads. Jack alighted off his horse, tied him to an oak-tree, then he put on his invisible cloak, under which he carried the sword of sharpness.

When he came up to the giant he made several strokes at him, but could not reach his body, but wounded his legs in many places; and he continued hacking till he had cut through the leg bones, and then down tumbled the giant, when he at once ran his sword of sharpness into his body and killed him.

The knight and his lady thanked Jack for their deliverance, and invited him to their castle.

'No,' said Jack, 'I cannot be satisfied until I have found out the habitation of this monster.'

So he remounted his horse and rode away, and in time came to a mountain. When he drew near he saw bones lying about, and knew that he was close to the dwelling of a giant. So he put on his invisible cloak, and ascended the mountain till he reached a cave, at the door of which sat a giant, who was saying: 'I wonder where my brother can be. He promised to bring a good fat knight and a plump lady for our day's meal.'

The giant was a hideous monster, with eyes as fierce as those of a wild boar; he had shaggy cheeks and a long beard, the hairs of which were like wire.

Jack walked up to him, and aimed a blow with his sword, which cut off the giant's nose. He jumped up, yelling, and looked about him, but could not see his adversary. Jack now sprang on the giant's seat, and aimed at his back, and pierced him through, so that he uttered a groan and died.

Jack then cut off his head, and sent it along with that of his brother to King Arthur.

Having thus slain these two monsters, Jack entered the cavern, and passed through several chambers in succession, till he reached one in which was a boiling caldron, and a table ready set for the giants to eat their meal on it. He now heard doleful cries of captives, and following the sound, came to a cavern all round the walls of which were cages in which a number of persons were kept.

When they saw him, they cried out: 'Are you also come to be put in a cage and fattened for food?'

Jack replied: 'Fear nothing, I am come to release you all. I have killed the two giants, and have sent their heads to King Arthur.'

The poor prisoners shouted with joy when they heard this—they had expected only death. Jack now undid the doors of their cages and let them out. Jack next went into the treasure cave of the giants and found there many bags full of money. This he divided equally among the captives he had released, and then bade them all return to their homes.

Jack now went to the castle of the knight and his lady whom he had delivered, and was received with great joy. The knight made a great feast for Jack, and at the conclusion presented him with a ring in which was a picture of his deliverance of him and the lady from the giant, and these lines beneath:—

'Behold in dire distress were we,
  Under a giant's fierce command;
  But there obtained our liberty
  By valiant Jack's victorious hand.'

Hardly had the ring been presented, and the guests had applauded, before into the hall rushed a messenger to say that Hundel, a savage giant,

with two heads, having heard of the death of his
brethren, was coming full of fury, and with great
strides, to take revenge. This news put a stop to
all mirth, and a shudder ran through the company.
Jack, nothing daunted, drew his sword of sharpness, and said, 'Let him come! Let the guests
assemble on the battlements of the castle and see
how I will deal with this fellow.'
To this they all agreed.
Now round the castle was a moat that was
very deep, and was crossed by a drawbridge to
the gates. Jack ordered this drawbridge to be
lowered, and set some men to saw the beams
nearly through. Then, putting on his invisible
cloak, and taking his sword, he went against the
giant, who was turning his noses—for he had two
—in every direction, and was snuffing the breeze
and saying—

'Fee-fo-fum,
 I smell the blood of an Englishman.
 Whether he be alive, or whether he be dead,
 I'll grind his bones to make my bread.'

When Jack heard this he said: 'You must catch
me first.'
'Where are you?' asked the giant looking about.
Then Jack threw off his cloak of invisibility, and
put on his shoes of swiftness and ran. The giant
came pounding after him, making the earth shake
under his tramp. Jack made him run after him
three times round the castle, that the guests
might have a good sight of the monster. Then,
with a sudden dart, he crossed the drawbridge
and ran in at the gate. The giant at once pursued
him; but no sooner was he in the middle of the
bridge, than the beams that had been nearly sawn
through gave way, and he fell headlong into the
moat.
Jack then ordered a strong rope to be brought

him, and he cast nooses round the giants' heads, and by the aid of horses drew him up to the edge of the moat, and then cut off his two heads.

All the spectators rejoiced, and praised Jack for his great cleverness and courage. He remained two or three days with his host, and then set off in search of fresh adventures.

He travelled over hill and dale unmolested till he reached the foot of a great mountain, were he saw a little hut, at the door of which he knocked. The door opened and a venerable old man with a snow-white beard stood there. Jack respectfully asked if he might be sheltered for the night.

The old man was a hermit, and he invited him in, and set before him some bread and fruit. Whilst he was eating, the hermit said: 'I perceive that you are the brave Cornishman who has destroyed so many giants. Now on the top of this mountain is an enchanted castle, kept by a giant called Galligant, who, by the help of a vile magician, gets many knights and ladies into his castle, where he changes them into owls, ravens, bats, and other noxious birds and animals. I lament, above all, the fate of a duke's daughter, whom they seized whilst walking in her father's garden, and they have turned her into a deer. Many knights have tried to destroy the enchantment and deliver her, yet none have been able to do so, because of two fiery dragons that guard the entrance to the castle. But you have got the cloak of invisibility, and can pass them by unperceived. On the gates of the castle you will find engraved some words that will tell you how you may break the enchantment.'

Jack promised that, in the morning, at the risk of his life, he would attempt this adventure. Accordingly next day he put on the cloak of invisibility, and ascended the mountain-side.

He saw the two dragons, but because of his mantle they could not see him, and he passed between

192

them unmolested. On the castle gate hung a golden trumpet, and under it was written these lines—

'Whoever can this trumpet blow
Will cause the giant's overthrow.'

As soon as Jack had read this he seized the trumpet, and blew such a shrill blast, that the gates burst open, and the walls of the castle trembled.

The giant and magician now knew that their evil course was at an end, and they stood biting their thumbs and shaking with fear.

Jack, with his sword of sharpness, soon killed the giant, but it was a less easy matter to subdue the magician, for he turned himself into various shapes.

Jack did not know what had become of him, and till the magician was overcome, those who had been transformed by him could not be released. But he put on his cap of wisdom, and at once discovered that the magician had changed himself into a little ant that was creeping away between his feet. He immediately raised his foot to stamp on him, when the magician became a hare and fled like an arrow. Jack put on his shoes of swiftness and went after him, when all at once the magician changed into a knot of thread. Jack knew him, because he had on his cap of wisdom, so with his sword of sharpness, he cut the knot, and the magician was dead.

Then all the knights and ladies who had been transformed into noxious birds resumed their proper forms, as did also the duke's daughter, who thanked Jack on her knees for her deliverance.

The head of the giant Galligant was sent to King Arthur, who invited Jack to his court, made him knight of the Round Table, and gave him to wife the daughter of the duke whom he had delivered.

# THE THREE BEARS

IT happened that on a time there lived in a wood three bears; and of these one was a GREAT BIG BEAR, the second was a MIDDLE-SIZED BEAR, and the third was a WEE WEE BEAR. Each slept in his own bed, and naturally so, for the
GREAT BIG BEAR there was a GREAT BIG BED, and also, quite naturally, for the
MIDDLE-SIZED BEAR there was a MIDDLE-SIZED BED, and, you can see for yourself, if you have common intelligence, for the
WEE WEE BEAR there was provided a WEE WEE BED. But that was not all: each had his own chair to sit in, and naturally so, for the
GREAT BIG BEAR there was a GREAT BIG CHAIR, and also, quite naturally, for the
MIDDLE-SIZED BEAR there was a MIDDLE-SIZED CHAIR, and also, in accordance with the dictates of common sense, for the
WEE WEE BEAR there was provided a WEE WEE CHAIR. That does not complete what has to be told. There goes more to the story than that. Each bear had a pot out of which to eat his porridge, and the
GREAT BIG BEAR had a GREAT BIG POT,

194

and also, in accordance with the eternal fitness of things, the MIDDLE-SIZED BEAR had a MIDDLE-SIZED POT, and there was for the WEE WEE BEAR only a WEE WEE POT.

One day after they had poured out their porridge they scalded their tongues with it. That is to say, the GREAT BIG BEAR scalded his GREAT LONG TONGUE, and the MIDDLE-SIZED BEAR scalded his MEDIUM TONGUE, and the WEE WEE BEAR scalded his WEENIE WEENIE TONGUE. So they resolved to walk out arm and arm into the wood and listen to the whistling of the birds whilst their porridge cooled.

Now, whilst they were out, a little girl came into the cottage, and seeing that there was good porridge smoking on the table, and no one there to eat it, she tripped in, as she was very hungry, and first she tasted the porridge of the GREAT BIG BEAR, and found it so hot that she burnt her mouth, so she went to the second pot and tasted them, and then also after having taken a little, she thrust the pot from her, as it was too cold. Lastly she went to the pot of the WEE WEE BEAR, and that was just right, so she ate it all up. Then the little maiden, having satisfied her hunger, felt tired with her walk, so she went to sit down, and first she sat in the chair of the GREAT BIG BEAR, but she found it was too hard for her. She did not like it, so she got up and tried the chair of the MIDDLE-SIZED BEAR, and that she thought too soft, so she quickly jumped up out of that and tried the chair of the WEE WEE BEAR, and that was exactly right, neither too hard nor too soft; and she sat in it till she sat through the seat and came plump on the ground. Then the little maiden went upstairs into the bedchamber in which the Three Bears slept. And first she lay down on the bed of the GREAT BIG BEAR, but it was too high at the head for her, so she got off it and tried next the bed of the MIDDLE-SIZED BEAR, and found it was too low in the head for her, so she got off that and went to the bed of the WEE WEE BEAR, and that was exactly right. She had no sooner laid her head on the pillow than she dropped asleep.

By this time the three bears had heard enough of the whistling of the birds, and they thought that their porridge would be cool enough ; so they came home to breakfast. Now the little girl had been careless, and had left the spoon standing in the pot of the GREAT BIG BEAR, so he roared out lustily—

'SOMEBODY HAS BEEN AT MY PORRIDGE !'

And then the MIDDLE-SIZED BEAR looked at his, and saw that the spoon was standing in that also, so he exclaimed with a growl—

'SOMEBODY HAS BEEN AT MY PORRIDGE !'

Then the WEE WEE BEAR looked at his, and found that his porridge was all gone and the spoon licked clean also, so he said—

'SOMEBODY HAS BEEN AT MY PORRIDGE AND HAS EATEN IT ALL UP !'

Upon this the three bears, seeing that some one had invaded their house whilst out together arm in arm, looking at buttercups and hearing the birds whistle, began to peer about, and very soon the GREAT BIG BEAR roared out at the top of his voice—

'SOMEBODY HAS BEEN SITTING IN MY CHAIR !'

for the little girl had not arranged the cushions after having sat on the chair. Then the MIDDLE-SIZED BEAR exclaimed with a growl—

'SOMEBODY HAS BEEN SITTING IN MY CHAIR !'

for the cushions there also were all in disorder.

But the WEE WEE BEAR soon saw that the seat of his chair was sat through, so he whimpered out—

'SOMEBODY HAS BEEN SITTING IN MY CHAIR AND HAS SAT THE BOTTOM THROUGH!'

Then the three bears thought it requisite to make further search, and they walked upstairs, 'majores priores,' as the classic Romans would have said, that is to say, biggest first. Now when the GREAT BIG BEAR came to his bed he saw that the pillow had been pushed on one side, so he boohed out—

'SOMEBODY HAS BEEN IN MY BED!'

and the MIDDLE-SIZED BEAR saw that the pillow in his had been pushed up into one lump. So he said—

'SOMEBODY HAS BEEN IN MY BED!'

But the WEE WEE BEAR standing by his bed was so astonished that at first he could say nothing at all. At last he piped out—

'SOMEBODY HAS BEEN IN MY BED AND IS LYING IN IT NOW!'

The little maid had heard the bellowing of the GREAT BIG BEAR, but had been so fast asleep that the sound had not woke her; and she had heard the middle voice of the MIDDLE-SIZED BEAR, and that also had not woke her, she was so very sleepy; but when she heard the sharp little squeaky voice of the WEE WEE BEAR, she jumped up at once, and there she saw the three bears before her, glowering at her as if they wanted to eat her, and licking their lips, and stretching out their claws.

She was a little miss of a ready wit; so she turned to the first and made a profound CURTSY down to the very ground, and said with the greatest deference—

'MISTER BEAR, I pray you FORBEAR!'

197

and she made a nice little graceful CURTSY to the second, and said with a pitiful voice—

'MISTER BEAR, I pray you FORBEAR!'

and then sharp she gave a little BOB OF A BOW to the WEE WEE BEAR, and caught him a WEE WEE BOX on his WEE WEE EAR, and said—

'LITTLE BEARIKINS, I don't care whether you FORBEAR or not!'

and away, down the stairs and out at the door, and away away—to her mammy home she ran.
Then the three bears looked at each other, and the first said—

'DEAR!'

and the second said—

'DEAR!'

and the third, rubbing his ear, said—
'DEAR!'

and all together concluded that little girls of the nineteenth century were so impudent that it was no longer possible for well-conducted bears to live in the forests of Old England.

# TOM THUMB

IN the days of King Arthur there lived a ploughman and his wife who wished greatly to have a son; so the man went to Merlin, the enchanter, and told him that he and his wife had been married for twenty years and had no children, and that they longed to have a little son, even if he were 'no bigger than his thumb.'

'Go home and you will find that you have one,' said the enchanter; and when the man returned to his house, he found his wife nursing a tiny tiny baby, who grew to be the size of the ploughman's thumb, but never grew much bigger.

The fairy Queen Vivienne was invited to the christening, and named him Tom Thumb.

An oak-leaf hat he had for crown;
His shirt of web by spiders spun;
With jacket wove of thistledown;
His breeches were of feathers done.
His stockings of apple rind, they tie
With eyelash from his mother's eye:
His shoes were made of mouse's skin
Turned with the downy hair within.

Tom was a healthy and happy baby. His parents were very fond of him; although he was so small yet their love for him was very great. They used to hold him on their palms till he was old enough to toddle, and then they placed him on the table. They were afraid to let him run on the floor lest he should be trodden on.

He was mischievous for all his small size, and as he grew to be a boy of twelve he was always at some prank or other.

When Tom was old enough to play with other boys, he delighted to do so, but then he was ever at some mad prank or other.

At that time boys were wont to play with cherry-stones instead of marbles, and when Tom had lost all his own cherrystones, he used to creep into the bags of his playfellows, fill his pockets, and crawl out again without their noticing what he was about, and join in the game once more.

One day, however, as he was issuing from a bag of cherrystones, where he had been stealing as usual, the boy whose bag he had entered chanced to see him.

'Ho-ho!' exclaimed the lad; 'so—Tom Thumb, then you are at your usual pranks. Now I have caught you stealing my cherrystones. I have long suspected you. As I have got you I shall punish you.' Then he drew the string of the bag tight round Tom's neck and shook the bag well, so that the cherrystones rattled against and bruised Tom's little body and thighs and legs. He screamed for pain, and begged to be released, and promised that he never would steal again.

One day that he had been at his pranks he was shut up in a pin box. This hurt him greatly, and next day he resolved to revenge himself. He took a number of glasses and hung them on a sunbeam. The other boys tried to do the same, but failed and broke all the glasses, and were severely whipped for having done this.

One day while his mother was making a batter-

pudding, Tom stood on the edge of the bowl holding
a candle in one hand so that he might see that the
pudding was properly made. But as he tried to
balance himself on one toe, when his mother's back
was turned he slipped and went head foremost
into the pudding. His mother did not know this
and continued stirring the pudding, and put it
and him into the pot.

But Tom no sooner felt the hot water than he
danced like one mad, and his mother was so frightened to see the pudding bouncing about that she
thought it was bewitched, and she hastily gave it
to a tinker who was passing the door.

The tinker was delighted with his present; but as
he was getting over a stile, Tom shouted out from
the middle of the pudding, 'Hallo, Pickins!' and
this so terrified the tinker that he flung away the
pudding in the field, and it broke to pieces, and
Tom escaped. Tom then cleaned himself of the
flour that stuck to him, and walked home to his
mother, who had been in great distress because
she could not find him. She gave him a lecture
not to be rash and get where he would be in mischief, and kissed him, and was very rejoiced to
have him again.

One day he climbed up the side of the cream-pan
and tumbled in, and would have been drowned
had not his screams brought his mother to his aid.
Another time he was lost, and after seeking for
him everywhere, the poor woman saw his head
popping out of the salt-box which hung against
the wall, and he came out as if covered over with
hoar-frost.

When his mother went into the fields to milk the
cow, then she was wont to tie him to a thistle lest
he should run away and get into mischief.

If a bee came that way, then Tom, who was armed
with a needle, fought it and carried off its honey.

When a butterfly came that way, if Tom had not

been tied to the thistle, he would certainly have
jumped on its back and tried if he could be carried
away a sail in the air.
One day a field-mouse came and looked at him.
Tom was afraid of the mouse, so he called to his
mother, who came up, and the mouse darted away.
One day whilst Tom was tied to the thistle, the
cow seeing his oakleaf cap, took poor Tom and
the thistle at one mouthful.

But, being missed, his mother went
   Calling him everywhere,
'Where art thou, Tom? Where art thou, Tom?'
   Quoth he, 'Here, mother, here!
Within the red cow's mouth am I
   Full nearly swallowed up,'
Which made his mother weep and sigh
   That thus the cow should sup.

Tom kicked and scratched till the cow dropped
him from her mouth. His mother caught him in
her apron as he was falling, or he would have been
greatly hurt.
One day Tom went with his father into the fields
a-ploughing; and the father made him a whip of
barley straw wherewith to drive the oxen, but
Tom's foot slipped and he fell into the furrow,
without the father observing it.
A crow flying by saw the barley straw, stooped and
carried Tom off to the top of a giant's castle.
The giant took Tom in the palm of his hand and
laughed much to see how small he was. Tom
had his little sword of a needle at his side and he
pricked the giant with it, and he shook his hand,
and Tom gave a jump and went out at the window
and fell into the sea, where a fish swallowed him.
The fish was soon after caught, and brought to
the castle of King Arthur. His steward bought it
and ordered the cook to boil it for dinner. When
the cook was opening the fish, to his great aston-

ishment out jumped Tom, quite delighted to be free again. He was taken before the king, who made Tom his dwarf, and he soon became a great favourite at court, where he delighted every one by his gambols.

Long time he lived in jollity,
  Beloved of the court,
And none like Tom was so esteemed
  Among the better sort.

The queen Gueniver was especially delighted with the little man, and made him dance a galliard on her left hand. His performance was so satisfactory that King Arthur gave him a ring which he wore about his waist as a girdle.
When he was out with the king, if rain came on he would creep up the sleeve of Arthur, and lie there till the shower was over.
One day Tom, who could not forget his poor father and mother, asked King Arthur to grant him leave to go and visit them. The king readily agreed, and taking him into his treasury, told him to carry away with him as much money as he could for his poor parents. This made him caper for joy. He found that the only coin he could carry was a threepenny piece.

And so away goes lusty Tom,
  With threepence at his back,
A heavy burden which did make
  His very bones to crack.

Tom remained three days with the old couple, and feasted on a hazel-nut so extravagantly that he grew ill.
King Arthur became impatient to have his dwarf back again, so his mother took a sort of tube, through which people blew darts at birds to kill them, and she put Tom in and blew through it, and blew him back to court.

203

He was received by the king with every token of
affection and delight, and tournaments were proclaimed in his honour.

Thus he at tilt and tournament
  Was entertained so,
That all the rest of Arthur's knights
  Did him much pleasure show.

As Tom's clothes had suffered much in the batter-
pudding and in the furrow, and in the inside of the
fish, the king ordered him a new suit of clothes,
and gave him a mouse to ride.

Of butterfly's wings his shirt was made,
  His boots of chicken's hide ;
And by a nimble fairy blade,
Well learned in the tailoring trade,
  His clothing was supplied.
A needle dangled by his side ;
A dapper mouse he used to ride :
  Thus strutted Tom in stately pride !

Tom used to go out hunting on his mouse with
the king and the knights.
Arthur also ordered a little chair to be made, in
order that Tom might sit on his table, and he gave
him as well a carriage drawn by six white mice.
At last the queen got jealous of Tom, because the
king made so much of him, and she determined to
be rid of him, and when the king was away she
had him shut up in prison in a mouse-trap, but he
managed to squeeze himself between the bars, and
seeing a lame butterfly he climbed on its back, and
the butterfly carried him away. However, in passing over the sea he became giddy and fell off,
when he was again swallowed by a fish, which
was caught and set out for sale in the town of Rye,
where a steward haggled for it with the fisherman
who had caught it.

Amongst the rest a steward came
  Who would the salmon buy,
And other fish that he did name,
  But he would not comply.

The steward said, 'You are so stout,
  If so, I 'll not buy any.'
So then out called Tom Thumb aloud,
  ' Sir, give another penny !'

At this they all began to start
  To hear the sudden joke ;
Nay, some were frightened to the heart,
  They thought the dead fish spoke.

The steward made no more ado
  But bid a penny more,
'Because,' he said, 'I never knew
  A fish to speak before.'

When the fish was opened out came Tom again,
and he remained in the kitchen at Rye, and was a
great object of diversion to the servants.
One day he was put in the window, when a great
spider observed him and came down to him. Tom
made a gallant fight, yet the spider's poisonous
breath at last overcame him.

He fell dead on the ground where he stood,
And the spider sucked every drop of his blood.

When the tidings came to King Arthur he was
very sorry, and went into mourning, he and all his
knights.

Such were his deeds and noble acts,
  In Arthur's court they shone,
As like in all the world beside
  Was hardly seen or known.

For him King Arthur and his knights
   Full forty days did mourn,
And in remembrance of his name
   That was so wondrous born,

He built a tomb of marble gray
   And year by year did come
To celebrate the tragic death
   And burial of Tom Thumb.

His fame still lives in England here
   Among the country sort;
Of him our wives and children small
   Tell tales of pleasant sport.

# THE WHITE CAT

NCE upon a time there reigned a king over a certain kingdom, who had three sons, so clever and gallant, that he began to fear that they might be impatient to reign in the kingdom before he was dead.

Now the king, although growing old, had no idea of abdicating his position and power, so he thought that the best way for him to manage under the circumstances would be for him to divert the minds of his sons by setting them tasks which would keep them well occupied.

Accordingly he sent for them, and addressing them kindly, he said—

'My dear sons, you no doubt perceive that my age is advanced, and that I am not able to occupy myself with the affairs of state as I did when I was younger. I am anxious that the wants of my subjects should not be overlooked through failure of my powers, accordingly I have resolved to lay down the reins of government as soon as I am satisfied that I can have that which will amuse and content me when I retire into private life. Now, I have been considering that a pretty, frisky, faithful little dog would prove excellent company; accordingly I am prepared to surrender my crown and

207

throne to that one among you, my sons, who furnishes me with the most acceptable little dog.'

The three princes were exceedingly surprised at their father's sudden fancy for a little dog, but by his announcement a chance of succession to the throne was opened to the two younger, who in the ordinary course of affairs would have had no such chance; they therefore gladly accepted the commission, and the eldest, fearing to be deprived of his rights, was fain also to start in quest of a perfect dog.

They resolved, before they separated, to meet each other and go together before the king, in a year and a day from that at which they started on their several journeys.

Each now took a different road, and the two elder brothers met with many adventures; but as those of the youngest were the most interesting, you shall hear only of them.

This prince was young, light-hearted, and very handsome; he was well educated; and as for his courage, it was boundless.

Hardly a day passed without his purchasing dogs, big and small, and of every description, mastiffs, bull-dogs, staghounds, spaniels, beagles, lap-dogs. Whenever he had bought a pretty one, he was sure next moment to be offered another that was still prettier, and then he had to get rid of those he had already purchased, and to buy that which took his fancy last; it was, as can well be understood, quite impossible for him, who was alone, to travel the country with a thousand dogs about him.

He journeyed on from day to day, not knowing whither he was going, till one day at nightfall he found himself in a large and gloomy forest. He completely lost his way, and what made matters worse was that a thunderstorm came on and the rain poured down in torrents. He took

the first path that offered, and after a while he
saw a glimmer of light before him, and hoped he
was approaching a cottage where he could obtain
shelter.
Guided by the light he presently found himself
before the gates of a beautiful castle. The door
was of gold inlaid with carbuncles, and it was the
glow of these precious stones which had shone
through the forest and had drawn him on.

The walls of the castle were of porcelain in the
most dainty colours; but the Prince was so wet
that he could not hesitate or halt to admire; he
went up to the door and there beheld a deer's foot
hanging by a chain of diamonds, and he wondered
who could inhabit such a marvellous castle.

'They cannot fear robbers greatly here,' said he;
'what is there to prevent any one from walking off
with this chain, and picking out these carbuncles,
and so enriching himself for life?'

He pulled the deer's foot and immediately a bell
sounded, which by the softness of its tone he concluded to be of silver. Then the door flew open,
but the Prince could see no one as porter, only a
number of hands appeared in the air, each holding
a torch. He was so greatly astonished that he
stood still, until he felt hands draw him forward
and thrust him on from behind, so that though
somewhat uneasy, he could hardly help going on.
With his hand on the hilt of his sword, ready for
whatever might happen, he entered a hall paved
with deep blue stone called lapis lazuli, and heard
voices singing sweetly—

'Fear no more the flitting hands,
    They your lightest wish obey.
If you dread not Cupid's bands,
    Safely in the palace stay.'

The Prince now lost all fear; he was confident
that where so warm a welcome was offered no

evil was intended. Accordingly, guided by the mysterious hands, he went to a door of coral, that opened of its own accord, and gave admittance into an apartment lined with mother-of-pearl, out of which opened a number of other rooms, sparkling with numerous candles, and full of the most beautiful pictures and precious objects that charmed the Prince's eyes and bewildered his mind. At last, weary of gazing at so many wondrous objects, he cast himself down in an easy chair he saw drawn up near a bright wood fire; and at once the delicate hands began to remove his wet, muddy garments, and other hands produced fresh ones made of the richest stuffs, embroidered with gold and picked out with jewels. He could not fail to admire everything he saw, and the graceful manner in which the hands attended on him.

When he was quite ready, and looked fresh and radiant in the costly suit he had assumed, the hands conducted him to a splendid room, on the walls of which in tapestry was shown the story of Puss in Boots. The table was spread for supper, and two golden plates were laid opposite each other, with golden forks and spoons. The sideboard was magnificently furnished with gold and silver salvers, ewers, and much beautiful glass. The Prince stood hesitating, not knowing whether to sit down at table or not, when suddenly there entered a dozen cats carrying lutes, who took up their places at one end of the room, and struck the strings of their instruments, and mewed out the most astounding cat-song imaginable to the accompaniment of their lutes. The Prince was obliged to stop his ears at the caterwauling, but he laughed so heartily that he could not keep them closed.

'What odd thing will happen next?' said he to himself; and at the same moment, the door at the

end of the hall opened, and there entered a tiny
figure covered with a long black veil, marshalled by
two cats wearing black velvet mantles, and
carrying swords of state. They were followed by
a train of other cats, which carried cages full of rats
and mice.

The Prince was so much astonished that he rubbed
his eyes, thinking he was dreaming, but the little
figure came up to him, threw back the veil, and
disclosed the loveliest white cat conceivable.
She looked very young and very sad. In a gentle
voice that went straight to the Prince's heart she
said—

'King's son, you are welcome. The Queen of the
Cats rejoices to see and salute you.'

'Madam Puss!' answered the Prince, with a bow,
'I thank you for your kindly reception; but surely
you can be no common pussy-cat. The magnificence and state that surround you convince me to
the contrary.'

'King's son,' said the White Cat, 'I am unac-
customed to compliments. Let supper be served
and the musicians cease their strains, as apparently, sir, you do not relish their music.'

Then the mysterious hands began to serve supper,
and first they put on the table two dishes, one
containing roast pigeons and the other fricasseed
mice.

The Prince declined the latter dish with horror;
but the White Cat assured him that her cook had
special orders to serve him with entirely different
food from herself, and that he need not fall to on
rats or mice unless he had a mind to. The Prince,
confident that she would not deceive him, at once
began his dinner on the roast pigeon.

Presently he observed that the little paw of the
White-Cat which was next him was adorned with
a bracelet from which hung a miniature portrait.
When the White Cat saw that he was desirous of

211

examining it, she passed it to him, and he was enchanted to see that it represented an extremely handsome young man who was remarkably like himself.

The White Cat sighed as he looked at it, and looked more depressed in spirits than before. The Prince forbore asking questions, lest he should pain her, and turned to talk of other matters. He found the White Cat very intelligent, well read, and well versed in politics.

After supper they retired into another room, which was fitted up as a theatre, and cats acted there and danced for the amusement of the Prince and the White Cat.

After a while the Queen of the Cats rose from her seat, bade the Prince a graceful adieu, wished him a good night and peaceful sleep, and withdrew.

Thereupon the hands reappeared and conducted him into a room he had not seen hitherto, hung with tapestry made of butterfly wings of every hue; there were mirrors reaching to the floor, and a cozy white bed with curtains round it tied up with pink ribbons.

The Prince retired to bed, and very soon fell fast asleep. Next morning he was awakened by a noise outside his window, and on looking out saw that a number of cats were in the courtyard, some leading greyhounds, others blowing horns.

Presently the hands reappeared and dressed the Prince in a complete hunting suit of green and silver. Then they threw open the door, and he was conducted below, where he saw the White Cat in a green riding-habit mounted on an ape, ready for hunting. The hands brought up a wooden horse for the Prince to mount. He did not see that he would have much sport riding on a wooden horse; however, as the White Cat seemed to expect it, he threw himself on its back, where-

212

upon the wooden horse began to prance and show his paces.

The White Cat on her ape went up trees in quest of eagle nests; but the Prince had rare sport on his wooden horse, and never enjoyed a hunt more in all his life.

After a while the whole party returned to the castle, and the Prince and the White Cat supped together as on the previous evening. When it was over, the cat offered him some ruby wine in a crystal goblet. Directly he had tasted it, he forgot his home, forgot that he was looking for a little dog, forgot everything, except his happiness in the society of the White Cat.

So the time passed, in every kind of amusement, until the year was nearly gone. The Prince had forgotten all about meeting his brothers, and appearing before his father, but the White Cat knew when he was bound to return, and said to him one day—

'Are you aware, my good friend, that you have only three days left in which to find a little dog for your father? Already your brothers have provided themselves with beautiful little dogs.'

Then all at once the Prince recollected everything, and cried out—

'What can have affected my memory that I should forget a matter of such supreme importance! My whole future depends on it. Even supposing that I were to find a little dog worthy to win me a kingdom, where should I find a horse swift enough to convey me home within the three days?'

The White Cat, seeing he was sore troubled, said to him—

'King's son, be not anxious and distressed. I am your friend, and will assist you to the uttermost of my power. You can continue here a day, as the wooden horse will convey you the entire distance to your father's realm in twelve hours.'

213

'I thank you, gracious Cat,' said the Prince, 'but what advantage will that be to me, if I have not a a dog suitable to present to his majesty, my father?'

'See here,' said the White Cat, holding up an acorn. 'In this is a prettier one than exists even at the dog star.'

'Oh! dear White Cat!' exclaimed the Prince, 'why do you make fun of me?'

Then he heard distinctly a little bow-wow! bow-wow! inside the acorn.

The Prince was delighted, for a dog enclosed in an acorn must indeed be a beauty. He wanted to take it out and look at it, but this the White Cat would not allow. She said that the little dog must on all accounts be preserved from the chance of catching a chill on the journey; and the Prince saw that in this as in all else, there was reason in what the Cat said. He thanked her heartily, and was quite sad when it was necessary for him to part from her.

'The days,' said he, 'have flown in your charming society. I would it were possible for me to take you with me.'

The White Cat shook her head and gave a faint mee-aw in answer.

The Prince was the first to be at the meeting-place, where it was agreed that the brothers should assemble before proceeding to the palace, and great was their amusement and astonishment to see the wooden horse, painted with great red spots, and with a brush of hair on its arched neck, standing in the courtyard, stiff and stark as if it had just come out of a toy-shop. The Prince met his brothers joyously, and they told him their adventures, but he was very reticent about his, and they did not think much of the dog that ran at his heels, and which was that he had with him when received into the White Cat's palace.

The elder brothers carried in baskets two little
dogs, so delicate that they hardly dared to touch
them. As for the dog that attended the youngest,
he was all covered with mud from his journey.

When they reached the palace, every one crowded
to welcome them as they ascended to the royal
hall, and when the two brothers presented their
little dogs, no one could resolve which was the
most beautiful.

They were already arranging between themselves
what disposition they would make of the kingdom,
when the youngest, stepping forward, bowed to his
father, and presented him with the acorn. The
king, much astonished, opened it carefully and out
there ran on his hand the tiniest, dearest little mite
of a dog imaginable. The king was so surprised
that he let it drop. But the dog was not hurt. It
at once began to skip about, pirouette and caper,
and even to stand on its head.

The king did not know what to say, for it was
quite impossible that any dog could be found to
surpass this little creature. Nevertheless, as he
was in no hurry to resign his crown, he said to his
sons that as they had been so successful this time,
they must be set another task, and must find
him a piece of muslin so fine that it could be
drawn through the eye of a needle.

If it had not been that the elder brothers had been
worsted by the youngest, it may well be believed
they would not have been disposed to set out
again; however, by this new task set them, they
were afforded another chance, so they accepted it.

The youngest mounted his wooden horse, it tossed
its head, threw out its legs, and bore him at full
speed to the palace of his dear White Cat.

Every door of the castle stood wide open, every
window was illumined, and the hands appeared
waving a welcome to him. His horse was taken
from him, and he was conducted into the castle.

The White Cat was lying by the fire in a basket on a cushion of white silk. She sprang up at his approach, and said—

'I did not expect you back quite so soon, king's son!'

Then he patted and stroked her and scratched her under the chin, and she purred; and he told her of his successful journey, and how he had come back to ask her assistance to procure him that which was now demanded by the king, and which it was not possible for him to procure elsewhere.

The White Cat looked grave, and replied that she would consider the matter, and consult with some spinster cats in the castle who were very skilful.

Then the hands appeared carrying torches, and conducted the Prince and the White Cat to a long gallery which overlooked the river, from the windows of which they saw a magnificent display of fireworks. After that they supped, and the Prince appreciated his supper much more than the fireworks, for he was hungry with his long ride.

So the time passed as before, just as pleasantly and just as quickly. The Prince often marvelled to find the cat so agreeable a companion, so well read, and so able to talk intelligently about matters. He once ventured to ask her how as a cat this was possible. She replied, with a sad smile—

'King's son, do not ask me. I am unable to give you the explanation you desire.'

The Prince was so happy that he did not trouble himself to take account of the time as it passed, but the White Cat did not forget, and one day she said to him—

'It is now within two days of that on which you are bound to appear before your father. This time you shall travel in better style.'

Then she showed him a gilded coach enamelled

with the most beautiful pictures. It was drawn
by twelve snow-white horses, harnessed four
abreast; their trappings, as were those of the
carriage, were of flame-colour, embroidered with
diamonds. Numerous guards followed all in
flame-coloured livery.
'Go,' said the White Cat, 'and when you appear
before the king in such state, he will surely give
up his crown. Take this walnut, but do not open
it until you arrive at your destination, lest the
wind should blow away its contents, or mud from
the carriage wheels stain it.'
'Lovely White Cat,' said the Prince, 'how can I
thank you sufficiently for your goodness to me?
Only tell me you desire it, and I will abandon the
thought of succeeding my father in his kingdom
and remain here with you.'
'King's son,' she answered, 'you have a good
heart to say this, and to care for a little white cat,
that is good for naught but catching mice; but
you must not stay. Good-bye.'
The Prince kissed her paw and departed.
The carriage spun along, faster than had travelled
the wooden horse; but this time the Prince arrived
so late that he found his brothers had already
proceeded to the palace to display the pieces of
muslin they had procured.
These were indeed very fine; they would pass
through a ring, and the eye of a packing needle:
but the king sent for a particular needle kept
among the Crown jewels that had an eye so small,
that every one saw at a glance that the stuffs provided could not possibly pass through it.
At that moment a flourish of trumpets was heard,
and the youngest son of the king entered. His
father and brothers were amazed at his magnificence, and after he had greeted them he produced
the walnut and opened it, fully expecting to find
the muslin. Instead of that he found a hazel-

217

nut. He cracked this, and therein lay a cherry-stone.

Every one looked on in astonishment, and the king was congratulating himself that all chance of the task being accomplished was at an end, when the Prince broke the cherry-stone, and drew out only its kernel. He divided the kernel, and in that was a grain of wheat. He opened the grain of wheat, and found a millet seed. Then he became concerned, and muttered: 'O White Cat, you have been making mock of me!'

At that moment he felt a cat's claw give his hand a scratch, and hoping that this was meant as an encouragement, he opened the millet seed and drew out of it a piece of muslin four hundred ells long, woven finer than gossamer, in the loveliest patterns; and when the needle was brought, it passed through the eye without any difficulty.

The king was aghast, and the two elder princes felt their discomfiture, for nobody could deny that this was the most marvellous piece of muslin that had ever been woven.

Then, after some consideration, the king said to his sons: 'Nothing is more grateful to me in my old age than to see your willingness to oblige me. Go out once more, and whoever, at the end of a year and a day, brings back the loveliest princess, shall marry her, and shall, without further delay, receive the crown, and reign upon my throne in my place. For, it is obvious to the meanest intellect that my successor must be a married man.'

The Prince thought he was hardly treated, as he had earned the kingdom fairly twice over, but he would not argue the point with his father, moreover he was impatient to return to the White Cat. Accordingly he mounted his gilded chariot, and swift as the wind it sped, throwing up clouds of dust in people's eyes, and bore him direct to the castle of the White Cat.

This time she was ready expecting him, and had caused her attendant cats to strew the road with flowers, and aromatic herbs and woods and gums were burnt in braziers on each side of the way.

The White Cat awaited him seated on a balcony. 'Well, king's son,' said she, on his arrival, 'you have again returned without your crown.'

'Madam,' answered he, 'thanks to your kind assistance I have twice earned it. But the fact is my father is so unwilling to part with it that I really do not care to have it.'

'Never mind,' she said, 'you can but do your best to deserve it. You shall take back with you a lovely princess whom I will find for you. In the meantime let us amuse ourselves. I have ordered to-night a battle between my cats and the water-rats, on purpose to give you entertainment. My cats, it is true, are somewhat at a disadvantage, for they dislike water, and the rats will naturally seek to carry on the conflict on their native element.'

So they walked together on a terrace and saw the battle. The cats were in ships made of cork. The rats were in half ostrich shells. The fight was obstinate and protracted. The rats threw themselves into the water and then the cats could not follow them. The rats were finally routed, but by no means exterminated. Many live on to the present day.

The Prince passed the year as he had passed the others, in hunting, fishing, and playing at chess with the White Cat. He could not forbear asking her how it was that she was able to talk; but she answered that it was not in her power at that time to explain to him many things that surprised him. Nothing passes so quickly as happy days, and if the White Cat had not been careful to remember the time when the Prince was bound to return to his father, he would have forgotten it.

She warned him of it the day before, and told him
that it remained only with him to obtain one of the
most beautiful princesses in the world; but in order
to do this, he must cut off her head and tail, and
throw them into the fire.

'What!' cried the Prince, 'my lovely, my dear
White Cat! shall I who have received so many
favours from you, be so wicked, so ungrateful, as
to sacrifice you? You say this merely to try me,
whether I am heartless and selfish——'

'No, indeed,' interrupted the White Cat; 'son of
a king, I know well your generous nature, and
that it will cut you to the heart to seem to act
towards me in a barbarous manner. Nevertheless,
do as I bid you; it is necessary, not for your own
happiness only, but also for mine.'

The Prince's eyes filled with tears, and he could
hardly bring his mind to do what he was bidden.
He said all the tender things he could think of
to dissuade the cat from urging him to it; but she
obstinately answered that she wished to die by
his hand, and that unless he did as she required,
she would be condemned to a hopeless and protracted age of misery.

At last, most reluctantly, and with averted head
and trembling hand, the Prince drew his sword
and smote. He cut off her head at one blow, and
with the next hewed off her tail. Then picking
them up, he threw them into the fire.

Instantly there was a blaze and a flash, and the
whole apartment was filled with light and the most
delicious fragrance. In the midst of the light he
saw a most lovely maiden. At the same moment
the door opened, and a company of knights and
ladies entered, each carrying a cat's skin.

With every token of joy they surrounded the
Princess, kissed her hand, and congratulated her
on being once more restored to her natural form.
She received them most graciously, and then

220

requested them to allow her a few moments in which to converse alone with the Prince, to whom she would unfold her history, and explain much that had hitherto perplexed him.

'My dear king's son,' said she, 'you were right in supposing me to be something superior to an ordinary cat. My father reigned over six kingdoms. My mother, the queen, was an admirable woman, but, unfortunately for me, of an inquisitive turn of mind, and restless in her habits.

'When I was only a few weeks old, she obtained the king's permission to visit a certain forest and palace, of which many wondrous tales were told, and she felt that she could have no peace of mind till she had ascertained what truth there was in these tales. She set off with a large retinue, and in course of time reached the forest, and saw that it was traversed by a road leading to a superb palace, the gates of which were closed, but through the railings my mother could see the most delicious and varied fruit. Many of the fruits were quite new to her, and such as she did know, infinitely surpassed those which grew in her own gardens. She at once resolved to taste this fruit, and was well assured she would not have a moment's happiness till she had done so. She ordered her servants to knock at the palace doors, and to rattle the gates and ring the bell; no answer was however given to these summonses. She therefore insisted on ladders being applied to the walls of the garden, that she might climb over them, to get at the fruit. But it was soon found that the walls stretched themselves in proportion to the length of the ladders applied to them, so that it was quite impossible to surmount them.

'The queen was in despair, but as night was coming on she had her tent planted outside the gates, resolved to spend the night there, and renew her attempt on the following morning. In the middle of the night she was suddenly aroused, and saw to her astonishment a little, ugly, old woman at her bedside, who was plucking at her ear.

'The queen, my mother, sat up in bed very frightened; then the old woman said to her: "You are a very tiresome, persevering, and meddlesome person, not to leave me and my sisters alone in our palace, but to insist on eating our fruit. I will give you as much of the latter as you desire, on one condition, which is that you let us have your daughter to bring up as our own?"

'The queen, my mother, answered, "Dear madam, is there nothing else you will have? I can give you most admirable receipts for making conserves of your fruit, and even for pickling the walnuts. Will not that do as well? If not, you shall have half of the kingdoms my husband reigns over."

'The fairy answered: "We want neither your receipts nor your realms; we will have nothing else but your little daughter. We will make her as happy as the day is long, and give her everything her heart can desire."

'"It is a hard condition," said the queen, my mother, but inasmuch as she was an exceedingly inquisitive and — it must be admitted — a greedy woman, she at last consented.

'Then the old fairy took her into the palace, and though it was still night, the queen, my mother, could plainly see that it was more magnificent than anything she had ever beheld. But my dear Prince,' said the White Cat, 'of this you can judge yourself, for you are now in the very palace into which my mother was introduced.

'The old fairy said to her: "Will you gather the fruit yourself, or shall I call it to come to you?"

'My mother answered that it would be less trouble and more interesting if it came when called.

'Thereupon the little old woman screamed out:

"Apricots, peaches, nectarines, cherries, plums, greengages, pears, grapes, apples, oranges, lemons, gooseberries, currants, raspberries, come! come! come!"

'Instantly from every tree down hopped the fruit and ran—and ran—just like chickens coming to be fed, and the queen ate as much as she liked, and found every kind of fruit passing good.

'The old fairy now gave her gilded baskets in which to carry away as much fruit as she liked, and she laded all her mules and servants with it. Then she reminded the queen, my mother, of the agreement; and next morning the queen returned to her kingdom, nibbling at the fruit all the way.

'However, it must not be supposed that she did not regret her bargain, when she saw me in my cradle on her return. She was afraid to tell the king what she had done, and she tried to deaden her remorse by eating fruit all day long.

'Presently there arrived at the palace five frightful little dwarfs sent by the fairies to fetch me; and then the queen was obliged to tell the king, my father, all she had promised. He was, of course, very angry, and ordered his guards to surround and cut the dwarfs to pieces. But as fast as they were chopped up they came together again, and persisted in their demand, as though nothing incommoded by the maltreatment to which they were exposed. Then the fairies came in a flaming chariot drawn by sea-horses, took up my cradle, placed it between them, and went away, carrying me.

'I grew up surrounded by everything that was beautiful and rare, and learning everything that is ever taught to a princess, but without any companions save a parrot and a little dog, who could both talk, and receiving every day a visit from one of the old fairies, who caressed me and spoke kindly to me, and assured me of her and her sisters' protection, so long as I remained in the

223

palace and enchanted wood. I was solemnly and
repeatedly warned that if I attempted to escape,
the most dreadful calamity would befall me.

'One day as I was pulling out the drawers, and
turning over the contents of the cabinets in the
palace, I found a bracelet, to which hung a miniature portrait of a very handsome young man.

'I could not keep my eyes off this picture. You
must understand, Prince, that hitherto I had seen
no men, and no women even, except the old fairies.
Next time one of these latter visited me, I asked
what that was which was represented in the
miniature. She was much vexed at my asking,
and said it was a picture of a sort of monkey that
lived in foreign parts. Then I said, innocently,
I should much like to see such monkeys. The
fairy said I must never think of such a thing, or
dreadful misfortunes would happen.

'However, I found I could take no pleasure in
anything; I could not sleep by night, I was always
anxious and longing to see these extraordinary
monkeys. I told this to one of the fairies, and she
said with a sigh: "I see there is some of the inquisi-
tiveness of your mother in you. You will come to
a dreadful misfortune unless you overcome it." I
said no more to the fairies, but I thought now of
nothing but how I might escape from the palace
and enchanted wood into Monkeyland.

'One day I put my purpose into execution, I got
away alone from the castle, and ran through the
wood, and was just about to pass the last tree
when the three fairy sisters appeared before me.
They were very angry, and said that I had rushed
on the doom which they had cautioned me against.
Now there was no help for it, I must be transformed into a white cat; but they said they would
give me a retinue of the lords and ladies of my
father's court in the same form; and they would
render invisible, all but their hands, the ladies and

lords of the bedchamber, and all such as attended
on the personal comforts of the king and queen,
both of whom were now dead.
'As they laid me under the enchantment, the fairy
sisters told me all my story, and warned me that
my only chance of release from the shape of a cat

was to win the love of a prince who should exactly
resemble the portrait on the bracelet I had found,
and having won that, to induce him to cut off
my cat's head and tail and throw them into the
fire.'
'You have indeed won my love,' said the Prince.

'And I am delighted to find you are such a fascinating monkey,' said the Princess. 'Now it is time for you to return to your father.'

So the Prince gave her his hand and led her down the stairs to the chariot; and they started on the journey. As the Princess was as clever and agreeable in conversation as she was beautiful, the time passed very pleasantly.

When they approached the castle, the Princess stepped into a crystal sedan with a little door in it with silken curtains before it, and this crystal sedan chair was carried by her guards. All the people wondered what it could contain.

The princes, the elder brothers, were on the terrace of the palace, each conducting a charming princess. On seeing their youngest brother they hastened to meet him, and asked if he had brought a beautiful lady with him.

'Well,' said he, 'I could find none superior to a lovely white cat.'

'A cat!' said they; 'were you afraid that the mice would eat up the palace?'

The courtiers now hastened before the king to announce that the three princes were approaching. 'Are they bringing fair ladies with them?' asked the king.

'Fairer are not to be found,' was the answer; at hearing which he was much displeased.

The two elder princes made haste to show their beautiful princesses. The king received them very graciously, and said that really each was so beautiful it would not be possible for him to decide between them, for he was as gallant an old man as he was cunning.

Then he looked at his youngest son, and said: 'So! this time you have failed!'

'Not altogether, your majesty,' said the Prince; 'if you will condescend to look at my little white cat in her crystal cage, who meeaws so prettily,

226

and gambols so playfully, you cannot fail to be
pleased.'

The king smiled, and went to open the sedan
chair itself, when all at once, the Princess
touched a spring and it flew apart, and she stood
in the midst, like the sun bursting from clouds.
Her fair hair was spread over her shoulders, and
hung in shining tresses to her feet; on her head
was a crown of roses; her gown of thin gauze
was lined with rose-coloured taffety; she curtsied
low to the king, who, in the excess of his admiration, clapped his hands, and said: 'This is indeed
the matchless beauty who deserves to wear the
crown.'

'Sire!' said she, 'I am not come to deprive you of
your kingdom, which you rule with such sagacity.
I am queen over six. Allow me to present one to
each of your elder sons; then there will remain
four for my dear young Prince and myself. What
with the housekeeping—that will be as much as
we can manage.'

The king and all the courtiers gave vent to their
joy and astonishment in loud and repeated cheers.
Indeed the king kept on hurrahing! and shouting
One cheer more! till he became purple in the face,
and had to be carried out and given a cooling
draught—lest he should have an apoplexy.

The marriages of all the three couples were
immediately solemnized, and the court spent
several months in rejoicings. Then they set out,
each for his own dominions, and all considered
that their happiness was due to the beautiful,
wise White Cat.

IN the olden times there lived a king whose daughters were all beautiful: but the youngest was the most beautiful of all.

Near the king's castle was a large and gloomy forest, and in the midst stood an old lime-tree, below which was a well, the water of which was clear as crystal. People thought much of this well; they said that the water came up from the heart of the earth, and was good for all kinds of sicknesses, and they used on May Day to put a wreath of flowers round it.

The king's daughter often went to this well, and one day as she was there—it was May Day, and all the well was set about with flowers—as she leaned to smell the flowers, and look down into the water, a gold ball with which she was playing fell out of her hand and tumbled into the well.

Then she was very unhappy, and sat beside the well crying.

Then, all at once, she heard a voice from the water that called out: 'Why do you weep, king's daughter?'

She looked about her, and saw a frog popping its ugly head out of the water.

228

'O you ugly creature,' said she; 'I am crying because I have lost my golden ball that has slipped away from me and has fallen into the well.'
'Be still and do not cry,' answered the frog; 'I can help you, but if I restore the ball, what will you do for me?'
'Dear good frog,' said she, 'I will give you my rings and necklaces.'
The frog answered: 'Rings and necklaces I want not.'
'Then,' said she, 'I will give you my silk dresses.'
'Silk dresses I value not,' said the frog.  'They would be spoiled by the water.'
'I will give you lollipops,' said the princess.
'They would melt in the water,' answered the frog.
'I will give you my little gold watch,' said she.
'The water would stop the works,' said he.
'Then you shall have my little red shoes,' said she.
'They are too large for my feet,' he answered.
'Then the gold comb with which I fasten up my back hair,' she said.
'I have no back hair—never had, never shall,' replied the frog.
'What then can satisfy you?' she asked, and began to weep again.
The frog answered: 'If you will love me, and let me be your companion and playfellow, and sit at your table, and eat off your plate, and drink out of your cup, and sit on your shoulder, and whisper into your ear, and sleep on your little bed, then and only then will I dive down and bring up your golden ball.'
'I will promise all this,' said the princess, 'if you will only get me my precious ball.'  But she thought to herself: 'What is this silly frog saying? Let him remain in the water and associate with efts and newts, and not seek to mix in human society.'

229

Now the frog, as soon as he had received her
promise, drew his head under water, and dived.
Presently up he came to the surface with the ball
in his mouth, and threw it on the grass.

The king's daughter was full of joy. She picked
up the ball, and forgot even to thank the frog. She
turned to run away. 'Stay! stay!' called the frog;
'take me with you, I cannot walk as fast as you do.'

But all his croaking was in vain. The king's daughter would not hear it, but, hastening home, soon forgot the poor frog, who was obliged to leap back into the fountain.

Next day, when the princess was sitting at table with her father and all his court, and was eating from her little golden plate, something was heard coming up the marble stairs, splish, splash! splish, splash! and when it arrived at the top, it knocked at the door, and a voice was heard calling: 'Open the door, youngest daughter of a king!' So she rose and went to see who was calling for her; and when she opened the door and caught sight of the frog, she shut it again with great haste, and went back to her place at the table, looking deadly pale. When the king saw how frightened she was, he asked her whether there was an ogre at the door, who wanted to eat her.

'Oh, no!' she answered; 'it is not an ogre, but an ugly wet frog.'

'And what does the frog want with you?' asked her father.

'My father,' she answered, 'as I was at the well yesterday, I dropped my golden ball into it, and the ball sank to the bottom. I cried greatly, and then a frog came to the surface, and promised to restore to me the ball if I would make him my playfellow, and suffer him to eat off my plate, drink out of my cup, sit on my shoulder and sleep on my bed. Now he has left the well and is come here.'

Then the frog was heard calling at the door—

'Open the door, my honey, my heart,
    Open the door, my dear.
Remember the oath atwixt us both,
    Adown by the wellhead clear.'

The king said: 'A promise is a promise, whether made to prince or beggar, to man or toad.'

So the king's daughter went to the door and opened it. Splish, splash! splish, splash! in waddled the frog and stood by the princess's chair. She sat down and looked very white, and her heart beat fast. Then the frog said—

'Lift me on your lap, my honey, my heart,
 Lift me on your lap, my dear.
Remember the words to me you spake,
 Adown by the wellhead clear.'

So the princess stooped and took up the frog and set it on her lap and put her hands on the table. Then the frog said—

'Give me to eat of your dainty meat,
 From your golden plate, my dear.
Remember the oath atwixt us both,
 Adown by the wellhead clear.'

232

So she was obliged to let the frog feed from off her plate. The courtiers looked on and were very astonished. As for the princess, she could eat not another bite. Then said the frog—

'Give me of your cup, that I may sup,
    Of your golden cup, my dear.
Remember the oath betwixt us both,
    Adown by the wellhead clear.'

Then she put the cup to the cold lips of the frog, and he drank a little drop, but after that she could not take any draught from the cup.
Then when the frog had eaten and drunken to his satisfaction, all the court rose from table and retired to the drawing-room, and the princess would have walked away, and dropped the frog on the floor. But the frog cried out—

'Take me on your shoulder, my honey, my heart,
Take me on your shoulder, dear.
Remember the oath betwixt us both,
Adown by the wellhead clear.'

So the Princess was obliged to take up the frog and set him on her shoulder, and then he put his cold lips to her ear, and said—

'Fair maid, do not weep, 'tis time to sleep,
    Carry me to the bed, my dear.
Remember the oath betwixt us both,
    Adown by the wellhead clear.'

At this the king's daughter began to cry. She could not bear to think of the clammy cold frog on her beautiful clean white counterpane, and she thought that whilst she was asleep he might hop on to her face and wake her with fright. But indeed she did not think she could sleep at all with the nasty creature in her room.
But the king was angry at her reluctance. He said again, that what she had promised must be

233

observed. To break a promise was dishonourable in a poor man, it was most disgraceful in one of royal blood.

So she went to her room, with the frog squatted on her shoulder, and when there, she threw him on her counterpane.

Then the frog said—

'Chop off my head, my honey, my heart,
  Come, chop off my head, my dear.
If you love me strong, be speedy, not long,
  And chop off my head without fear.'

The princess was greatly alarmed, but she got an axe and chopped, and cut off the head of the frog. Then all at once there stood before her a beautiful prince, and all traces of the frog had disappeared. And he told her how that he had been transformed into a frog by a witch, and that he could never have recovered his own shape again, unless some young girl had promised to let him eat out of her plate, drink out of her cup, sit on her shoulder, and sleep on her bed.

The princess was so delighted that she ran and called her father and mother and all the court. And they all sat down to table again, and ate a second supper, for delight and surprise had made them all hungry again; and at this second supper it was agreed that the princess and the prince should be married.

Next day, when the sun rose, a carriage drawn by eight white horses with golden harness drove up to the door of the palace, and behind the carriage stood trusty Henry, the servant of the young prince. When his master was transformed into a frog, trusty Henry had grieved so greatly that he had bound three iron hoop-bands round his heart, for fear lest it should break with grief. Now he came with the carriage to take the prince back to his own country, and the faithful fellow helped in the bride and bridegroom, and then mounted the seat behind, full of joy at his master's recovery of his proper form.

They had not proceeded very far before the prince and princess heard a crack as though one of the carriage springs had given way.

The prince put his head out of the window and asked trusty Henry what was broken.

His servant answered: 'It is nothing in or about the carriage, dear master, but one of the bands has given way that I had bound round my heart when I was in grief because you were changed into a frog.'

Twice afterwards, on the journey, they heard the same noise, and each time the prince thought that some portion of the carriage had given way; but it was only the breaking of the bands that bound the heart of trusty Henry.

Thenceforth all lived in happiness.

# NOTES

**JACK AND THE BEAN STALK.—** This is probably a genuine old English folk-tale. A trace of it is to be found in the Sage of Olaf Tryg-vason. In dream he is said to have climbed a tree and got into a land of marvels above the clouds. The tree is Ygdrasil, the World Tree that supports the firmament above.

The giant who lives above the cloud floor is Odin or Wuotan with his single eye, and with his wife Freya.

Wuotan is possessed of the red hen that lays the golden egg every morn, that is the red dawn of which the sun is born; the harp that plays of itself, which is the wind; and the money and jewel bags, which are the clouds that drop fertilising showers.

**PUSS IN BOOTS.—**This story was taken by Perrault from the first of the 11th Night of Straparola, whose collection of Tales was printed at Venice in 1550 and 1554. Straparola himself borrowed from earlier writers.

**CINDERELLA.—**This story is given by Perrault; its counterparts are to be found in every European folk-store of tales. An exhaustive notice of all the analogues has been published by the Folklore Society. The English form of the tale, 'Catskin,' has been displaced by the French 'Cinderella.'

237

I hope to give 'Catskin' in 'The Oldest English Fairy Tales.' In German the story is 'Aschenputtel.' It was certainly known in Germany at the beginning of the 16th century, for it is referred to by Thomas Murner in 1515. In Scotland Cinderella was called Assiepet or Ashiepattle.

There are traces of the story in very remote antiquity: Strabo (**xxii.** 808) tells the story of Rhodopis, who by losing her slipper became Queen of Egypt, and the same tale is referred to by Aelian (Hist. var. xiii. 33).

The tale is this. Rhodopis was one day bathing, when an eagle picked up one of her sandals and flew away with it, and dropped it in the lap of the Egyptian King, as he was administering justice at Memphis. Surprised at its smallness and beauty, he had no rest till he found the owner of the sandal, and then he raised her from the basest and most despised condition to be his queen.

The old German Heldenlied of Gudran is but a version of the Ashputel fable. Perrault took his story from the Pentamerone.

**VALENTINE AND ORSON.**—This is one of the latest of the cycle of metrical French Romances, turning about Charlemagne and his family. It was written in prose on the reign of Charles VIII. It first appeared in print at Lyons in 1489. Again in 1495. It was translated into Italian and published at Venice in 1558. In England it was printed by Copland as 'The hystorie of the two valyante brethern Valentyne and Orson'; no date. Again in 1637, 1649, 1688, 1694. It was published in Dutch in Holland, and even found entry into Iceland. It was dramatised by Lope de Vega in Spain. In Germany it was printed at Frankfurt-am-Main in 1572, and at Basle in 1604. I have not thought it advisable to alter much the somewhat stilted style of this tale, which is characteristic of its origin.

238

**LITTLE RED RIDING-HOOD.**—One of Perrault's tales. The germ of this story may perhaps be traced in the Edda. In that is told the story of Thorr visiting the Thursr dressed in female garments, and representing himself as Freyja, whom the Thursr has asked in marriage. At the wedding banquet Thorr drinks three barrels of mead. 'Never did I see bride eat and drink so much,' said the dismayed bridegroom. Then the Thursr attempted to kiss his bride, and raised the veil. 'Never did I see such fiery eyes before!' he exclaimed, and staggered back. Then he brought his hammer and laid it on his bride's knee, who at once struck him dead with it.

Little Red Riding-hood is found in Germany, in Portugal, in Italy, etc.

**THE SLEEPING BEAUTY.**—One of Perrault's tales. This is the Dornröschen of Grimm. This is almost certainly a nature-myth of the earth sleeping in winter till kissed by the warm rays of the Spring sun, and it betokens a Northern origin. The spindle is the sleep-thorn wherewith in the Norse myth the Valkyrie Brunnhild was sent to sleep by Odin. In the ancient myth the Sleeping Beauty was surrounded by the wabberlohe, or wall of flame, till Sigurd came and released her. This myth has acquired fresh vitality from its adoption into Wagner's marvellous cycle of opera, the Ring of the Niebelungen. Perrault took the tale from the Pentamerone.

**THE BABES IN THE WOOD.**—A genuine old English tale based on a ballad.

**PRETTY MARUSCHKA.**—A Sclavonic tale. It is properly Slovakian, and is given by Wenzig in his 'West Slawischer Märchenschatz,' 1857. The story has a mythological importance, on account

239

**NOTES** of the impersonation of the Twelve Months represented as seated round the great central fire of the sun. The fire-wheel occurs in traditional usage, not only in Sclavonic but also in Gaulish lands.

**BEAUTY AND THE BEAST.**—One of Mme. de Beaumont's tales, and it is the only one of hers that has lived, and it has lived for one reason only, that it is not an original creation of her brain, but is based on an universally-known myth of a woman, loving and consenting to union with a transformed prince who has a monstrous shape. Very generally the sexes are reversed, and the young lady is transformed into a serpent or a dragon. I know a certain precipice in the Montafun Thal, in the Alps, where a maiden changed into the form of a monstrous toad, with poison dribbling from her lips, was said to be doomed to squat in a cave till a youth would kiss her on the mouth.

**THE YELLOW DWARF.**—One of the Countess D'Aulnoy's tales. At bottom this is the same story as Grimm's Rumpelstilskin, which is a very old one, and is referred to by Fischart in his 'Gargantua,' 1575. Mme. D'Aulnoy spoiled a good story. All the portion of it relative to the King of the Gold Mines is her addition. The fact was that she did not understand the significance of the task set to discover the name of the dwarf, and so she cut that away and substituted some trash of her own for it. The result has been that a good folk-tale has suffered, and 'The Yellow Dwarf' has never attained the popularity of some of her other tales, in which she has more faithfully followed tradition. The demand of the Dwarf for the Queen's daughter enters into a whole string of fairy tales, and refers back to the date when the fair-haired Gaul or Briton or Teuton had overcome the dusky Ugric

race which had occupied the land previously.
Marriage was strictly forbidden between the conquerors and the conquered, but the Ugric autoc-
thones were regarded as invested with supernatural
powers, and with superior skill in the working of
metals, and when they rendered services to their
conquerors, often demanded in recompense one of
their daughters in marriage. I have not rewritten
'The Yellow Dwarf.' I could not endure to do this,
so dissatisfied do I feel with Mme. D'Aulnoy for
having spoiled a good story. Let any one compare
this version with Grimm's 'Rumpelstilskin,' and
he will see at once the immeasurable superiority of
the latter. I myself read both as a child, and I
have never forgotten Rumpelstilskin, and I never
have been able to recall 'The Yellow Dwarf.'

HOP-O'-MY-THUMB.—One of Perrault's tales.
It is a version of the story which appears in its
earliest form in the 'Odyssey,' of Ulysses and Poly-
phemus. Grimm in his 'Die Saga von Polyphem,'
Berlin, 1857, has given eleven variants. In 'Henderson's Northern Folk-lore,' 2nd ed. 1879, pp. 195-6,
is a Yorkshire variant I picked up near Thirsk,
where the giant's grave was pointed out, and the
mill in which the giant was killed, and where also
the sword was shown with which the giant was
killed. Recently the tumulus has been destroyed.
It contained a prehistoric stone kist, probably of
the neolithic age, along with bones, so that the
burial was before inceneration took place. Moreover it was an oblong barrow and not circular.
Unhappily no person of education was present
when the tumulus was demolished.

DON'T KNOW.—A Hungarian folk-tale from the
collection of George Gaal, translated by Stier,
Pesth, n.d.
The affinity of sympathy between the prince and

his horse is not an uncommon feature in such tales. The story of the service to the King of England, and of the mysterious horses on which the prince rides to hunt and to deliver the king from his foes, occurs also in the far older tale of 'Robert the Devil,' which can be traced back to the early Middle Ages, and to which indeed William the Conqueror is said to have alluded before the battle of Hastings in his address to his soldiers.

MIRANDA; OR, THE ROYAL RAM.—A tale by Mme. D'Aulnoy. The story became a favourite for issue in chap-book form in England. It is a variant of 'Beauty and the Beast,' and is without any distinguishing merit.

BLUE-BEARD.—One of Perrault's admirable tales. It has been supposed that the story was based on the crimes and execution of the infamous De Retz, but I do not think that there is evidence that this was the case. Fatal curiosity occurs in several folk-tales.

THE FAIR MAID WITH GOLDEN LOCKS. —This capital story is by Mme. D'Aulnoy, but is not wholly original. She has made use of the favourite tale of the Thankful Beasts and the story of the Tasks, and has welded the two happily together. The Tasks are introduced into 'Cupid and Psyche.'

JACK THE GIANT KILLER.—This is a genuine old English chap-book tale, and is to be compared with others in other languages where a man of small stature, by his adroitness and superior wits, overcomes men larger and more powerful than himself. It is probably a reminiscence of a struggle between two races, the one small and the other of greater bulk.

THE THREE BEARS.—A tale by Southey.

TOM THUMB.—Another English tale, a mere play of the fancy. It is found in chap-books and in metrical form. Stories of same character among the Greeks: of Philytas, a poet of Cos, it was related that he carried lead in his shoes to save him from being blown away; and of Archestratus, that when taken by the enemy and weighed, he was found to be no heavier than an obolus.

THE WHITE CAT.—A tale by Mme. D'Aulnoy and imperishable. It combines the folk-tale of setting tasks and that of transformation into animal form. To that is added the task of cutting off head and tail, as in 'The Frog Prince.' The use of cold steel has been regarded as a means of disenchantment ever since the introduction of iron. The race of bronze workers, who used weapons of this amalgam, was conquered by the Celt with his implements of war of tempered steel, and the subjugated race regarded the new metal with feelings of terror, as something altogether super-natural.

The fairies who enchant are in most stories the members of the subjugated race. It is possible enough that transformation into bear, or frog, or cat may originally have meant no more than adoption into a tribe of which bear or frog or cat was the totem. Or it may mean, that in the race regarded as endowed with supernatural powers, the clothing was of skins, bear or cat-skin, or even—as with the Ainu—fish-skin; and that the man of the higher race, by means of his steel sword, recovered one of the members of his own race who had been carried away and adopted into the clan of the inferior race.

THE FROG PRINCE.—A very ancient folk-tale.

**NOTES**    Professor Max Müller believes it to be due to a blunder in the interpretation of words:—that the story represents the Sun beloved by the Dawn; in Sanskrit the words for sun and for frog are almost the same. But this is mere fantasy. The Sanskrit is not a parent language to our European Aryan tongues, but a sister tongue, and later in form than some of the latter. His theory may be dismissed without further consideration.

The story of 'The Frog Prince' is told by Halliwell, in his 'Popular Rhymes and Nursery Tales,' 1849. There is a Scotch version of the tale, 'The Well o' the Warld's End,' given by Chambers in his 'Popular Rhymes of Scotland.' The story is found in Germany, and is given by Grimm. There is clear evidence that anciently the tale was told in England in ballad form, and now only fragments of the metrical version remain. Professor Child, in his collection of British Ballads, gives an exhaustive account of the various forms in which this tale is found.

Printed by T. and A. CONSTABLE
Printers to Her Majesty: Edinburgh

# A CATALOGUE OF BOOKS
# PUBLISHED BY METHUEN
# AND COMPANY: LONDON
# 36 ESSEX STREET
# W.C.

## CONTENTS

MARCH 1905

# A CATALOGUE OF
# MESSRS. METHUEN'S
## PUBLICATIONS

Colonial Editions are published of all Messrs. METHUEN's Novels issued
at a price above 2s. 6d., and similar editions are published of some works of
General Literature. These are marked in the Catalogue. Colonial editions
are only for circulation in the British Colonies and India.

An asterisk denotes that a book in the Press.

## PART I.—GENERAL LITERATURE

**Abbot (Jacob).** See Little Blue Books.

**Acatos (M. J.),** Modern Language Master at King Edward School, Birmingham.
See Junior School Books.

**Adams (Frank).** JACK SPRATT. With 24 Coloured Pictures. *Super Royal 16mo.* 2s.

**Adeney (W. F.),** M.A. See Bennett and Adeney.

**Æschylus.** See Classical Translations.

**Æsop.** See Illustrated Pocket Library.

**Ainsworth (W. Harrison).** See Illustrated Pocket Library.

*****Alderson (J. P.).** MR. ASQUITH. With Portraits and Illustrations. *Demy 8vo.* 7s. 6d. net.

**Alexander (William),** D.D., Archbishop of Armagh. THOUGHTS AND COUNSELS
OF MANY YEARS. Selected by J. H. BURN, B.D. *Demy 16mo.* 2s. 6d.

**Alken (Henry).** THE NATIONAL SPORTS OF GREAT BRITAIN. With descriptions in English and French. With 51 Coloured Plates. *Royal Folio. Five Guineas net.*
See Illustrated Pocket Library.

**Allen (Jessie).** See Little Books on Art.

**Allen (J. Romilly),** F.S.A. See Antiquary's Books.

**Almack (E.).** See Little Books on Art.

**Amherst (Lady).** A SKETCH OF EGYPTIAN HISTORY FROM THE EARLIEST
TIMES TO THE PRESENT DAY. With many Illustrations, some of which are in
Colour. *Demy 8vo.* 10s. 6d. net.

**Anderson (F. M.).** THE STORY OF THE BRITISH EMPIRE FOR CHILDREN.
With many Illustrations. *Crown 8vo.* 2s.

**Andrewes (Bishop).** PRECES PRIVATAE. Edited, with Notes, by F. E. BRIGHTMAN,
M.A., of Pusey House, Oxford. *Crown 8vo.* 6s.

**Aristophanes.** THE FROGS. Translated into English by E. W. HUNTINGFORD, M.A.,
Professor of Classics in Trinity College, Toronto. *Crown 8vo.* 2s. 6d.

**Aristotle.** THE NICOMACHEAN ETHICS. Edited, with an Introduction and Notes,
by JOHN BURNET, M.A., Professor of Greek at St. Andrews. *Demy 8vo.* 10s. 6d. net.

**Ashton (R.).** See Little Blue Books.

**Atkins (H. G.).** See Oxford Biographies.

**Atkinson (C. M.).** JEREMY BENTHAM. *Crown 8vo.* 5s.
A biography of this great thinker, and an estimate of his work and influence.

**Atkinson (T. D.).** A SHORT HISTORY OF ENGLISH ARCHITECTURE. With
over 200 Illustrations by the Author and others. *Fcap. 8vo.* 3s. 6d. net.

**Aurelius (Marcus).** See Methuen's Universal Library.

**Austen (Jane).** See Little Library and Methuen's Universal Library.

**Aves (Ernest).** See Books on Business.

**Bacon (Francis).** See Little Library and Methuen's Universal Library.

**Baden-Powell (R. S. S.),** Major-General. THE DOWNFALL OF PREMPEH. A Diary
of Life in Ashanti, 1895. With 21 Illustrations and a Map. *Third Edition. Large
Crown 8vo.* 6s.
A Colonial Edition is also published.

THE MATABELE CAMPAIGN, 1896. With nearly 100 Illustrations. *Fourth and Cheaper Edition. Large Crown 8vo. 6s.*
A Colonial Edition is also published.

**Baker (W. G.), M.A.** See Junior Examination Series.

**Baker (Julian L.), F.I.C., F.C.S.** See Books on Business.

**Balfour (Graham). THE LIFE OF ROBERT LOUIS STEVENSON.** *Second Edition. Two Volumes. Demy 8vo. 25s. net.*
A Colonial Edition is also published.

**Bally (S. E.).** See Commercial Series.

**Banks (Elizabeth L.). THE AUTOBIOGRAPHY OF A 'NEWSPAPER GIRL.** With a Portrait of the Author and her Dog. *Second Edition. Crown 8vo. 6s.*
A Colonial Edition is also published.

**Barham (R. H.).** See Little Library.

**Baring-Gould (S.).** Author of 'Mehalah,' etc. **THE LIFE OF NAPOLEON BONAPARTE.** With over 450 Illustrations in the Text, and 12 Photogravure Plates. *Gilt top. Large quarto. 36s.*

THE TRAGEDY OF THE CÆSARS. With numerous Illustrations from Busts Gems, Cameos, etc. *Fifth Edition. Royal 8vo. 10s. 6d. net.*

A BOOK OF FAIRY TALES. With numerous Illustrations and Initial Letters by ARTHUR J. GASKIN. *Second Edition. Crown 8vo. Buckram. 6s.*

A BOOK OF BRITTANY. With numerous Illustrations. *Crown 8vo. 6s.*
Uniform in scope and size with Mr. Baring-Gould's well-known books on Devon, Cornwall, and Dartmoor.

OLD ENGLISH FAIRY TALES. With numerous Illustrations by F. D. BEDFORD. *Second Edition. Crown 8vo. Buckram. 6s.*
A Colonial Edition is also published.

THE VICAR OF MORWENSTOW: A Biography. A new and Revised Edition. With a Portrait. *Crown 8vo. 3s. 6d.*
A completely new edition of the well-known biography of R. S. Hawker.

DARTMOOR: A Descriptive and Historical Sketch. With Plans and numerous Illustrations. *Crown 8vo. 6s.*

THE BOOK OF THE WEST. With numerous Illustrations. *Two volumes.* Vol. I. Devon. *Second Edition.* Vol. II. Cornwall. *Second Edition. Crown 8vo. 6s. each.*

A BOOK OF NORTH WALES. With numerous Illustrations. *Crown 8vo. 6s.*
This book is uniform with Mr. Baring-Gould's books on Devon, Dartmoor, and Brittany.

*A BOOK OF SOUTH WALES. With many Illustrations. *Crown 8vo. 6s.*

A BOOK OF GHOSTS. With 8 Illustrations by D. Murray Smith. *Second Edition. Crown 8vo. 6s.*
A Colonial Edition is also published.

OLD COUNTRY LIFE. With 67 Illustrations. *Fifth Edition. Large Crown 8vo. 6s.*

*AN OLD ENGLISH HOME. With numerous Plans and Illustrations. *Cr. 8vo. 2s. 6d. net.*

*YORKSHIRE ODDITIES AND STRANGE EVENTS. *Fifth Edition. Crown 8vo. 2s. 6d. net.*

*STRANGE SURVIVALS AND SUPERSTITIONS. *Third Edition. Cr. 8vo. 2s. 6d. net.*
A Colonial Edition is also published.

A GARLAND OF COUNTRY SONG: English Folk Songs with their Traditional Melodies. Collected and arranged by S. BARING-GOULD and H. F. SHEPPARD. *Demy 4to. 6s.*

SONGS OF THE WEST: Traditional Ballads and Songs of the West of England, with their Melodies. Collected by S. BARING-GOULD, M.A., and H. F. SHEPPARD, M.A. In 4 Parts. *Parts I., II., III., 2s. 6d. each.* Part IV., 4s. *In One Volume, French Morocco, 10s. net.; Roan, 15s.*
See also The Little Guides.

**Barker (Aldred F.),** Author of 'Pattern Analysis,' etc. See Textbooks of Technology.

**Barnes (W. E.), D.D.,** Hulsaean Professor of Divinity at Cambridge. See Churchman's Bible.

**Barnett (Mrs. P. A.).** See Little Library.

**Baron (R. R. N.), M.A. FRENCH PROSE COMPOSITION.** *Crown 8vo. 2s. 6d. Key, 3s. net.* See also Junior School Books.

**Barron (H. M.), M.A.,** Wadham College, Oxford. **TEXTS FOR SERMONS.** With a Preface by Canon SCOTT HOLLAND. *Crown 8vo. 3s. 6d.*

**Bastable (C. F.), M.A.,** Professor of Economics at Trinity College, Dublin. See Social Questions Series.

**Batson (Mrs. Stephen). A BOOK OF THE COUNTRY AND THE GARDEN.** Illustrated by F. CARRUTHERS GOULD and A. C. GOULD. *Demy 8vo. 10s. 6d.*

A CONCISE HANDBOOK OF GARDEN FLOWERS. *Fcap. 8vo. 3s. 6d.*

*Batten (Loring W.), Ph.D., S.T.D., Rector of St. Mark's Church, New York; sometime Professor in the Philadelphia Divinity School. THE HEBREW PROPHET. *Crown 8vo.* *3s. 6d. net.*

Beaman (A. Hulme). PONS ASINORUM; OR, A GUIDE TO BRIDGE. *Second Edition. Fcap. 8vo. 2s.*

Beard (W. S.). See Junior Examination Series.
EASY EXERCISES IN ARITHMETIC. Arranged by. *Cr. 8vo.* Without Answers, 1s. With Answers, 1s. 3d.

Beckford (Peter). THOUGHTS ON HUNTING. Edited by J. OTHO PAGET, and Illustrated by G. H. JALLAND. *Second and Cheaper Edition. Demy 8vo. 6s.*

Beckford (William). See Little Library.

Beeching (H. C.), M.A., Canon of Westminster. See Library of Devotion.

Behmen (Jacob). THE SUPERSENSUAL LIFE. Edited by BERNARD HOLLAND. *Fcap. 8vo. 3s. 6d.*

Belloc (Hilaire). PARIS. With Maps and Illustrations. *Crown 8vo. 6s.*

Bellot (H. H. L.), M.A. THE INNER AND MIDDLE TEMPLE. With numerous Illustrations. *Crown 8vo. 6s. net.*
See also L. A. A. Jones.

Bennett (W. H.), M.A. A PRIMER OF THE BIBLE. *Second Edition. Crown 8vo. 2s. 6d.*

**Bennett (W. H) and Adeney (W. F.).** A BIBLICAL INTRODUCTION. *Second Edition. Crown 8vo. 7s. 6d.*

Benson **(Archbishop).** GOD'S BOARD: Communion Addresses. *Fcap. 8vo. 3s. 6d. net.*

Benson (A. C.), M.A. See Oxford Biographies.

Benson (R. M.). THE WAY OF HOLINESS: a Devotional Commentary on the 119th Psalm. *Crown 8vo. 5s.*

Bernard (E. R.), M.A., Canon of Salisbury. THE ENGLISH SUNDAY. *Fcap. 8vo. 1s. 6d.*

Bertouch (Baroness de). THE LIFE OF FATHER IGNATIUS, O.S.B., THE MONK OF LLANTHONY. With Illustrations. *Demy 8vo. 10s. 6d. net.*
A Colonial Edition is also published.

Bethune-Baker (J. F.), M.A., Fellow of Pembroke College, Cambridge. See Handbooks of Theology.

Bidez (M.). See Byzantine Texts.

Biggs (C. R. D.), D.D. See Churchman's Bible.

Bindley (T. Herbert), B.D. THE OECUMENICAL DOCUMENTS OF THE FAITH. With Introductions and Notes. *Crown 8vo. 6s.*
A historical account of the Creeds.

Binyon (Laurence). THE DEATH OF ADAM, AND OTHER POEMS. *Crown 8vo. 3s. 6d. net.*

Birnstingl (Ethel). See Little Books on Art.

Blair (Robert). See Illustrated Pocket Library.

Blake (William). See Illustrated Pocket Library and Little Library.

Blaxland (B.), M.A. See Library of Devotion.

Bloom (T. Harvey), M.A. SHAKESPEARE'S GARDEN. With Illustrations. *Fcap. 8vo. 3s. 6d.; leather. 4s. 6d. net.*

Blouet (Henri). See The Beginner's Books.

Boardman (T. H.). See Text Books of Technology.

Bodley (J. E. C.). Author of 'France.' THE CORONATION OF EDWARD VII. *Demy 8vo. 21s. net.* By Command of the King.

Body (George), D.D. THE SOUL'S PILGRIMAGE: Devotional Readings from his published and unpublished writings. Selected and arranged by J. H. BURN, B.D. F.R.S.E. *Pott 8vo. 2s. 6d.*

Bona (Cardinal). See Library of Devotion.

Boon (F. C.). See Commercial Series.

Borrow (George). See Little Library.

Bos (J. Ritzema). AGRICULTURAL ZOOLOGY. Translated by J. R. AINSWORTH DAVIS, M.A. With an Introduction by ELEANOR A. ORMEROD, F.E.S. With 155 Illustrations. *Crown 8vo. Third Edition. 3s. 6d.*

Botting (C. G.), B.A. EASY GREEK EXERCISES. *Crown 8vo. 2s.* See also Junior Examination Series.

Boulton (E. S.). GEOMETRY ON MODERN LINES. *Crown 8vo. 2s.*

Bowden (E. M.). THE IMITATION OF BUDDHA: Being Quotations from Buddhist Literature for each Day in the Year. *Fourth Edition. Crown 16mo. 2s. 6d.*

**Boyle (W.).** CHRISTMAS AT THE ZOO. With Verses by W. BOYLE and 24 Coloured Pictures by H. B. NEILSON. *Super Royal 16mo.* 2s.

**Brabant (F. G.),** M.A. See The Little Guides.

**Brodrick (Mary) and Morton (Anderson).** A CONCISE HANDBOOK OF EGYPTIAN ARCHÆOLOGY. With many Illustrations. *Crown 8vo.* 3s. 6d.

**Brooke (A. S.),** M.A. SLINGSBY AND SLINGSBY CASTLE. With many Illustrations. *Crown 8vo.* 7s. 6d.

**Brooks (E. W.).** See Byzantine Texts.

**Brown (P. H.),** Fraser Professor of Ancient (Scottish) History at the University of Edinburgh. SCOTLAND IN THE TIME OF QUEEN MARY. *Demy 8vo.* 7s. 6d. net.

**Browne (Sir Thomas).** See Methuen's Universal Library.

**Brownell (C. L.).** THE HEART OF JAPAN. Illustrated. *Third Edition. Crown 8vo.* 6s.; also *Demy 8vo.* 6d.
A Colonial Edition is also published.

**Browning (Robert).** See Little Library.

**Buckland (Francis T.).** CURIOSITIES OF NATURAL HISTORY. With Illustrations by HARRY B. NEILSON. *Crown 8vo.* 3s. 6d.

**Buckton (A. M.).** THE BURDEN OF ENGELA: a Ballad-Epic. *Third Edition. Crown 8vo.* 3s. 6d. net.

EAGER HEART: A Mystery Play. *Third Edition. Crown 8vo.* 1s. net.

**Budge (E. A. Wallis).** THE GODS OF THE EGYPTIANS. With over 100 Coloured Plates and many Illustrations. *Two Volumes. Royal 8vo.* £3, 3s. net.

**Bull (Paul),** Army Chaplain. GOD AND OUR SOLDIERS. *Crown 8vo.* 6s.
A Colonial Edition is also published.

**Bulley (Miss).** See Social Questions Series.

**Bunyan (John).** THE PILGRIM'S PROGRESS. Edited, with an Introduction, by C. H. FIRTH, M.A. With 39 Illustrations by R. ANNING BELL. *Cr. 8vo.* 6s. See also Library of Devotion and Methuen's Universal Library.

**Burch (G. J.),** M.A., F.R.S. A MANUAL OF ELECTRICAL SCIENCE. With numerous Illustrations. *Crown 8vo.* 3s.

**Burgess (Gelett).** GOOPS AND HOW TO BE THEM. With numerous Illustrations. *Small 4to.* 6s.

**Burke (Edmund).** See Methuen's Universal Library.

**Burn (A. F.),** D.D., Prebendary of Lichfield. See Handbooks of Theology.

**Burn (J. H.),** B.D. See Library of Devotion.

**Burnand (Sir F. C.).** RECORDS AND REMINISCENCES, PERSONAL AND GENERAL. With many Illustrations. *Demy 8vo. Two Volumes. Third Edition.* 25s. net.
A Colonial Edition is also published.

**Burns (Robert),** THE POEMS OF. Edited by ANDREW LANG and W. A. CRAIGIE. With Portrait. *Third Edition. Demy 8vo, gilt top.* 6s.

**Burnside (W. F.),** M.A. OLD TESTAMENT HISTORY FOR USE IN SCHOOLS. *Crown 8vo.* 3s. 6d.

**Burton (Alfred).** See Illustrated Pocket Library.

**Butler (Joseph).** See Methuen's Universal Library.

**Caldecott (Alfred),** D.D. See Handbooks of Theology.

**Calderwood (D. S.),** Headmaster of the Normal School, Edinburgh. TEST CARDS IN EUCLID AND ALGEBRA. In three packets of 40, with Answers. 1s. each. Or in three Books, price 2d., 2d., and 3d.

**Cambridge (Ada) [Mrs. Cross].** THIRTY YEARS IN AUSTRALIA. *Demy 8vo.* 7s. 6d.
A Colonial Edition is also published.

**Canning (George).** See Little Library.

**Capey (E. F. H.).** See Oxford Biographies.

**Careless (John).** See Illustrated Pocket Library.

**Carlyle (Thomas).** THE FRENCH REVOLUTION. Edited by C. R. L. FLETCHER, Fellow of Magdalen College, Oxford. *Three Volumes. Crown 8vo.* 18s.

THE LIFE AND LETTERS OF OLIVER CROMWELL. With an Introduction by C. H. FIRTH, M.A., and Notes and Appendices by Mrs. S. C. LOMAS. *Three Volumes. Demy 8vo.* 18s. net.

**Carlyle (R. M. and A. J.),** M.A. See Leaders of Religion.

**Chamberlin (Wilbur B.).** ORDERED TO CHINA. *Crown 8vo.* 6s.
A Colonial Edition is also published.

**Channer (C. C.) and Roberts (M. E.).** LACE-MAKING IN THE MIDLANDS, PAST AND PRESENT. With 16 full-page Illustrations. *Crown 8vo.* 2s. 6d.

**Chatterton (Thomas).** See Methuen's Universal Library.

**Chesterfield (Lord),** THE LETTERS OF, TO HIS SON. Edited, with an Introduction by C. STRACHEY, and Notes by A. CALTHROP. *Two Volumes. Cr. 8vo.* 12s.

**Christian (F. W.)** THE CAROLINE ISLANDS. With many Illustrations and Maps. *Demy 8vo.* 12s. 6d. net.

**Cicero.** See Classical Translations.

**Clarke (F. A.),** M.A. See Leaders of Religion.

**Cleather (A. L.) and Crump (B.).** RICHARD WAGNER'S MUSIC DRAMAS: Interpretations, embodying Wagner's own explanations. *In Four Volumes. Fcap 8vo.* 2s. 6d. each.

VOL. I.—THE RING OF THE NIBELUNG.

VOL. II.—PARSIFAL, LOHENGRIN, and THE HOLY GRAIL.

**Clinch (G.)** See The Little Guides.

**Clough (W. T.),** Head of the Physical Department East Ham Technical College. See Junior School Books.

**Coast (W. G),** B.A. EXAMINATION PAPERS IN VERGIL. *Crown 8vo.* 2s.

**Cobb (T.).** See Little Blue Books.

**Collingwood (W. G.),** M.A. THE LIFE OF JOHN RUSKIN. With Portraits. *Second and Cheap Edition. Cr. 8vo.* 6s. Also a Popular Edition. *Cr. 8vo.* 2s. 6d. net.

**Collins (W. E.),** M.A. See Churchman's Library.

**Colonna.** HYPNEROTOMACHIA POLIPHILI UBI HUMANA OMNIA NON NISI SOMNIUM ESSE DOCET ATQUE OBITER PLURIMA SCITU SANE QUAM DIGNA COMMEMORAT. An edition limited to 350 copies on handmade paper. *Folio. Three Guineas net.*

**Combe (William).** See Illustrated Pocket Library.

**Cook (A. M.),** M.A. See E. C. Marchant.

**Cooke-Taylor (R. W.).** See Social Questions Series.

**Corelli (Marie).** THE PASSING OF THE GREAT QUEEN : A Tribute to the Noble Life of Victoria Regina. *Small 4to.* 1s.

A CHRISTMAS GREETING. *Sm. 4to.* 1s.

**Corkran (Alice).** See Little Books on Art.

**Cotes (Rosemary).** DANTE'S GARDEN. With a Frontispiece. *Second Edition. Fcap. 8vo. cloth* 2s. 6d.; *leather,* 3s. 6d. net.

BIBLE FLOWERS. With a Frontispiece and Plan. *Fcap. 8vo.* 2s. 6d. net.

**Cowley (Abraham).** See Little Library.

**Cox (J. Charles),** LL.D., F.S.A. See Little Guides.

**Cox (Harold),** B.A. See Social Questions Series.

**Crabbe (George).** See Little Library.

**Craigie (W. A.).** A PRIMER OF BURNS. *Crown 8vo.* 2s. 6d.

**Craik (Mrs.).** See Little Library.

**Crashaw (Richard).** See Little Library.

**Crawford (F. G.).** See Mary C. Danson.

**Crouch (W.)** BRYAN KING. With a Portrait. *Crown 8vo.* 2s. 6d. net.

**Cruikshank (G.)** THE LOVING BALLAD OF LORD BATEMAN. With 11 Plates. *Crown 16mo.* 1s. 6d. net.

From the edition published by C. Tilt, 1811.

**Crump (B.).** See A. L. Cleather.

**Cunliffe (F. H. E.),** Fellow of All Souls' College, Oxford. THE HISTORY OF THE BOER WAR. With many Illustrations, Plans, and Portraits. *In 2 vols. Quarto.* 15s. each.

**Cutts (E. L.),** D.D. See Leaders of Religion.

**Daniell (G. W.),** M.A. See Leaders of Religion.

**Danson (Mary C.) and Crawford (F. G.).** FATHERS IN THE FAITH. *Small 8vo.* 1s. 6d.

**Dante.** LA COMMEDIA DI DANTE. The Italian Text edited by PAGET TOYNBEE, M.A., D.Litt. *Crown 8vo.* 6s. See also Paget Toynbee, Little Library, and Methuen's Universal Library.

**Darley (George).** See Little Library.

**Davenport (Cyril).** See Connoisseur's Library and Little Books on Art.

**Dawson (A. J.).** MOROCCO. Being a bundle of jottings, notes, impressions, tales, and tributes. With many Illustrations. *Demy 8vo.* 10s. 6d. net.

**Deane (A. C.).** See Little Library.

**Delbos (Leon).** THE METRIC SYSTEM. *Crown 8vo.* 2s.

**Demosthenes :** THE OLYNTHIACS AND PHILIPPICS. Translated upon a new principle by OTHO HOLLAND *Crown 8vo.* 2s. 6d.

**Demosthenes.** AGAINST CONON AND CALLICLES. Edited with Notes and Vocabulary, by F. DARWIN SWIFT, M.A. *Fcap. 8vo. 2s.*

**Dickens (Charles).** See Illustrated Pocket Library.

**Dickinson (Emily).** POEMS. First Series. *Crown 8vo. 4s. 6d. net.*

**Dickinson (G. L.),** M.A., Fellow of King's College, Cambridge. THE GREEK VIEW OF LIFE. *Third Edition. Crown 8vo. 2s. 6d.*

**Dickson (H. N.),** F.R.S.E., F.R.Met. Soc. METEOROLOGY. Illustrated. *Crown 8vo. 2s. 6d.*

**Dilke (Lady).** See Social Questions Series.

**Dillon (Edward).** See Connoisseur's Library.

**Ditchfield (P. H.),** M.A., F.S.A. ENGLISH VILLAGES. Illustrated. *Crown 8vo. 2s. 6d. net.*

THE STORY OF OUR ENGLISH TOWNS. With an Introduction by AUGUSTUS JESSOPP, D.D. *Second Edition. Crown 8vo. 6s.*

OLD ENGLISH CUSTOMS : Extant at the Present Time. An Account of Local Observances, Festival Customs, and Ancient Ceremonies yet Surviving in Great Britain. *Crown 8vo. 6s.*

**Dixon (W. M.),** M.A. A PRIMER OF TENNYSON. *Second Edition. Crown 8vo. 2s. 6d.*

ENGLISH POETRY FROM BLAKE TO BROWNING. *Second Edition. Crown 8vo. 2s. 6d.*

**Dole N. H.).** FAMOUS COMPOSERS. With Portraits. *Two Volumes. Demy 8vo. 12s. net.*

**Dowden (J.),** D.D., Lord Bishop of Edinburgh. See Churchman's Library.

**Drage (G.)** See Books on Business.

**Driver (S. R.),** D.D., Canon of Christ Church, Regius Professor of Hebrew in the University of Oxford. SERMONS ON SUBJECTS CONNECTED WITH THE OLD TESTAMENT. *Crown 8vo. 6s.* See also Westminster Commentaries.

**Dryhurst (A. R.).** See Little Books on Art.

**Duguid (Charles),** City Editor of the *Morning Post*, Author of the 'Story of the Stock Exchange,' etc. See Books on Business.

**Duncan (S. J.) (Mrs. COTES),** Author of 'A Voyage of Consolation.' ON THE OTHER SIDE OF THE LATCH. *Second Edition. Crown 8vo. 6s.*

**Dunn (J. T.),** D.Sc., **and Mundella (V. A.).** GENERAL ELEMENTARY SCIENCE. With 114 Illustrations. *Crown 8vo. 3s. 6d.*

**Dunstan (A. E.),** B.Sc., Head of the Chemical Department, East Ham Technical College. See Junior School Books.

*****Durham (The Earl of).** A REPORT ON CANADA. With an Introductory Note. *Demy 8vo. 4s. 6d. net.*

**Dutt (W. A.).** A POPULAR GUIDE TO NORFOLK. *Medium 8vo. 6d. net.*

THE NORFOLK BROADS. With coloured and other Illustrations by FRANK SOUTHGATE. *Large Demy 8vo. 21s. net.* See also The Little Guides.

**Earle (John),** Bishop of Salisbury. MICROCOSMOGRAPHE, OR A PIECE OF THE WORLD DISCOVERED ; IN ESSAYES AND CHARACTERS. *Post 16mo. 2s net.* Reprinted from the Sixth Edition published by Robert Allot in 1633.

**Edwards (Clement).** See Social Questions Series.

**Edwards (W. Douglas).** See Commercial Series.

*****Edwards (Betham).** HOME LIFE IN FRANCE. With many Illustrations. *Demy 8vo. 7s. 6d. net.*

**Egan (Pierce).** See Illustrated Pocket Library.

**Egerton (H. E.),** M.A. A HISTORY OF BRITISH COLONIAL POLICY. *Demy 8vo. 12s. 6d.* A Colonial Edition is also published.

**Ellaby (C. G.).** See The Little Guides.

**Ellerton (F. G.).** See S. J. Stone.

**Ellwood (Thomas),** THE HISTORY OF THE LIFE OF. Edited by C. G. CRUMP, M.A. *Crown 8vo. 6s.*

**Engel (E.).** A HISTORY OF ENGLISH LITERATURE : From its Beginning to Tennyson. Translated from the German. *Demy 8vo. 7s. 6d. net.*

**Fairbrother (W. H.),** M.A. THE PHILOSOPHY OF T. H. GREEN. *Second Edition. Crown 8vo. 3s. 6d.*

FELISSA ; OR, THE LIFE AND OPINIONS OF A KITTEN OF SENTIMENT. With 12 Coloured Plates. *Post 16mo. 2s. 6d. net. (5½ × 3½).* From the edition published by J. Harris, 1811.

8 MESSRS. METHUEN'S CATALOGUE

**Farrer (Reginald).** THE GARDEN OF ASIA. *Second Edition.* *Crown 8vo.* *6s.*
A Colonial Edition is also published.
**Ferrier (Susan).** See Little Library.
**Fidler (T. Claxton),** M. Inst. C.E., Professor of Engineering, University College, Dundee in the University of St. Andrews. See Books on Business.
**Fielding (Henry).** See Methuen's Universal Library.
**Finn (S. W.),** M.A. See Junior Examination Series.
**Firth (C. H.),** M.A. CROMWELL'S ARMY: A History of the English Soldier during the Civil Wars, the Commonwealth, and the Protectorate. *Crown 8vo.* *6s.*
**Fisher (G. W.),** M.A. ANNALS OF SHREWSBURY SCHOOL. With numerous Illustrations. *Demy 8vo.* *10s. 6d.*
**FitzGerald (Edward).** THE RUB'AIYAT OF OMAR KHAYYAM. Printed from the Fifth and last Edition. With a Commentary by Mrs. STEPHEN BATSON, and a Biography of Omar by E. D. Ross. *Crown 8vo.* *6s.* See also Miniature Library.
**Flecker (W. H.),** M.A., D.C.L., Headmaster of the Dean Close School, Cheltenham. THE STUDENT'S PRAYER BOOK. Part I. MORNING AND EVENING PRAYER AND LITANY. With an Introduction and Notes. *Crown 8vo.* *2s. 6d.*
**Flux (A. W.),** M.A., William Dow Professor of Political Economy in M'Gill University, Montreal: sometime Fellow of St. John's College, Cambridge, and formerly Stanley-Jevons Professor of Political Economy in the Owens Coll., Manchester. ECONOMIC PRINCIPLES. *Demy 8vo.* *7s. 6d. net.*
**Fortescue (Mrs. G.)** See Little Books on Art.
**Fraser (David).** A MODERN CAMPAIGN; OR, WAR AND WIRELESS TELE-GRAPHY IN THE FAR EAST. Illustrated. *Crown 8vo.* *6s.*
**Fraser (J. F.).** ROUND THE WORLD ON A WHEEL. With 100 Illustrations. *Third Edition Crown 8vo.* *6s.*
A Colonial Edition is also published.
**French (W.).** See Textbooks of Technology.
**Freudenreich (Ed. von).** DAIRY BACTERIOLOGY. A Short Manual for the Use of Students. Translated by J. R. AINSWORTH DAVIS, M.A. *Second Edition.* *Revised.* *Crown 8vo.* *2s. 6d.*
**Fulford (H. W.),** M.A. See Churchman's Bible.
**C. G., and F. C. G.** JOHN BULL'S ADVENTURES IN THE FISCAL WONDER-LAND. By CHARLES GEAKE. With 46 Illustrations by F. CARRUTHERS GOULD. *Second Edition.* *Crown 8vo.* *2s. 6d. net.*
**Gallichan (W. M.).** See The Little Guides.
**Gambado (Geoffrey, Esq.).** See Illustrated Pocket Library.
**Gaskell (Mrs.).** See Little Library.
**Gasquet,** the Right Rev. Abbot, O.S.B. See Antiquary's Books.
**George (H. B.),** M.A., Fellow of New College, Oxford. BATTLES OF ENGLISH HISTORY. With numerous Plans. *Fourth Edition.* Revised, with a new Chapter including the South African War. *Crown 8vo.* *6s.*
A HISTORICAL GEOGRAPHY OF THE BRITISH EMPIRE. *Crown 8vo.* *3s. 6d.*
**Gibbins (H. de B.),** Litt.D., M.A. INDUSTRY IN ENGLAND: HISTORICAL OUTLINES. With 5 Maps. *Third Edition.* *Demy 8vo.* *10s. 6d.*
A COMPANION GERMAN GRAMMAR. *Crown 8vo.* *1s. 6d.*
THE INDUSTRIAL HISTORY OF ENGLAND. *Tenth Edition.* Revised. With Maps and Plans. *Crown 8vo.* *3s.*
ENGLISH SOCIAL REFORMERS. *Second Edition.* *Crown 8vo.* *2s. 6d.*
See also Commercial Series and Social Questions Series.
**Gibbon (Edward).** THE DECLINE AND FALL OF THE ROMAN EMPIRE. A New Edition, edited with Notes, Appendices, and Maps, by J. B. BURY, M.A., Litt.D., Regius Professor of Greek at Cambridge. *In Seven Volumes.* *Demy 8vo.* *Gilt top, 8s. 6d. each.* *Also, Crown 8vo.* *6s. each.*
MEMOIRS OF MY LIFE AND WRITINGS. Edited, with an Introduction and Notes, by G. BIRKBECK HILL, LL.D. *Crown 8vo.* *6s.*
See also Methuen's Universal Library.
**Gibson (E. C. S.),** D.D., Vicar of Leeds. See Westminster Commentaries, Handbooks of Theology, and Oxford Biographies.
**Gilbert (A. R.).** See Little Books on Art.
**Godfrey (Elizabeth).** A BOOK OF REMEMBRANCE. *Fcap. 8vo.* *2s. 6d. net.*
**Godley (A. D.),** M.A., Fellow of Magdalen College, Oxford. LYRA FRIVOLA. *Third Edition.* *Fcap. 8vo.* *2s. 6d.*
VERSES TO ORDER. *Second Edition.* *Fcap. 8vo.* *2s. 6d.*
SECOND STRINGS. *Fcap. 8vo.* *2s. 6d.*

**Goldsmith (Oliver).** THE VICAR OF WAKEFIELD. With 24 Coloured Plates by T. ROWLANDSON. *Royal 8vo. One Guinea net.*
Reprinted from the edition of 1817. Also *Fcap. 32mo.* With 10 Plates in Photogravure by Tony Johannot. *Leather,* 2s. 6d. net. See also Illustrated Pocket Library and Methuen's Universal Library.

**Goudge (H. L.),** M.A., Principal of Wells Theological College. See Westminster Commentaries.

**Graham (P. Anderson).** See Social Questions Series.

**Granger (F. S.),** M.A., Litt.D. PSYCHOLOGY. *Second Edition. Crown 8vo.* 2s. 6d.
THE SOUL OF A CHRISTIAN. *Crown 8vo.* 6s.

**Gray (E. M'Queen).** GERMAN PASSAGES FOR UNSEEN TRANSLATION. *Crown 8vo.* 2s. 6d.

**Gray (P. L.),** B.Sc., formerly Lecturer in Physics in Mason University College, Birmingham. THE PRINCIPLES OF MAGNETISM AND ELECTRICITY: an Elementary Text-Book. With 181 Diagrams. *Crown 8vo.* 3s. 6d.

**Green (G. Buckland),** M.A., Assistant Master at Edinburgh Academy, late Fellow of St. John's College, Oxon. NOTES ON GREEK AND LATIN SYNTAX. *Crown 8vo.* 3s. 6d.

**Green (E. T.),** M.A. See Churchman's Library.

**Greenidge (A. H. J.),** M.A. A HISTORY OF ROME: During the Later Republic and the Early Principate. *In Six Volumes. Demy 8vo.* Vol. I. (133-104 B.C.). 10s. 6d. net.

**Greenwell (Dora).** See Miniature Library.

**Gregory (R. A.)** THE VAULT OF HEAVEN. A Popular Introduction to Astronomy. With numerous Illustrations. *Crown 8vo.* 2s. 6d.

**Gregory (Miss E. C.).** See Library of Devotion.

**Greville Minor.** A MODERN JOURNAL. Edited by J. A. SPENDER. *Crown 8vo.* 3s. 6d. net.

**Grinling (C. H.).** A HISTORY OF THE GREAT NORTHERN RAILWAY, 1845-95. With Illustrations. Revised, with an additional chapter. *Demy 8vo.* 10s. 6d.

**Grubb (H. C.).** See Textbooks of Technology.

**Guiney (Louisa I.).** HURRELL FROUDE: Memoranda and Comments. Illustrated. *Demy 8vo.* 10s. 6d. net.

**Gwynn (M. L.).** A BIRTHDAY BOOK. *Royal 8vo.* 12s.

**Hackett (John),** B.D. A HISTORY OF THE ORTHODOX CHURCH OF CYPRUS. With Maps and Illustrations. *Demy 8vo.* 15s. net.

**Haddon (A. C.),** Sc.D., F.R.S. HEAD-HUNTERS, BLACK, WHITE, AND BROWN. With many Illustrations and a Map. *Demy 8vo.* 15s.

**Hadfield (R. A.).** See Social Questions Series.

**Hall (R. N.) and Neal (W. G.).** THE ANCIENT RUINS OF RHODESIA. With numerous Illustrations. *Second Edition, revised. Demy 8vo.* 10s. 6d. net.

**Hall (R. N.).** GREAT ZIMBABWE. With numerous Plans and Illustrations. *Royal 8vo.* 21s. net.

**Hamilton (F. J.),** D.D. See Byzantine Texts.

**Hammond (J. L.).** CHARLES JAMES FOX: A Biographical Study. *Demy 8vo.* 10s. 6d.

**Hannay (D.).** A SHORT HISTORY OF THE ROYAL NAVY, FROM EARLY TIMES TO THE PRESENT DAY. Illustrated. *Two Volumes. Demy 8vo.* 7s. 6d. each. Vol. I. 1200-1688.

**Hannay (James O.),** M.A. THE SPIRIT AND ORIGIN OF CHRISTIAN MONASTICISM. *Crown 8vo.* 6s.
THE WISDOM OF THE DESERT. *Crown 8vo.* 3s. 6d. net.

**Hare, (A. T.),** M.A. THE CONSTRUCTION OF LARGE INDUCTION COILS. With numerous Diagrams. *Demy 8vo.* 6s.

**Harrison (Clifford).** READING AND READERS. *Fcap. 8vo.* 2s. 6d.

**Hawthorne (Nathaniel).** See Little Library.
HEALTH, WEALTH AND WISDOM. *Crown 8vo.* 1s. net.

**Heath (Frank R.).** See The Little Guides.

**Heath (Dudley).** See Connoisseur's Library.

**Hello (Ernest).** STUDIES IN SAINTSHIP. Translated from the French by V. M. CRAWFORD. *Fcap 8vo.* 3s. 6d.

**Henderson (B. W.),** Fellow of Exeter College, Oxford. THE LIFE AND PRINCIPATE OF THE EMPEROR NERO. With Illustrations. *Demy 8vo.* 10s. 6d. net.

**Henderson (T. F.).** See Little Library and Oxford Biographies.

**Henley (W. E.).** ENGLISH LYRICS. *Second Edition. Crown 8vo.* 2s. 6d. net.

**Henley (W. E.) and Whibley (C.).** A BOOK OF ENGLISH PROSE. *Crown 8vo. Buckram, gilt top.* 6s.

**Henson (H. H.),** B.D., Canon of Westminster. APOSTOLIC CHRISTIANITY: As Illustrated by the Epistles of St. Paul to the Corinthians. *Crown 8vo.* 6s.

A 2

LIGHT AND LEAVEN: HISTORICAL AND SOCIAL SERMONS. *Crown 8vo. 6s.*
DISCIPLINE AND LAW. *Fcap. 8vo. 2s. 6d.*
**Herbert (George).** See Library of Devotion.
**Herbert of Cherbury (Lord).** See Miniature Library.
**Hewins (W. A. S.),** B.A. ENGLISH TRADE AND FINANCE IN THE SEVEN-TEENTH CENTURY. *Crown 8vo. 2s. 6d.*
**Heywood (W.).** PALIO AND PONTE: A Book of Tuscan Games. Illustrated. *Royal 8vo. 21s. net.*
**Hilbert (T.).** See Little Blue Books.
**Hill (Clare),** Registered Teacher to the City and Guilds of London Institute. See Textbooks of Technology.
**Hill (Henry),** B.A., Headmaster of the Boy's High School, Worcester, Cape Colony. A SOUTH AFRICAN ARITHMETIC. *Crown 8vo. 3s. 6d.*
    This book has been specially written for use in South African schools.
**Hillegas (Howard C.).** WITH THE BOER FORCES. With 24 Illustrations. *Second Edition. Crown 8vo. 6s.*
**Hobhouse (Emily).** THE BRUNT OF THE WAR. With Map and Illustrations. *Crown 8vo. 6s.*
    A Colonial Edition is also published.
**Hobhouse (L. T.),** Fellow of C.C.C., Oxford. THE THEORY OF KNOWLEDGE. *Demy 8vo. 10s. 6d. net.*
**Hobson (J. A.),** M.A. INTERNATIONAL TRADE: A Study of Economic Principles. *Crown 8vo. 2s. 6d. net.* See also Social Questions Series.
**Hodgkin (T.),** D.C.L. See Leaders of Religion.
**Hogg (Thomas Jefferson).** SHELLEY AT OXFORD. With an Introduction by R. A. STREATFEILD. *Fcap. 8vo. 2s. net.*
**Holden-Stone (G. de).** See Books on Business.
**Holdich (Sir T. H.),** K.C.I.E. THE INDIAN BORDERLAND: being a Personal Record of Twenty Years. Illustrated. *Demy 8vo. 10s. 6d. net.*
**Holdsworth (W. S.),** M.A. A HISTORY OF ENGLISH LAW. *In Two Volumes. Vol. I. Demy 8vo. 10s. 6d. net.*
**Holyoake (G. J.).** See Social Questions Series.
**Hoppner.** See Little Galleries.
**Horace.** See Classical Translations.
**Horsburgh (E. L. S.),** M.A. WATERLOO: A Narrative and Criticism. With Plans. *Second Edition. Crown 8vo. 5s.* See also Oxford Biographies.
**Horth (A. C.),** Master of Art and Manual Training Departments, Roan School, Greenwich. See Textbooks of Technology.
**Horton (R. F.),** D.D. See Leaders of Religion.
**Hosie (Alexander).** MANCHURIA. With Illustrations and a Map. *Second Edition. Demy 8vo. 7s. 6d. net.*
**How (F. D.).** SIX GREAT SCHOOLMASTERS. With Portraits and Illustrations. *Demy 8vo. 7s. 6d.*
**Howell (G.).** See Social Questions Series.
**Hudson (Robert).** MEMORIALS OF A WARWICKSHIRE VILLAGE. With many Illustrations. *Demy 8vo. 15s. net.*
**Hughes (C. E.).** THE PRAISE OF SHAKESPEARE. An English Anthology. With a Preface by SIDNEY LEE. *Demy 8vo. 3s. 6d. net.*
**Hughes (Thomas).** TOM BROWN'S SCHOOLDAYS. With an Introduction and Notes by VERNON RENDALL. *Leather. Royal 32mo. 2s. 6d. net.*
**Hutchinson (Horace G.).** THE NEW FOREST. Described by. Illustrated in colour with 50 Pictures by WALTER TYNDALE and 4 by Miss LUCY KEMP WELCH. *Large Demy 8vo. 21s. net.*
**Hutton (A. W.),** M.A. See Leaders of Religion.
**Hutton (R. H.).** See Leaders of Religion.
**Hutton (W. H.),** M.A. THE LIFE OF SIR THOMAS MORE. With Portraits. *Second Edition. Crown 8vo. 5s.* See also Leaders of Religion.
**Hyett (F. A.).** A SHORT HISTORY OF FLORENCE. *Demy 8vo. 7s. 6d. net.*
**Ibsen (Henrik).** BRAND. A Drama. Translated by WILLIAM WILSON. *Third Edition. Crown 8vo. 3s. 6d.*
**Inge (W. R.),** M.A., Fellow and Tutor of Hertford College, Oxford. CHRISTIAN MYS-TICISM. The Bampton Lectures for 1899. *Demy 8vo. 12s. 6d. net.* See also Library of Devotion.
**Innes (A. D.),** M.A. A HISTORY OF THE BRITISH IN INDIA. With Maps and Plans. *Crown 8vo. 6s.*

**Langbridge (F.)** M.A. BALLADS OF THE BRAVE: Poems of Chivalry, Enterprise, Courage, and Constancy. *Second Edition. Crown 8vo. 2s. 6d.*
**Law (William).** See Library of Devotion.
**Leach (Henry).** THE DUKE OF DEVONSHIRE. A Biography. With 12 Illustrations. *Demy 8vo. 12s. 6d. net.*
  A Colonial Edition is also published.
*\*Lee (Captain L. Melville).* A HISTORY OF POLICE IN ENGLAND. *Crown 8vo. 3s. 6d. net.*
**Leigh (Percival).** THE COMIC ENGLISH GRAMMAR. Embellished with upwards of 50 characteristic Illustrations by JOHN LEECH. *Post 16mo. 2s. 6d. net.*
**Lewes (V. B.),** M.A. AIR AND WATER. Illustrated. *Crown 8vo. 2s. 6d.*
**Lisle (Fortunée de).** See Little Books on Art.
**Littlehales (H.).** See Antiquary's Books.
**Lock (Walter),** D.D., Warden of Keble College. ST. PAUL, THE MASTER-BUILDER. *Second Edition. Crown 8vo. 3s. 6d.* See also Leaders of Religion.
**Locke (John).** See Methuen's Universal Library.
**Locker (F.).** See Little Library.
**Longfellow (H. W.)** See Little Library.
**Lorimer (George Horace).** LETTERS FROM A SELF-MADE MERCHANT TO HIS SON. *Twelfth Edition. Crown 8vo. 6s.*
  A Colonial Edition is also published.
OLD GORGON GRAHAM. *Second Edition. Crown 8vo. 6s.*
  A Colonial Edition is also published.
**Lover (Samuel).** See Illustrated Pocket Library
**E. V. L.** and **C. L. G.** ENGLAND DAY BY DAY : Or, The Englishman's Handbook to Efficiency. Illustrated by GEORGE MORROW. *Fourth Edition. Fcap. 4to. 1s. net.*
  A burlesque Year-Book and Almanac.
**Lucas (E. V.).** THE LIFE OF CHARLES LAMB. With numerous Portraits and Illustrations. *Two Vols. Demy 8vo. 21s. net.*
**Lucian.** See Classical Translations.
**Lyde (L. W.),** M.A. See Commercial Series.
**Lydon (Noel S.).** See Junior School Books.
**Lyttelton (Hon. Mrs. A.).** WOMEN AND THEIR WORK. *Crown 8vo. 2s. 6d.*
**M. M.** HOW TO DRESS AND WHAT TO WEAR. *Crown 8vo. 1s. net.*
**Macaulay (Lord).** CRITICAL AND HISTORICAL ESSAYS. Edited by F. C. MONTAGUE, M.A. *Three Volumes. Cr. 8vo. 18s.*
  The only edition of this book completely annotated.
**M'Allen (J. E. B.),** M.A. See Commercial Series.
**MacCulloch (J. A.).** See Churchman's Library.
**MacCunn (F.).** See Leaders of Religion.
**McDermott, (E. R.),** Editor of the *Railway News*, City Editor of the *Daily News*. See Books on Business.
**M'Dowall (A. S.).** See Oxford Biographies.
**Mackay (A. M.).** See Churchman's Library.
**Magnus (Laurie),** M.A. A PRIMER OF WORDSWORTH. *Crown 8vo. 2s. 6d.*
**Mahaffy (J. P.),** Litt.D. A HISTORY OF THE EGYPT OF THE PTOLEMIES. Fully Illustrated. *Crown 8vo. 6s.*
**Maitland (F. W.),** LL.D., Downing Professor of the Laws of England in the University of Cambridge. CANON LAW IN ENGLAND. *Royal 8vo. 7s. 6d.*
**Malden (H. E.),** M.A. ENGLISH RECORDS. A Companion to the History of England. *Crown 8vo. 3s. 6d.*
THE ENGLISH CITIZEN : HIS RIGHTS AND DUTIES. *Crown 8vo. 1s. 6d.*
**Marchant (E. C.),** M.A., Fellow of Peterhouse, Cambridge. A GREEK ANTHOLOGY. *Second Edition. Crown 8vo. 3s. 6d.*
**Marchant (E. C.),** M.A., and **Cook (A. M.),** M.A. PASSAGES FOR UNSEEN TRANSLATION. *Second Edition. Crown 8vo. 3s. 6d.*
**Marlowe (Christopher).** See Methuen's Universal Library.
**Marr (J. E.),** F.R.S., Fellow of St John's College, Cambridge. THE SCIENTIFIC STUDY OF SCENERY. *Second Edition.* Illustrated. *Crown 8vo. 6s.*
AGRICULTURAL GEOLOGY. With numerous Illustrations. *Crown 8vo. 6s.*
**Marvell (Andrew).** See Little Library.
**Maskell (A.)** See Connoisseur's Library.
**Mason (A. J.),** D.D. See Leaders of Religion.
**Massee (George).** THE EVOLUTION OF PLANT LIFE: Lower Forms. With Illustrations. *Crown 8vo. 2s. 6d.*

**Masterman (C. F. G.),** M.A. TENNYSON AS A RELIGIOUS TEACHER. *Cr. 8vo.* ·6s.

**May (Phil).** THE PHIL MAY ALBUM. *Second Edition. 4to. 1s. net.*

**Mellows (Emma S.).** A SHORT STORY OF ENGLISH LITERATURE. *Crown 8vo.* 3s. 6d.

**Michell (E. B).** THE ART AND PRACTICE OF HAWKING. With 3 Photogravures by G. E. LODGE, and other Illustrations. *Demy 8vo. 10s. 6d.*

*Millais (J. G.).** THE LIFE AND LETTERS OF SIR JOHN EVERETT MILLAIS, President of the Royal Academy. With 319 Illustrations, of which 9 are in Photogravure. *New Edition. Demy 8vo. 7s. 6d. net.*

**Millais (Sir John Everett).** See Little Galleries.

**Millis (C. T.),** M.I.M.E., Principal of the Borough Polytechnic College. See Textbooks of Technology.

**Milne (J. G.),** M.A. A HISTORY OF ROMAN EGYPT. Fully Illustrated. *Crown 8vo. 6s.*

**Milton, John,** THE POEMS OF, BOTH ENGLISH AND LATIN, Compos'd at several times. Printed by his true Copies.

The Songs were set in Musick by Mr. HENRY LAWES, Gentleman of the Kings Chappel, and one of His Majesties Private Musick.

Printed and publish'd according to Order.

Printed by RUTH RAWORTH for HUMPHREY MOSELEY, and are to be sold at the signe of the Princes Armes in Pauls Churchyard, 1645.

See also Little Library and Methuen's Universal Library.

**Minchin (H. C.),** M.A. See Little Galleries.

**Mitchell (P. Chalmers),** M.A. OUTLINES OF BIOLOGY. Illustrated. *Second Edition. Crown 8vo. 6s.*

A text-book designed to cover the Schedule issued by the Royal College of Physicians and Surgeons.

**'Moil (A.).'** See Books on Business.

**Moir (D. M.).** See Little Library.

**Moore (H. E.).** See Social Questions Series.

**Moran (Clarence G.).** See Books on Business.

**More (Sir Thomas).** See Methuen's Universal Library.

**Morfill (W. R.),** Oriel College, Oxford. A HISTORY OF RUSSIA FROM PETER THE GREAT TO ALEXANDER II. With Maps and Plans. *Crown 8vo. 3s. 6d.*

**Morich (R. J.),** late of Cl'ton College. See School Examination Series.

**Morris (J. E.).** See The Little Guides.

**Morton (Miss Anderson).** See Miss Brodrick.

**Moule (H. C. G.),** D.D., Lord Bishop of Durham. See Leaders of Religion.

**Muir (M. M. Pattison),** M.A. THE CHEMISTRY OF FIRE. The Elementary Principles of Chemistry. Illustrated. *Crown 8vo. 2s. 6d.*

**Mundella (V. A),** M.A. See J. T. Dunn.

**Munro (R.),** LL.D. See The Antiquary's Books.

**Naval Officer (A).** See Illustrated Pocket Library.

**Neal (W. G.).** See R. N. Hall.

**Newman (J. H.) and others.** See Library of Devotion.

**Nichols (J. B. B.).** See Little Library.

**Nicklin (T.),** M.A. EXAMINATION PAPERS IN THUCYDIDES. *Crown 8vo. 2s.*

**Nimrod.** See Illustrated Pocket Library.

**Northcote (James),** R.A. THE CONVERSATIONS OF JAMES NORTHCOTE, R.A., AND JAMES WARD. Edited by ERNEST FLETCHER. With many Portraits. *Demy 8vo. 10s. 6d.*

*Norway (A. H.),** Author of 'Highways and Byways in Devon and Cornwall.' NAPLES. With 24 Coloured Illustrations by MAURICE GREIFFENHAGEN. A New Edition. *Crown 8vo. 6s.*

**Novalis.** THE DISCIPLES AT SAÏS AND OTHER FRAGMENTS. Edited by Miss UNA BIRCH. *Fcap. 8vo. 3s. 6d.*

**Oliphant (Mrs.).** See Leaders of Religion.

**Oman (C. W. C.),** M.A., Fellow of All Souls', Oxford. A HISTORY OF THE ART OF WAR. Vol. II.: The Middle Ages, from the Fourth to the Fourteenth Century. Illustrated. *Demy 8vo. 10s. 6d net.*

**Ottley (R. L.),** D.D., Professor of Pastoral Theology at Oxford and Canon of Christ Church. See Handbooks of Theology and Leaders of Religion.

**Owen (Douglas),** Barrister-at-Law, Secretary to the Alliance Marine and General Assurance Company. See Books on Business.

**Oxford (M. N.),** of Guy's Hospital. A HANDBOOK OF NURSING. *Second Edition. Crown 8vo. 3s. 6d.*

**Pakes (W. C. C.).** THE SCIENCE OF HYGIENE. With numerous Illustrations. *Demy 8vo. 15s.*

**Palmer (Frederick).** WITH KUROKI IN MANCHURIA. With many Illustrations. *Second Edition. Demy 8vo. 7s. 6d. net.*
   A Colonial Edition is also published.

**Parker (Gilbert).** A LOVER'S DIARY: SONGS IN SEQUENCE. *Fcap. 8vo. 5s.*

**Parkinson (John).** PARADISI IN SOLE PARADISUS TERRESTRIS, OR A GARDEN OF ALL SORTS OF PLEASANT FLOWERS. *Folio. £3, 5s. net.*
   Also an Edition of 90 copies on Japanese vellum. *Ten Guineas net.*

**Parmenter (John).** HELIO-TROPES, OR NEW POSIES FOR SUNDIALS, 1625. Edited by PERCIVAL LANDON. *Quarto. 3s. 6d. net.*

**Parmentier (Prof. Léon).** See Byzantine Texts.

**Pascal.** See Library of Devotion.

**Paston (George).** SOCIAL CARICATURES OF THE EIGHTEENTH CENTURY. *Imperial Quarto. £2, 12s. 6d. net.* See also Little Books on Art and Illustrated Pocket Library.

**Paterson (W. R.)** (Benjamin Swift). LIFE'S QUESTIONINGS. *Crown 8vo. 3s. 6d. net.*

**Patterson (A. H.).** NOTES OF AN EAST COAST NATURALIST. Illustrated in Colour by F. SOUTHGATE. *Second Edition. Cr. 8vo. 6s.*

**Peacock (N.).** See Little Books on Art.

**Pearce (E. H.), M.A.** ANNALS OF CHRIST'S HOSPITAL. With many Illustrations. *Demy 8vo. 7s. 6d.*

**Peary (R. E.),** Gold Medallist of the Royal Geographical Society. NORTHWARD OVER THE GREAT ICE. With over 800 Illustrations. *2 vols. Royal 8vo. 32s. net.*

**Peel (Sidney),** late Fellow of Trinity College, Oxford, and Secretary to the Royal Commission on the Licensing Laws. PRACTICAL LICENSING REFORM. *Second Edition. Crown 8vo. 1s. 6d.*

**Peters (J. P.), D.D.** See Churchman's Library.

**Petrie (W. M. Flinders), D.C.L., LL.D.,** Professor of Egyptology at University College. A HISTORY OF EGYPT, FROM THE EARLIEST TIMES TO THE PRESENT DAY. Fully Illustrated. *In six volumes. Crown 8vo. 6s. each.*
   VOL. I. PREHISTORIC TIMES TO XVITH DYNASTY. *Fifth Edition.*
   VOL. II. THE XVIITH AND XVIIITH DYNASTIES. *Fourth Edition.*
   VOL. III. XIXTH TO XXXTH DYNASTIES.
   VOL. IV. THE EGYPT OF THE PTOLEMIES. J. P. MAHAFFY, Litt.D.
   VOL. V. ROMAN EGYPT. J. G. MILNE, M.A.
   VOL. VI. EGYPT IN THE MIDDLE AGES. STANLEY LANE-POOLE, M.A.

RELIGION AND CONSCIENCE IN ANCIENT EGYPT. Fully Illustrated. *Crown 8vo. 2s. 6d.*

SYRIA AND EGYPT, FROM THE TELL EL AMARNA TABLETS. *Crown 8vo. 2s. 6d.*

EGYPTIAN TALES. Illustrated by TRISTRAM ELLIS. *In Two Volumes. Crown 8vo. 3s. 6d. each.*

EGYPTIAN DECORATIVE ART. With 120 Illustrations. *Crown 8vo. 3s. 6d.*

**Phillips (W. A.).** See Oxford Biographies.

**Phillpotts (Eden).** MY DEVON YEAR. With 38 Illustrations by J. LEY PETHYBRIDGE. *Second and Cheaper Edition. Large Crown 8vo. 6s.*

**Pienaar (Philip).** WITH STEYN AND DE WET. *Second Edition. Crown 8vo. 3s. 6d.*

**Plautus.** THE CAPTIVI. Edited, with an Introduction, Textual Notes, and a Commentary, by W. M. LINDSAY, Fellow of Jesus College, Oxford. *Demy 8vo. 10s. 6d. net.*

**Plowden-Wardlaw (J. T.), B.A.,** King's Coll. Camb. See School Examination Series.

**Pocock (Roger).** A FRONTIERSMAN. *Third Edition. Crown 8vo. 6s.*
   A Colonial Edition is also published.

**Podmore (Frank).** MODERN SPIRITUALISM. *Two Volumes. Demy 8vo. 21s. net.* A History and a Criticism.

**Poer (J. Patrick Le).** A MODERN LEGIONARY. *Crown 8vo. 6s.*
   A Colonial Edition is also published.

**Pollard (Alice).** See Little Books on Art.

**Pollard (A. W.).** OLD PICTURE BOOKS. With many Illustrations. *Demy 8vo. 7s. 6d. net.*

**Pollard (Eliza F.).** See Little Books on Art.

**Pollock (David), M.I.N.A.,** Author of 'Modern Shipbuilding and the Men engaged in it, etc., etc. See Books on Business.

**Potter (M. C.), M.A., F.L.S.** A TEXT-BOOK OF AGRICULTURAL BOTANY. Illustrated. *Second Edition. Crown 8vo. 4s. 6d.*

**Potter Boy (An Old).** WHEN I WAS A CHILD. *Crown 8vo. 6s.*

**Pradeau (G.).** A KEY TO THE TIME ALLUSIONS IN THE DIVINE COMEDY. With a Dial. *Small quarto. 3s. 6d.*

**France (G.).** See R. Wyon.

**Prescott (O. L.).** ABOUT MUSIC, AND WHAT IT IS MADE OF. *Crown 8vo. 3s. 6d. net.*

**Price (L. L.),** M.A., Fellow of Oriel College, Oxon. A HISTORY OF ENGLISH POLITICAL ECONOMY. *Fourth Edition. Crown 8vo. 2s. 6d.*

**Primrose (Deborah).** A MODERN BŒOTIA. *Crown 8vo. 6s.*

PROTECTION AND INDUSTRY. By various Writers. *Crown 8vo. 1s. 6d. net.*

**Pugin and Rowlandson.** THE MICROCOSM OF LONDON, OR LONDON IN MINIA-TURE. With 104 Illustrations in colour. *In Three Volumes. Small 4to. £3, 3s. net.*

**'Q' (A. T. Quiller Couch).** THE GOLDEN POMP. A Procession of English Lyrics. *Second Edition. Crown 8vo. 2s. 6d. net.*

**Quevedo Villegas.** See Miniature Library.

**G.R. and E.S.** THE WOODHOUSE CORRESPONDENCE. *Crown 8vo. 6s.*

**Rackham (R. B.),** M.A. See Westminster Commentaries.

**Randolph (B. W.),** D.D., Principal of the Theological College, Ely. See Library of Devotion.

**Rannie (D. W.),** M.A. A STUDENT'S HISTORY OF SCOTLAND. *Cr. 8vo. 3s. 6d.*

**Rashdall (Hastings),** M.A., Fellow and Tutor of New College, Oxford. DOCTRINE AND DEVELOPMENT. *Crown 8vo. 6s.*

**Rawstorne (Lawrence, Esq.).** See Illustrated Pocket Library.

**A Real Paddy.** See Illustrated Pocket Library.

**Reason (W.),** M.A. See Social Questions Series.

**Redfern (W. B.),** Author of 'Ancient Wood and Iron Work in Cambridge,' etc. ROYAL AND HISTORIC GLOVES AND ANCIENT SHOES. Profusely Illustrated in colour and half-tone. *Quarto, £2, 2s. net.*

**Reynolds.** See Little Galleries.

**Roberts (M. E.).** See C. C. Channer.

**Robertson, (A.),** D.D., Lord Bishop of Exeter. REGNUM DEI. The Bampton Lectures of 1901. *Demy 8vo. 12s. 6d. net.*

**Robertson (C. Grant),** M.A., Fellow of All Souls' College, Oxford, Examiner in the Honour School of Modern History, Oxford, 1901-1904. SELECT STATUTES, CASES, AND CONSTITUTIONAL DOCUMENTS, 1660-1832. *Demy 8vo. 10s. 6d. net.*

**\*Robertson (Sir G. S.)** K.C.S.I. CHITRAL: The Story of a Minor Siege. With numerous Illustrations, Map and Plans. *Fourth Edition. Crown 8vo. 2s. 6d. net.*

**Robinson (A. W.),** M.A. See Churchman's Bible.

**Robinson (Cecilia).** THE MINISTRY OF DEACONESSES. With an Introduction by the late Archbishop of Canterbury. *Crown 8vo. 3s. 6d.*

**Rochefoucauld (La).** See Little Library.

**Rodwell (G.),** B.A. NEW TESTAMENT GREEK. A Course for Beginners. With a Preface by WALTER LOCK, D.D., Warden of Keble College. *Fcap. 8vo. 3s. 6d.*

**Roe (Fred).** ANCIENT COFFERS AND CUPBOARDS: Their History and Description. With many Illustrations. *Quarto. £3, 3s. net.*

**Rogers (A. G. L.),** M.A., Editor of the last volume of 'The History of Agriculture and Prices in England.' See Books on Business.

**Romney.** See Little Galleries.

**Roscoe (E. S.).** ROBERT HARLEY, EARL OF OXFORD. Illustrated. *Demy 8vo. 7s. 6d.* This is the only life of Harley in existence. See also The Little Guides.

**Rose (Edward).** THE ROSE READER. With numerous Illustrations. *Crown 8vo. 2s. 6d. Also in 4 Parts. Parts I. and II. 6d. each ; Part III. 8d. ; Part IV. 10d.*

**Rubie (A. E.),** D.D., Head Master of College, Eltham. See Junior School Books.

**Russell (W. Clark).** THE LIFE OF ADMIRAL LORD COLLINGWOOD. With Illustrations by F. BRANGWYN. *Fourth Edition. Crown 8vo. 6s.* A Colonial Edition is also published.

**St. Anselm.** See Library of Devotion.

**St. Augustine.** See Library of Devotion.

**'Saki' (H. Munro).** REGINALD. *Second Edition. Fcap. 8vo. 2s. 6d. net.*

**Sales (St. Francis de).** See Library of Devotion.

**Salmon (A. L.).** A POPULAR GUIDE TO DEVON. *Medium 8vo. 6d. net.* See also The Little Guides.

**Sargeaunt (J.),** M.A. ANNALS OF WESTMINSTER SCHOOL. With numerous Illustrations. *Demy 8vo. 7s. 6d.*

**Sathas (C.).** See Byzantine Texts.

**Schmitt (John).** See Byzantine Texts.
**Scott, (A. M.)** WINSTON SPENCER CHURCHILL. With Portraits and Illustrations.
*Crown 8vo.* 3s. 6d.
**Seeley (H. G.)** F.R.S. DRAGONS OF THE AIR. With many Illustrations. *Cr. 8vo.* 6s.
**\*Selincourt (E. de),** M.A. THE POEMS OF JOHN KEATS. With an Introduction
and Notes, and a Portrait in Photogravure. *Demy 8vo.* 7s. 6d. net.
**Sells (V. P.),** M.A. THE MECHANICS OF DAILY LIFE. Illustrated. *Cr. 8vo.* 2s. 6d.
**Selous (Edmund).** TOMMY SMITH'S ANIMALS. Illustrated by G. W. Ord.
*Third Edition. Fcap. 8vo.* 2s. 6d.
**Settle (J. H.).** ANECDOTES OF SOLDIERS. *Crown 8vo.* 3s. 6d. net.
A Colonial Edition is also published.
**Shakespeare (William).**
THE FOUR FOLIOS, 1623; 1632; 1664; 1685. Each *Four Guineas net,* or a complete
set, *Twelve Guineas net.*
**The Arden Shakespeare.**
*Demy 8vo.* 2s. 6d. net each volume. General Editor, W. J. Craig. An Edition of
Shakespeare in single Plays. Edited with a full Introduction, Textual Notes, and a
Commentary at the foot of the page.
HAMLET. Edited by Edward Dowden, Litt.D.
ROMEO AND JULIET. Edited by Edward Dowden, Litt.D.
KING LEAR. Edited by W. J. Craig.
JULIUS CAESAR. Edited by M. Macmillan, M.A.
THE TEMPEST. Edited by Moreton Luce.
OTHELLO. Edited by H. C. Hart.
TITUS ANDRONICUS. Edited by H. B. Baildon.
CYMBELINE. Edited by Edward Dowden.
THE MERRY WIVES OF WINDSOR. Edited by H. C. Hart.
A MIDSUMMER NIGHT'S DREAM. Edited by H. Cuningham.
KING HENRY V. Edited by H. A. Evans.
ALL'S WELL THAT ENDS WELL. Edited by W. O. Brigstocke.
THE TAMING OF THE SHREW. Edited by R. Warwick Bond.
TIMON OF ATHENS. Edited by K. Deighton.
**The Little Quarto Shakespeare.** Edited by W. J. Craig. With Introductions and Notes.
*Pott 16mo. In 40 Volumes. Leather, price* 1s. net each volume.
See also Methuen's Universal Library.
**Sharp (A.).** VICTORIAN POETS. *Crown 8vo.* 2s. 6d.
**Sharp (Mrs. E. A.).** See Little Books on Art.
**Shedlock (J. S.).** THE PIANOFORTE SONATA: Its Origin and Development.
*Crown 8vo.* 5s.
**Shelley (Percy B.).** ADONAIS; an Elegy on the death of John Keats, Author of
'Endymion,' etc. Pisa. From the types of Didot, 1821. 2s. net.
See also Methuen's Universal Library.
**Sherwell (Arthur),** M.A. See Social Questions Series.
**\*Shipley (Mary E.).** AN ENGLISH CHURCH HISTORY FOR CHILDREN.
With a Preface by the Bishop of Gibraltar, late Professor of Ecclesiastical History at King's
College, London. With Maps and Illustrations. Part I. *Crown 8vo.* 2s. 6d. net.
**Sichel (Walter).** DISRAELI: A Study in Personality and Ideas. With 3 Portraits.
*Demy 8vo.* 12s. 6d. net.
A Colonial Edition is also published.
See also Oxford Biographies.
**Sime (J.).** See Little Books on Art.
**Simonson (G. A.).** FRANCESCO GUARDI. With 41 Plates. *Royal folio.* £2, 2s. net.
**Sketchley (R. E. D.).** See Little Books on Art.
**Skipton (H. P. K.).** See Little Books on Art.
**Sladen (Douglas).** SICILY. With over 200 Illustrations. *Crown 8vo.* 5s. net.
**Small (Evan),** M.A. THE EARTH. An Introduction to Physiography. Illustrated.
*Crown 8vo.* 2s. 6d.
**Smallwood, (M. G.).** See Little Books on Art.
**Smedley (F. E.).** See Illustrated Pocket Library.
**Smith (Adam).** THE WEALTH OF NATIONS. Edited with an Introduction and
numerous Notes by Edwin Cannan, M.A. *Two volumes. Demy 8vo.* 21s. net.
See also Methuen's Universal Library.
**Smith (Horace and James).** See Little Library.
**Snell (F. J.).** A BOOK OF EXMOOR. Illustrated. *Crown 8vo.* 6s.
**Sophocles.** See Classical Translations.

**Sornet (L. A.),** Modern Language Master at King Edward School, Birmingham.
See Junior School Books.

**South (Wilton E.), M.A.** See Junior School Books.

**Southey (R.)** ENGLISH SEAMEN. Edited, with an Introduction, by DAVID HANNAY.
Vol. I. (Howard, Clifford, Hawkins, Drake, Cavendish). *Second Edition. Crown 8vo. 6s.*
Vol. II. (Richard Hawkins, Grenville, Essex, and Raleigh). *Crown 8vo. 6s.*

**Spence (C. H.),** M.A., Clifton College. See School Examination Series.

**Spooner (W. A.),** M.A., Warden of New College, Oxford. See Leaders of Religion.

**Stanbridge (J. W.),** B.D., late Canon of York, and sometime Fellow of St. John's College, Oxford. See Library of Devotion.

**'Stancliffe.'** GOLF DO'S AND DONT'S. *Second Edition. Fcap. 8vo. 1s.*

**Stedman (A. M. M.), M.A.**

INITIA LATINA: Easy Lessons on Elementary Accidence. *Seventh Edition. Fcap. 8vo. 1s.*

FIRST LATIN LESSONS. *Eighth Edition. Crown 8vo. 2s.*

FIRST LATIN READER. With Notes adapted to the Shorter Latin Primer and Vocabulary. *Sixth Edition revised. 18mo. 1s. 6d.*

EASY SELECTIONS FROM CÆSAR. The Helvetian War. *Second Edition. 18mo. 1s.*

EASY SELECTIONS FROM LIVY. Part I. The Kings of Rome. 18mo. *Second Edition. 1s. 6d.*

EASY LATIN PASSAGES FOR UNSEEN TRANSLATION. *Tenth Edition. Fcap. 8vo. 1s. 6d.*

EXEMPLA LATINA. First Exercises in Latin Accidence. With Vocabulary. *Third Edition. Crown 8vo. 1s.*

EASY LATIN EXERCISES ON THE SYNTAX OF THE SHORTER AND REVISED LATIN PRIMER. With Vocabulary. *Ninth and Cheaper Edition, rewritten. Crown 8vo. 1s. 6d. Original Edition. 2s. 6d.* KEY, *3s. net.*

THE LATIN COMPOUND SENTENCE: Rules and Exercises. *Second Edition. Crown 8vo. 1s. 6d.* With Vocabulary. *2s.*

NOTANDA QUAEDAM: Miscellaneous Latin Exercises on Common Rules and Idioms. *Fourth Edition. Fcap. 8vo. 1s. 6d.* With Vocabulary. *2s.* Key, *2s. net.*

LATIN VOCABULARIES FOR REPETITION: Arranged according to Subjects. *Twelfth Edition. Fcap. 8vo. 1s. 6d.*

A VOCABULARY OF LATIN IDIOMS. 18mo. *Second Edition. 1s.*

STEPS TO GREEK. *Second Edition, revised. 18mo. 1s.*

A SHORTER GREEK PRIMER. *Crown 8vo. 1s. 6d.*

EASY GREEK PASSAGES FOR UNSEEN TRANSLATION. *Third Edition, revised. Fcap. 8vo. 1s. 6d.*

GREEK VOCABULARIES FOR REPETITION. Arranged according to Subjects. *Third Edition. Fcap. 8vo. 1s. 6d.*

GREEK TESTAMENT SELECTIONS. For the use of Schools. With Introduction, Notes, and Vocabulary. *Third Edition. Fcap. 8vo. 2s. 6d.*

STEPS TO FRENCH. *Sixth Edition. 18mo. 8d.*

FIRST FRENCH LESSONS. *Sixth Edition, revised. Crown 8vo. 1s.*

EASY FRENCH PASSAGES FOR UNSEEN TRANSLATION. *Fifth Edition. revised. Fcap. 8vo. 1s. 6d.*

EASY FRENCH EXERCISES ON ELEMENTARY SYNTAX. With Vocabulary. *Fourth Edition. Crown 8vo. 2s. 6d.* KEY, *3s. net.*

FRENCH VOCABULARIES FOR REPETITION: Arranged according to Subjects. *Twelfth Edition. Fcap. 8vo. 1s.*

**Steel (R. Elliott),** M.A., F.C.S. THE WORLD OF SCIENCE. Including Chemistry, Heat, Light, Sound, Magnetism, Electricity, Botany, Zoology, Physiology, Astronomy, and Geology. 147 Illustrations. *Second Edition. Crown 8vo. 2s. 6d.* See also School Examination Series.

**Stephenson (C.),** of the Technical College, Bradford, and **Suddards (F.)** of the Yorkshire College, Leeds. ORNAMENTAL DESIGN FOR WOVEN FABRICS. Illustrated. *Demy 8vo. Second Edition. 7s. 6d.*

**Stephenson (J.),** M.A. THE CHIEF TRUTHS OF THE CHRISTIAN FAITH. *Crown 8vo. 3s. 6d.*

**Sterne (Laurence).** See Little Library.

**Sterry (W.),** M.A. ANNALS OF ETON COLLEGE. With numerous Illustrations. *Demy 8vo. 7s. 6d.*

**Steuart (Katherine).** BY ALLAN WATER. *Second Edition. Crown 8vo. 6s.*

**Stevenson (R. L.).** THE LETTERS OF ROBERT LOUIS STEVENSON TO HIS FAMILY AND FRIENDS. Selected and Edited, with Notes and Introductions, by SIDNEY COLVIN. *Sixth and Cheaper Edition. Crown 8vo. 12s.*

A 3

LIBRARY EDITION. *Demy 8vo.* 2 *vols.* 25s. *net.*
    A Colonial Edition is also published.
VAILIMA LETTERS. With an Etched Portrait by WILLIAM STRANG. *Fourth Edition.*
*Crown 8vo. Buckram.* 6s.
    A Colonial Edition is also published.
THE LIFE OF R. L. STEVENSON. See G. Balfour.
**Stevenson (M. I.).** FROM SARANAC TO THE MARQUESAS. Being Letters written
by Mrs. M. I. STEVENSON during 1887-8 to her sister, Miss JANE WHYTE BALFOUR. With
an Introduction by GEORGE W. BALFOUR, M.D., LL.D., F.R.S.S. *Crown 8vo.* 6s. *net.*
    A Colonial Edition is also published.
**Stoddart (Anna M.).** See Oxford Biographies.
**Stone (E. D.),** M.A., late Assistant Master at Eton. SELECTIONS FROM THE
ODYSSEY. *Fcap. 8vo.* 1s. 6d.
**Stone (S. J.).** POEMS AND HYMNS. With a Memoir by F. G. ELLERTON, M.A.
With Portrait. *Crown 8vo.* 6s.
**Straker (F.),** Assoc. of the Institute of Bankers, and Lecturer to the London Chamber of
Commerce. See Books on Business.
**Streane (A. W.),** D.D. See Churchman's Bible.
**Stroud (H.),** D.Sc., M.A., Professor of Physics in the Durham College of Science, Newcastle-
on-Tyne. See Textbooks of Technology.
**Strutt (Joseph).** THE SPORTS AND PASTIMES OF THE PEOPLE OF
ENGLAND. Illustrated by many engravings. Revised by J. CHARLES COX, LL.D., F.S.A.
*Quarto.* 21s. *net.*
**Stuart (Capt. Donald).** THE STRUGGLE FOR PERSIA. With a Map. *Crown 8vo.* 6s.
**Sturch (F.),** Manual Training Instructor to the Surrey County Council. SOLUTIONS TO
THE CITY AND GUILDS QUESTIONS IN MANUAL INSTRUCTION DRAW-
ING. *Imp. 4to.* 2s.
**Suckling (Sir John).** FRAGMENTA AUREA: a Collection of all the Incomparable
Peeces, written by. And published by a friend to perpetuate his memory. Printed by his
own copies.
    Printed for HUMPHREY MOSELEY, and are to be sold at his shop, at the sign of the Princes
Arms in St. Paul's Churchyard, 1646.
**Suddards (F.).** See C. Stephenson.
**Surtees (R. S.).** See Illustrated Pocket Library.
**Swift (Jonathan).** THE JOURNAL TO STELLA. Edited by G. A. AITKEN. *Cr. 8vo.* 6s.
**Symes (J. E.),** M.A. THE FRENCH REVOLUTION. *Second Edition. Crown 8vo.* 2s. 6d.
**Syrett (Netta).** See Little Blue Books.
**Tacitus.** AGRICOLA. With Introduction, Notes, Map, etc. By R. F. DAVIS, M.A.,
late Assistant Master at Weymouth College. *Fcap. 8vo.* 2s.
GERMANIA. By the same Editor. *Fcap. 8vo.* 2s. See also Classical Translations.
**Tauler (J.).** See Library of Devotion.
**Taunton (E. L.).** A HISTORY OF THE JESUITS IN ENGLAND. With Illustra-
tions. *Demy 8vo.* 21s. *net.*
**Taylor (A. E.).** THE ELEMENTS OF METAPHYSICS. *Demy 8vo.* 10s. 6d. *net.*
**Taylor (F. G.),** M.A. See Commercial Series.
**Taylor (I. A.).** See Oxford Biographies.
**Taylor (T. M.),** M.A., Fellow of Gonville and Caius College, Cambridge. A CONSTI-
TUTIONAL AND POLITICAL HISTORY OF ROME. *Crown 8vo.* 7s. 6d.
**Tennyson (Alfred, Lord).** THE EARLY POEMS OF. Edited, with Notes and an
Introduction, by J. CHURTON COLLINS, M.A. *Crown 8vo.* 6s.
IN MEMORIAM, MAUD, AND THE PRINCESS. Edited by J. CHURTON COLLINS, M.A.
*Crown 8vo.* 6s. See also Little Library.
**Terry (C. S.).** See Oxford Biographies.
**Terton (Alice).** LIGHTS AND SHADOWS IN A HOSPITAL. *Crown 8vo.* 3s. 6d.
**Thackeray (W. M.).** See Little Library.
**Theobald (F. W.),** M.A. INSECT LIFE. Illustrated. *Second Ed. Revised. Cr. 8vo.* 2s. 6d.
**Thompson (A. H.).** See The Little Guides.
**Tileston (Mary W.).** DAILY STRENGTH FOR DAILY NEEDS. *Tenth Edition.*
*Fcap. 8vo.* 2s. 6d. *net.* Also editions in superior binding 5s. and 6s.
**Tompkins (H. W.),** F.R.H.S. See The Little Guides.
**Townley (Lady Susan).** MY CHINESE NOTE-BOOK. With 16 Illustrations and 2
Maps. *Third Edition. Demy 8vo.* 10s. 6d. *net.*
    A Colonial Edition is also published.
**Toynbee (Paget),** M.A., D.Litt. DANTE STUDIES AND RESEARCHES. *Demy
8vo.* 10s. 6d. *net.* See also Oxford Biographies.

**Trench (Herbert).** DEIRDRE WED: and Other Poems. *Crown 8vo.* 5s.
**Trevelyan (G. M.),** Fellow of Trinity College, Cambridge. ENGLAND UNDER THE STUARTS. With Maps and Plans. *Demy 8vo.* 10s. 6d. *net.*
**Troutbeck (G. E.).** See The Little Guides.
**Tuckwell (Gertrude).** See Social Questions Series.
**Twining (Louisa).** See Social Questions Series.
**Tyler (E. A.),** B.A., F.C.S., Head of Chemical Department, Swansea Technical College. See Junior School Books.
**Tyrell-Gill (Frances).** See Little Books on Art.
**Vaughan (Henry).** See Little Library.
**Voegelin (A.),** M.A. See Junior Examination Series.
**Wade (G. W.),** D.D. OLD TESTAMENT HISTORY. With Maps. *Third Edition.* *Crown 8vo.* 6s.
**Wagner (Richard).** See A. L. Cleather.
**Wall (J. C.)** DEVILS. Illustrated by the Author and from photographs. *Demy 8vo.* 4s. 6d. *net.* See also The Antiquary's Books.
**Walters (H. B.).** See Little Books on Art.
**Walton (Izaac) and Cotton (Charles).** See Illustrated Pocket Library, Methuen's Universal Library, and Little Library.
**Warmelo (D. S. Van).** ON COMMANDO. With Portrait. *Crown 8vo.* 3s. 6d.
**Waterhouse (Mrs. Alfred).** WITH THE SIMPLE-HEARTED: Little Homiliesto Women in Country Places. *Small Pott 8vo.* 2s. *net.* See also Little Library.
**Weatherhead (T. C.),** M.A. EXAMINATION PAPERS IN HORACE. *Crown 8vo.* 2s. See also Junior Examination Series.
**Webb (W. T.).** See Little Blue Books.
**Webber (F. C.).** See Textbooks of Technology.
**Wells (Sidney H.).** See Textbooks of Technology.
**Wells (J.),** M.A., Fellow and Tutor of Wadham College. OXFORD AND OXFORD LIFE. By Members of the University. *Third Edition* *Crown 8vo.* 3s. 6d.
A SHORT HISTORY OF ROME. *Fifth Edition.* With 3 Maps. *Cr. 8vo.* 3s. 6d.
    This book is intended for the Middle and Upper Forms of Public Schools and for Pass Students at the Universities. It contains copious Tables, etc. See also The Little Guides.
**Wetmore (Helen C.).** THE LAST OF THE GREAT SCOUTS ('Buffalo Bill'). With Illustrations. *Second Edition.* *Demy 8vo.* 6s.
**Whibley (C.).** See Henley and Whibley.
**Whibley (L.),** M.A., Fellow of Pembroke College, Cambridge. GREEK OLIGARCHIES: THEIR ORGANISATION AND CHARACTER. *Crown 8vo.* 6s.
**Whitaker (G. H.),** M.A. See Churchman's Bible.
**White (Gilbert).** THE NATURAL HISTORY OF SELBORNE. Edited by L. C. MIALL, F.R.S., assisted by W. WARDE FOWLER, M.A. *Crown 8vo.* 6s. See also Methuen's Universal Library.
**Whitfield (E. E.).** See Commercial Series.
**Whitehead (A. W.).** GASPARD DE COLIGNY. With many Illustrations. *Demy 8vo.* 12s. 6d. *net.*
**Whitley (Miss).** See Social Questions Series.
**Whyte (A. G.),** B.Sc., Editor of *Electrical Investments.* See Books on Business.
**Wilberforce (Wilfrid)** See Little Books on Art.
**Wilde (Oscar).** DE PROFUNDIS. *Crown 8vo.* 5s. *net.*
    Also a Limited Edition on Japanese Vellum. *Demy 8vo.* £2, 2s. *net*; and a Limited Edition on hand-made paper. *Demy 8vo.* 21s. *net.* A Colonial Edition is also published.
**Wilkins (W. H.),** B.A. See Social Questions Series.
**Wilkinson (J. Frome).** See Social Questions Series.
**Williamson (W.).** THE BRITISH GARDENER. Illustrated. *Demy 8vo.* 10s. 6d.
**Williamson (W.),** B.A. EASY DICTATION AND SPELLING. *Third Edition.* *Fcap. 8vo.* 1s. See also Junior Examination Series and Junior School Books.
**Wilmot-Buxton (E. M.).** MAKERS OF EUROPE. *Crown 8vo.* *Third Edition.* 3s. 6d
    A Text-book of European History for Middle Forms.
THE ANCIENT WORLD. With Maps and Illustrations. *Crown 8vo.* 3s. 6d.
    See also The Beginner's Books.
**Wilson (Bishop).** See Library of Devotion.
**Wilson (Beckles).** LORD STRATHCONA: the Story of his Life. Illustrate 8vo. 7s. 6d.
    A Colonial Edition is also published.
**Wilson (A. J.),** Editor of the *Investor's Review*, City Editor of the *Daily* Books on Business.
**Wilson (H. A.).** See Books on Business.

**Wilton (Richard)**, M.A.   LYRA PASTORALIS: Songs of Nature, Church, and Home. *Pott 8vo.* *2s. 6d.*
   A volume of devotional poems.
**Winbolt (S. E.)**, M.A., Assistant Master in Christ's Hospital.   EXERCISES IN LATIN ACCIDENCE.   *Crown 8vo.* *1s. 6d.*
   An elementary book adapted for Lower Forms to accompany the Shorter Latin Primer.
LATIN HEXAMETER VERSE: An Aid to Composition. *Crown 8vo.* *3s. 6d.* KEY, *5s. net.*
**Windle (B. C. A.)**, D.Sc., F.R.S.   See Antiquary's Books and The Little Guides.
**Winterbotham (Canon)**, M.A., B.Sc., LL.B.   See Churchman's Library.
**Wood (J. A. E.)**.   See Textbooks of Technology.
**Wordsworth (Christopher)**.   See Antiquary's Books.
**Wordsworth (W.)**.   See Little Library.
**Wordsworth (W.) and Coleridge (S. T.)**.   See Little Library.
**Wright (Arthur)**, M.A., Fellow of Queen's College, Cambridge.   See Churchman's Library.
**Wright (Sophie)**.   GERMAN VOCABULARIES FOR REPETITION. *Fcap. 8vo.* *1s. 6d.*
*\*Wrong, (George M.)**, Professor of History in the University of Toronto.   THE EARL OF ELGIN.   With Illustrations. *Demy 8vo.* *7s. 6d. net.*
**Wylde (A. B.)**.   MODERN ABYSSINIA.   With a Map and a Portrait. *Demy 8vo.* *15s. net.*
**Wyndham (G.)**, M.P.   THE POEMS OF WILLIAM SHAKESPEARE.   With an Introduction and Notes. *Demy 8vo. Buckram, gilt top.* *10s. 6d.*
**Wyon (R.) and Prance (G.)**.   THE LAND OF THE BLACK MOUNTAIN.   Being a description of Montenegro.   With 40 Illustrations. *Crown 8vo.* *6s.*
   A Colonial Edition is also published.
**Yeats (W. B.)**.   AN ANTHOLOGY OF IRISH VERSE. *Revised and Enlarged Edition. Crown 8vo.* *3s. 6d.*
**Yendis (M.)**.   THE GREAT RED FROG.   A Story told in 40 Coloured Pictures. *Fcap. 8vo.* *1s. net.*
**Young (Filson)**.   THE COMPLETE MOTORIST.   With 138 Illustrations. *Third Edition. Demy 8vo.* *12s. 6d. net.*
**Young (T. M.)**.   THE AMERICAN COTTON INDUSTRY: A Study of Work and Workers.   With an Introduction by ELIJAH HELM, Secretary to the Manchester Chamber of Commerce. *Crown 8vo. Cloth, 2s. 6d. ; paper boards, 1s. 6d.*
**Zenker (E. V.)**.   ANARCHISM. *Demy 8vo.* *7s. 6d.*
**Zimmern (Antonia)**.   WHAT DO WE KNOW CONCERNING ELECTRICITY? *Crown 8vo.* *1s. 6d. net.*

## Antiquary's Books, The

General Editor, J. CHARLES COX, LL.D., F.S.A.

A series of volumes dealing with various branches of English Antiquities; comprehensive and popular, as well as accurate and scholarly.

ENGLISH MONASTIC LIFE.   By the Right Rev. Abbot Gasquet, O.S.B.   Illustrated. *Second Edition, revised. Demy 8vo.* *7s. 6d. net.*
REMAINS OF THE PREHISTORIC AGE IN ENGLAND.   By B. C. A. Windle, D.Sc., F.R.S.   With numerous Illustrations and Plans. *Demy 8vo.* *7s. 6d. net.*
OLD SERVICE BOOKS OF THE ENGLISH CHURCH.   By Christopher Wordsworth, M.A., and Henry Littlehales.   With Coloured and other Illustrations. *Demy 8vo.* *7s. 6d. net.*
CELTIC ART.   By J. Romilly Allen, F.S.A.   With numerous Illustrations and Plans. *Demy 8vo.* *7s. 6d. net.*
*ARCHÆOLOGY AND FALSE ANTIQUITIES.   By R. Munro, LL.D.   With numerous Illustrations. *Demy 8vo.* *7s. 6d. net.*
SHRINES OF BRITISH SAINTS.   By J. C. WALL.   With numerous Illustrations and Plans. *Demy 8vo.* *7s. 6d. net.*

## Beginner's Books, The

FRENCH RHYMES.   By Henri Blouet.   Illustrated. *Fcap. 8vo.* *1s.*
STORIES FROM ENGLISH HISTORY.   By E. M. Wilmot-Buxton, Author of 'Makers of ' *Fcap. 8vo.* *1s.*

## Business, Books on

A series . . . *Crown 8vo.* *2s. 6d. net.*
financial act . . . umes dealing with all the most important aspects of commercial and
   The volumes are intended to treat separately all the considerable

industries and forms of business, and to explain accurately and clearly what they do and how they do it. The first Twelve volumes are—

PORTS AND DOCKS. By Douglas Owen.
RAILWAYS. By E. R. McDermott.
THE STOCK EXCHANGE. By Chas. Duguid. *Second Edition.*
THE BUSINESS OF INSURANCE. By A. J. Wilson.
THE ELECTRICAL INDUSTRY: LIGHTING, TRACTION, AND POWER. By A. G. Whyte, B.Sc.
THE SHIPBUILDING INDUSTRY. By David Pollock, M.I.N.A.
THE MONEY MARKET. By F. Straker.
THE BUSINESS SIDE OF AGRICULTURE. By A. G. L. Rogers, M.A.
LAW IN BUSINESS. By H. A. Wilson.
THE BREWING INDUSTRY. By Julian L. Baker, F.I.C., F.C.S.
THE AUTOMOBILE INDUSTRY. By G. de H. Stone.
MINING AND MINING INVESTMENTS. By 'A. Moil.'
*THE BUSINESS OF ADVERTISING. By Clarence G. Moran, Barrister-at-Law. Illustrated.
*TRADE UNIONS. By G. Drage.
*CIVIL ENGINEERING. By T. Claxton Fidler, M.Inst. C.E. Illustrated.
*THE COAL INDUSTRY. By Ernest Aves. Illustrated.

## Byzantine Texts

### Edited by J. B. BURY, M.A., Litt.D.

A series of texts of Byzantine Historians, edited by English and foreign scholars.

ZACHARIAH OF MITYLENE. Translated by F. J. Hamilton, D.D., and E. W. Brooks. *Demy 8vo. 12s. 6d. net.*
EVAGRIUS. Edited by Léon Parmentier and M. Bidez. *Demy 8vo. 10s. 6d. net.*
THE HISTORY OF PSELLUS. Edited by C. Sathas. *Demy 8vo. 15s. net.*
ECTHESIS CHRONICA. Edited by Professor Lambros. *Demy 8vo. 7s. 6d. net.*
THE CHRONICLE OF MOREA. Edited by John Schmitt. *Demy 8vo. 15s. net.*

## Churchman's Bible, The

### General Editor, J. H. BURN, B.D., F.R.S.E.

A series of Expositions on the Books of the Bible, which will be of service to the general reader in the practical and devotional study of the Sacred Text.

Each Book is provided with a full and clear Introductory Section, in which is stated what is known or conjectured respecting the date and occasion of the composition of the Book, and any other particulars that may help to elucidate its meaning as a whole. The Exposition is divided into sections of a convenient length, corresponding as far as possible with the divisions of the Church Lectionary. The Translation of the Authorised Version is printed in full, such corrections as are deemed necessary being placed in footnotes.

THE EPISTLE TO THE GALATIANS. Edited by A. W. Robinson, M.A. *Second Edition. Fcap. 8vo. 1s. 6d. net.*
ECCLESIASTES. Edited by A. W. Streane, D.D. *Fcap. 8vo. 1s. 6d. net.*
THE EPISTLE TO THE PHILIPPIANS. Edited by C. R. D. Biggs, D.D. *Fcap 8vo. 1s. 6d. net.*
THE EPISTLE OF ST. JAMES. Edited by H. W. Fulford, M.A. *Fcap. 8vo 1s. 6d. net.*
ISAIAH. Edited by W. E. Barnes, D.D. *Two Volumes. Fcap. 8vo. 2s. net each.* With Map.
THE EPISTLE OF ST. PAUL THE APOSTLE TO THE EPHESIANS. Edited by G. H. Whitaker, M.A. *Fcap. 8vo. 1s. 6d. net.*

## Churchman's Library, The

### General Editor, J. H. BURN, B.D., F.R.S.E.,

A series of volumes upon such questions as are occupying the attention of Church people at the present time. The Editor has enlisted the services of a band of scholars, who, having made a special study of their respective subjects, are in a position to furnish the best results of modern research accurately and attractively.

THE BEGINNINGS OF ENGLISH CHRISTIANITY. By W. E. Collins, M.A. With Map. *Crown 8vo. 3s. 6d.*
SOME NEW TESTAMENT PROBLEMS. By Arthur Wright, M.A. *Crown 8vo. 6s.*

THE KINGDOM OF HEAVEN HERE AND HEREAFTER. By Canon Winterbotham, M.A., B.Sc., LL.B. *Crown 8vo.* 3s. 6d.
THE WORKMANSHIP OF THE PRAYER BOOK: Its Literary and Liturgical Aspects. By J. Dowden, D.D. *Second Edition. Crown 8vo.* 3s. 6d.
EVOLUTION. By F. B. Jevons, M.A., Litt.D. *Crown 8vo.* 3s. 6d.
THE OLD TESTAMENT AND THE NEW SCHOLARSHIP. By J. W. Peters, D.D. *Crown 8vo.* 6s.
THE CHURCHMAN'S INTRODUCTION TO THE OLD TESTAMENT. By A. M. Mackay, B.A. *Crown 8vo.* 3s. 6d.
THE CHURCH OF CHRIST. By E. T. Green, M.A. *Crown 8vo.* 6s.
COMPARATIVE THEOLOGY. By J. A. MacCulloch. *Crown 8vo.* 6s.

## Classical Translations

Edited by H. F. Fox, M.A., Fellow and Tutor of Brasenose College, Oxford.

*Crown 8vo.*

**A series** of Translations from the Greek and Latin Classics. The Publishers have enlisted the services of some of the best Oxford and Cambridge Scholars, and it is their intention that the series shall be distinguished by literary excellence as well as by scholarly accuracy.

ÆSCHYLUS—Agamemnon, Choephoroe, Eumenides. Translated by Lewis Campbell, LL.D. 5s.
CICERO—De Oratore I. Translated by E. N. P. Moor, M.A. 3s. 6d.
CICERO—Select Orations (Pro Milone, Pro Mureno, Philippic II., in Catilinam). Translated by H. E. D. Blakiston, M.A. 5s.
CICERO—De Natura Deorum. Translated by F. Brooks, M.A. 3s. 6d.
CICERO—De Officiis. Translated by G. B. Gardiner, M.A. 2s. 6d.
HORACE—The Odes and Epodes. Translated by A. D. Godley, M.A. 2s.
LUCIAN—Six Dialogues (Nigrinus, Icaro-Menippus, The Cock, The Ship, The Parasite, The Lover of Falsehood). Translated by S. T. Irwin, M.A. 3s. 6d.
SOPHOCLES—Electra and Ajax. Translated by E. D. A. Morshead, M.A. 2s. 6d.
TACITUS—Agricola and Germania. Translated by R. B. Townshend. 2s. 6d.
THE SATIRES OF JUVENAL. Translated by S. G. Owen. 2s. 6d.

## Commercial Series, Methuen's

Edited by H. DE B. GIBBINS, Litt.D., M.A.

*Crown 8vo.*

A series intended to assist students and young men preparing for a commercial career, by supplying useful handbooks of a clear and practical character, dealing with those subjects which are absolutely essential in the business life.

COMMERCIAL EDUCATION IN THEORY AND PRACTICE. By E. E. Whitfield, M.A. 5s.
An introduction to Methuen's Commercial Series treating the question of Commercial Education fully from both the point of view of the teacher and of the parent.
BRITISH COMMERCE AND COLONIES FROM ELIZABETH TO VICTORIA. By H. de B. Gibbins, Litt.D., M.A. *Third Edition.* 2s.
COMMERCIAL EXAMINATION PAPERS. By H. de B. Gibbins, Litt.D., M.A. 1s. 6d.
THE ECONOMICS OF COMMERCE. By H. de B. Gibbins, Litt.D., M.A. 1s. 6d.
A GERMAN COMMERCIAL READER. By S. E. Bally. With Vocabulary. 2s.
A COMMERCIAL GEOGRAPHY OF THE BRITISH EMPIRE. By L. W. Lyde, M.A. *Fourth Edition.* 2s.
A COMMERCIAL GEOGRAPHY OF FOREIGN NATIONS. By F. C. Boon, B.A. 2s.
A PRIMER OF BUSINESS. By S. Jackson, M.A. *Third Edition.* 1s. 6d.
COMMERCIAL ARITHMETIC. By F. G. Taylor, M.A. *Third Edition.* 1s. 6d.
FRENCH COMMERCIAL CORRESPONDENCE. By S. E. Bally. With Vocabulary. *Third Edition.* 2s.
GERMAN COMMERCIAL CORRESPONDENCE. By S. E. Bally. With Vocabulary. 2s. 6d.
A FRENCH COMMERCIAL READER. By S. E. Bally. With Vocabulary. *Second Edition.* 2s.
PRECIS WRITING AND OFFICE CORRESPONDENCE. By E. E. Whitfield, M.A. *Second Edition.* 2s.
A GUIDE TO PROFESSIONS AND BUSINESS. By H. Jones. 1s. 6d.
THE PRINCIPLES OF BOOK-KEEPING BY DOUBLE ENTRY. By J. E. B. M'Allen, M.A. 2s.
COMMERCIAL LAW. By W. Douglas Edwards. 2s.

## Connoisseur's Library, The
*Wide Royal 8vo.  25s. net.*

A sumptuous series of 20 books on art, written by experts for collectors, superbly illustrated in photogravure, collotype, and colour. The technical side of the art is duly treated. The first volumes are—

MEZZOTINTS. By Cyril Davenport. With 40 Plates in Photogravure.
PORCELAIN. By Edward Dillon. With 19 Plates in Colour, 20 in Collotype, and 5 in Photogravure.
*MINIATURES. By Dudley Heath. With 9 Plates in Colour, 15 in Collotype, and 15 in Photogravure.
*IVORIES. By A. Maskell. With 80 Plates in Collotype and Photogravure.

## Devotion, The Library of
With Introductions and (where necessary) Notes.
*Small Pott 8vo, cloth, 2s. ; leather, 2s. 6d. net.*

The masterpieces of devotional literature. The books are furnished with such Introductions and Notes as may be necessary to explain the standpoint of the author and the obvious difficulties of the text, without unnecessary intrusion between the author and the devout mind.

THE CONFESSIONS OF ST. AUGUSTINE. Edited by C. Bigg, D.D. *Third Edition.*
THE CHRISTIAN YEAR. Edited by Walter Lock, D.D. *Second Edition.*
THE IMITATION OF CHRIST. Edited by C. Bigg, D.D. *Fourth Edition.*
A BOOK OF DEVOTIONS. Edited by J. W. Stanbridge. B.D. *Second Edition.*
LYRA INNOCENTIUM. Edited by Walter Lock, D.D.
A SERIOUS CALL TO A DEVOUT AND HOLY LIFE. Edited by C. Bigg, D.D. *Second Edition.*
THE TEMPLE. Edited by E. C. S. Gibson, D.D.
A GUIDE TO ETERNITY. Edited by J. W. Stanbridge, B.D.
THE PSALMS OF DAVID. Edited by B. W. Randolph, D.D.
LYRA APOSTOLICA. Edited by Canon Scott Holland and Canon H. C. Beeching, M.A.
THE INNER WAY. By J. Tauler. Edited by A. W. Hutton, M.A.
THE THOUGHTS OF PASCAL. Edited by C. S. Jerram, M.A.
ON THE LOVE OF GOD. By St. Francis de Sales. Edited by W. J. Knox-Little, M.A.
A MANUAL OF CONSOLATION FROM THE SAINTS AND FATHERS. Edited by J. H. Burn, B.D.
THE SONG OF SONGS. Edited by B. Blaxland, M.A.
THE DEVOTIONS OF ST. ANSELM. Edited by C. C. J. Webb, M.A.
GRACE ABOUNDING. By John Bunyan. Edited by S. C. Freer, M.A.
BISHOP WILSON'S SACRA PRIVATA. Edited by A. E. Burn, B.D.
LYRA SACRA: A Book of Sacred Verse. Edited by H. C. Beeching, M.A, Canon of Westminster.
A DAY BOOK FROM THE SAINTS AND FATHERS. Edited by J. H. Burn, B.D.
HEAVENLY WISDOM. A Selection from the English Mystics. Edited by E. C. Gregory.
LIGHT, LIFE, and LOVE. A Selection from the German Mystics. Edited by W. R. Inge, M.A.

## Illustrated Pocket Library of Plain and Coloured Books, The
*Fcap 8vo.  3s. 6d. net each volume.*

A series, in small form, of some of the famous illustrated books of fiction and general literature. These are faithfully reprinted from the first or best editions without introduction or notes.

### COLOURED BOOKS

OLD COLOURED BOOKS. By George Paston. With 16 Coloured Plates. *Fcap. 8vo.* 2s. net.
THE LIFE AND DEATH OF JOHN MYTTON, ESQ. By Nimrod. With 18 Coloured Plates by Henry Alken and T. J. Rawlins. *Third Edition.* 3s. 6d. net.
  Also a limited edition on large Japanese paper. 30s. net.
THE LIFE OF A SPORTSMAN. By Nimrod. With 35 Coloured Plates by Henry Alken. 3s. 6d. net.
  Also a limited edition on large Japanese paper. 30s. net.
HANDLEY CROSS. By R. S. SURTEES. With 17 Coloured Plates and 100 Woodcuts in the Text by John Leech. 3s. 6d. net.
  Also a limited edition on large Japanese paper. 30s. net.
MR. SPONGE'S SPORTING TOUR. By R. S. Surtees. With 13 Coloured Plates and 90 Woodcuts in the Text by John Leech. 3s. 6d. net.
  Also a limited edition on large Japanese paper. 30s. net.

JORROCKS' JAUNTS AND JOLLITIES. By R. S. Surtees. With 15 Coloured Plates by H. Alken. 3s. 6d. net.
   Also a limited edition on large Japanese paper. 30s. net.
   This volume is reprinted from the extremely rare and costly edition of 1843, which contains Alken's very fine Illustrations instead of the usual ones by Phiz.
ASK MAMMA. By R. S. Surtees. With 13 Coloured Plates and 70 Woodcuts in the Text by John Leech. 3s. 6d. net.
   Also a limited edition on large Japanese paper. 30s. net.
THE ANALYSIS OF THE HUNTING FIELD. By R. S. Surtees. With 7 Coloured Plates by Henry Alken, and 43 Illustrations on Wood. 3s. 6d. net.
THE TOUR OF DR. SYNTAX IN SEARCH OF THE PICTURESQUE. By William Combe. With 30 Coloured Plates by T. Rowlandson. 3s. 6d. net.
   Also a limited edition on large Japanese paper. 30s. net.
THE TOUR OF DOCTOR SYNTAX IN SEARCH OF CONSOLATION. By William Combe. With 24 Coloured Plates by T. Rowlandson. 3s. 6d. net.
   Also a limited edition on large Japanese paper. 30s. net.
THE THIRD TOUR OF DOCTOR SYNTAX IN SEARCH OF A WIFE. By William Combe. With 24 Coloured Plates by T. Rowlandson. 3s. 6d. net.
   Also a limited edition on large Japanese paper. 30s. net.
THE HISTORY OF JOHNNY QUAE GENUS: the Little Foundling of the late Dr. Syntax. By the Author of 'The Three Tours.' With 24 Coloured Plates by Rowlandson. 3s. 6d. net.
   Also a limited edition on large Japanese paper. 30s. net.
THE ENGLISH DANCE OF DEATH, from the Designs of T. Rowlandson, with Metrical Illustrations by the Author of 'Doctor Syntax.' Two Volumes. 7s. net.
   This book contains 76 Coloured Plates.
   Also a limited edition on large Japanese paper. 30s. net.
THE DANCE OF LIFE: A Poem. By the Author of 'Doctor Syntax.' Illustrated with 26 Coloured Engravings by T. Rowlandson. 3s. 6d. net.
   Also a limited edition on large Japanese paper. 30s. net.
LIFE IN LONDON: or, the Day and Night Scenes of Jerry Hawthorn, Esq., and his Elegant Friend, Corinthian Tom. By Pierce Egan. With 36 Coloured Plates by I. R. and G. Cruikshank. With numerous Designs on Wood. 3s. 6d. net.
   Also a limited edition on large Japanese paper. 30s. net.
*REAL LIFE IN LONDON: or, the Rambles and Adventures of Bob Tallyho, Esq., and his Cousin, The Hon. Tom Dashall. By an Amateur (Pierce Egan). With 31 Coloured Plates by Alken and Rowlandson, etc. Two Volumes. 7s. net.
THE LIFE OF AN ACTOR. By Pierce Egan. With 27 Coloured Plates by Theodore Lane, and several Designs on Wood. 3s. 6d. net.
THE VICAR OF WAKEFIELD. By Oliver Goldsmith. With 24 Coloured Plates by T. Rowlandson. 3s. 6d. net.
   Also a limited edition on large Japanese paper. 30s. net.
   A reproduction of a very rare book.
THE MILITARY ADVENTURES OF JOHNNY NEWCOME. By an Officer. With 15 Coloured Plates by T. Rowlandson. 3s. 6d. net.
THE NATIONAL SPORTS OF GREAT BRITAIN. With Descriptions and 51 Coloured Plates by Henry Alken. 3s. 6d. net.
   Also a limited edition on large Japanese paper. 30s. net.
   This book is completely different from the large folio edition of 'National Sports' by the same artist, and none of the plates are similar.
THE ADVENTURES OF A POST CAPTAIN. By A Naval Officer. With 24 Coloured Plates by Mr. Williams. 3s. 6d. net.
GAMONIA: or, the Art of Preserving Game; and an Improved Method of making Plantations and Covers, explained and illustrated by Lawrence Rawstorne, Esq. With 15 Coloured Plates by T. Rawlins. 3s. 6d. net.
AN ACADEMY FOR GROWN HORSEMEN: Containing the completest Instructions for Walking, Trotting, Cantering, Galloping, Stumbling, and Tumbling. Illustrated with 27 Coloured Plates, and adorned with a Portrait of the Author. By Geoffrey Gambado, Esq. 3s. 6d. net.
REAL LIFE IN IRELAND, or, the Day and Night Scenes of Brian Boru, Esq., and his Elegant Friend, Sir Shawn O'Dogherty. By a Real Paddy. With 19 Coloured Plates by Heath, Marks, etc. 3s. 6d. net.
THE ADVENTURES OF JOHNNY NEWCOME IN THE NAVY. By Alfred Burton. With 16 Coloured Plates by T. Rowlandson 3s. 6d. net.
*THE OLD ENGLISH SQUIRE: A Poem. By John Careless, Esq. With 20 Coloured Plates after the style of T. Rowlandson.

## PLAIN BOOKS

THE GRAVE: A Poem. By Robert Blair. Illustrated by 12 Etchings executed by Louis Schiavonetti from the original Inventions of William Blake. With an Engraved Title Page and a Portrait of Blake by T. Phillips, R.A. 3s. 6d. net.

The illustrations are reproduced in photogravure. Also a limited edition on large Japanese paper, with India proofs and a duplicate set of the plates. 15s. net.

ILLUSTRATIONS OF THE BOOK OF JOB. Invented and engraved by William Blake. 3s. 6d. net.

These famous Illustrations—21 in number—are reproduced in photogravure. Also a limited edition on large Japanese paper, with India proofs and a duplicate set of the plates. 15s. net.

ÆSOP'S FABLES. With 380 Woodcuts by Thomas Bewick. 3s. 6d. net.

WINDSOR CASTLE. By W. Harrison Ainsworth. With 22 Plates and 87 Woodcuts in the Text by George Cruikshank. 3s. 6d. net.

THE TOWER OF LONDON. By W. Harrison Ainsworth. With 40 Plates and 58 Woodcuts in the Text by George Cruikshank. 3s. 6d. net.

FRANK FAIRLEGH. By F. E. Smedley. With 30 Plates by George Cruikshank. 3s. 6d. net.

HANDY ANDY. By Samuel Lover. With 24 Illustrations by the Author. 3s. 6d. net.

THE COMPLEAT ANGLER. By Izaak Walton and Charles Cotton. With 14 Plates and 77 Woodcuts in the Text. 3s. 6d. net.

This volume is reproduced from the beautiful edition of John Major of 1824.

THE PICKWICK PAPERS. By Charles Dickens. With the 43 Illustrations by Seymour and Phiz, the two Buss Plates, and the 32 Contemporary Onwhyn Plates. 3s. 6d. net.

## Junior Examination Series

### Edited by A. M. M. STEDMAN, M.A. Fcap. 8vo. 1s.

This series is intended to lead up to the School Examination Series, and is intended for the use of teachers and students, to supply material for the former and practice for the latter. The papers are carefully graduated, cover the whole of the subject usually taught, and are intended to form part of the ordinary class work. They may be used *vivâ voce* or as a written examination.

JUNIOR FRENCH EXAMINATION PAPERS. By F. Jacob, M.A.

JUNIOR LATIN EXAMINATION PAPERS. By C. G. Botting, M.A. *Third Edition.*

JUNIOR ENGLISH EXAMINATION PAPERS. By W. Williamson, M.A.

JUNIOR ARITHMETIC EXAMINATION PAPERS. By W. S. Beard. *Second Edition.*

JUNIOR ALGEBRA EXAMINATION PAPERS. By S. W. Finn, M.A.

JUNIOR GREEK EXAMINATION PAPERS. By T. C. Weatherhead, M.A.

JUNIOR GENERAL INFORMATION EXAMINATION PAPERS. By W. S. Beard.

JUNIOR GEOGRAPHY EXAMINATION PAPERS. By W. G. Baker, M.A.

JUNIOR GERMAN EXAMINATION PAPERS. By A. Voegelin, M.A.

## Junior School-Books, Methuen's

### Edited by O. D. INSKIP, LL.D., and W. WILLIAMSON, B.A.

A series of elementary books for pupils in lower forms, simply written by teachers of experience.

A CLASS-BOOK OF DICTATION PASSAGES. By W. Williamson, B.A. *Tenth Edition.* Cr. 8vo. 1s. 6d.

THE GOSPEL ACCORDING TO ST. MATTHEW. Edited by E. Wilton South, M.A. With Three Maps. Crown 8vo. 1s. 6d.

THE GOSPEL ACCORDING TO ST. MARK. Edited by A. E. Rubie, D.D. With Three Maps. Crown 8vo. 1s. 6d.

A JUNIOR ENGLISH GRAMMAR. By W. Williamson, B.A. With numerous passages for parsing and analysis, and a chapter on Essay Writing. *Second Edition.* Crown 8vo. 2s.

A JUNIOR CHEMISTRY. By E. A. Tyler, B.A., F.C.S. With 73 Illustrations. *Second Edition.* Crown 8vo. 2s. 6d.

THE ACTS OF THE APOSTLES. Edited by A. E. Rubie, D.D. Crown 8vo. 2s.

A JUNIOR FRENCH GRAMMAR. By L. A. Sornet and M. J. Acatos. Crown 8vo. 2s.

ELEMENTARY EXPERIMENTAL SCIENCE. PHYSICS by W. T. Clough, A.R.C.S. CHEMISTRY by A. E. Dunstan, B.Sc. With 2 Plates and 154 Diagrams. Crown 8vo. 2s.

A JUNIOR GEOMETRY. By Noel S. Lydon. With 230 Diagrams. Crown 8vo. 2s.

*A JUNIOR MAGNETISM AND ELECTRICITY. By W. T. Clough. With many Illustrations. Crown 8vo. 2s. 6d.

*ELEMENTARY EXPERIMENTAL CHEMISTRY. By A. E. Dunstan, B.Sc. With many Illustrations. Crown 8vo. 2s.

*A JUNIOR FRENCH PROSE. By R. R. N. Baron, M.A. Crown 8vo. 2s.

*THE GOSPEL ACCORDING TO ST. LUKE. With an Introduction and Notes by William Williamson, B.A. With Three Maps. Crown 8vo. 1s. 6d.

## Leaders of Religion

Edited by H. C. BEECHING, M.A., Canon of Westminster. *With Portraits.*

*Crown 8vo. 2s. net.*

A series of short biographies of the most prominent leaders of religious life and thought of all ages and countries.

CARDINAL NEWMAN. By R. H. Hutton.
JOHN WESLEY. By J. H. Overton, M.A.
BISHOP WILBERFORCE. By G. W. Daniell, M.A.
CARDINAL MANNING. By A. W. Hutton, M.A.
CHARLES SIMEON. By H. C. G. Moule, D.D.
JOHN KEBLE. By Walter Lock, D.D.
THOMAS CHALMERS. By Mrs. Oliphant.
LANCELOT ANDREWES. By R. L. Ottley, D.D. *Second Edition.*
AUGUSTINE OF CANTERBURY. By E. L. Cutts, D.D.

WILLIAM LAUD. By W. H. Hutton, M.A. *Second Edition.*
JOHN KNOX. By F. MacCunn. *Second Edition.*
JOHN HOWE. By R. F. Horton, D.D.
BISHOP KEN. By F. A. Clarke, M.A.
GEORGE FOX, THE QUAKER. By T. Hodgkin, D.C.L.
JOHN DONNE. By Augustus Jessopp, D.D.
THOMAS CRANMER. By A. J. Mason, D.D.
BISHOP LATIMER. By R. M. Carlyle and A. J. Carlyle, M.A.
BISHOP BUTLER. By W. A. Spooner, M.A.

## Little Blue Books, The

General Editor, E. V. LUCAS.

*Illustrated. Demy 16mo. 2s. 6d.*

A series of books for children. The aim of the editor is to get entertaining or exciting stories about normal children, the moral of which is implied rather than expressed.

1. THE CASTAWAYS OF MEADOWBANK. By Thomas Cobb.
2. THE BEECHNUT BOOK. By Jacob Abbott. Edited by E. V. Lucas.
3. THE AIR GUN. By T. Hilbert.
4. A SCHOOL YEAR. By Netta Syrett.
5. THE PEELES AT THE CAPITAL. By Roger Ashton.
6. THE TREASURE OF PRINCEGATE PRIORY. By T. Cobb.
7. MRS. BARBERRY'S GENERAL SHOP. By Roger Ashton.
8. A BOOK OF BAD CHILDREN. By W. T. Webb.
9. THE LOST BALL. By Thomas Cobb.

## Little Books on Art

*With many Illustrations. Demy 16mo. 2s. 6d. net.*

A series of monographs in miniature, containing the complete outline of the subject under treatment and rejecting minute details. These books are produced with the greatest care. Each volume consists of about 200 pages, and contains from 30 to 40 illustrations, including a frontispiece in photogravure.

GREEK ART. H. B. Walters.
BOOKPLATES. E. Almack.
REYNOLDS. J. Sime.
ROMNEY. George Paston.
WATTS. Miss R. E. D. Sketchley.
LEIGHTON. Alice Corkran.
VELASQUEZ. Wilfrid Wilberforce and A. R. Gilbert.
GREUZE AND BOUCHER. Eliza F. Pollard.
VANDYCK. M. G. Smallwood.

TURNER. F. Tyrell-Gill.
DÜRER. Jessie Allen.
HOPPNER. H. P. K. Skipton.
HOLBEIN. Mrs. G. Fortescue.
BURNE-JONES. Fortunée de Lisle.
REMBRANDT. Mrs. E. A. Sharp.
COROT. Alice Pollard and Ethel Birnstingl.
MILLET. Netta Peacock.
*RAPHAEL. A. R. Dryhurst.
*ILLUMINATED MSS. J. W. Bradley.

## Little Galleries, The

*Demy 16mo. 2s. 6d. net.*

A series of little books containing examples of the best work of the great painters. Each volume contains 20 plates in photogravure, together with a short outline of the life and work of the master to whom the book is devoted.

A LITTLE GALLERY OF REYNOLDS.
A LITTLE GALLERY OF ROMNEY.
A LITTLE GALLERY OF HOPPNER.
A LITTLE GALLERY OF MILLAIS.
A LITTLE GALLERY OF ENGLISH POETS.

## Little Guides, The

*Small Pott 8vo, cloth, 2s. 6d. net.; leather, 3s. 6d. net.*

OXFORD AND ITS COLLEGES. By J. Wells, M.A. Illustrated by E. H. New. *Fourth Edition.*
CAMBRIDGE AND ITS COLLEGES. By A. Hamilton Thompson. *Second Edition.* Illustrated by E. H. New.
THE MALVERN COUNTRY. By B. C. A. Windle, D.Sc., F.R.S. Illustrated by E. H. New.
SHAKESPEARE'S COUNTRY. By B. C. A. Windle, D.Sc., F.R.S. Illustrated by E. H. New. *Second Edition.*
SUSSEX. By F. G. Brabant, M.A. Illustrated by E. H. New.
WESTMINSTER ABBEY. By G. E. Troutbeck. Illustrated by F. D. Bedford.
NORFOLK. By W. A. Dutt. Illustrated by B. C. Boulter.
CORNWALL. By A. L. Salmon. Illustrated by B. C. Boulter.
BRITTANY. By S. Baring-Gould. Illustrated by J. Wylie.
HERTFORDSHIRE. By H. W. Tompkins, F.R.H.S. Illustrated by E. H. New.
THE ENGLISH LAKES. By F. G. Brabant, M.A. Illustrated by E. H. New.
KENT. By G. Clinch. Illustrated by F. D. Bedford.
ROME By C. G. Ellaby. Illustrated by B. C. Boulter.
THE ISLE OF WIGHT. By G. Clinch. Illustrated by F. D. Bedford.
SURREY. By F. A. H. Lambert. Illustrated by E. H. New.
BUCKINGHAMSHIRE. By E. S. Roscoe. Illustrated by F. D. Bedford.
SUFFOLK. By W. A. Dutt. Illustrated by J. Wylie.
DERBYSHIRE. By J. C. Cox, LL.D., F.S.A. Illustrated by J. C. Wall.
THE NORTH RIDING OF YORKSHIRE. By J. E. Morris. Illustrated by R. J. S. Bertram.
HAMPSHIRE. By J. C. Cox. Illustrated by M. E. Purser.
SICILY. By F. H. Jackson. With many Illustrations by the Author.
*DORSET. By Frank R. Heath. Illustrated.
*CHESHIRE. By W. M. Gallichan. Illustrated by Elizabeth Hartley.

## Little Library, The

With Introductions, Notes, and Photogravure Frontispieces.
*Small Pott 8vo. Each Volume, cloth, 1s. 6d. net; leather, 2s. 6d. net.*

A series of small books under the above title, containing some of the famous works in English and other literatures, in the domains of fiction, poetry, and belles lettres. The series also contains volumes of selections in prose and verse.

The books are edited with the most sympathetic and scholarly care. Each one contains an introduction which gives (1) a short biography of the author; (2) a critical estimate of the book. Where they are necessary, short notes are added at the foot of the page.

Each volume has a photogravure frontispiece, and the books are produced with great care.

ENGLISH LYRICS, A LITTLE BOOK OF. Anon.
PRIDE AND PREJUDICE. By Jane Austen. Edited by E. V. Lucas. *Two Volumes.*
NORTHANGER ABBEY. By Jane Austen. Edited by E. V. Lucas.
THE ESSAYS OF LORD BACON. Edited by Edward Wright.
THE INGOLSBY LEGENDS. By R. H. Barham. Edited by J. B. Atlay. *Two Volumes.*
A LITTLE BOOK OF ENGLISH PROSE. Edited by Mrs. P. A. Barnett.
THE HISTORY OF THE CALIPH VATHEK. By William Beckford. Edited by E. Denison Ross.
SELECTIONS FROM WILLIAM BLAKE. Edited by M. Perugini.
LAVENGRO. By George Borrow. Edited by F. Hindes Groome. *Two Volumes.*
THE ROMANY RYE. By George Borrow. Edited by John Sampson.
SELECTIONS FROM THE EARLY POEMS OF ROBERT BROWNING. Edited by W. Hall Griffin, M.A.
SELECTIONS FROM THE ANTI-JACOBIN; with George Canning's additional Poems. Edited by Lloyd Sanders.
THE ESSAYS OF ABRAHAM COWLEY. Edited by H. C. Minchin.
SELECTIONS FROM GEORGE CRABBE. Edited by A. C. Deane.
JOHN HALIFAX GENTLEMAN. By Mrs. Craik. Edited by Annie Matheson. *Two Volumes.*
THE ENGLISH POEMS OF RICHARD CRAWSHAW. Edited by Edward Hutton.
THE INFERNO OF DANTE. Translated by H. F. Cary. Edited by Paget Toynbee, M.A., D.Litt.
THE PURGATORIO OF DANTE. Translated by H. F. Cary. Edited by Paget Toynbee, M.A., D.Litt.

THE PARADISO OF DANTE. Translated by H. F. Cary. Edited by Paget Toynbee, M.A., D.Litt.
SELECTIONS FROM THE POEMS OF GEORGE DARLEY. Edited by R. A. Streatfeild.
A LITTLE BOOK OF LIGHT VERSE. Edited by A C. Deane.
MARRIAGE. By Susan Ferrier. Edited by Miss Goodrich Freer and Lord Iddesleigh. *Two Volumes.*
THE INHERITANCE. By Susan Ferrier. Edited by Miss Goodrich Freer and Lord Iddesleigh. *Two Volumes.*
CRANFORD. By Mrs. Gaskell. Edited by E. V. Lucas. *Second Edition.*
THE SCARLET LETTER. By Nathaniel Hawthorne. Edited by Percy Dearmer.
A LITTLE BOOK OF SCOTTISH VERSE. Edited by T. F. Henderson.
POEMS. By John Keats. With an Introduction by L. Binyon and Notes by J. MASEFIELD.
EOTHEN. By A. W. Kinglake. With an Introduction and Notes. *Second Edition.*
ELIA, AND THE LAST ESSAYS OF ELIA. By Charles Lamb. Edited by E. V. Lucas.
LONDON LYRICS. By F. Locker. Edited by A. D. Godley, M.A. A reprint of the First Edition.
SELECTIONS FROM LONGFELLOW. Edited by L. M. Faithfull.
THE POEMS OF ANDREW MARVELL. Edited by E. Wright.
THE MINOR POEMS OF JOHN MILTON. Edited by H. C. BEECHING, **M.A.**
MANSIE WAUCH. By D. M. Moir. Edited by T. F. Henderson.
A LITTLE BOOK OF ENGLISH SONNETS. Edited by J. B. B. Nichols.
THE MAXIMS OF LA ROCHEFOUCAULD. Translated by Dean Stanhope. Edited by G. H. Powell.
REJECTED ADDRESSES. By Horace and James Smith. Edited by A. D. Godley, M.A.
A SENTIMENTAL JOURNEY. By Laurence Sterne. Edited by H. W. Paul.
THE EARLY POEMS OF ALFRED TENNYSON. Edited by J. Churton Collins, M.A.
IN MEMORIAM. By Alfred, Lord Tennyson. Edited by H. C. Beeching, M.A.
THE PRINCESS. By Alfred, Lord Tennyson. Edited by Elizabeth Wordsworth.
MAUD. By Alfred, Lord Tennyson. Edited by Elizabeth Wordsworth.
VANITY FAIR. By W. M. Thackeray. Edited by S. Gywnn. *Three Volumes.*
PENDENNIS. By W. M. Thackeray. Edited by S. Gwynn. *Three Volumes.*
ESMOND. By W. M. Thackeray. Edited by S. Gwynn.
CHRISTMAS BOOKS. By W. M. Thackeray. Edited by S. Gwynn.
THE POEMS OF HENRY VAUGHAN. Edited by Edward Hutton.
THE COMPLEAT ANGLER. By Izaak Walton. Edited by J. Buchan.
A LITTLE BOOK OF LIFE AND DEATH. Edited by Mrs. Alfred Waterhouse. *Sixth Edition.*
SELECTIONS FROM WORDSWORTH. Edited by Nowell C. Smith.
LYRICAL BALLADS. By W. Wordsworth and S. T. Coleridge. Edited by George Sampson.

## Miniature Library, Methuen's

Reprints in miniature of a few interesting books which have qualities of humanity, devotion, or literary genius.

EUPHRANOR: A Dialogue on Youth. By Edward FitzGerald. From the edition published by W. Pickering in 1851. *Demy 32mo, Leather, 2s. net.*
POLONIUS: or Wise Saws and Modern Instances. By Edward FitzGerald. From the edition published by W. Pickering in 1852. *Demy 32mo. Leather, 2s. net.*
THE RUBAIYAT OF OMAR KHAYYAM. By Edward FitzGerald. From the 1st edition of 1859. *Second Edition. Leather, 2s. net.*
THE LIFE OF EDWARD, LORD HERBERT OF CHERBURY. Written by himself. From the edition printed at Strawberry Hill in the year 1764. *Medium 32mo. Leather, 2s. net.*
THE VISIONS OF DOM FRANCISCO QUEVEDO VILLEGAS, Knight of the Order of St. James. Made English by R. L. From the edition printed for H. Herringman 1668. *Leather, 2s. net.*
POEMS. By Dora Greenwell. From the edition of 1848. *Leather, 2s. net.*

## The Oxford Biographies

*Fcap. 8vo. Each volume, cloth, 2s. 6d. net; leather, 3s. 6d. net.*

These books are written by scholars of repute, who combine knowledge and literary skill with the power of popular presentation. They are illustrated from authentic material.

DANTE ALIGHIERI. By Paget Toynbee, M.A., D.Litt. With 12 Illustrations. *Second Edition.*
SAVONAROLA. By E. L. S. Horsburgh, M.A. With 12 Illustrations. *Second Edition.*
JOHN HOWARD. By E. C. S. Gibson, D.D., Vicar of Leeds. With 12 Illustrations.

TENNYSON. By A. C. BENSON, M.A. With 9 Illustrations.
WALTER RALEIGH. By I. A. Taylor. With 12 Illustrations.
ERASMUS. By E. F. H. Capey. With 12 Illustrations.
THE YOUNG PRETENDER. By C. S. Terry. With 12 Illustrations.
ROBERT BURNS. By T. F. Henderson. With 12 Illustrations.
CHATHAM. By A. S. M'Dowall. With 12 Illustrations.
ST. FRANCIS OF ASSISI. By Anna M. Stoddart. With 16 Illustrations.
CANNING. By W. A. Phillips. With 12 Illustrations.
BEACONSFIELD. By Walter Sichel. With 12 Illustrations.
GOETHE. By H. G. Atkins. With 12 Illustrations.

## School Examination Series

### Edited by A. M. M. STEDMAN, M.A. *Crown 8vo. 2s. 6d.*

FRENCH EXAMINATION PAPERS. By A. M. M. Stedman, M.A. *Thirteenth Edition.*
  A KEY, issued to Tutors and Private Students only to be had on application to the
  Publishers. *Fifth Edition. Crown 8vo. 6s. net.*
LATIN EXAMINATION PAPERS. By A. M. M. Stedman, M.A. *Twelfth Edition.*
  KEY (*Fourth Edition*) issued as above. *6s. net.*
GREEK EXAMINATION PAPERS. By A. M. M. Stedman, M.A. *Seventh Edition.*
  KEY (*Second Edition*) issued as above. *6s. net.*
GERMAN EXAMINATION PAPERS. By R. J. Morich. *Fifth Edition.*
  KEY (*Second Edition*) issued as above. *6s. net.*
HISTORY AND GEOGRAPHY EXAMINATION PAPERS. By C. H. Spence, M.A. *Second Edition.*
PHYSICS EXAMINATION PAPERS. By R. E. Steel, M.A., F.C.S.
GENERAL KNOWLEDGE EXAMINATION PAPERS. By A. M. M. Stedman, M.A. *Fourth Edition.*
  KEY (*Third Edition*) issued as above. *7s. net.*
EXAMINATION PAPERS IN ENGLISH HISTORY. By J. Tait Plowden-Wardlaw, B.A.

## Social Questions of To-day

### Edited by H. DE B. GIBBINS, Litt.D., M.A. *Crown 8vo. 2s. 6d.*

A series of volumes upon those topics of social, economic, and industrial interest that are foremost in the public mind.

Each volume is written by an author who is an acknowledged authority upon the subject with which he deals.

TRADE UNIONISM—NEW AND OLD. By G. Howell. *Third Edition.*
THE CO-OPERATIVE MOVEMENT TO-DAY. By G. J. Holyoake. *Fourth Edition.*
MUTUAL THRIFT. By J. Frome Wilkinson, M.A.
PROBLEMS OF POVERTY. By J. A. Hobson, M.A. *Fourth Edition.*
THE COMMERCE OF NATIONS. By C. F. Bastable, M.A. *Third Edition.*
THE ALIEN INVASION. By W. H. Wilkins, B.A.
THE RURAL EXODUS. By P. Anderson Graham.
LAND NATIONALIZATION. By Harold Cox, B.A.
A SHORTER WORKING DAY. By H. de Gibbins and R. A. Hadfield.
BACK TO THE LAND. An Inquiry into Rural Depopulation. By H. E. Moore.
TRUSTS, POOLS, AND CORNERS. By J. Stephen Jeans.
THE FACTORY SYSTEM. By R. W. Cooke-Taylor.
THE STATE AND ITS CHILDREN. By Gertrude Tuckwell.
WOMEN'S WORK. By Lady Dilke, Miss Bulley, and Miss Whitley.
SOCIALISM AND MODERN THOUGHT. By M. Kauffmann.
THE PROBLEM OF THE UNEMPLOYED. By J. A. Hobson, M.A.
LIFE IN WEST LONDON. By Arthur Sherwell, M.A. *Third Edition.*
RAILWAY NATIONALIZATION. By Clement Edwards.
WORKHOUSES AND PAUPERISM. By Louisa Twining.
UNIVERSITY AND SOCIAL SETTLEMENTS. By W. Reason, M.A.

## Technology, Textbooks of

### Edited by PROFESSOR J. WERTHEIMER, F.I.C.
### *Fully Illustrated.*

HOW TO MAKE A DRESS. By J. A. E. Wood. *Third Edition. Crown 8vo. 1s. 6d.*
CARPENTRY AND JOINERY. By F. C. Webber. *Third Edition. Crown 8vo. 3s. 6d.*
PRACTICAL MECHANICS. By Sidney H. Wells. *Second Edition. Crown 8vo. 3s. 6d.*

PRACTICAL PHYSICS. By H. Stroud, D.Sc., M.A. *Crown 8vo.* 3s. 6d.
MILLINERY, THEORETICAL AND PRACTICAL. By Clare Hill. *Second Edition. Crown 8vo.* 2s.
PRACTICAL CHEMISTRY. Part I. By W. French, M.A. *Crown 8vo. Second Edition.* 1s. 6d.
PRACTICAL CHEMISTRY. Part II. By W. French, M.A., and T. H. Boardman, M.A *Crown 8vo.* 1s. 6d.
TECHNICAL ARITHMETIC AND GEOMETRY. By C. T. Millis, M.I.M.E. *Crown 8vo.* 3s. 6d.
AN INTRODUCTION TO THE STUDY OF TEXTILE DESIGN. By Aldred F. Barker. *Demy 8vo.* 7s. 6d.
BUILDERS' QUANTITIES. By H. C. Grubb. *Crown 8vo.* 4s. 6d.
*METAL WORK (REPOUSSÉ). By A. C. Horth. *Crown 8vo.* 3s. 6d.

## Theology, Handbooks of

### Edited by R. L. OTTLEY, D.D., Professor of Pastoral Theology at Oxford, and Canon of Christ Church, Oxford.

The series is intended, in part, to furnish the clergy and teachers or students of Theology with trustworthy Text-books, adequately representing the present position of the questions dealt with; in part, to make accessible to the reading public an accurate and concise statement of facts and principles in all questions bearing on Theology and Religion.

THE XXXIX. ARTICLES OF THE CHURCH OF ENGLAND. Edited by E. C. S. Gibson, D.D. *Third and Cheaper Edition in one Volume. Demy 8vo.* 12s. 6d.
AN INTRODUCTION TO THE HISTORY OF RELIGION. By F. B. Jevons, M.A., Litt.D. *Third Edition. Demy 8vo.* 10s. 6d.
THE DOCTRINE OF THE INCARNATION. By R. L. Ottley, D.D. *Second and Cheaper Edition. Demy 8vo.* 12s. 6d.
AN INTRODUCTION TO THE HISTORY OF THE CREEDS. By A. E. Burn, B.D. *Demy 8vo.* 10s. 6d.
THE PHILOSOPHY OF RELIGION IN ENGLAND AND AMERICA. By Alfred Caldecott, D.D. *Demy 8vo.* 10s. 6d.
A HISTORY OF EARLY CHRISTIAN DOCTRINE. By J. F. Bethune Baker, M.A. *Demy 8vo.* 10s. 6d.

## Methuen's Universal Library

### EDITED BY SIDNEY LEE. *In Sixpenny Volumes.*

MESSRS. METHUEN are preparing a new series of reprints containing both books of classical repute, which are accessible in various forms, and also some rarer books, of which no satisfactory edition at a moderate price is in existence. It is their ambition to place the best books of all nations, and particularly of the Anglo-Saxon race, within the reach of every reader. All the great masters of Poetry, Drama, Fiction, History, Biography, and Philosophy will be represented. Mr. Sidney Lee will be the General Editor of the Library, and he will contribute a Note to each book.

The characteristics of METHUEN'S UNIVERSAL LIBRARY are five :—

1. SOUNDNESS OF TEXT. A pure and unabridged text is the primary object of the series, and the books will be carefully reprinted under the direction of competent scholars from the best editions. In a series intended for popular use not less than for students, adherence to the old spelling would in many cases leave the matter unintelligible to ordinary readers, and, as the appeal of a classic is universal, the spelling has in general been modernised.

2. COMPLETENESS. Where it seems advisable, the complete works of such masters as Milton Bacon, Ben Jonson and Sir Thomas Browne will be given. These will be issued in separate volumes, so that the reader who does not desire all the works of an author will have the opportunity of acquiring a single masterpiece.

3. CHEAPNESS. The books will be well printed on good paper at a price which on the whole is without parallel in the history of publishing. Each volume will contain from 100 to 350 pages, and will be issued in paper covers, Crown 8vo, at Sixpence net. In a few cases a long book will be issued as a Double Volume at One Shilling net.

4. CLEARNESS OF TYPE. The type will be a very legible one.

5. SIMPLICITY. There will be no editorial matter except a short biographical and bibliographical note by Mr. Sidney Lee at the beginning of each volume.

The volumes may also be obtained in cloth at One Shilling net, or in the case of a Double Volume at One and Sixpence net. Thus TOM JONES may be bought in a Double paper volume at One Shilling net, or in one cloth volume at 1s. 6d. net.

The Library will be issued at regular intervals after the publication of the first six books, all of which will be published together. Due notice will be given of succeeding issues. The orders of publication will be arranged to give as much variety of subject as possible, and the volume composing the complete works of an author will be issued at convenient intervals.

These are the early Books, all of which are in the Press.

THE WORKS OF WILLIAM SHAKESPEARE. In 10 volumes.
Vol. I.—The Tempest; The Two Gentlemen of Verona; The Merry Wives of Windsor; Measure for Measure; The Comedy of Errors.
Vol. II.—Much Ado About Nothing; Love's Labour's Lost; A Midsummer Nights' Dream; The Merchant of Venice; As You Like It.
Vol. III.—The Taming of the Shrew; All's Well that Ends Well; Twelfth Night; The Winter's Tale.

THE PILGRIM'S PROGRESS. By John Bunyan.

THE NOVELS OF JANE AUSTEN. In 5 volumes.
Vol. I.—Sense and Sensibility.

THE ENGLISH WORKS OF FRANCIS BACON, LORD VERULAM.
Vol. I.—Essays and Counsels and the New Atlantis.

THE POEMS AND PLAYS OF OLIVER GOLDSMITH.

ON THE IMITATION OF CHRIST. By Thomas à Kempis.

THE WORKS OF BEN JOHNSON. In about 12 volumes.
Vol. I.—The Case is Altered; Every Man in His Humour; Every Man out of His Humour.

THE PROSE WORKS OF JOHN MILTON.
Vol. I.—Eikonoklastes and The Tenure of Kings and Magistrates.

SELECT WORKS OF EDMUND BURKE.
Vol. I.—Reflections on the French Revolution
Vol. II.—Speeches on America.

THE WORKS OF HENRY FIELDING.
Vol. I.—Tom Jones. (Double Volume.)
Vol. II.—Amelia. (Double Volume.)

THE POEMS OF THOMAS CHATTERTON. In 2 volumes.
Vol. I.—Miscellaneous Poems.
Vol. II.—The Rowley Poems.

THE MEDITATIONS OF MARCUS AURELIUS. Translated by R. Graves.

THE HISTORY OF THE DECLINE AND FALL OF THE ROMAN EMPIRE. By Edward Gibbon. In 7 volumes.
The Notes have been revised by J. B. Bury, Litt.D.

THE PLAYS OF CHRISTOPHER MARLOWE.
Vol. I.—Tamburlane the Great; The Tragical History of Doctor Faustus.
Vol. II.—The Jew of Malta; Edward the Second; The Massacre at Paris; The Tragedy of Dido.

THE NATURAL HISTORY AND ANTIQUITIES OF SELBORNE. By Gilbert White.

THE COMPLETE ANGLER. In 2 volumes.
Vol. I.—By Izaak Walton.
Vol. II.—Part 2, by Cotton, and Part 3 by Venables.

THE POEMS OF PERCY BYSSHE SHELLEY. In 4 volumes.
Vol. I.—Alastor; The Daemon of the World; The Revolt of Islam, etc.

THE WORKS OF SIR THOMAS BROWNE. In 6 volumes.
Vol. I.—Religio Medici and Urn Burial.

THE POEMS OF JOHN MILTON. In 2 volumes.
Vol. I.—Paradise Lost.
Vol. II.—Miscellaneous Poems and Paradise Regained.

HUMPHREY CLINKER. By T. G. Smollett.

SELECT WORKS OF SIR THOMAS MORE.
Vol. I.—Utopia and Poems.

THE ANALOGY OF RELIGION, NATURAL AND REVEALED. By Joseph Butler, D.D.

ON HUMAN UNDERSTANDING. By John Locke. In 3 volumes.

THE POEMS OF JOHN KEATS. In 2 volumes.

THE DIVINE COMEDY OF DANTE. The Italian Text edited by Paget Toynbee, M.A., D.Litt. (A Double Volume.)

## Westminster Commentaries, The

General Editor, WALTER LOCK, D.D., Warden of Keble College, Dean Ireland's Professor of Exegesis in the University of Oxford.

The object of each commentary is primarily exegetical, to interpret the author's meaning to the present generation. The editors will not deal, except very subordinately, with questions of textual criticism or philology; but, taking the English

text in the Revised Version as their basis, they will try to combine a hearty accept-
ance of critical principles with loyalty to the Catholic Faith.

THE BOOK OF GENESIS. Edited with Introduction and Notes by S. R. Driver, D.D. *Third Edition. Demy 8vo. 10s. 6d.*

THE BOOK OF JOB. Edited by E. C. S. Gibson, D.D. *Second Edition. Demy 8vo. 6s.*

THE ACTS OF THE APOSTLES. Edited by R. B. Rackham, M.A. *Demy 8vo. Second and Cheaper Edition. 10s. 6d.*

THE FIRST EPISTLE OF PAUL THE APOSTLE TO THE CORINTHIANS. Edited by H. L. Goudge, M.A. *Demy 8vo. 6s.*

THE EPISTLE OF ST. JAMES. Edited with Introduction and Notes by R. J. Knowling, M.A. *Demy 8vo. 6s.*

# PART II.—FICTION

## Marie Corelli's Novels
### Crown 8vo. 6s. each.

A ROMANCE OF TWO WORLDS. *Twenty-Fifth Edition.*

VENDETTA. *Twenty-First Edition.*

THELMA. *Thirty-First Edition.*

ARDATH: THE STORY OF A DEAD SELF. *Fifteenth Edition.*

THE SOUL OF LILITH. *Twelfth Edition.*

WORMWOOD. *Fourteenth Edition.*

BARABBAS: A DREAM OF THE WORLD'S TRAGEDY. *Thirty-Ninth Edition.*
'The tender reverence of the treatment and the imaginative beauty of the writing have reconciled us to the daring of the conception. This "Dream of the World's Tragedy" is a lofty and not inadequate paraphrase of the supreme climax of the inspired narrative.'—*Dublin Review.*

THE SORROWS OF SATAN. *Forty-Eighth Edition.*
'A very powerful piece of work. . . . The conception is magnificent, and is likely to win an abiding place within the memory of man. . . . The author has immense command of language, and a limitless audacity. . . . This interesting and remarkable romance will live long after much of the ephemeral literature of the day is forgotten. . . . A literary phenomenon . . . novel, and even sublime.'—W. T. STEAD in the *Review of Reviews.*

THE MASTER CHRISTIAN. [165th Thousand.
'It cannot be denied that "The Master Christian" is a powerful book; that it is one likely to raise uncomfortable questions in all but the most self-satisfied readers, and that it strikes at the root of the failure of the Churches—the decay of faith—in a manner which shows the inevitable disaster heaping up. . . The good Cardinal Bonpré is a beautiful figure, fit to stand beside the good Bishop in "Les Misérables." It is a book with a serious purpose expressed with absolute unconventionality and passion . . . And this is to say it is a book worth reading.'—*Examiner.*

TEMPORAL POWER: A STUDY IN SUPREMACY. [150th Thousand.
'It is impossible to read such a work as "Temporal Power" without becoming convinced that the story is intended to convey certain criticisms on the ways of the world and certain suggestions for the betterment of humanity. . . . If the chief intention of the book was to hold the mirror up to shams, injustice, dishonesty, cruelty, and neglect of conscience, nothing but praise can be given to that intention.'—*Morning Post.*

GOD'S GOOD MAN: A SIMPLE LOVE STORY. *Sixth Edition.*

## Anthony Hope's Novels
### Crown 8vo. 6s. each.

THE GOD IN THE CAR. *Tenth Edition.*
'A very remarkable book, deserving of critical analysis impossible within our limit; brilliant, but not superficial; well considered, but not elaborated; constructed with the proverbial art that conceals, but yet allows itself to be enjoyed by readers to whom fine literary method is a keen pleasure.'—*The World.*

A CHANGE OF AIR. *Sixth Edition.*
'A graceful, vivacious comedy, true to human nature. The characters are traced with a masterly hand.'—*Times.*

A MAN OF MARK. *Fifth Edition.*
'Of all Mr. Hope's books, "A Man of Mark" is the one which best compares with The Prisoner of Zenda.'—*National Observer.*

THE CHRONICLES OF COUNT ANTONIO. *Fifth Edition.*
'It is a perfectly enchanting story of love and chivalry, and pure romance. The Count is the most constant, desperate, and modest and tender of lovers, a peerless gentleman, an intrepid fighter, a faithful friend, and a magnanimous foe.'—*Guardian.*
PHROSO. Illustrated by H. R. MILLAR. *Sixth Edition.*
'The tale is thoroughly fresh, quick with vitality, stirring the blood.'—*St. James's Gazette.*
SIMON DALE. Illustrated. *Sixth Edition.*
'There is searching analysis of human nature, with a most ingeniously constructed plot. Mr. Hope has drawn the contrasts of his women with marvellous subtlety and delicacy.' —*Times.*
THE KING'S MIRROR. *Fourth Edition.*
'In elegance, delicacy, and tact it ranks with the best of his novels, while in the wide range of its portraiture and the subtilty of its analysis it surpasses all his earlier ventures.' —*Spectator.*
QUISANTE. *Fourth Edition.*
'The book is notable for a very high literary quality, and an impress of power and mastery on every page.'—*Daily Chronicle.*
THE DOLLY DIALOGUES.

## W. W. Jacobs' Novels
### *Crown 8vo. 3s. 6d. each*

MANY CARGOES. *Twenty-Seventh Edition.*
SEA URCHINS. *Eleventh Edition.*
A MASTER OF CRAFT. Illustrated. *Sixth Edition.*
'Can be unreservedly recommended to all who have not lost their appetite for wholesome laughter.'—*Spectator.*
'The best humorous book published for many a day.'—*Black and White.*
LIGHT FREIGHTS. Illustrated. *Fourth Edition.*
'His wit and humour are perfectly irresistible. Mr. Jacobs writes of skippers, and mates, and seamen, and his crew are the jolliest lot that ever sailed.'—*Daily News.*
'Laughter in every page.'—*Daily Mail.*

## Lucas Malet's Novels
### *Crown 8vo. 6s. each.*

COLONEL ENDERBY'S WIFE. *Third Edition.*
A COUNSEL OF PERFECTION. *New Edition.*
LITTLE PETER. *Second Edition.* 3s. 6d.
THE WAGES OF SIN. *Fourteenth Edition.*
THE CARISSIMA. *Fourth Edition.*
THE GATELESS BARRIER. *Fourth Edition.*
'In "The Gateless Barrier" it is at once evident that, whilst Lucas Malet has preserved her birthright of originality, the artistry, the actual writing, is above even the high level of the books that were born before.'—*Westminster Gazette.*
THE HISTORY OF SIR RICHARD CALMADY. *Seventh Edition.* A Limited Edition in Two Volumes. *Crown 8vo.* 12s.
'A picture finely and amply conceived. In the strength and insight in which the story has been conceived, in the wealth of fancy and reflection bestowed upon its execution, and in the moving sincerity of its pathos throughout, "Sir Richard Calmady" must rank as the great novel of a great writer.'—*Literature.*
'The ripest fruit of Lucas Malet's genius. A picture of maternal love by turns tender and terrible.'—*Spectator.*
'A remarkably fine book, with a noble motive and a sound conclusion.'—*Pilot.*

## Gilbert Parker's Novels
### *Crown 8vo. 6s. each.*

PIERRE AND HIS PEOPLE. *Fifth Edition.*
'Stories happily conceived and finely executed. There is strength and genius in Mr Parker's style.'—*Daily Telegraph.*
MRS. FALCHION. *Fifth Edition.*
'A splendid study of character.'—*Athenæum.*
THE TRANSLATION OF A SAVAGE. *Second Edition.*
THE TRAIL OF THE SWORD. Illustrated. *Eighth Edition.*
'A rousing and dramatic tale. A book like this is a joy inexpressible.'—*Daily Chronicle.*

WHEN VALMOND CAME TO PONTIAC: The Story of a Lost Napoleon. *Fifth Edition.*
'Here we find romance—real, breathing, living romance. The character of Valmond is drawn unerringly.'—*Pall Mall Gazette.*

AN ADVENTURER OF THE NORTH : The Last Adventures of 'Pretty Pierre.' *Third Edition.*
'The present book is full of fine and moving stories of the great North.'—*Glasgow Herald.*

THE SEATS OF THE MIGHTY. Illustrated. *Thirteenth Edition.*
'Mr. Parker has produced a really fine historical novel.'—*Athenæum.*
'A great book.'—*Black and White.*

THE BATTLE OF THE STRONG : a Romance of Two Kingdoms. Illustrated. *Fourth Edition.*
'Nothing more vigorous or more human has come from Mr. Gilbert Parker than this novel.'—*Literature.*

THE POMP OF THE LAVILETTES. *Second Edition.* 3*s.* 6*d.*
'Unforced pathos, and a deeper knowledge of human nature than he has displayed before.'—*Pall Mall Gazette.*

## Arthur Morrison's Novels
### *Crown 8vo. 6s. each.*

TALES OF MEAN STREETS. *Sixth Edition.*
'A great book. The author's method is amazingly effective, and produces a thrilling sense of reality. The writer lays upon us a master hand. The book is simply appalling and irresistible in its interest. It is humorous also ; without humour it would not make the mark it is certain to make.'—*World.*

A CHILD OF THE JAGO. *Fourth Edition.*
'The book is a masterpiece.'—*Pall Mall Gazette.*

TO LONDON TOWN. *Second Edition.*
'This is the new Mr. Arthur Morrison, gracious and tender, sympathetic and human.'—*Daily Telegraph.*

CUNNING MURRELL.
'Admirable. . . Delightful humorous relief . . . a most artistic and satisfactory achievement.'—*Spectator.*

THE HOLE IN THE WALL. *Third Edition.*
'A masterpiece of artistic realism. It has a finality of touch that only a master may command.'—*Daily Chronicle.*
'An absolute masterpiece, which any novelist might be proud to claim.'—*Graphic.*
'"The Hole in the Wall" is a masterly piece of work. His characters are drawn with amazing skill. Extraordinary power.'—*Daily Telegraph.*

## Eden Phillpotts' Novels
### *Crown 8vo. 6s. each.*

LYING PROPHETS.

CHILDREN OF THE MIST. *Fifth Edition.*

THE HUMAN BOY. With a Frontispiece. *Fourth Edition.*
'Mr. Phillpotts knows exactly what school-boys do, and can lay bare their inmost thoughts ; likewise he shows an all-pervading sense of humour.'—*Academy.*

SONS OF THE MORNING. *Second Edition.*
'A book of strange power and fascination.'—*Morning Post.*

THE STRIKING HOURS. *Second Edition.*
'Tragedy and comedy, pathos and humour, are blended to a nicety in this volume.'—*World.*
'The whole book is redolent of a fresher and ampler air than breathes in the circumscribed life of great towns.'—*Spectator.*

THE RIVER. *Third Edition.*
'"The River" places Mr. Phillpotts in the front rank of living novelists.'—*Punch.*
'Since "Lorna Doone" we have had nothing so picturesque as this new romance.'—*Birmingham Gazette.*
'Mr. Phillpotts's new book is a masterpiece which brings him indisputably into the front rank of English novelists.'—*Pall Mall Gazette.*
'This great romance of the River Dart. The finest book Mr. Eden Phillpotts has written.'—*Morning Post.*

THE AMERICAN PRISONER. *Third Edition.*

THE SECRET WOMAN. *Second Edition.*

## S. Baring-Gould's Novels

*Crown 8vo. 6s. each.*

ARMINELL. *Fifth Edition.*
URITH. *Fifth Edition.*
IN THE ROAR OF THE SEA. *Seventh Edition.*
CHEAP JACK ZITA. *Fourth Edition.*
MARGERY OF QUETHER. *Third Edition.*
THE QUEEN OF LOVE. *Fifth Edition.*
JACQUETTA. *Third Edition.*
KITTY ALONE. *Fifth Edition.*
NOÉMI. Illustrated. *Fourth Edition.*
THE BROOM-SQUIRE. Illustrated. *Fourth Edition.*
DARTMOOR IDYLLS.

THE PENNYCOMEQUICKS. *Third Edition.*
GUAVAS THE TINNER. Illustrated. *Second Edition.*
BLADYS. Illustrated. *Second Edition.*
DOMITIA. Illustrated. *Second Edition.*
PABO THE PRIEST.
WINIFRED. Illustrated. *Second Edition.*
THE FROBISHERS.
ROYAL GEORGIE. Illustrated.
MISS QUILLET. Illustrated.
LITTLE TU'PENNY. *A New Edition.* 6d.
CHRIS OF ALL SORTS.
IN DEWISLAND. *Second Edition.*

## Robert Barr's Novels

*Crown 8vo. 6s. each.*

IN THE MIDST OF ALARMS. *Third Edition.*
  'A book which has abundantly satisfied us by its capital humour.'—*Daily Chronicle.*
THE MUTABLE MANY. *Second Edition.*
  'There is much insight in it, and much excellent humour.'—*Daily Chronicle.*
THE VICTORS.
THE COUNTESS TEKLA. *Third Edition.*
  'Of these mediæval romances, which are now gaining ground, "The Countess Tekla" is the very best we have seen.'—*Pall Mall Gazette.*
THE LADY ELECTRA. *Second Edition.*
THE TEMPESTUOUS PETTICOAT.

## E. Maria Albanesi's Novels

*Crown 8vo. 6s. each.*

SUSANNAH AND ONE OTHER. *Fourth Edition.*
THE BLUNDER OF AN INNOCENT. *Second Edition.*
CAPRICIOUS CAROLINE. *Second Edition.*
LOVE AND LOUISA. *Second Edition.*
PETER, A PARASITE.

## B. M. Croker's Novels

*Crown 8vo. 6s. each.*

ANGEL. *Fourth Edition.*
PEGGY OF THE BARTONS. *Sixth Edit.*
THE OLD CANTONMENT.

A STATE SECRET. *Third Edition.*
JOHANNA. *Second Edition.*
THE HAPPY VALLEY. *Second Edition.*

## J. H. Findlater's Novels

*Crown 8vo. 6s. each.*

THE GREEN GRAVES OF BALGOWRIE. *Fifth Edition.*

## Mary Findlater's Novels

*Crown 8vo. 6s.*

A NARROW WAY. *Third Edition.*
OVER THE HILLS.

THE ROSE OF JOY. *Second Edition.*

## Robert Hichens' Novels

*Crown 8vo. 6s. each.*

THE PROPHET OF BERKELEY SQUARE. *Second Edition.*
TONGUES OF CONSCIENCE. *Second Edition.*
FELIX. *Fourth Edition.*
THE WOMAN WITH THE FAN. *Fifth Edition.*
BYEWAYS. 3s. 6d.
THE GARDEN OF ALLAH *Seventh Edition.*

## Henry James's Novels
*Crown 8vo. 6s. each.*

THE SOFT SIDE. *Second Edition.*
THE BETTER SORT.

THE AMBASSADORS. *Second Edition.*
THE GOLDEN BOWL.

## Mary E. Mann's Novels
*Crown 8vo. 6s. each.*

OLIVIA'S SUMMER. *Second Edition.*
A LOST ESTATE. *A New Edition.*
THE PARISH OF HILBY. *A New Edition.*
*THE PARISH NURSE.
GRAN'MA'S JANE.
MRS. PETER HOWARD.

A WINTER'S TALE. *A New Edition.*
ONE ANOTHER'S BURDENS. *A New Edition.*
THERE WAS ONCE A PRINCE. Illustrated. 3s. 6d.
WHEN ARNOLD COMES HOME. Illustrated. 3s. 6d.

## W. Pett Ridge's Novels
*Crown 8vo. 6s. each.*

LOST PROPERTY. **Second** *Edition.*
ERB. *Second Edition.*
A SON OF THE STATE. 3s. **6d.**

A BREAKER OF LAWS. 3s. 6d.
MRS. GALER'S BUSINESS.
SECRETARY TO BAYNE, M.P. 3s. 6d.

## Adeline Sergeant's Novels
*Crown 8vo. 6s. each.*

THE MASTER OF BEECHWOOD.
BARBARA'S MONEY. *Second Edition.*
ANTHEA'S WAY.
THE YELLOW DIAMOND. *Second Edition.*
UNDER SUSPICION.

THE LOVE THAT OVERCAME.
THE ENTHUSIAST.
ACCUSED AND ACCUSER. *Second Edition.*
THE PROGRESS OF RACHEL.
THE MYSTERY OF THE MOAT.

---

**Albanesi (E. Maria).** See page 35.

**Anstey (F.),** Author of 'Vice Versâ.' A BAYARD FROM BENGAL. Illustrated by BERNARD PARTRIDGE. *Third Edition. Crown 8vo.* 3s. 6d.

**Bacheller (Irving),** Author of 'Eben Holden.' DARREL OF THE BLESSED ISLES *Third Edition. Crown 8vo.* 6s.

**Bagot (Richard).** A ROMAN MYSTERY. *Third Edition. Crown 8vo.* 6s.

**Balfour (Andrew).** See Shilling Novels.

**Baring-Gould (S.).** See page 35 and Shilling Novels.

**Barlow (Jane).** THE LAND OF THE SHAMROCK. *Crown 8vo.* 6s. See also Shilling Novels.

**Barr (Robert).** See page 35 and Shilling Novels.

**Begbie (Harold).** THE ADVENTURES OF SIR JOHN SPARROW. *Crown 8vo.* 6s.

**Belloc (Hilaire).** EMMANUEL BURDEN, MERCHANT. With 36 Illustrations by G. K. CHESTERTON. *Second Edition. Crown 8vo.* 6s.

**Benson (E. F.).** See Shilling Novels.

**Benson (Margaret).** SUBJECT TO VANITY. *Crown 8vo.* 3s. 6d.

**Besant (Sir Walter).** See Shilling Novels.

**Bowles (C. Stewart).** A STRETCH OFF THE LAND. *Crown 8vo.* 6s.

**Bullock (Shan. F.).** THE SQUIREEN. *Crown 8vo.* 6s.
THE RED LEAGUERS. *Crown 8vo.* 6s.
See also Shilling Novels.

**Burton (J. Bloundelle).** THE YEAR ONE: A Page of the French Revolution. Illustrated. *Crown 8vo.* 6s.
THE FATE OF VALSEC. *Crown 8vo.* 6s.
A BRANDED NAME. *Crown 8vo.* 6s.
See also Shilling Novels.

**Capes (Bernard),** Author of 'The Lake of Wine.' THE EXTRAORDINARY CONFESSIONS OF DIANA PLEASE. *Third Edition. Crown 8vo.* 6s.

**Chesney (Weatherby).** THE BAPTST RING. *Crown 8vo.* 6s.
THE TRAGEDY OF THE GREAT EMERALD. *Crown 8vo.* 6s.

THE MYSTERY OF A BUNGALOW. *Second Edition. Crown 8vo. 6s.*
Clifford (Hugh). A FREE LANCE OF TO-DAY. *Crown 8vo. 6s.*
Clifford (Mrs. W. K.). See also Shilling Novels and Books for Boys and Girls.
Cobb (Thomas). A CHANGE OF FACE. *Crown 8vo. 6s.*
Cobban (J. Maclaren). See Shilling Novels.
Corelli (Marie). See page 32.
Cotes (Mrs. Everard). See Sara Jeannette Duncan.
Cotterell (Constance). THE VIRGIN AND THE SCALES. *Crown 8vo. 6s.*
Crane (Stephen) and Barr (Robert). THE O'RUDDY. *Crown 8vo. 6s.*
Crockett (S. R.), Author of 'The Raiders,' etc. LOCHINVAR. Illustrated. *Second Edition. Crown 8vo. 6s.*
THE STANDARD BEARER. *Crown 8vo. 6s.*
Croker (B. M.). See page 35.
Dawson (A. J.). DANIEL WHYTE. *Crown 8vo. 3s. 6d.*
Doyle (A. Conan), Author of 'Sherlock Holmes,' 'The White Company,' etc. ROUND THE RED LAMP. *Ninth Edition. Crown 8vo. 6s.*
Duncan (Sara Jeannette) (Mrs. Everard Cotes). THOSE DELIGHTFUL AMERI-CANS. Illustrated. *Third Edition. Crown 8vo. 6s.*
THE POOL IN THE DESERT. *Crown 8vo. 6s.*
A VOYAGE OF CONSOLATION. *Crown 8vo. 3s. 6d.*
Findlater (J. H.). See page 35 and Shilling Novels.
Findlater (Mary). See page 35.
Fitzpatrick (K.) THE WEANS AT ROWALLAN. Illustrated. *Crown 8vo. 6s.*
Fitzstephen (Gerald). MORE KIN THAN KIND. *Crown 8vo. 6s.*
Fletcher (J. S.). LUCIAN THE DREAMER. *Crown 8vo. 6s.*
DAVID MARCH. *Crown 8vo. 6s.*
Francis (M. E.). See Shilling Novels.
Fraser (Mrs. Hugh), Author of 'The Stolen Emperor.' THE SLAKING OF THE SWORD. *Crown 8vo. 6s.*
Gallon (Tom), Author of 'Kiddy.' RICKERBY'S FOLLY. *Crown 8vo. 6s.*
Gerard (Dorothea), Author of 'Lady Baby.' THE CONQUEST OF LONDON. *Second Edition. Crown 8vo. 6s.*
HOLY MATRIMONY. *Second Edition. Crown 8vo. 6s.*
MADE OF MONEY. *Crown 8vo. 6s.*
THE BRIDGE OF LIFE. *Crown 8vo. 6s.*
Gerard (Emily). THE HERONS' TOWER. *Crown 8vo. 6s.*
Gissing (George), Author of 'Demos,' 'In the Year of Jubilee,' etc. THE TOWN TRAVELLER. *Second Edition. Crown 8vo. 6s.*
THE CROWN OF LIFE. *Crown 8vo. 6s.*
Glanville (Ernest). THE INCA'S TREASURE. Illustrated. *Crown 8vo. 3s. 6d.*
Gleig (Charles). BUNTER'S CRUISE. Illustrated. *Crown 8vo. 3s. 6d.*
Goss (C. F.). See Shilling Novels.
Herbertson (Agnes G.). PATIENCE DEAN. *Crown 8vo. 6s.*
Hichens (Robert). See page 35.
Hobbes (John Oliver), Author of 'Robert Orange.' THE SERIOUS WOOING. *Crown 8vo. 6s.*
Hope (Anthony). See page 32.
Hough (Emerson). THE MISSISSIPPI BUBBLE. Illustrated. *Crown 8vo. 6s.*
Hyne (C. J. Cutcliffe), Author of 'Captain Kettle.' MR. HORROCKS, PURSER. *Third Edition. Crown 8vo. 6s.*
Jacobs (W. W.). See page 33.
James (Henry). See page 36.
Janson (Gustaf). ABRAHAM'S SACRIFICE. *Crown 8vo. 6s.*
Keays (H. A. Mitchell). HE THAT EATETH BREAD WITH ME. *Crown 8vo. 6s.*
Lawless (Hon. Emily). See Shilling Novels.
Lawson (Harry), Author of 'When the Billy Boils.' CHILDREN OF THE BUSH. *Crown 8vo. 6s.*
Levett-Yeats (S.). ORRAIN. *Second Edition. Crown 8vo. 6s.*
Linden (Annie). A WOMAN OF SENTIMENT. *Crown 8vo. 6s.*
Linton (E. Lynn). THE TRUE HISTORY OF JOSHUA DAVIDSON, Christian and Communist. *Twelfth Edition. Medium 8vo. 6d.*
Long (J. Luther), Co-Author of 'The Darling of the Gods.' MADAME BUTTERFLY. *Crown 8vo. 3s. 6d.*
SIXTY JANE. *Crown 8vo. 6s.*
Lyall (Edna). DERRICK VAUGHAN, NOVELIST. *42nd Thousand. Cr. 8vo. 3s. 6d.*

M'Carthy (Justin H.), Author of ' If I were King.' THE LADY OF LOYALTY HOUSE.
  *Third Edition. Crown 8vo. 6s.*
THE DRYAD. *Crown 8vo. 6s.*
Mackie (Pauline Bradford). THE VOICE IN THE DESERT. *Crown 8vo. 6s.*
Macnaughtan (S.). THE FORTUNE OF CHRISTINA MACNAB. *Third Edition.*
  *Crown 8vo. 6s.*
Malet (Lucas). See page 33.
Mann (Mrs. M. E.). See page 36.
Marriott (Charles), Author of ' The Column. GENEVRA. *Second Edition. Cr. 8vo. 6s.*
Marsh (Richard). THE TWICKENHAM PEERAGE. *Second Edition. Crown 8vo. 6s.*
A METAMORPHOSIS. *Crown 8vo. 6s.*
GARNERED. *Crown 8vo. 6s.*
A DUEL. *Crown 8vo. 6s.*
Mason (A. E. W.), Author of ' The Courtship of Morrice Buckler,' ' Miranda of the Balcony,
  etc. CLEMENTINA. Illustrated. *Crown 8vo. Second Edition. 6s.*
Mathers (Helen), Author of ' Comin' thro' the Rye.' HONEY. *Fourth Edition.*
  *Crown 8vo. 6s.*
GRIFF OF GRIFFITHSCOURT. *Crown 8vo. 6s.*
Meade (L. T.). DRIFT. *Crown 8vo. 6s.*
RESURGAM. *Crown 8vo. 6s.*
Meredith (Ellis). HEART OF MY HEART. *Crown 8vo. 6s.*
'Miss Molly' (The Author of). THE GREAT RECONCILER. *Crown 8vo. 6s.*
Mitford (Bertram). THE SIGN OF THE SPIDER. Illustrated. *Sixth Edition*
  *Crown 8vo. 3s. 6d.*
IN THE WHIRL OF THE RISING. *Third Edition. Crown 8vo. 6s.*
THE RED DERELICT. *Crown 8vo. 6s.*
Montresor (F. F.), Author of ' Into the Highways and Hedges.' THE ALIEN. *Third*
  *Edition. Crown 8vo. 6s.*
Morrison (Arthur). See page 34.
Nesbit (E.). (Mrs. E. Bland). THE RED HOUSE. Illustrated. *Fourth Edition.*
  *Crown 8vo. 6s.*
THE LITERARY SENSE. *Crown 8vo. 6s.*
Norris (W. E.). THE CREDIT OF THE COUNTY. Illustrated. *Second Edition.*
  *Crown 8vo. 6s.*
THE EMBARRASSING ORPHAN. *Crown 8vo. 6s.*
NIGEL'S VOCATION. *Crown 8vo. 6s.*
LORD LEONARD THE LUCKLESS. *Crown 8vo. 6s.*
BARHAM OF BELTANA. *Crown 8vo. 6s.*
Oliphant (Mrs.). See Shilling Novels.
Ollivant (Alfred). OWD BOB, THE GREY DOG OF KENMUIR. *Seventh Edition.*
  *Crown 8vo. 6s.*
Oppenheim (E. Phillips). MASTER OF MEN. *Third Edition. Crown 8vo. 6s.*
Oxenham (John), Author of ' Barbe of Grand Bayou.' A WEAVER OF WEBS.
  *Second Edition. Crown 8vo. 6s.*
THE GATE OF THE DESERT. *Crown 8vo. 6s.*
Pain (Barry). THREE FANTASIES. *Crown 8vo. 1s.*
LINDLEY KAYS. *Third Edition. Crown 8vo. 6s.*
Parker (Gilbert). See page 23.
Pemberton (Max). THE FOOTSTEPS OF A THRONE. Illustrated. *Third Edition.*
  *Crown 8vo. 6s.*
I CROWN THEE KING. With Illustrations by Frank Dadd and A. Forrestier.
  *Crown 8vo. 6s.*
Penny (Mrs. F. E.). See Shilling Novels.
Phillpotts (Eden). See page 34 and Shilling Novels.
Pickthall (Marmaduke). SAID THE FISHERMAN. *Fifth Edition. Crown 8vo. 6s.*
BRENDLE. *Crown 8vo. 6s.*
Pryce (Richard). WINIFRED MOUNT. *A New Edition. Crown 8vo. 6s.*
'Q,' Author of ' Dead Man's Rock.' THE WHITE WOLF. *Second Edition. Crown*
  *8vo. 6s.*
Queux (W. le). THE HUNCHBACK OF WESTMINSTER. *Third Edition. Crown*
  *8vo. 6s.*
THE CLOSED BOOK. *Second Edition. Crown 8vo. 6s.*
THE VALLEY OF THE SHADOW. Illustrated. *Crown 8vo. 6s.*
Rhys (Grace). THE WOOING OF SHEILA. *Second Edition. Crown 8vo. 6s.*
THE PRINCE OF LISNOVER. *Crown 8vo. 6s.*

**Rhys (Grace) and Another.** THE DIVERTED VILLAGE. With Illustrations by DOROTHY GWYN JEFFREYS. *Crown 8vo.* 6s.

**Ridge (W. Pett).** See page 36.

**Ritchie (Mrs. David G.).** THE TRUTHFUL LIAR. *Crown 8vo.* 6s.

**Roberts (C. G. D.).** THE HEART OF THE ANCIENT WOOD. *Crown 8vo.* 3s. 6d.

*Robertson (Frances Forbes).** THE TAMING OF THE BRUTE. *Crown 8vo.* 6s.

**Russell (W. Clark).** MY DANISH SWEETHEART. Illustrated. *Fourth Edition Crown 8vo.* 6s.

ABANDONED. *Second Edition. Crown 8vo.* 6s.

HIS ISLAND PRINCESS. Illustrated. *Crown 6vo.* 6s.

**Sergeant (Adeline).** See page 36.

**Shannon (W. F.).** THE MESS DECK. *Crown 8vo.* 3s. 6d.

JIM TWELVES. *Second Edition. Crown 8vo.* 3s. 6d.

**Sonnichsen (Albert).** DEEP SEA VAGABONDS. *Crown 8vo.* 6s.

**Stringer (Arthur).** THE SILVER POPPY. *Crown 8vo.* 6s.

**Sutherland (Duchess of).** See Shilling Novels.

**Swan (Annie).** See Shilling Novels.

**Tanqueray (Mrs. B. M.).** THE ROYAL QUAKER. *Crown 8vo.* 6s.

**Thompson (Vance).** SPINNERS OF LIFE. *Crown 8vo.* 6s.

**Waineman (Paul).** BY A FINNISH LAKE. *Crown 8vo.* 6s.

THE SONG OF THE FOREST. *Crown 8vo.* 6s. See also Shilling Novels.

**Watson (H. B. Marriott).** ALARUMS AND EXCURSIONS. *Crown 8vo.* 6s.

CAPTAIN FORTUNE. *Second Edition. Crown 8vo.* 6s.

**Wells (H. G.)** THE SEA LADY. *Crown 8vo.* 6s.

**Weyman (Stanley),** Author of 'A Gentleman of France.' UNDER THE RED ROBE With Illustrations by R. C. WOODVILLE. *Eighteenth Edition. Crown 8vo.* 6s.

**White (Stewart E.).** Author of 'The Blazed Trail.' CONJUROR'S HOUSE. A Romance of the Free Trail. *Second Edition. Crown 8vo.* 6s.

**White (Percy).** THE SYSTEM. *Second Edition. Crown 8vo.* 6s.

**Williamson (Mrs. C. N.),** Author of 'The Barnstormers.' PAPA. *Second Edition. Crown 8vo.* 6s.

THE ADVENTURE OF PRINCESS SYLVIA. *Crown 8vo.* 3s. 6d.

THE WOMAN WHO DARED. *Crown 8vo.* 6s.

THE SEA COULD TELL. *Second Edition. Crown 8vo.* 6s.

THE CASTLE OF THE SHADOWS. *Crown 8vo.* 6s.

**Williamson (C. N. and A. M.).** THE LIGHTNING CONDUCTOR: Being the Romance of a Motor Car. Illustrated. *Tenth Edition. Crown 8vo.* 6s.

THE PRINCESS PASSES. Illustrated. *Second Edition. Crown 8vo.* 6s.

## Methuen's Shilling Novels

### *Cloth, 1s. net.*

ENCOURAGED by the great and steady sale of their Sixpenny Novels, Messrs. Methuen have determined to issue a new series of fiction at a low price under the title of 'METHUEN'S SHILLING NOVELS.' These books are well printed and well bound in *cloth*, and the excellence of their quality may be gauged from the names of those authors who contribute the early volumes of the series.

Messrs. Methuen would point out that the books are as good and as long as a six shilling novel, that they are bound in cloth and not in paper, and that their price is One Shilling *net*. They feel sure that the public will appreciate such good and cheap literature, and the books can be seen at all good booksellers.

The first volumes are—

**Adeline Sergeant.** A GREAT LADY.

**Richard Marsh.** MARVELS AND MYSTERIES.

**Tom Gallon.** RICKERBY'S FOLLY.

**H. B. Marriott-Watson.** THE SKIRTS OF HAPPY CHANCE.

**Bullock (Shan F.).** THE BARRYS.

THE CHARMERS.

**Gissing (George).** THE CROWN OF LIFE.

**Francis (M. E.).** MISS ERIN.

**Sutherland (Duchess of).** ONE HOUR AND THE NEXT.

**Burton (J. Bloundelle).** ACROSS THE SALT SEAS.

**Oliphant (Mrs.).** THE PRODIGALS.

**Balfour (Andrew).** VENGEANCE IS MINE.

Barr (Robert), Author of 'The Countess Tekla.' THE VICTORS.
Penny (Mrs. F. A.). A MIXED MARRIAGE.
Hamilton (Lord Ernest). MARY HAMILTON.
Glanville (Ernest). THE LOST REGIMENT.
Benson (E. F.), Author of 'Dodo.' THE CAPSINA.
Goss (C. F.). THE REDEMPTION OF DAVID CORSON.
Findlater (J. H.), Author of 'The Green Graves of Balgowrie.' A DAUGHTER OF STRIFE.
Cobban (J. M.) THE KING OF ANDAMAN.
Clifford (Mrs. W. K.). A WOMAN ALONE.
Phillpotts (Eden). FANCY FREE.

## Books for Boys and Girls.

### Crown 8vo.　3s. 6d.

THE GETTING WELL OF DOROTHY. By Mrs. W. K. Clifford. Illustrated by Gordon Browne. Second Edition.

THE ICELANDER'S SWORD. By S. Baring-Gould.

ONLY A GUARD-ROOM DOG. By Edith E. Cuthell.

THE DOCTOR OF THE JULIET. By Harry Collingwood.

LITTLE PETER. By Lucas Malet. Second Edition.

MASTER ROCKAFELLAR'S VOYAGE. By W. Clark Russell.

THE SECRET OF MADAME DE MONLUC. By the Author of " Mdlle. Mori."

SYD BELTON; Or, the Boy who would not go to Sea. By G. Manville Fenn.

THE RED GRANGE. By Mrs. Molesworth.

A GIRL OF THE PEOPLE. By L. T. Meade.

HEPSY GIPSY. By L. T. Meade. 2s. 6d.

THE HONOURABLE MISS. By L. T. Meade.

## The Novels of Alexandre Dumas.

### Price 6d. Double Volumes, 1s.

THE THREE MUSKETEERS. With a long Introduction by Andrew Lang. Double volume.

THE PRINCE OF THIEVES. Second Edition.

ROBIN HOOD. A Sequel to the above.

THE CORSICAN BROTHERS.

GEORGES.

CROP-EARED JACQUOT; JANE; Etc.

TWENTY YEARS AFTER. Double volume.

AMAURY.

THE CASTLE OF EPPSTEIN.

THE SNOWBALL, and SULTANETTA.

CECILE; OR, THE WEDDING GOWN.

ACTÉ.

THE BLACK TULIP.

THE VICOMTE DE BRAGELONNE.
　Part 1. Louis de la Vallière. Double Volume.
　Part II. The Man in the Iron Mask. Double Volume.

THE CONVICT'S SON.

THE WOLF-LEADER.

NANON; OR, THE WOMEN'S WAR. Double volume.

PAULINE; MURAT; AND PASCAL BRUNO.

THE ADVENTURES OF CAPTAIN PAMPHILE.

FERNANDE.

GABRIEL LAMBERT.

THE REMINISCENCES OF ANTONY.

CATHERINE BLUM.

THE CHEVALIER D'HARMENTAL.

SYLVANDIRE.

THE FENCING MASTER.

*CONSCIENCE.

*THE REGENT'S DAUGHTER. A Sequel to Chevalier d'Harmental.

### Illustrated Edition.

THE THREE MUSKETEERS. Illustrated in Colour by Frank Adams. 2s. 6d.

THE PRINCE OF THIEVES. Illustrated in Colour by Frank Adams. 2s.

ROBIN HOOD THE OUTLAW. Illustrated in Colour by Frank Adams. 2s.

THE CORSICAN BROTHERS. Illustrated in Colour by A. M. M'Lellan. 1s. 6d.

FERNANDE. Illustrated in Colour by Munro Orr.

THE BLACK TULIP. Illustrated in Colour by A. Orr.

GEORGES. Illustrated in Colour by Munro Orr. 2s.

TWENTY YEARS AFTER. Illustrated in Colour by Frank Adams. 3s.

AMAURY. Illustrated in Colour by Gordon Browne. 2s.

THE SNOWBALL, and SULTANETTA. Illustrated in Colour by Frank Adams. 2s.

*THE VICOMTE DE BRAGELONNE. Part 1. Illustrated in Colour by Frank Adams.

*CROP-EARED JACQUOT; JANE; Etc. Illustrated in Colour by Gordon Browne.

*THE CASTLE OF EPPSTEIN. Illustrated in Colour by Stewart Orr.

*ACTÉ. Illustrated in Colour by Gordon Browne.

*CECILE; OR, THE WEDDING GOWN. Illustrated in Colour by D. Murray Smith.

*THE ADVENTURES OF CAPTAIN PAMPHILE. Illustrated in Colour by Frank Adams.

*THE WOLF-LEADER. Illustrated in Colour by Frank Adams. 1s. 6d.